THE MASK OF ARES

GODSWAR
Volume 1

Ryk E. Spoor

THE MASK OF ARES

Histria SciFi & Fantasy

Las Vegas ◊ London ◊ New York ◊ Palm Beach

Published in the United States of America by
Histria Books
7181 N. Hualapai Way, Ste. 130-86
Las Vegas, NV 89166 USA
HistriaBooks.com

Histria SciFi & Fantasy is an imprint of Histria Books encompassing outstanding, innovative works in the genres of science fiction and fantasy. Titles published under the imprints of Histria Books are distributed in the United States and Canada by Simon & Schuster and worldwide through Unified Book Distribution. We appreciate your support of copyright by purchasing an authorized edition of this book and for respecting intellectual property laws by not reproducing, scanning, or otherwise distributing any part of it by any means without permission. You are supporting authors and enabling Histria Books to continue publishing books for everyone.

All rights reserved. No part of this book may be reprinted or reproduced or utilized in any form or by any electronic, mechanical or other means, now known or hereafter invented, including photocopying and recording, or in any information storage or retrieval system, without the permission in writing from the Publisher. No part of this book may be used or reproduced in any manner for the purpose of training artificial intelligence technologies or systems.

This is a work of fiction. Names, characters, places, and incidents either are the product of the author's imagination or are used fictitiously, and any resemblance to actual persons, living or dead, business establishments, events, or locales is entirely coincidental.

First Edition

Library of Congress Control Number: 2025944115

ISBN 978-1-59211-690-4 (softbound)
ISBN 978-1-59211-712-3 (eBook)

Copyright © 2026 by Ryk E. Spoor

This novel is dedicated to two people. First, to Masami Kurumada, creator of *Saint Seiya*. Anyone who knows me can recognize that *Saint Seiya* was one of the major inspirations for Aegeia and the God-Warriors, though much has been changed in both broad and fine. But the inspiration remains – and was more than just inspiration for my writing. It would not be a terrible overstatement to say that *Saint Seiya* is one of the reasons Kathleen and I are married. Thank you, Kurumada-sama, for the inspiration of your heroes.

Second, to the late David Hargrave, creator of *The Arduin Grimoire* and its sequels. Arduin was one of the most powerful influences on the development of Zarathan, and in one of the main characters one can see a very specific influence. A salute to you and Arduin!

Author's Note

My world of Zarathan is something of a potpourri of all fantasy elements, and some SF ones as well, as readers of the Balanced Sword trilogy know. This is intentional. Few of the elements that *look* familiar are exactly what they appear to be, and even references to real-world people, places, or things are changed to make them work as I want them to in my stories.

This is of course the case with the pseudo-Greek elements of the country of Aegeia. Readers should recognize that in NO WAY is this story intended to reflect any real aspects of Grecian history, culture, or mythology. In-universe, it's assumed that the Earthly versions of the pantheons seen herein were in some way inspired or derived from those of Aegeia, but this is obviously untrue in real life. Readers who know some more personal details of my history will also recognize another source for Aegeia and some of its features, but those, too, have been changed to fit my world and my story.

Prologue
Ares and Athena

The door swung open to reveal a most beloved figure, and Ares was on his feet immediately, sweeping Athena into his arms for a hug and a kiss on the cheek. "Sister! Oh, I'm *so* glad you stopped by!"

As with all the gods of the Aegeian pantheon, what the Lady of Wisdom *looked* like varied – on the mortal world, with whatever body she was incarnate, and here, with the viewer's own interpretation of what they sensed. To Ares, she looked like a tall, well-muscled woman, broad of shoulder, high of brow, gray or green of eye, with tumbling, uncontrollable curls of bronze cascading around a strongly defined face, a shade darker and considerably more olive in tone than the hair. Her dark brows rose in aristocratic arches above a very slightly curved nose.

Ares knew that when *she* looked at him, she saw a man slightly taller than she, with skin more bronze than olive, black hair, and a long face that allowed for exaggerated expressions of joy or sorrow or rage, dressed in a fancy set of robes that mimicked the armor of his deific persona.

"How could I *not* stop by before I must leave?" she asked, smiling back.

The words jolted him, sent a momentary spurt of denial through him. "What? No, darling, it *can't* be that late... can it?"

"I'm afraid so, brother mine. I know you lose track of time, but it really *is* that time. The Cycle begins anew, and none too soon."

"Oh, Thunder and Fire, I've got so much to *do*! Deimos... *Deimos*, there you are, look, get my favorite sister something – Essence of Song, perhaps?" She flashed a smile both to him and to the small, blade-thin, blond youth who had emerged at Ares' call. "Yes, Essence of Song, I knew it was one of your favorites! By the other *pantheons*, why didn't you *warn* me?"

She accepted the glass of sparkling, singing light from Deimos. "I *did*, you scatterbrain. Twice in the past decade."

"Oh." Vague memory broke through. "Oh, yes, you did. Forgive me, 'Thena, I'm every bit the scatterbrain. Time to stop that, though, the Cycle calls, I've got to get in tune with who I *am* this time. I'm supposed to be down and incarnate before *you*, right?"

She rolled her eyes. "Yes, of *course* you are. That's why I had to stop by, I saw your invitation to a party next month and I *knew* you—"

"The *party*, oh no, I'll have to cancel! How embarrassing." Ares cringed inwardly, thinking of all the apologies he was going to have to write. *Battles are so much easier than facing your own* faux pas. "So you're not *really* leaving just yet?"

"No, not yet." She smiled again. "I'll make sure you have the usual head start. We have our conflict to play out, after all."

"What of Father…?" As always, he felt a momentary spark of hope, quashed again when Athena shook her head.

"It's been *Cycles*, Ares," she said gently. "I don't know if he's ever coming back. If he is… well, no one knows where he went, or why. But he's definitely not here for this Cycle, so we have to play out the script as it lies."

He sighed. "Well, we have time for a few drinks, and dinner, and conversation. Now that you've recalled me to myself a bit, I realize it's been a decade or three. What *have* you been up to?"

***

"You seem cheered, Lord Ares," Deimos said, helping Phobos – a woman as dark all over as Deimos was pale, and twice as broad – clear up the table and get the dishes put away. "I'd thought the approach of the Cycle might depress your spirits."

"Oh, it does, on occasion, but my sister never fails to lift them. You'll come to see that yourself, if you make it a few Cycles."

"I certainly hope I will!"

His companion echoed that sentiment, looking nervous.

Ares shook his head, grinning, and stood, casting the fancy robes aside as he headed for a huge, gold-inlaid closet at the far side of the room. "I hope so as well, but do not fear; the roles of Deimos and Phobos are strenuous, truly, but even if the cost of the Art is to die on the stage of the world, rest assured that your spirits will be caught with the most gracious gentleness and conveyed directly to Elysium. But the last pair performed for, oh, many Cycles indeed before they were forced to pass to their reward. You'll meet them, I'm sure – wouldn't want their advice to be lost, you know."

"But you do not pass, Lord?"

"Me? Well... not as you might, no," he admitted, flinging the doors wide and studying the arms and armor displayed, in glittering array, within. *Which ones? What is the spirit of this age? Please don't let it be one in which I'm a crude ravager, those are so boring. Easy to play, but deathly dull, and I despise dull.*

"No, not quite as you might," he repeated. "The outline of the contest – between the God of War and Passion on one side, and the Goddess of War and Wisdom on the other – you both know well already, of course. And in the climax of the Great Work, often I must fall, usually to my sister's hand, though sometimes to the God-Warriors themselves. But as the High Gods, we are known to be merely felled for the moment, to rise inevitably again. Others, alas, often pass beyond the living world and do not easily return."

"But... Elysium *is* real, yes?" Phobos asked, her voice tense and uncertain.

He turned from the closet and crossed the distance in three quick strides, dropping to his knees before her and taking both her hands. "Lady Phobos, I had not realized... you were a traveler, an Adventurer, but not *of* us, of course, when you found yourself caught up in the... recruitment, shall we say. What were you? A follower of ours, or...?

"Honestly?" She grinned hesitantly. "Chromaias and the Four. Kharianda was my main patron among the gods."

He gave a nod. "Ahh, of course. One of our strongest allies among the other gods, along with Terian and the King of Dragons. And Lady Kharianda herself, ahh, a fine one for a great warrior to follow. I suppose she must have transferred her blessing to us when you were Chosen." He concentrated, smiled. "Yes, I can remember it now. The end of a prior Cycle is always a bit blurry when a new one is about to begin, but yes, she did; her favor still follows you."

He frowned. "But where was I? Oh! Yes, my lady, Elysium is as real as this palace you stand within, as real as the world you left behind and will return to with me. You need not fear death; my arm – the arms of all of us of Aegeia – is about you and shall guide you there, if need be."

He looked into her eyes, saw that his words had reached her, and nodded, stood again and resumed his contemplation of the costumes. "Remind me, Lady, before we leave; I shall have a word with the Lord of the Underworld and he will show you Elysium – and your predecessors, that you may know that the word 'reward' is real and true – as it is for all mortals who are forced to a final performance in the Great Play." He rubbed his chin. "But for now, you may both retire. I'll finish that cleaning, no need to trouble yourselves. I've work to do, a performance to contemplate."

"As you wish, Lord Ares." The two bowed – he could see it from the corner of his eye – and departed, shutting the golden doors behind them.

After another ten minutes, he sighed and turned to the various dishes left. "Somehow, I'm not quite... *getting* this Cycle's... oh, *vibe*," he murmured to himself. "Should have started meditating on it a year ago. Now I have to catch up. Poor Athena, she has to put up with this *every* Cycle. I really need to do better. Maybe some kind of automated alarm... I'm sure Hephaestus could put one together. Yes, I'll talk to him about that on the morrow."

Naturally, he *could* have cleaned everything up with a gesture – a trivial exercise for even the least of gods, after all – but that wasn't *style*. You had to get your hands dirty – had to do the work *yourself* – or what work was it, really?

And there was a certain pleasure in scrubbing dirt away, leaving something clean and sparkling for another day. He hummed and let his mind wander for a bit.

Really, he looked forward to the beginning of every Cycle. The ageless performance, the Eternal Play that helped affirm the places of the gods for the mortals they served, and in turn reinforced the power that made them gods... it was the very core of Aegeia, and he took great joy in the fact that he could serve in such a crucial role, teaching people the dangers of passion and anger uncontrolled, while reminding them of that same passion within themselves! The other gods of the Pantheon played their parts, certainly (well, alas, not Father, not these many Cycles past), but he and Athena had long since become the centerpieces, the core and crucial contest and conflict that drove the entire play.

There were, of course, the *other* gods – the hundreds and more that watched over, manipulated, defended, or exploited the other peoples of Zarathan – but while they might have more freedom in some ways, and in the case of a few, greater *power*, they did lack one thing: resistance to the effects of the legendary Chaoswars. The Cycle *did* resist those effects – not completely, but more than any other power on Zarathan. The Goddess of Wisdom retained much knowledge that the others lost. It was, Ares thought, a fair trade that their Father had arranged, harnessing the powers underlying the Chaoswars to create a faster, controlled Cycle.

And the Cycle *did* also allow them to learn and adapt to their worshipers, as their needs and beliefs and perceptions of the gods changed. It changed the Great Script, enough to keep the Play fresh over all these repetitions. It even had given them flexibility and presence of... power, one might say... sufficient to project themselves occasionally to Zahralandar, the sister world now cut off almost entirely from magic, and leave at least a hint of the existence of the gods, along with the few other deities who detected the momentary opportunity by fortune or fate.

Yes, *now* he was starting to anticipate the role!

He did allow himself to cheat the *tiniest* bit and dried the dishes with a gesture, so he could put them away quickly. He bobbled one, nearly dropped it, caught it *just* before it hit, and sighed with relief.

These dishes – unlike most to be found throughout Olympia – were in fact real, solid objects, brought from Zarathan's surface, just like Deimos and Phobos had been. Much of Olympia was the stuff of gods, thoughts and primal energy made real, yet seen through the lens of individual perception. Ares preferred, in his own quarters, to have a lot of mortal, solid artifacts; they were ideal performance props, reminding him of the essence of the world he served, and that served him as the perfect stage.

And that was true of his costumes, of course. He returned to that closet. But this time, almost instantly, his eye was drawn to a flamboyant suit of armor. He felt a smile broadening. *Oh, my, what fun I will have! Such potential for being a complete and utter scenery-chewer this time!*

The undergarments and padding were, of course, kept with every suit, so he could don the armor immediately. With the armor came the weapons; while the ancient tradition equipped him with a simple sword and spears and such, *this* version of the role gave him an almost ridiculously massive sword, a battleaxe, a jagged-pointed spear, and other over-the-top accoutrements.

He couldn't help chuckling as he put them on. They would be effective, of course – Hephaestus and the god-power could make a scythe as swift and deadly as a rapier, a stylus strike as viciously as a lance. He wondered if Athena would be as exaggerated in her heroism, or be deliberately more understated, to provide dramatic contrast. It was hard to guess; it was, after all, the mortals' souls who wrote the ultimate script, but even *they* couldn't explain, exactly, *why* the changes were made. They simply... *were*.

He heard the door open quietly, turned to see a familiar slender form.

Deimos bowed. "I wanted to make sure you would require no more of us tonight."

"I thank you, but no, I believe I am content for now. You would be wise to go to your rest – the role has begun to speak to me, and the curtain will be rising soon!"

Deimos smiled back. "I look forward to learning my role."

"It is well." He looked down, adjusting his harness *just* so.

It was only the instincts of a thousand battles that saved him, a flicker of too-fast motion just at the edge of awareness – a motion that *should* have been sensed, should have been *anticipated*, by the god-power, but *was not*.

Still, he was Ares, God of War, and he was armed and armored, and his sword caught the blade scant inches from his chest, whipped around, sent the black blade flying, and nearly took Deimos' head from his body; the youth bent back, supple as a willow-wand, and Ares' weapon passed not a hair's breadth from his nose, shaving stray golden hairs that had failed to fall as fast as their owner.

Ares leapt back, calling his shield with a simple effort of will; an assassin, once committed, had no choice but to press on. "What treachery is this, Deimos?"

"Oh, treachery *long* planned, Ares," the slender yellow-haired youth answered, an uncharacteristically savage grin on his face. "Longer than I wanted, honestly," he went on, and Ares saw the ebony blade fly back to Deimos' hand. "You've spent *years* doing nothing but your idiotic parties and plays... *Demons*, but I have been wondering how a useless fop like you could *possibly* be the God of War." The smile sharpened. "But it seems you *are* more than a popinjay, eh?"

Ares reached out his senses... and immediately knew something was terribly, terribly wrong. To all appearances, Deimos was but an ordinary human. But that should not be true; he had been enhanced when selected, and even leaving that aside, no ordinary human could possibly have *entered* Olympia without much help.

Could he have had help? Are there any here who would truly wish me ill? The thought was terribly upsetting, but with an assassin in his chambers, it was a necessary thought.

But even if he admitted the possibility that one of the others of the Pantheon wanted him dead, the idea that they'd send a mortal, even a very, very *skilled* mortal, was ludicrous.

Deimos darted in, so fast that human eyes could never have followed him, and Ares backpedaled, barely able to parry the storm of strikes; then his assailant withdrew, and they circled, each seeking a weakness. *And he is definitely no human. Yet I sense no power from him. He moves at speeds beyond mortal, strikes with the force of a giant in the frame of a child, yet I sense…*

A chill of horror crept down his spine. Few indeed were the beings who could use their power so well, yet hide it so perfectly. He concentrated, sent out a pulse of the godspower in the form of a message, an alarm, precisely and only attuned to his sister.

The alarm – the very power that composed it – vanished in midair.

And now I know my adversary.

He called the power up, keeping it *within* himself, not allowing it to go beyond the bounds of his body. With the speed of Zeus' lightning, he streaked back into the armory, pursued by the thing calling itself Deimos. His right hand released his sword, reached out, caught up another blade, as his left arm raised the red-and-gold shield, took a blow from the black knife. The blade carved three inches into the rim of the shield – but that bound it for just the briefest moment.

And in that instant his new sword – glittering, pure silver – struck, cleaving Deimos' head in twain.

For a moment he stood, staring down at the grisly sections of his assailant's head, each hanging from part of the neck, then withdrew the sword.

The body staggered back, then, impossibly, flipped away from him, the head *re-forming* and smiling, the teeth now longer, shining, glistening like crystal. "Oh, very *good*, Ares, you're not so bad as I thought!" The voice wavered on the edge of a laugh; it *did* giggle, and the sound was oh, very not sane.

Ares felt the horror closing in on him. *How? I was* sure *that would kill it! Did I guess wrong? But then what…?*

His knees wobbled, and without warning it was nearly impossible to stand, as though…

"…as though your very strength was being drained? *Precisely*, Ares!" There was now just a line, a faint scar, down the center of Deimos' head. "Oh, you *did* think fast, *bravo* for your performance!" A slow series of claps, with the mouth broadening, teeth growing longer. "You were even... *almost*... right."

The transformation accelerated, and the figure loomed up above Ares. He fought desperately to move, to escape, but now he was on his knees. It bent down, immense, sparkling fangs inches from the throat of the god, and breathed out three more words, the breath hot and hungry.

"But *only* almost."

Chapter 1
A Pause Before Leaving

"Our mission ended some days ago, Ingram."

Ingram Camp-Bel kept himself from jumping in startlement only because he was *used* to Quester managing to surprise him. The seven-foot-tall Iriistiik was incredibly quiet despite size and his insectoid, chitinous armor. "We agreed to stay and help."

After almost two years together, Ingram could read Quester's expressions — which combined posture, gestures of antennae, and particular scents — almost as well as he could human, and what he smelled now was a tolerant amusement. "*You wanted to stay and help, and I did not gainsay you. But the Vantages are well moved into their new home, and aside from that first night, there has been nothing of note.*"

"Urelle and Kyri lost their parents, and *then* their brother," Ingram said, with an inward twinge at the thought of his own family. "No one knows who or what did it, and if it, or they, are after the family — they could be just a week or two behind."

"I note you don't mention Lady Victoria."

Ingram snorted. "*That* old woman can protect herself."

The antennae waved and the cutting jaws *click-clacked*. "I can make no argument there. And they have already begun hiring a household. Do they truly need us anymore? Adventurers," a wave of the shining-black hand with its three clawed fingers, "are usually expected to Adventure. Unless you contemplate a change of profession to house guard?"

"Not sure I want to stay in one place all the time... but the beds and food are better, you have to admit that."

"Truth."

"I can't *believe* you *did* this!" a girl's voice shouted from across the hall. There was a window-rattling *thud* of a door slamming, and Ingram turned to see Urelle Vantage practically running up the stairs, tears in her huge gray eyes, ebony-shining hair streaming behind her. She skidded slightly as she hit the top, but caught herself and stormed into her own room, slamming that door as well.

Ingram found himself halfway up the stairs, mouth open, before he realized that, firstly, he had no idea what to say since he didn't know what was going on, and second, it wasn't his business, and third, *he* was supposed to be standing watch, and he couldn't do that looking at a closed door.

"What was *that* about?" he murmured as he returned to his post before the front window. He ignored the tilt of head and scent of mingled snowberry and cinnamon that was Quester's equivalent of a knowing grin.

"Obviously Lady Victoria has done *something* to meet with her disapproval," Quester said. "Not, naturally, that it is any of our concern."

"More that I've *failed* to do something," came the precise, if weary, voice of Victoria Vantage. The elegant, slender figure of their employer stood outlined in the door of her own room, from which Urelle had fled. "You may have noticed that Kyri did not come home this evening."

"I did, in fact, but I presumed she had business in town," Ingram said. "Not true?"

"Now that most of the day has passed, I can tell you that she will not be returning, at least not in the foreseeable future."

"What? You all just got here! Where's she gone off to?"

The tall woman regarded the two of them for a moment, black-and-silver hair adding a severity to her penetrating blue gaze – a gaze which lingered on the Guild patches on both their shoulders.

"She has just become Guilded, as are you," she said finally. "And felt there was some pressing business to attend—"

"Lady's *Spear*, she's gone back to Evanwyl for vengeance," Ingram heard himself say, and knew even as he said it that it *had* to be true.

One narrow eyebrow quirked upward. "Well, you *do* have the instincts for this job, I will allow. Not *quite* as simple as all that, young Ingram, but as a general idea, it will do. Kyri has found herself... Called, if you follow me."

Ingram nodded. "Like the God-Warriors back home," he said, remembering a particular face he had not seen in a long time and missed, badly.

"And young Urelle resents having been left out," Quester said.

"I am afraid…" Victoria shook her head with a rueful smile. "I am afraid she is far too much a Vantage to accept that she should simply stay back where she is safe."

"I'd think you'd be glad," Ingram ventured. "Being angry and wanting to *do* something… lot better than she was when we started."

He remembered his first sight of Urelle Vantage – a tiny figure in the carriage, face unnaturally pale beneath brown skin, gray eyes as dead as winter sunlight glinting on ice, staring blankly into the distance. *Just recovered from her parents being killed, started to come out of her shell, then her brother's slaughtered a few hundred yards from home.*

Victoria's gaze dropped, then she nodded. "Oh, far better, yes."

A belated shock hit Ingram. "Wait. Kyri *just* became Guilded? She didn't have a patch yesterday! That's… that's faster than *we* got it, and we took the expedited route!"

Victoria chuckled quietly. "Yes, it is a bit sudden. Come, let us sit down."

"I'm on guard—"

"I am *quite* sure we shall be safe enough in the side room, young Camp-Bel."

Well, she *was* the boss. Quester was already following her, so Ingram shrugged and went after them.

Victoria gestured at the standing teapot, which began steaming instantly. "A convenient trick one learns on the road," she said in answer to Ingram's blink of surprise. "Allow me to pour."

She served each of them in turn, then sat in the high-backed chair usually reserved for her use. "As I said, Kyri was Called. As Adventurers yourselves, and ones who have helped protect Kyri and myself as well as little Urelle, I feel it is no more than you have earned to know that her Call came from Myrionar Itself, after she discovered who was truly responsible for the murders of her parents and her brother." She gazed at them, that eyebrow arched again.

Ingram glanced at Quester, who suddenly stiffened. In his head, he heard the faint voice of his friend through the link they had forged over the last year or two: *Ah. It is all too clear now. You understand, do you not, Ingram?*

He thought; obviously both Victoria *and* Quester thought he had enough information to see the obvious. *They didn't know who'd done it before we came. Then Kyri… well, she got so upset she just ran off into the Forest Sea, which was a crazy thing to do. She was lucky she came back alive. Whatever she found out made her so upset that she couldn't even* think.

Kyri being Chosen *did* explain that moment he'd seen her the other day, where it looked like her hair was blue and gold, with a flash of silver-white over her forehead. She must have colored it black again afterward. *Blue, silver, gold – Myrionar's colors. Victoria says it was* Myrionar *who chose Kyri, but that makes no sense; the representatives of Myrionar are...*

"Ares' *Balls*," he breathed. "The *Justiciars*?"

"It *does* seem insane, doesn't it?" Victoria said. "The Justiciars are the chosen of a god. How could they betray the very *ideals* of the god they serve? But the evidence is far too strong to deny. And Myrionar confirmed Kyri's deductions Itself."

Quester dipped his antennae in a nod, moderated by a scent of vinegar and pine. "That she has a driving mission, that is understood; and, too, that it would be unwise for her younger sister to follow her without a god's support. But still the mystery of her becoming Guilded in less than one day remains."

"Good fortune is the answer – she chose well in her relatives and their acquaintances. One of them happens to be the Marshal of Hosts for the King, who is also an old Adventuring friend of mine. With him as a direct sponsor, she could get her patch in a matter of an hour or two."

Ingram almost dropped his teacup. "You know the *Marshal of Hosts*?"

"I do – as do you, I think."

"I've never been to the Palace," Ingram objected.

"Neither have I," Quester said. "The only Sauran either of us has ever met – as far as I am aware – is one named Toron, who administered the practical portion of our examination. I was given to understand he was retired from Adventuring, but still a visitor to the Guild."

"And right you were. But old Bridgebreaker, as we used to call him, just didn't bring up his *other* job. That's very much his way. He was meeting you as a fellow Guild member, not as an official of the Crown. But when I mentioned your name, and especially that you were travelling with an Iriistiik, he remembered you well."

Ingram stared. "He... Oh, *Cycles*! He *mentioned* that the adventure they used to test us... that when *he'd* gone through the real original of that adventure, his friend Victoria had been furious at him for missing her brother's wedding..."

"And yes, I was! Oh, my, that takes me back." She sipped at her tea, a faraway smile momentarily touching her face, eyes shining in memory; Ingram thought it made her look decades younger.

She blinked the reminiscence away. "In any event, now you understand what has happened, and why Urelle is so upset. I cannot, in honesty, blame her. In her position, I'd be furious with me as well. But…"

"…but she's the last of your family," Ingram said. He felt an ache in his chest, the longing he always had to keep at bay, for a family that could never quite be his. "Camp-Bels understand that. Kyri's taking a dangerous road. I hope she knows what she's doing."

"When the gods direct us, we have to assume *they* know what they're doing," Victoria said dryly. "If this had been solely *her* idea, I assure you I would never have let her leave. But Myrionar Itself made her Its true Justiciar and laid Its command upon her – a command she accepted." She sighed. "I would not take it amiss if both of you were to say a prayer or two for her."

"I will remember her to the Lady," Ingram promised. He looked at Quester.

"And I, as well, shall make sure Shargamor hears my prayers for her." The insectoid gave a smooth bow and ripple of antennae.

"I thank you both, then." She stood. "It *is* getting a bit late – Urelle should have been asleep before now, but she always waited to say good night to Kyri, and thus… this." She glanced up the stairs, in the direction of Urelle's closed door. "Keep an eye out, if you would? I would not put it *entirely* past my youngest niece to pack up and attempt to head out on the road herself."

And that *would be really, really bad.* Oh, the Great Road itself was reasonably safe, but even it had its dangerous stretches, and several hundred miles before Evanwyl it grew more and more damaged until there was no Great Road at all. Even a pretty capable young wizard like Urelle would be in real danger at that point – as their recent journey *from* Evanwyl had proven.

"You can count on us, ma'am," he said emphatically. "We'll make sure she doesn't go anywhere."

"Thank you, Ingram." She crossed the front hall, heading towards her room.

Ingram looked at Quester. "You know what *that* means."

A buzz-sigh from his friend. "One of us must keep an eye on the windows upstairs."

"Hope she hasn't left *yet*."

"I will go. If I am not back, take it that I am certain she has not yet left precipitously, and thus I am watching."

"Got it. Assuming she hasn't already taken off, I'll come relieve you in... about four hours." That'd be long enough to get a decent nap in.

"Understood." Quester bowed and disappeared out the front door.

Ingram sighed and headed to his own room. *Best get rest while I can!*

Chapter 2
A Night Seeking Answers

Urelle drifted down through the air, the airwing enchantment fading away. *Still, that's brought me almost half a mile from the house. Should be enough.*

She was still furious, though a part of her – an increasingly *annoying* part of her – was starting to sound like Auntie Victoria and telling her that this was a really bad idea. Still... "They could have *trusted* me!" she muttered, as her toes touched down on the leafy floor of the Forest Sea.

"Like your aunt could trust you to stay in your room?"

At the voice from behind her, Urelle gasped and spun, fingers already grasping the fabric of reality before the fact that she *knew* that voice penetrated. She lowered her hand and banished the threatening glow, staring at Ingram Camp-Bel. The little lavender-haired youth was leaning on his *anai-k'ota* casually, as though...

...*as though he'd been* waiting *for her.*

Belated realization of his words struck, and she felt a hot blush on her cheeks. "That's not—" She bit back the words. "I didn't *say* I was staying in my room," she said after a moment.

Ingram nodded. "No, I didn't hear you do so. But given that you aren't allowed outside the estate defenses after full dark, the *expectation* that you'd stay was reasonable."

"Not *your* business!" She turned and stalked away, farther into the forest.

She didn't hear his footsteps, but a sigh behind her made it clear he was following.

"And *how* did you find me this fast? You can't fly!"

"That's true. But I've had to deal with flying things more than once. I saw you leave the window—"

"I was *cloaked!*"

"To normal sight, yes." He tapped the peculiar goggles on his face. "Not to what the Founder called 'infra-red.' There, you still glow like a beacon."

That was a pointed reminder of the fact that magic was only as useful as your understanding of the *rest* of the world. The Camp-Bel's "Founder" had left the clan a lot of interesting technological devices. "Ugh. Still, I *was* flying."

"Yes, and that was certainly the right tactical choice. Quester can jump and glide, but not fly, and without warning he would never have been able to reach your altitude and catch you." He was walking next to her now, and even as he talked, his gaze swept across the entirety of the forest, watching. "Still, you relied on being able to evade sight and physical pursuit too much. You traveled in a straight line, telling me where you were going; since we *have* traveled together for quite a while, I had a good idea of your current achievements as a wielder of magic, so I guessed how far out your airwing would run out, and sprinted there at top speed."

That told her a lot about just how fast Ingram was. *He sure doesn't shame the Camp-Bel name.*

Of course, she knew that from their journey here. At first, she hadn't been able to pay much attention, but she did remember the first time she'd seen him. He'd looked in the carriage, where she was sitting – immobile, unable to think of anything except horror – and stepped in, waiting until she finally found the will to turn her gaze to him.

Then he'd said: "I am Ingram Camp-Bel, Zarathanton Guilded. Lady Urelle Vantage, my companion Quester and I will protect you on your journey. I promise and pledge to keep you safe."

And to her utter astonishment, he *had*. As she had allowed herself to emerge, slowly, from the second great loss of her life, she remembered flashes: Ingram and Quester battling a massive figure of stone, a thing born of corrupted elemental power; Ingram dueling one of the half-human, half-demon guards at the border of fallen Dalthunia, a tiny, lavender-haired waif before the nine-foot soldier, but a waif who evaded every blow as though made of smoke and dreams, and then struck with the force of a smith's hammer, staggering the soldier; the *anai-k'ota* coming apart into multiple chain-linked sections and whirling, singing and humming a song of death as the young Adventurer cut his way through a swarm of *elikzia* ants. Even Aunt Victoria had murmured her appreciation of his skill once. "That young man will go far," she had said, "if he doesn't get himself killed first."

And he's here to protect me again. From the Forest Sea.

It penetrated, then — that she was *in the Forest Sea*, the jungle that enveloped much of the central portion of the continent, a wilderness from which even trained Adventurers often did not emerge.

That part of her that sounded like Auntie was *definitely* louder. And the angry part... was a lot more like the worried part.

She looked over at Ingram, and now she could see the tension in him, his body ready to launch like an arrow from a bow. "Where's Quester?"

"He had to stay back. We're guarding the house too, after all."

By Myrionar, I probably am *an idiot.* "I can't believe you outran my airwing."

"Airwing's not *that* fast compared to other flight tricks, and you were fighting a headwind," he said, sounding at once proud and embarrassed. He glanced at her. "Can we go back now?"

Urelle let the rest of her anger fade. But there was still something else left: necessity. She had to ask a question and discover if there was an answer. "Not yet. But... could you come with me?"

His tension eased the slightest bit. "If you have to keep going? You can't get *rid* of me."

Urelle let a tiny giggle escape — it might have been the first laugh of any kind she'd had since Rion had died. "Okay. Somewhere ahead there's a clearing. Kyri found it. I don't know exactly how far, but she ran to it when she was upset."

"You want to find the *same* clearing, in the *dark*? Your sister's a big woman; if she was running half-berserk she could've gone a *long* way that night."

"I know." She sighed, then grasped reality gently, muttered the words that focused her will, and a faint glow emanated from her, illumining the space around them without making them blind to the rest of the shadowy dark beyond. "Easier to see now. And you can see in the dark already. I think we can find it. I *have* to find it."

Ingram shook his head. "Kyri being called doesn't mean you will be. And location wouldn't mean anything to a god, would it?"

"It means *something*. Otherwise why would gods focus on temples? There's some that *only* manifest in their temples."

He shrugged. "We can try. I'll give us two hours to find this clearing. Don't know how we'll be sure it's the *right* one."

"If I find it I'll know. Not," she added as he gave her another look, "because I assume Myrionar will answer. Because Kyri broke her Balance necklace when she was there. She didn't throw it away, but there's going to be a piece – a link or two – of the chain still there."

She saw his mouth quirk upward. "Ah. And you're familiar with her necklace, so you can use that connection to sense the remnants. Okay, I'll accept that. Still, two hours. No more."

Urelle gave him a brief bow, acknowledging both his limit and his tolerance.

They spoke little afterward; they'd already made more than enough noise. No need to attract any *more* attention, at least until they reached their destination.

It wasn't long before she started following in Ingram's footsteps; the boy was *experienced* in moving through the jungle without leaving traces, and he knew the general direction better than she did. *I've spent... a lot of time studying, not so much in my other training.* She wasn't *incompetent* – Lythos wouldn't have tolerated it – but she knew, just from watching Ingram duck below a branch smoothly, never touching it with even a single strand of his lavender hair, that there was a world of difference between *learning* a thing, and *doing* the thing in the real world.

Still, he turned to her at one point and gave her a quick smile. *You're doing well,* that smile said, and maybe something like *it's all okay,* too.

She smiled back, trying to convey two kinds of *thank you* in one expression. *He's easy to smile at,* she thought, and wondered at the thought.

There were scuttlings and strange, hollow, echoing calls in the distance, and whispers of other sounds in the dark. Once something snarled, a ripping, ringing sound, and began a charge, but she unloosed a quick, sharp barrage of pure force in its direction, and it turned and fled; some time later, Ingram pulled her back and gestured, showing her the nearly-invisible, ghostly thread dangling from far above. "Forestfisher," he mouthed, and she shuddered, seeing the wet glitter of the toxic line and imagining the huge, long-legged spider-thing waiting above. They gave it a wide berth.

At last, the undergrowth thickened, as it often did at the edges of the forest where light could penetrate, and they broke through into a wide, starlight-silvered clearing. "This had better be it," Ingram murmured. "It's been an hour and a half."

She nodded, then closed her eyes. She brought the vision of Kyri's Balanced Sword pendant clearly into her mind, then envisioned each of its links, glittering silver in her mind's eye. Then she reached out into the clearing, calling Reality to echo Vision.

Three glittering sparks answered her; she ran forward, knelt, and caught one up before the eldritch light faded. "There," she said, showing it to Ingram.

"That... okay, that's impressive. I'd have thought it would take longer. You just ran right up and picked something the size of a grass-grain off the ground. You were right, we found the right place. And we probably shouldn't have, so... good luck."

She nodded, feeling her heart beating faster – she wanted to say with anticipation, but now that she was being honest with herself, with fear and maybe guilt, too.

I'm here now, it's a little late to be thinking maybe I shouldn't have come at all.

She looked around, trying to decide *where...*

And there it was; a depression, a crushed place in the thick leaves and grasses covering the clearing, with the indentations of two knees so clearly visible she could imagine her sister, sobbing in rage and sorrow and heartbreak.

Urelle swallowed, then, standing with one foot where each knee had been, raised her eyes and saw the Balanced Sword, the stars representing the Sword and Balance twinkling brightly and immutably down. She reached inside her shirt and brought out her own Balanced Sword and raised it to its stellar mirror above.

"Myrionar, I lost no less than my sister!" she shouted, and her voice echoed across the clearing, making Ingram jump. "My mother, my father, my brother, my faith in the Justiciars who betrayed us! Now you send my sister away *alone*? What justice for me, for Aunt Victoria who has cared for us, protected us? If Kyri is the first of the new Justiciars, then let *me* be the second! She is a warrior; I am a *wizard*! There will be magics ranged against her, and *someone* has to protect her!"

She raised the symbol higher. "You asked her to have faith, be true to You – I will do the same! Just..." and suddenly she found no more anger, no more fine words, only worry and truth: "...just... let me protect my sister." *Not be the one who has to be protected.* "Let me do something to *help.*"

The clearing was silent, save only for the distant movements of the forest creatures. She stood there, pendant held aloft, for long minutes, waiting. She focused on the stars, begging, pleading, *demanding* that there be an answer.

But no answer came. The warm wind blew gently but impersonally through her hair, the stars glittered, as distant as ever. No spectral voice spoke, no thoughts came unbidden, no signs.

She let her arm drop at last and sagged to the ground, feeling tears start from her eyes, and desperately tried to suppress them. But she couldn't; now she knew. Kyri would walk her road alone, and have to face the Justiciars by herself. Face whatever had made their corruption *possible* by herself.

Leaving her alone.

A gentle hand touched her shoulder. "I'm sorry, Urelle."

She reached up and gripped Ingram's fingers. "It's... not your fault."

"No," he said. "But it still hurts to see you sad."

She sniffled. "Auntie didn't want me to do this."

"She was probably afraid this would happen," Ingram said. Then he chuckled.

"What's funny?" she demanded, a dim spark of combined anger and curiosity breaking through her worry and grief.

"She was probably *also* afraid that this *wouldn't* happen. That Myrionar *would* accept you."

"But that's..." she started to say *stupid*, but stopped.

"Yeah," he said. "Worried you'd be hurt by not being accepted... and even more worried how badly you'd be hurt if you went down the same path."

She glanced up, saw conflict on his face, but when his eyes met hers, his resolve firmed. "Look. You and Kyri, you're the last family your aunt has in the world. You're not alone. You still have *her*. If you go..." He shrugged. "Sometimes you *do* have to go," he said after a moment. "But don't ever forget how precious it is to have a family that loves you like she does."

She heard something behind that – an echo of pain and regret that told her *Ingram* had either never had that, or had somehow lost it. *Stop pitying yourself, Urelle*, she told herself firmly.

She stood up and glanced once more towards the Balanced Sword.

For an instant – just one instant – the stars glittered warmer, a red-orange like a perfect fire in a fireplace, and she felt a phantom caress on her face, a touch of lips on her forehead.

The message needed no words. She knew she was not Chosen – not for this, anyway. But she knew Myrionar had heard her. And that she was still loved.

She blinked back new tears and turned to the south. "Let's go home."

Chapter 3
A Perilous Favor

"I will be meditating in my chambers," Ares said to Phobos. "Please, no interruptions unless it is a matter of life and death."

Or it will surely become *one,* he thought as Phobos bowed deeply to him.

Ares – or, now that he was in private, he who had *taken* Ares for himself – barred the door, both with physical bolts and a touch of godspower. Even the new Deimos and Phobos knew very little about what he did when he was "meditating." They were, of course, aware that he was in no way the *true* Ares, but they neither knew nor, in truth, *wanted* to know exactly what he was or what his goals were.

Demons, after all, needed few explanations to assist in corruption and destruction.

But *he*... ahh, he had far more important goals than the mere breaking of the Aegeian Cycles, than the ultimate death of the Lady of Wisdom, Athena, and the rest of her little pantheon. This was, truth be told, more a... *proof of concept*, a demonstration. If it succeeded – and success was now very, very near, a scant year or three at the outside – everything he had hoped for would be his.

With great difficulty he fought down the smile of hunger and joy, the anticipation. *Do not be the child who turns to run with the ball before it has been caught!* Failure here would be *disastrous*. Yes, success seemed perilously near, but he had staked *everything* on this project.

He would be very wise to remember that when speaking with the one who held judgment in his hands.

Emotions held in check now, face calm and composed, he sat at the great desk and took up the scroll from its hidden compartment – the golden scroll that opened to a mirror-finish and slotted so neatly into the space before him. "I am here," he said to his reflection.

A moment only, and the reflection rippled, darkened, became a window into a very different room, a dimly-lit space from which another face – open, cheerful, blond of hair and blue of eye – smiled at him.

"Ahhh," said the other. "Punctual as always, Raiagamor."

"I strive to please my... forebear."

"Take a care," said the other, still smiling. "My acceptance of our kinship is still undecided – as you must well know."

"With all respect, Majesty, there is no denying you are my forebear in some manner. All that I seek is to prove my worthiness to stand with the Elders, for all that I number so many fewer years."

The smile curled, acknowledging, perhaps, a small point. "True, and an ambitious claim it is."

"Yet you have already found... some inspiration, some intriguing new thoughts, in my own invention of the moment, have you not, Majesty?"

A laugh both warm and chilling. "True, true! My current plan draws quite some inspiration from yours. But of that we have spoken enough. You were granted my aid thrice, once for each of the pleas your mother spoke on your behalf. You were pleased, I take it, with the first?"

"Your reading of the Cards was... most useful, yes, Majesty," Raiagamor-Ares said, bowing his head. "I was, I believe, able to address the... weakness it described, and also use that approach to solidify my hold in other ways."

"Excellent. I am always pleased when my services are appreciated. So you have called upon me a second time; what service do you require of me?"

"If Your Majesty would be so kind, I would query the Cards another time."

"Indeed? A bold course you chart, child. The Cards always speak true, yes... but when queried in succession they seek, more and more, to mislead the querent." The smile glittered with amused malice. "They were, after all, meant to serve a rather different hand than mine."

"I would hope that their memory might fade in ten years, enough that I might chance another question or three."

"They may, they may well. And you are, after all, on a schedule that does not allow you the luxury of waiting a century between moves."

His King produced – from whence, Raiagamor could not say – a deck of ancient cards, made for one with large hands indeed, four inches across and seven or so long; the ivory sides of the deck were just slightly touched with yellow, but otherwise the Cards were pristine. Their backs showed an intricate pattern in deep blue and gold, a pattern that made Raiagamor uncomfortable to view; he noticed that even his King did not gaze long at it. "Then ask. Up to three, you understand, as you have spoken, and as no more than three would be safe even for me."

"Understood." He waited until the King had placed the cards before him in the proper way. "Then I would ask... other than the opponents I already know, are there others I must deal with if I am to triumph?"

"An excellent question." The deceptively-human hands reached out, shuffled the cards without effort, cut them, shuffled again, and then dealt out a querent's diamond – four cards surrounding a central one.

The faces of the Cards, as always, were obscured to him; either the Cards refused to allow any but their user to view them clearly or – far more likely – his Majesty had no intention of allowing him to learn anything more of this most potent tool.

"And... a *most* interesting answer. There *is* another obstacle," he touched the central card, "as clearly indicated by the Barred Door. Between you and your goal," he flipped over the card above the central card, "is a courageous woman, as indicated by the Sword-Maiden. One who is touched by true Power of one sort or another, as shown by," another card turned, to the right hand, "the Phoenix in Flight. *Most* interesting."

His hand moved down, flicked over the third card around the perimeter. "A woman of great knowledge, or perhaps talent and skill, as shown by the Scroll and Pen." He flipped the last card. "And what is this? How very intriguing. Your opponent is also one who knows not her own power, as represented by the Blind Monk."

That was a surprising array of indicators... but one should always be cautious about alternatives. "Do all of these cards refer to the *same* person?"

The King smiled. "Yes; that requires no other reading."

A courageous woman; that was obvious. No one seeking to oppose him in *any* guise would be anything else. But the Sword-Maiden also indicated one not merely courageous, but themselves a warrior at heart. Still unremarkable, taken by itself. But touched by true Power, now, that was more rare. Added to that, great knowledge or skill and, at the same time one who did not know their own power...

Perhaps someone young, then, who has learned much in study or training, but not yet achieved full awareness of themselves... or perhaps had that knowledge withheld *from them...*

No. It could not...

He forced *that* thought to die unfinished. Believing something could not be, simply because you *thought* it shouldn't be? That was the way to ruin. But oh, if it *was* true, oh, the *blood* that would run...

"My second question, then, my King: this individual... is she the *same* girl-child that was indicated by the *earlier* readings?"

That was a simple question, and a single card was turned. "The Rising Sun says yes."

He let out a hiss and felt his form waver from that of Ares, knew his eyes glowed inhumanly for a moment. "It seems there are those who will need *severe* reprimands in the ranks," he murmured, smiling at the thought while feeling his anger *blazing*.

But control, control! He must restrain himself. The prize he sought, the right to call the King by a very different title, *that* would come not merely from success but from *control* in all things. The King valued little more highly than perfect control.

"...but that is an internal matter," he finished, once more Ares in perfection. "All I need ask, then, is where is she? How might I find her, that she be removed?"

"But of course, the natural question." The King once more shuffled the Cards and went to turn one over... then hesitated. "Curious. The Cards refuse."

"They will not answer the question?" Raiagamor was stunned. He knew the *peril* of the Cards, but he had never heard, even in rumor, that they had failed to answer.

"Hmmm. No. No, they will answer... Oh, I see." He extended his hand towards Raiagamor, and his hand emerged from the scroll, holding the Cards before the false Ares' startled eyes. "The answer lies within the Card you select, it appears."

At this range, the power of the Cards smote his senses with threat and promise so intense it was both drug and warning of danger. *Now I know why even the King is wary of them.* He reached out cautiously, using his own senses to try and grasp the currents of fate that wove about the Cards.

Without volition, his hand dipped down, plucked a card from the bottom third of the deck, and placed it face-up before him.

He recoiled for a moment, for gazing directly into his were the gray-green eyes of Athena – a sight he had no intention of allowing to come to pass in life. He relaxed the slightest fraction as the card shifted and the eyes, too, shifted, no longer directly focused on him. "Athena?"

The King had risen and was peering through the scroll. "Is *that* what you see? Of course, it would make sense."

"What do you see, then, my King?"

"I see the Card of the Flying Arrows. In this context, it means your target is in motion, traveling or about to travel far. There is no one location that can be given."

Now that he concentrated, he could sense... a *connection*. The concept of *Athena* resonated with his questions. Naturally; the Cycle demanded Athena's God-Warriors, and eventually the Incarnate Goddess herself. And between that thought, that concept, and the unknown girl or woman was some connection – a nascent God-Warrior? The Incarnate Form herself? Or even a priest, questing for either or both?

The Cards always answered truly – though they would seek to deceive, as the King warned. So this Card would tell him how to find...

He smiled. "Majesty, is it permitted that I cast a spell *using* this Card?"

"I believe that is, in fact, part of the Cards' answer to you, so yes; in this case you may."

He took forth a handful of coins – full golden Shields of Aegeia – and placed them on the mystical plaque. Then he called up both magic and godspower and gazed upon the Card, saw the *connection*, the resonance between the Card and the Concepts and the World itself. He caught up that resonance, that connection between the concept and the subject, and impressed it on the coins, *pouring* magic and the power of Ares into that connection until each and every Coin vibrated with the precise same resonance, sang with the same connection to some distant, unseen person.

With a swift gesture, he completed the enchantment, tying off the threads of magic and destiny so that the Coins themselves were linked to the target – to the woman who stood between him and the completion of his great work.

The King's fingers plucked the Card from beneath the Coins. "Well, that was entertaining. I hope you will find these answers... profitable. Feel free to call upon me – once more."

The scroll went blank, but there was no need for pleasantries between them. He knew that unless he succeeded, his forebear would not acknowledge him. But this – this was enough.

Traveling and never in one place, was she? Well, these Coins would guide his forces. They would close upon her and capture her, no matter where she was. Perhaps they should kill her upon... but no. They had failed to kill her before. He would not trust others to do the deed at a distance. Capture her, bring her somewhere he could *see*, and *then* have her killed.

In honesty, he would have preferred to do it himself, but he could not spare the time. Ares' presence was *necessary* now. The plan was in motion.

He gestured to the door, which opened. "Deimos," he called. "Phobos. Come. I have a task for you…"

Chapter 4
An Exercise and an Assassination

Quester leapt, evading the streak of bladed energy that burned waist-high through the air. But even as he did, Urelle's hand reached, formed a claw, and the very air *stretched*, as though she had grasped its substance like a rippling sheet and *pulled*.

A blast of air caught him in mid-jump, tore at his wings and body, tipped him over. He did not land with his usual grace, but tumbled like a human who had tripped over an unexpected branch; the impact caused air to whistle out of him in a high-pitched shriek.

Ingram had been closing on the girl from the other side, but *his* feet abruptly slipped out from under him; he scrabbled incredulously at the ground, but though it *appeared* to still be the grass and stone they had been sparring on, Quester saw Ingram's fingers fail to gain purchase. The girl simply stepped aside to let him pass, on his way to a full-speed collision with a boulder ahead of him.

But neither Ingram nor Quester were out of the match; and as Quester rolled to his feet, Ingram's arm snapped out, and the *anai-k'ota* broke apart, one of its crescent blades on a chain that whipped around Urelle's leg, jerking her from her feet and turning her into an anchor that slowed Ingram's headlong flight and pulled him from the unnaturally-slick surface.

Quester closed with the girl, even as the chain fell from her leg with startling ease. She gave a yelp of surprise and dove aside.

Almost he fell for the trick; but instead of smelling her scent growing more distant, he felt it getting *closer* than it should. *Illusion!*

He kicked out, and felt his leg connect with something that went *"Oooof!"* Urelle's duplicate disappeared, leaving the real girl sprawled on the ground, curling up around her stomach.

"Urelle! Are you all right?" Ingram said, dropping his weapon and running to her side. "Quester, you have to be *careful!*"

"I'm... all right. Just... got the wind knocked out of me," Urelle gasped, her face a shade paler than its normal dark-wood tint, leaning against Ingram for a moment. She swallowed and forced herself to stand, though she looked more than a bit wobbly. "Don't blame Quester. Happens in sparring, right?" She managed a smile.

"Indeed, Urelle," Quester replied. "And Ingram?"

"Yes?"

"Look down."

The lavender-haired boy saw a phantom knife protruding from his gut. He flushed darkly under his olive tan. "Oh."

"An excellent lesson," Victoria Vantage said from her seat on the overlook. "Urelle had not yielded, and you allowed your sentiment, and her apparent helplessness, to place you in the perfect position, young Camp-Bel. I think your trainers might be a trifle disappointed."

They'd give me a sound drubbing and assign me a week of drills, that's what they'd do, came Ingram's chagrined voice in his head.

In fairness, my friend, we are all friends here, and this is sparring, not life and death. But by the Nest and Wave and Forest, she plays her games to win!

A flash of Ingram's white smile. *She does that.*

"Still, you all did well. Not that I doubted your skills – you've proven them well enough on our way. But you sometimes see new things in practice."

Quester bowed, first to Victoria and then to Urelle. "And surely I have seen new things. You are a more formidable magician than we had suspected, Urelle. Versatile, indeed."

"I find the *speed* more impressive," Ingram said. "You pulled off a lot of spells in the middle of combat, in instants. You must have done a lot of work to optimize them, and a lot more practice to make them something you could do while people come charging at you."

Still rubbing her gut and moving a bit gingerly, Urelle smiled warmly at Ingram. "Well, yes, I was reading a lot of the, you know, classics—"

"—*The Seedling Heroes, Singer of Names, Armor of Chaos*, that kind of thing, right?" Quester had heard of one of those titles, and thought he knew a few similar titles, but he had never read any. *Perhaps I should.*

"Right! And if there's anything that just *jumps* out at you in those tales is that even the best wizard ends up with things right in her face eventually, so you've just *got* to be able to cast your spells fast and perfect, even when someone sticks a dagger in you."

"That is most certainly true," Victoria said. The tall woman looked down, then suddenly gave a grin and leapt from the overlook – a balcony at least ten feet off the ground – to land perfectly before them. "As the spellslingers I knew often learned the hard way."

"So, did you come down to join us?" Ingram asked.

"I am very tempted, young man. But I'm hardly dressed or equipped for the occasion." Her scent was definitely amused.

"I'll bet you have at least two weapons on you, and your dress there has at least a second-circle enchantment to protect it – and you," Ingram said.

Her eyebrows climbed high. "Indeed? And what odds would you give on that?"

"One weapon's in that... bracelet you wear," he said, pointing to a broad, elaborately-worked vinework of silver or platinum, set with green gems. "I don't know exactly *what* kind of weapon or how it's *in* something that small, but I'd bet... bet my *anai-k'ota* that it's there. And you've got a knife hidden under your skirts, strapped to the inside of your calf. Even odds you've got at least one more on you, too, maybe small of your back or in one of the little pouches at your waist.

"As far as the dress, it sheds dirt far too well, and the way you jumped showed you hadn't any worry about it getting damaged. Given that I know you pay attention to the condition of your clothes, even when on the road, that tells me they're magicked up in some way, and it's protective. Given that you're a former Adventurer and you aren't poor, you could afford..." his eyes narrowed, "...afford the best, and wow, that's *Artan* treesilk, so I'll up that guess, it's at least third-circle because anything less would be an insult to treesilk, which is stronger than steel to begin with."

Urelle was looking back and forth between them; Quester could sense her surprise... and that of Victoria Vantage, as well.

"You win full points," she said at last. "You are quite correct in every particular. I admit to being impressed. How?"

"Camp-Bel training. We are bodyguards and general protectors; being able to judge someone's potential as a threat, including telling how well armed and protected they are? That's absolutely *central* to our training. If you can judge your opponent well enough, you can defeat them. That's what..." Quester smelled a familiar half-melancholy, half-fond scent, "...what my best teacher told me."

"I would not go *quite* that far," Victoria said with a wry smile. "There were several times I judged my opponent *very* carefully, and my conclusion was that I was about to have my head and all my other extremities handed to me if I did not find a means to retreat with expediency. But your training certainly shows itself."

Ingram bowed, obviously pleased. *That partly makes up for my sparring stupidity.*

Only if you apply both *lessons in the field, my friend.*

A silent, rueful laugh of acknowledgement was the reply.

"Well," Victoria said, "I think we should have a—"

She broke off as a lightly-armored figure rounded the bend in the path leading to the new Vantage estate.

The figure was *running*, not merely at sprinting speed but at a pace that told of magical enhancement. Brown hair streamed out from beneath a protective helm, and despite his speed, it was evident that he was also alert to all around him. More worrisome to Quester was the fact that the man's armor was emblazoned with the stylized lightning bolt starburst that was the symbol of the Sauran King.

One of the King's Guard, Ingram thought at the same time. *With courier enchantments, I think.*

The man did not slacken his pace until he reached Victoria, at which point he came to an instant halt and saluted. "Lady Victoria Vantage, correct?" he asked.

The older woman returned the salute with a bow. "I am."

"The Marshal of Hosts sends his most urgent and earnest plea that you will attend him immediately at *T'Teranahm Chendoron.*"

Victoria's left eyebrow rose. "Toron wants me there *immediately*? What is the urgency?"

The man hesitated, glancing around at the others, eyes lingering with momentary surprise on Quester.

"I will be keeping no secrets from these unless I must, sir," Victoria went on, noting his gaze. "This is my niece and ward, Urelle Vantage, and these are my current aides and bodyguards, Zarathanton Guilded through examination by Toron himself."

He took a breath. "Understand, then, all of you, that what I am about to say has *not* been announced and will not be until it must be." He hesitated a moment, and Quester could scent a stunned dread, one made stronger by having to verbalize it. "The... The Sauran King is dead."

For a moment no one moved. No one spoke. Even Quester's mind seemed to have... frozen, unable to grasp the import of those words.

"*Dead?*" whispered Victoria.

The word seemed meaningless in context. The Sauran King of the State of the Dragon God had ruled since time out of mind – so long that even the incredibly long-lived *Artan* had none among them old enough to remember a time when he had not reigned, so long that at least two Chaoswars had passed since he had first ascended the throne, so long that his name was nearly forgotten, as there was no need of it; he was the King, had *always* been King, *would* always be King.

Quester managed, finally, to speak. "How?"

The messenger shook his head. "Still being investigated, sir. But... I think we can all understand that it was no natural event."

"An assassination, then," Ingram said, his face gray; that, Quester knew, was no surprise given the mission of the Camp-Bels; assassination of a ruler was the nightmare they all lived to prevent.

"It would seem so, sir. Lady Vantage?"

She gave a short, sharp nod. "Yes, of course, I will come directly. I presume the full wards have been activated, and thus why mortal runners are being sent?"

"Exactly, Ma'am."

"Then please continue on your business; I will ride to the Palace straightaway."

The messenger gave another salute, and then turned, speeding off back down the road.

"Athena's Shield protect us." Ingram's voice was barely audible. "Who would dare? Who *could?*"

"May Elbon and the Sixteen grant that we can find out," Victoria said, moving towards the small stables.

Urelle, too, was pale beneath the dark-wood complexion. "What's *happening* to the world? Mother, Father, and Rion murdered by the *Justiciars*, the Sauran King assassinated..."

"I do not know, child," Victoria said, throwing open the door and entering. She caressed the beak of the golden-plumed sithigorn inside, then led the swift riding-bird out. "But I will do my best to find out. I expect I won't be back until tomorrow morning. Close the gate behind me and lock it."

She vaulted smoothly onto the sithigorn's back and clucked a signal; instantly the bird bent forward and sprinted away, leaving a small trail of dust with its speed. In moments, bird and rider had disappeared.

Quester swung the gate shut and fastened it, feeling the wards rise about the estate, and turned back. His antennae tested the air nervously, but for what, he did not know. He could not imagine what else there was to fear.

But somehow, he thought, the worst was yet to come.

Chapter 5
An Unexpected Summoning

The night felt... *tense*, was the best way Ingram could put it. Here, several miles from Zarathanton itself, there was little light other than that of the stars and what spilled out from the windows of the sprawling mansion. And with nearly everyone asleep, there were few lights within. Even as he glanced back at the house, he saw another window go dark. Embrae, the Master of House, he thought. The taciturn woman had been hired only a week and a half ago, but already had organized the household admirably. *Partly by doing twelve-hour days. Good thing she's finally going to sleep tonight.*

But even with everyone asleep, the tension remained. The sounds of the Forest Sea were muted; the grass-singers still chirped and sang within the walls, but not as loudly, not as numerously, as just a night or three ago.

Ingram unslung the *anai-k'ota*. The feel of the cool metal in his hands was comforting. *Still, nothing should intrude upon us here. The wards are not nearly powerful enough to* stop *intrusion, but they are very good for* warning *us, and that is generally enough.* As he was on patrol, the wards were attuned to him.

He passed by the vegetable garden, absently scanning it for signs of disturbance – there were none, although it did look as though something was eating the burnroot leaves. *Better let Victoria and Isherr, the gardener, know.* The rows of vegetables were dim lines of rustling gray separated by strips of pooled blackness, except where the *vestitia*, or sparkleaf, lifted crinkled leaves that glittered with blue and gold pinpoints, making their rows a mass of harvestable constellations.

He passed into one of the small groves of trees on the estate. Whoever had owned it before Victoria purchased it had obviously valued shade and privacy, as the trees bordered all of the thirty-seven acres and were clumped here and there throughout the grounds, interspersed with bits of garden, meadow, and a small wetlands surrounding the spring that gave birth to a small, fast stream that coursed through the property to the south-southwest.

They really need more people if they want a secure watch. And stronger wards, something to keep things out *rather than just let you know when they've already come in.*

A chill and flash of light appeared before him. *The wards! Something's at the gate!*

He sprinted in that direction, listening, watching. But the locking wards remained intact, and there was – so far – no sign of any intrusion. A bell rang, signaling that someone requested admittance.

Who could there be at this *time of night? Lady Victoria? If so, why would she ring instead of just letting herself in? She has the key-wands.*

The gates came into view; Ingram gestured with his own key-wand and the lights outside of the gate brightened, showing a lone figure standing before the reinforced steel-and-ebonwood portals.

As Ingram came nearer, he could see that the man before the gates was broad and more compact than human – one of the *Odinsyrnen*. He was wearing a leather traveling coat, a wide-brimmed leather hat, and armored leather pants. *Obviously cool-spelled, or even an Odinsyrnen would be uncomfortable.* He noted a patch on the shoulder – similar to his own, but this one's background was of high gates surrounded by mountains. The only visible weapons were a pair of broad-bladed knives, one on each hip, but Ingram suspected this man had quite a few others.

"Ah. Someone's awake, then," the newcomer said, deep voice tired but cheerful. "Thought I might have to camp out until morning just to get an answer." He covered one eye and bowed. "Hengel, Guilded out of Hell's Edge, courier."

"If you'll turn and let me verify, Guildsman?" Ingram stretched the rod he had been given when he first gained his own patch. It glowed and chimed with white light and the great gates on the patch shimmered. "Thank you."

"Welcome. Sometimes wonder what the point is – never seen a fake Adventurer's Patch myself. Let me in, then?"

"A moment." The key-wand again, and the gates opened enough to admit the courier, who stepped through and let the portals shut behind him. "I've seen a fake. Or, rather, I saw a genuine Patch that had been stolen and was being used by someone else. Wand screamed fear and death and the Patch burst into flame." Ingram felt a grim smile curling his lips. "Oh, they work, believe me."

"Learn a new thing every day, don't I?" Hengel said. "Anyway, hope I'm not just heading back out on the next leg of this Loki-cursed quest, but probably am."

"Quest?"

"Aye, the Guild's been trying to run this delivery for *years*, last I heard." He reached into a pouch – one clearly larger within than without – and extracted a note, which he squinted at in the gate-light. "I'm looking for an Ingram Camp-Bel, Clan Camp-Bel of Aegeia, Zarathanton Guilded."

Ingram blinked in surprise. "Well, you're not just heading back out. I'm Ingram Camp-Bel."

"*You*? Heimdall's *Eyes*, I was expecting some ancient warrior, not some slip of a boy barely sword-high. I'll need to check your identity, of course."

"Of course." The other waved his own rod past Ingram's patch, verifying his Guild status, and then dug into the pouch again and extracted a flat, transparent crystal rectangle. Ingram felt his eyes widen; he hadn't seen one of those since…

"I'm told if you're the right guy, touching this little plate'll prove it."

Feeling as though the world were becoming distant, unreal, Ingram reached out and pressed his thumb onto the shining surface.

Instantly it glowed, gave a mellow tone, and the color shifted to pure green. "Well, give me stilts and call me a giant. You *are* the guy." It looked like Hengel was having trouble believing it as well. "Then I can finally put this as a completed mission."

He reached into his backpack and pulled out a small, simple metallic box, barely larger than Ingram's hand, with a symbol Ingram had known since he was a child inlaid on the top. Hengel placed the box in Ingram's hands – hands that were shaking – and bowed. "I'm not to see what you do with the thing, whether you open it or throw it away, so I'll bid you good-night, Ingram Camp-Bel."

"I… I thank you, Hengel. Should I… I mean, is there a cost…"

"To a fellow Guildsman? Nay, think no more of it."

Still, Ingram pressed two Scales into Hengel's hand. "For your trouble, and my thanks for the delivery. May… may the road be smooth and your way safe."

When the gate was once more closed and Ingram was alone, he moved away and sat down on one of the square stone blocks that lined the walkway, staring at the box. From the top surface, the symbol shone: stylized curves that represented a ship, a *starship*, in flight, against an ebony backdrop sprinkled with silver-shining stars, bracketed on each side by an open book. The symbol of *Rhyme and Reason*, the ship of the Founder.

Sent from Aegeia. Sent from the Clan. From the Clan to me.

Ingram couldn't believe it. He'd *left*. He'd *had* to leave, after what had happened, what he'd heard, what he'd learned. *He said it's been* years. *Do I open it?* If "years" was true, they must have sent it out within... weeks, months at the most, of the time he'd left. It had been chasing him from adventure to adventure. He and Quester had just never stopped long enough. Whatever reason they'd sent it, it couldn't be... *relevant* any longer.

Could it?

Couldn't it? asked the colder, more analytical side of himself. *I know what this is. I know what it almost* has *to be. I left without permission. I stole from the Clan, no matter what excuses I've given myself, what justifications I've made myself accept.*

His heart pounded faster and he felt sweat on his palms, making the metal box slick as it sat there in his trembling hands. Within would be an official note, written by Mother and Father... if not by the Captain directly. It would express the Clan's grave displeasure, and order him to return without delay for a trial, a court-martial, there to be stripped of Clan and kin.

It was a summons he could not refuse, nor one he could delay. Once read... he would be honor-bound to return by the swiftest means possible to Aegeia, to present himself to the Clan for judgment.

I could refuse to open it. If I never see it, if I never read it, I haven't been given the command. I can stay here, with Quester, with Urelle.

The thought itself was shocking. But it was seductive, and in its way true. *I don't know that's what's in here, I'm just guessing. I don't have to see it. If I don't see it, I'm not ignoring a command...*

He swallowed hard, then looked to his own shoulder. The Adventurer's Patch glimmered there. *Will I be so much a coward? How can I wear that symbol, take pride in being Guilded of Zarathanton, if I won't and can't face my own sins?*

He couldn't. That was the hardest truth, the simplest, yet most painful answer. If he wanted to retain any semblance of honor or pride, he couldn't ignore this message, one that had pursued him through the years and thousands of miles. Perhaps... perhaps even the dishonor of losing the Clan might not drive Quester away. They had traveled long and far together.

But he would not *deserve* Quester's regard – or that of other people he cared for – if he didn't face his own responsibilities.

With that thought – and before he could have any second thoughts – Ingram grasped the box firmly, thumbs touching the sides, and said "Ingram Camp-Bel, inducted on the third day of the seventh month of the tenth year of Cycle Three Hundred and Fourteen."

The box hummed and the top sprang back.

Shock and disbelief enveloped Ingram, numbing him with uncomprehending horror, blotting out anything except the thing that lay atop the folded paper within. Shining in polished gold and silver alloy, the figure of a bird of prey ascending, wings spread and raised above the narrow beaked head, a symbol of courage and spirit... and in this place, in this way, of something terrible and impossible.

Ingram! Ingram, what is it?

The voice within his head broke through his stunned disbelief. He heard a whirring of wings, saw Quester sailing through the air, weapons drawn. *What happens? How are we assailed?*

"I... it's nothing, Quester. We're safe," he said numbly.

"*Nothing?*" The buzzing voice shook with his friend's confused emotions. "My friend, never have I scented such shock and fear from you, not even when we faced the Darkness That Devours. What is that before you, that you cannot take your eyes from?"

"I..." He slammed the lid closed, although that could not in any way remove from him the memory of what he had seen, rose, and began walking. "A message. A message I cannot *believe*."

Quester studied him as they walked, great faceted eyes sparkling in the faint light from the stars. "Tell me. Tell me so I might understand, nest-brother."

He felt a sting in his eyes at that term, because he knew what that meant to Quester. "I... I did not... didn't leave my clan happily," he said finally.

The antennae dipped, there was a touch of lemon shading to cinnamon. "So I had guessed, from things said and unsaid. You were... exiled? Cast out?"

"Not... quite." *Might have been easier.* "I left on my own. Took things that... well, if I'd been *sent* on a mission by the Clan I would have perhaps been allowed to take them, but..."

"Ah." The insectoid face was hard to read, but the spike of tar and iron in his scent showed shock and disappointment. *I talked about the Clan, but I had already dishonored myself to the Clan. No wonder he is disappointed.*

They were near the house now, and Quester was a shadow against the darkness. Finally he spoke. "Why?"

Ingram ran one hand through his hair, feeling the old anger and betrayal and sadness, tears trying to force their way out. Finally, he sank down, leaning his back against the stone. "I was angry. So *furious* with them all, and especially M... Mother and Father."

"Why?" Quester asked again.

Ingram gave a snort of laughter, laughter without humor or lightness. "Because I heard a truth I wasn't supposed to hear. A truth I'd always suspected I'd hear if I listened."

Trying to tell Quester took him back, so that he could see it, could *hear* it all again. Barely recovered from that terrible day, his body finally whole, walking down the stairs quietly, carefully, so as to disturb no one, so he could go outside alone... and hearing his parents, their voices low but tense, with anger and fear, coming from the study, the door almost-but-not-quite closed.

"*...a complete disaster,*" his father had said. Ingram could see his dark face in his mind's eye, stern, worried.

"*I know. Ingram should never have been there,*" his mother said, and he could imagine her too, tense with worry, brown eyes watching her husband and partner, hair the color of dark-polished wood curling out of control from a tight ponytail.

"*He was* barred *from there. Forbidden! And* she *should have...*" His father sighed. "*But what else could we expect, Ianthe? Ingram was* raised *a Camp-Bel. He... he tries to be one of us.*"

"*He* is *one of us, Rastus!*" his mother retorted. "*Ever since—*"

"*He* cannot ever *be truly one of us, Ianthe,*" his father said, coldly. "*You... we... see him that way, but we know the truth, we saw the truth—*"

"*Don't,*" Ianthe said, even as Ingram began backing slowly away, a dull horror filling him at the knowledge that even his parents didn't truly see him as a Camp-Bel, no matter how much he had tried. "*Don't... I know. I know I should not think of him as our child...*"

Her voice faded as he turned and ran, as quietly and swiftly as he could, tears streaming silently down his face.

Ingram became aware that he had trailed off, that the night had been silent save for the grass-singers and the wind for long moments.

Then Quester's clawed hand came to rest gently on his shoulder, and he looked up to see the great-eyed head bent low. Ingram felt the feather-light touch of the two antennae, and for a moment could *sense* the aching sympathy of his friend. "Oh, nest-brother. What a terrible thing to learn, to hear, and a terrible way to learn it."

"I should have stayed, should have confronted them," Ingram said, unable to keep his self-directed anger and disgust from his voice. "Instead, I ran, got into the A&A – Armory and Archives – and took what I told myself was my rightful inheritance, my severance pay, whatever." He looked down. "I'm a coward and a thief, that's the truth, Quester."

His friend was quiet for a moment. "You are not a coward, Ingram Camp-Bel. Whatever you might have been in the past, you have never shown cowardice in my presence, in all the time we have been together. Nor have you stolen, or done any other thing that would dishonor our bond, or the Guild that is our family and home."

Ingram could no longer keep tears from spilling out. He let them come instead, crying quietly for the pain of the past and the faith of a friend he wasn't sure he deserved.

But when that was over, he felt... clearer. Ingram drew a long, shaky breath and looked up.

Quester nodded. "So, what is the message, then? That you return to be tried?"

He tried to laugh. "Ha. No, that was actually what I *thought* it would be. Instead..." He opened the box, showed the glittering winged symbol. "...instead, I've been sent the Captain's Insignia."

"I sense much significance within your mind, but I do not understand, myself."

"It can mean... a lot of things, depending on when and how it's presented. There are only four Insignias. One's worn by the Captain of the Clan at all times. The other three are... tokens of command, I guess. The Captain can hand them to people to allow them to speak with their authority, or can send them to someone as a command that cannot be disobeyed."

He looked down, afraid to touch the Insignia. "By sending this to me..." He felt the tears threaten to return "By sending this to me, they've already said *you are a Camp-Bel* to me, so loudly, so emphatically, that even *I* can't miss it. But they've also said *answer this call*, and I'm terrified what could possibly require them to call back a runaway who didn't even... didn't even measure up," he finished miserably.

"I find *that* hard to believe."

Ingram shook his head. "You never saw the *real* Camp-Bels. That's why a part of me always knew what I would hear, if I listened... don't they say that none who listen at doors will like what they hear? In any case..."

He picked up the Insignia, feeling a faint tingle as it sensed a new hand touching it... and accepted him. *I really am the one this is for. By Athena and her missing Father...*

Filled with trepidation, he picked up the paper beneath it. It was a small, folded note, sealed with his father's symbol. He broke the seal and read:

Return at once. Avoid well-traveled routes; danger is extreme; enemies may be seeking you. There are things you must know, that must not be written nor spoken outside of the Clan. This order remains in force no matter how long this message takes to reach you.

Be swift and be safe.

Lady and the Founder protect you.

Rastus, Clan Camp-Bel

Ingram stared at this brief note, trying to grasp all the implications. *Danger is extreme.* Rastus would not use a word like "extreme" lightly. *Things you must know.* What things? About his not being Camp-Bel? He knew about that – he had been adopted into the Clan because they felt responsible for what had happened to the rest of his family. What else? What terrible secret that could not even be *hinted* at in such a secure message?

"'This order remains in force no matter how long this message takes to reach you,'" he murmured, still disbelieving.

Quester nodded, antennae emphasizing the motion. "An order of grave import. What will you do?"

"Do?" He took a breath, then slapped his face with his hands twice, briskly. The shock and quick snap of pain cleared the confusion. "There's only one thing

I *can* do, Quester: go. As fast as I can by the less-traveled route, through wilderness if I have to."

"So we will leave tomorrow—"

"No, I have to leave *now*." He thought he heard a faint noise at that statement, but looking around, he saw no indication of anyone else; the house remained dark and quiet, and nothing else moved except the plants in the breeze.

"This..." he gestured to the box, "this is an *imperative*. By strict interpretation, if I was given this command in the middle of... of pulling a family from a flooded river, I would be expected to drop the rope and start on my journey." At Quester's abrupt head-tilt, he added, "Not that I *would*!"

"I would not think so. But I can feel the urgency. You cannot bring yourself to wait until the morrow, when Lady Vantage returns?"

Ingram shook his head, tension building within him. "No. No, I wish I could, but I can't. It's been two years reaching me. I know, one might say 'but then, what difference could a day make?', but I say, what if I return one day late? I have to go. I'll... I'll leave my own note. I don't know what she'll think of me for it, but you can tell her."

"Tell her? How could I do that, when we are already on our way?"

"Quester, this is *my* problem, maybe my trial! I can't ask—"

"You are my *nest-brother*," Quester said, with a strange combination of patience and annoyance. "What threatens you, threatens me. What duty calls to you, I must also answer that call. Unless you would repudiate that bond, then I, too, go with you."

He stared at Quester. "But... I *ran away*, Quester. I *stole* from my own Clan. I—"

"—you are considered still part of your Clan. Whatever you may have done or heard, they have sent you what is – by your own words – the highest symbol of your Nest, your Clan Camp-Bel. Would they send that to one who was only to be disgraced and punished?"

He found himself shivering, and for a moment he didn't know why. "N... no. No, they would just send me the recall, and tell me why."

"Then – no matter your own view of your actions – they still hold you in esteem, or at least in enough honor that no lesser call would suffice. Perhaps it *is* for some terrible purpose... but not, I think, one so petty and tragic."

"No. You're right." Now he understood the shivering. It was *fear*. Not fear for himself, but fear of the unknown, fear of what horrific secret might have impelled the Captain to call the renegade child home with such desperate emphasis.

"You're right," he said again, and it seemed the night shivered for him. "Let's go, then."

But as he turned to enter the Vantage mansion for the last time, he felt the fear recede; because no matter what, he would not face it alone.

Chapter 6
An Ominous Conversation

Urelle watched from her darkened window as the two passed out of the gate, her heart beating twice, three times its normal speed. *Ingram and Quester are* leaving!

She'd heard a lot of their discussion; enough to make her eyes sting at what had happened to Ingram, why he'd run away, and to be worried *very* much about what danger he was heading into. Quester was obviously worried too.

But they'll need my help!

That, another part of her mind told her, *is one of the most arrogant things you've ever thought.*

But it *wasn't*, not entirely. Ingram was dangerous – there wasn't any doubt about that – and with Quester, he was four times better. Yet neither of them was a *wizard*. If they were being followed by unknown enemies, they'd *need* someone who understood magic.

Oh, really? They were Adventurers, Guilded, before they met up with you. Two years or so, I think they said? If they really *needed a mage with them, wouldn't they have already found one? One with actual* experience *in the Adventuring game?*

Yet the rest of her felt – even more strongly – that Ingram needed her. Needed her *badly*.

Which, she had to admit, really didn't make sense. She was used to him, yes, and he was fun to have around, he'd been more than just fun when she was... was finding her way out of shock and darkness. He'd been an *anchor*, sometimes more so than her sister Kyri or Aunt Victoria, just because he *was* like her – small, studious, even if he was also more than capable of fighting, preferring to think rather than fight if he could.

She would miss him. Miss him *terribly*. But that was no reason to go following him. Her sensible side was right.

So why did she feel so clearly that it was *wrong*? Just because she didn't want him to go? Was she *that* pathetic, that she had to cling to everyone?

Even as she thought that, she knew it was, at least, *part* of the truth. She *did* want to hold on to the people around her. "I have *reason* to," she whispered to herself. Her parents. Rion. Kyri, on a deadly mission of justice and vengeance. And now Quester and Ingram.

Was that all? No. Even examining herself in the most coldly unflattering light didn't provide explanation for it all. Somehow a part of her was *convinced* she had to follow them.

Myrionar? Is it you? Are you telling me this is the reason I couldn't follow Kyri? Because I was supposed to follow him?

She stared out the window, craning her neck to see the portion of the Balanced Sword that could be seen above the roof. The stars remained their normal color. If it *was* Myrionar, it was not going to give her a sledgehammer of a sign.

If I don't have *a good reason, they'll chase me right back here anyway. And then it will be* my *fault that Ingram's delayed on his travel.* It was possible that, given the urgency Ingram had mentioned, he might not turn around – that he'd feel he had to continue on – but she couldn't bet on that. More likely, if that were the case, he'd order Quester to take her back and catch up with him later.

She sat there, debating with herself, for... well, she didn't know how long, staring out into the grounds towards the gate through which the tiny boy and towering insectoid had disappeared.

What finally roused her was motion, an almost-ignored motion of black against near-blackness. She focused on that location, then averted her eyes slightly; she knew that the edges of her vision were more sensitive to movement.

Something was there, near the gate. But there was – at least as of now – no reaction from the wards.

She sketched a pair of circles before her eyes and stretched her hand and mind outward. Her little adventure with Ingram had taught her one thing, at least – not to rely on ordinary sight alone.

As reality realigned itself to her will, the grounds sprang into sharp relief, as bright as an overcast day to her newly-enhanced vision.

Four figures, gathered in front of the gate. She brought out a spyglass and focused on them.

The four were dressed very similarly – in dark, tough travel clothing that showed ridges of armor underneath. Two wore tight-fitting helms that had wide visors protected by thin bars – good field of vision without sacrificing much defense – while the others were bareheaded. She couldn't quite make out the small insignia on their arms, but she *could* see that they were all armed – at least one with a rune-carved staff.

Amplifying light went pretty well. How about sound?

Improvising a spell was a lot harder than casting one you'd practiced, but in this case, she had the advantage of knowing – as Lythos and Sasha Rithair had emphasized – exactly *what* she wanted to change about reality, and how it might be accomplished. A wide, bowl-shaped surface, just *so*, focusing sound from its entire radius onto her ears…

There was a momentary swelling and chattering of sound – insects, scuttling little animals in the brush – and then she managed to envision the collecting surface pointed directly at the gate, while still keeping the sound funneled to her.

"…only residence anywhere *near* this area," one was saying.

"Check again," another said, the voice deeper. "This gate is warded; it's a fair-sized estate. We don't want to buy trouble we can't afford."

A sigh. "Very well." The one with the staff slung it over his back, reached into a pouch and pulled out something that glittered in the amplified light. He mumbled some words that Urelle couldn't quite make out, but she knew a spell when she heard one. The object glittered and moved for a few moments.

"Ares' *Sword*," the magician cursed. "Not there. The target's in motion… that direction, looks like, though it keeps wobbling, which it shouldn't. Maybe some kind of protective ward's confusing it."

"They weren't moving in that direction before. Something…" Another curse. "That courier. The Odinsyrnen we passed a bit ago."

"Some kind of message?"

"I would think so. Don't know what it could be to get someone to start out in the middle of the damned night, but moving, they are."

"But they had to start from here, right?" the deep voice said. "No reasonable alternative. Go much past here and we're in the Forest Sea. So they can't be far. If we move *now*, we might catch them!"

Urelle let the spells drop. She'd heard enough. Four people looking for someone who had been here? Swearing by Ares?

Pursuit was closer than Ingram or Quester dreamed.

Now she had a reason.

Then she turned and was packing as fast as she could. The small so-called "neverfull" backpack would have to do. It wouldn't hold *everything* maybe, but enough. Magical equipment and notes, reagents, materials ranging from powdered crystals to hairs from an Eonwyl and a tiny piece of the tooth of a *Nahm*, one of the lesser Dragons, a vial of forestfisher venom, dozens of others. Clothing. The training tent she'd gotten three years ago and used once.

She ran downstairs as quietly as she could, yanked open the healer's cabinet. *Can't take it all – wouldn't it be terrible if I did and someone got hurt?* Still, she could take several of the bottles and enchanted pads. Those also went into the bag, which was starting to hit its limits. *Food. Maybe we can get some along the way, but can't bet on it.* The pantry and coldbox yielded enough for several days. *Bet Aunt Victoria has some marching rations somewhere, but I don't know where.*

Then back upstairs. A part of her was still telling her this was very unwise, but this time she had an actual argument other than pure pique and selfishness. She stripped off her day clothes, yanked open the armoire, pulled down the spelled armorcloth outfit Auntie had gotten her just last year and got it on – *it's a little tight, I think I've grown a bit, have to do some minor resizing later* – hooked the access pouches to the belt, along with the crystal dagger that Daddy had carried when *he* was on Adventure.

Finally, her combat gloves and the quickstaff; the latter she secured inside her sleeve in the form of a small cylinder.

I've got everything I can get on short notice.

One last thing to do – add her own note. She dashed it off and was going to place it atop Ingram's, then reconsidered; Auntie would want the context first. She slid hers underneath Ingram's, then went back a final time to her room.

She took a deep breath and forced away all her self-doubts. *If there's ever a good reason, it's to save someone else.*

She stepped off the window ledge and soared up into the starlit night.

Chapter 7
A Warning and an Ambush

How much longer do you wish to continue tonight? Quester asked.

Ingram shrugged. *I was thinking of pushing through until tomorrow night, then rest. It gets us a good push forward and back onto a normal schedule. Unless you don't feel up to it?*

I was designed *to continue for days, if necessary. If you think you can handle it, little human, by all means, let us keep going until night again falls.*

Someday we'll find out which one of us would actually fall first, but this won't be the day.

There was genuine humor in that mental message, and that made Quester feel much better. Ingram was recovering from the shock and starting to sound like his old self.

Oh, there was no doubt a lot more to come – even when they'd been traveling, it had been clear that Ingram had a lot of secrets in his past, and Quester felt that there were questions he needed to ask soon – but his friend was no longer near a breaking point.

He flicked his antennae in amused disbelief. He would never have believed that it would hurt him so much to see a human in such pain... but then, until he met Ingram, the thought of considering one a nestmate had never occurred to him. Now that he thought on it, such things *had* been known before; the memory of the Mother before him showed him some other human faces in the tale of the Nests.

He barely repressed an annoyed buzz. *A thousand pieces of trivia are mine at a thought, yet understanding my purpose? Mother, why? Is it that I am so hopeless that I cannot understand what is completely obvious, or is there a reason that even I cannot yet know?*

At least the two of them could keep a good pace; his vision at night was vastly better than the human norm, and Ingram's goggles gave him more than adequate sight for this. Beneath the canopy of the Forest Sea, it was nearly dark as within a cave.

The growth became thicker abruptly. "Ha," muttered Ingram, "We're at the clear-cut."

A moment later they had burst out into the cleared area along the Great Road. Up to ten miles wide, it provided both safety and land for cultivation by those willing to live outside the protection of city walls. Farmers, hunters, and others who needed to make their living from the land often banded together to make safe retreats, small villages and fortresses, and they were also some of the best customers of the wandering Adventurer.

To the east, perhaps a mile off, was the dark bulk of just such a local fortress. To the west, beyond the horizon, the glow in the sky showed where Zarathanton itself sat, the greatest city in the world, so huge that its very lights could guide people to it from fifty miles away, perhaps more than two hundred thousand people in one walled city about the Palace of the Dragon King.

A city that now has no Dragon King within the palace itself. A sobering thought.

They'd come out before a pasture surrounded by high fences; it didn't take long, however, to find a door in the fence and pass through.

"Sithigorns," Ingram said; the figures of the large riding-birds were visible in the blue semidarkness beneath the bright stars. A few of them lifted their heads and gave querying burbles. Ingram grinned. "Cute things."

"So long as they do not see us as threats, perhaps. I do not want to be on the receiving end of their beaks or claws."

"No, that wouldn't be fun. But don't worry; these are obviously well cared for and happy. If we don't go right up to them, there won't be a problem."

"We could purchase a pair."

"I'm tempted, but we aren't really equipped or provisioned for mounts, and we might end up going through terrain that isn't friendly to them. Best to stay on foot."

"We will make good time across here," Quester said, spreading his antennae and tasting the air. "We could head to Zarathanton or perhaps directly to East Twin and take a ship south; that would bring us to your home as swiftly as might be."

Ingram shook his head emphatically. "No. You heard the message. I can't use any of the established routes, land or sea. Near as I can tell, they want me to get there without anyone even being sure I'm *close* to home. Why, I don't know, but it's pretty clear to me."

"So, what route do we take?"

"If nothing changes?" Ingram was silent for a few moments; his scent was that of someone thinking very hard. "As much dead south as we can manage, I think. That'll take us through the south reaches of the Forest Sea – hopefully no one will even think about us taking that route – and we'll come out on the coast east of Shipton. Then we can just follow the coast, skirting the west edge of Wisdom's Fortress and that'll take us straight to Aegis." His voice shifted on the last word, wistful and sad and eager at the same time.

"That is the capital of Aegeia, yes?"

Ingram gave a grimace. "Well... yes. For most purposes. Aegeia isn't... isn't always *one* country, exactly. Aegis and the surroundings are the main state, the gateway to get anywhere else, but the interior's got five other major cities, each claiming their section of the country – Lyra, Velos, Demati, Talaria, and Amoni Agapis. They've each got their own patron among the gods, and during the Cycle, they take sides until the Cycle's resolved. Then it's all one country until the next Cycle, under Athena's rule."

Quester considered that as they continued. "It seems... rather chaotic."

"I guess. From the outside it must. I was raised with it, so it seemed perfectly sensible to me when I was a kid." He sniffed. "Hey, what are you laughing about?"

"You are only, what, fifteen, perhaps? A child still, I would think, yet you speak like an elder. 'When I was a kid,' yes?"

"Oh, be quiet." Quester could see Ingram's grin even through the darkness. "That *is* kind of funny, though. You're right."

They hastened their footsteps, and in about an hour reached the smooth, hundred-yard-wide Great Road, its surface unblemished. What sort of enchantments or materials had been used in its making, Quester could not imagine; the Great Roads had endured since before the beginning of the Chaoswars, from the age of legend, half a million years before.

Crossing the Great Road was a matter of moments, and now they were in more ordered growth of trees, a tree farm providing lumber for cities and villages alike, with wide pathways through it that turned in graceful curves, to allow easy transport of logs when each section of trees was cut. Quester felt his antennae quiver; there were many magics active here to keep the trees growing swiftly and true, to exclude pests, and so on.

Which was likely why he did not sense something approaching until the air above him rippled. *Ingram!*

The young Adventurer rolled to one side and drew his weapon in one motion, even as the new figure dropped to the path before them.

Ingram froze. "*URELLE?*"

The scent from the girl was unmistakable – as were her exhaustion and triumph. "Found you!" she gasped, steadying herself against one of the tree-trunks. "You people move *fast*."

"You... You've been maintaining an airwing *all this time?*" Ingram was astonished, and Quester felt the same; maintaining a spell uninterrupted for hours was a very impressive feat of will and focus.

Astonishment gave way to a different emotion. "What in the name of Athena Herself are you *doing* here? Your aunt will *kill* me!"

"And me as well," Quester said. "Ingram, you may have to go on for a while alone. I will have to conduct Lady Urelle back to—"

"I am *not* going back yet!" She managed to straighten. "You're in danger – both of you. I came to warn you – and help if I can."

"But you..." The tang of frustration was overwhelming, but it faded as Ingram got control of himself. "What do you mean, danger?"

"Four people, I think all human. They have something that gives them a good idea of your direction, and they're marching to catch you right now. I heard one of them swear by Ares..." she hesitated, a smell of guilt mingled with determination, "...and since I heard a lot of your conversation, I have a good idea what that means."

"You heard... *ugh!*" Ingram ran his hand through his lavender hair. "All right. Four of them, you said?"

"Four. Two armored and equipped as warriors, one clearly a mage of some kind, the other I'm not sure; could be another mage or a channeler, or could just be someone who prefers speed and evasion to just wading in and taking a shot."

Quester tilted his head, then bowed in appreciation. "Perhaps we did not invite you, Lady Urelle, but your information is most timely. How close are they?"

"I think they're about three miles back right now, but they're hustling. They'll catch you about the point you reach the Forest Sea again, if nothing changes." She was following now, as Ingram had started walking again.

"Do they know about Quester?"

"I don't know. They weren't detailing their knowledge. I was lucky to hear as much as I did."

"True. Well, even if they do, they won't know about you. And three to four with a hidden weapon is a strong position for us. I think we should hustle ourselves, just enough so we have time to set up an ambush." He looked up at Quester.

After a few moments of thought, Quester nodded. "I see no better alternative. If they have some way of following you, we will have to deal with them sooner or later – most likely sooner."

"I could do something about that," Urelle said, "but not without a little time to work."

"Okay. We'll worry about getting you back to Victoria later. For now, let's move."

About an hour later they had reached the edge of the Forest Sea. "Here, Ingram. I believe this will be ideal."

The boy looked around and grinned; Urelle echoed him.

The terrain here dipped into a natural path, with banks above a small stream that led nearly due south. It was an excellent way to pass through this part of the Forest Sea heading in that direction. "You're right. This will work perfectly. We can take them from the ridge tops there," he gestured. "Let's walk down here about a hundred yards, then we'll get to the top and double back. Urelle, can you do that slippery-ground trick again?"

She nodded. "I definitely can."

"Then cast it *right* there, see? If you can make it cover enough area –"

She was nodding enthusiastically. "Then they'll slide into that shallow dip and it will be very hard for them to get out, at least for a few minutes. Yes!"

"Excellent thinking, Ingram. Then we can be in a position to fire from either side. If they will not yield, they will be in a very disadvantageous position. We may be able to capture them and get information rather than killing."

"I'd *much* rather do that, yes. The more information we can get…"

"Then let's do it," Urelle said.

Setting up did not take long. *If they're following our track, or even just a sense of our direction, they should come right down here,* Ingram thought.

I agree. This is by far our best chance.

The wind gently rustled the leaves, blowing from the north-northwest. *There is a good chance I will scent them as they approach.*

Good. Let Urelle know as soon as they're getting close. A flicker of concern. *And we make sure to protect her* first *if things get bad, right?*

Of course. She is still our responsibility, I suppose, as Victoria Vantage has hardly had time yet to read our note and accept our resignation.

Fifteen minutes passed quietly. Then the faintest scent touched his antennae. *Humans approaching. More than one, though it will take time to sort out the scents and be sure it is, in fact, four.* He nudged Urelle and whispered, "they are approaching. Prepare your spell."

Urelle nodded, and raised her hands, fingers poised.

As four figures came into view, making their way with deliberate speed down the little valley, Quester tensed himself for action. *Nearly there.*

A vibration through the air, and abruptly he smelled something else, close—

Multiple canisters fell from the air around them and shattered, discharging a blue vapor that billowed high and wide. He tasted something sharp, and his senses wavered, focus of eyes and mind blurring. He whirled, staggering, trying to bring his weapons to bear, but he could barely see anything.

Vague shapes moved towards him; Ingram stumbled upright somehow, *anai-k'ota* at the ready, but another wave of bluish vapor enveloped them; his friend fell where he stood, and despite all the desperate urgings of fear and loss, Quester slumped to the ground, his armored head striking the soft soil at an angle; and even though his eyes were always open, he saw no more.

Chapter 8
An Inevitable Return to Duty

Myrionar's Balance *I am tired.* Victoria sighed, shaking her head, as she let Chirrup trot towards home. The bird made soft noises in anticipation of arriving at its paddock, where there would be fresh greens and comfortable hay to lie in.

Victoria was looking forward to getting home too, but she doubted she'd be sleeping easily. It was, if anything, worse than she had imagined. It was, of course, bad enough – incomprehensibly bad – that the King had been killed. But the *way* in which he had been killed? Nightmarish. Slain on his own throne, apparently by something able to approach him without rousing the slightest suspicion, or able to move at utterly terrifying speeds, or able to teleport into one of the most heavily warded chambers in the entirety of Zarathan.

Old Bridgebreaker had the investigation underway, of course. The five *very* peculiar children who had been the last known to have seen him alive had gone, and naturally they were prime suspects. Victoria's heart said that they were not involved in this, but even if she was right, they might know something vital to the investigation. It did seem that poor Toron might have had a bit of luck in the two Adventurers who'd been present at the discovery, though she wouldn't get a chance to interview them to make sure until tomorrow; they'd been seen to quarters and were undoubtedly asleep before she arrived.

The gate slowly came into view. She sighed again. The worst of the situation was the chaos that would result once the news got out. Such a thing hadn't happened... well, ever. At least, not since the Fall, and no one really knew details of *that* time.

It was the work of about half an hour to get in, close the gate, see that Chirrup was properly rubbed down and fed, so the dawn was starting to lighten the darkness in the east. *Weighted* Balance, *and I need to be back at the Castle at some kind of reasonable hour.*

She almost missed it in her hurry to find her bed and get a few hours' rest; a pale rectangle against the dark wood of the hall table. But old instincts registered the anomaly and she halted, backed up. Two sheets of paper, one atop the other.

The first was from Ingram:

> *Lady Vantage,*
>
> *I am called away by an imperative summons of my Clan, one which brooks no hesitation — which technically includes even taking the time to write this note. I am, however, an Adventurer and one who had accepted employment from you; this requires you know why Quester and I are departing.*
>
> *It has been an honor and a pleasure to serve you and your household, and I wish we had been able to stay longer. I will always remember this time fondly, and hope you will also remember us well.*
>
> *Yours,*
>
> *Ingram Camp-Bel, Clan Camp-Bel*

Well, now, that was mysterious enough. Clan business that found him this far from his home, and so urgent he couldn't wait a few hours? She shook her head. *Good luck to you, young Ingram, Quester.*

The note from Urelle was even shorter:

> *Aunt Victoria,*
>
> *Ingram and Quester are in much more immediate danger than they know. I have to go warn them and help them. No time for more explanation. I'm sorry.*
>
> *Love,*
>
> *Urelle*

Victoria sat down hard, staring at that brief missive. *Gods above, what was the child thinking?* She'd gone off in the middle of the *night* for this?

But no, that was foolish. If she took what Urelle said at face value, the girl had discovered some objective evidence that the two were in danger, and — quite naturally, for a Vantage — decided that the only thing to do was to go immediately.

Had she been thinking that rationally? Easily enough determined.

A swift survey of the house, and especially Urelle's rooms, showed that she did seem to be acting rationally. She had clearly packed quickly but carefully, and it appeared that she'd taken everything a reasonable Adventurer under time pressure would. She smiled a bit at that; it was good to see the girl was keeping her head.

Or at least was in *that* sense. Would she have gone so quickly for any random person? Perhaps, but Victoria was hardly blind to the way in which the two younger people had been becoming closer. It was possible they didn't even notice it themselves.

In any event, it was a pretty situation, no matter how she looked at it. There wasn't the slightest chance that Urelle would leave the two voluntarily, assuming she caught up with them. Ingram... he would be driven to press onward. *Possibly* he would send Quester back with Urelle, although that would be quite a job in itself, making Urelle leave if she didn't want to; she did have the Vantage strength herself, after all, and her not-inconsiderable magical talent.

But that was all secondary, circling around the point without addressing it, and Victoria frowned at herself. *Am I that old, that I dance about a subject instinctively? Or am I so afraid for her that I don't want to think of it?*

The latter, she decided. Urelle thought there was a great and immediate danger, and the girl was neither stupid nor unobservant, so Victoria thought she could take that as a given truth. And that meant that – in all likelihood – her little niece was going into a trap meant to capture, or kill, a Camp-Bel and anyone who might be with him.

Urelle is in terrible danger.

The thought, finally expressed, constricted her chest. The loss of their parents had been terrible; Rion's death, horrific. Letting Kyri go on her god-ordained mission, heart-rending.

Losing little Urelle?

"Absolutely not!" she snapped. "There's no help for it; I have to catch up with all *three* of them."

There was no time to lose, no chance to rest. *Well, for that, at least, I have recourse.* Opening the chest that held all her old Adventurer's gear, she began unpacking it efficiently, pausing to extract a bottle from her healing kit and set it aside. The alchemical draught was expensive, difficult to make, and dangerous to use more than once or twice a month... but used occasionally, it would substitute completely for a good night's rest. Best to take it just before she set out; no telling how long she'd be on the road.

Her battle coat settled across her shoulders familiarly – perhaps a touch looser than it had been twenty, thirty years before. *Haven't kept myself at my peak, have I? Scarcely needed to, of course.* The bracelet Ingram had noted stayed, of course – she hadn't been separated from it and the weapon it concealed since she'd first won it in a lethal contest. From the chest she drew and put on other items, rings and jewelry, a simple coronet of platinum across her brow, armored boots, Enkanir's Gloves, all of them more than mere decoration; and as their mystic powers flowed back into her, Victoria felt herself standing even straighter, the world sharpening into greater focus, becoming lighter and stronger and faster.

She smiled. *I had forgotten this.* She glanced down at the Guild patch on her right arm; an instant of compressed reminiscence, where she seemed to re-live a thousand adventures, passed through her mind. She shook off nostalgia, dove back into the chest. A bow, a pair of red-metal throwing knives, and her neverfull pack – still filled with everything she'd need to travel. She kept it that way... just in case.

It seemed that such prudence was about to pay off.

With the pack on her back and all the rest of her equipment in place, she headed back downstairs. *Need to leave my own note for the staff. And somehow get my apology sent to Toron. He'll be disappointed, but he'll understand.* But by the *Balance*, how was she to make sure Kyri knew? The girl might be gone for a year or three, or be back in weeks. She couldn't imagine how Kyri might react if she came back to find her aunt and little sister gone without warning.

There was a chime in her ear. Someone was at the gate.

Urelle and the others? Perhaps she convinced them to come and at least tell me, get what help I can provide. It seemed unlikely, given the wording of Ingram's note, but possible. Or perhaps the immediate danger was taken care of, and Quester had brought her home somehow?

She hastened to the gate.

There was but one figure at the gate, and it was too tall for either Urelle or the young Camp-Bel, and far too human for Quester. As she got closer, the figure became clearer. No, not human... *Artan.*

"*Lythos?*" she said in astonishment, staring at the Vantage's *Sho-Ka-Taida*, Master of Arms. "I thought you went to rejoin your people?"

Then she saw how he stood – exhausted, his impeccably-polished armor dented and scratched, a new and raw scar on his face – and new horror began even before he spoke:

"My people... are no more."

Chapter 9
Three Friends in Peril

Ingram blinked his way slowly back to consciousness into a blurred world filled with a vaguely underwater green. The dim green light, he finally realized, was from sunlight filtering through the innumerable leaves of the Forest Sea.

Having made that determination, and finding his mind starting to gain some coherence, he blinked again and forced himself to focus.

He was sitting up, bound to and against something. From the feel – without raising his head – it felt like two somethings. Backs. Quester's and Urelle's, almost certainly. Moving only his eyes, he looked to one side and then the other. Yes, on the left his wrist was bound to Urelle's, and on the right to Quester's armored primary hand; out of the corner of his eye he saw other rope, which indicated that their captors had also efficiently bound Quester's second-hands.

They were also gagged, which didn't surprise him. Some mages, and others, could evoke power just by speaking. He thought there might also be power inhibiting cords wound through the ropes, but it was hard to tell. Either way, getting out of this was not going to be easy.

There were voices around him, and now he could finally make them out.

"…been tracking them this whole time!" A tenor voice, controlled but angry.

"You and all the others, yes. But you didn't *catch* them, did you?" That voice was deeper, a touch smug. "That was *our* group, and a good thing, too; they were laying for you, remember."

Both had familiar accents. *From Aegeia, definitely. Urelle was right. But this sounds like there were at least two groups hunting for me?*

He raised his head.

Eight people sat or stood in a rough circle a short distance off. They *all* fit the descriptions Urelle had given them. *All part of the same general force?* He didn't recognize the specifics of their outfits, but that didn't mean much; a private guard or secret operations group wouldn't publicize their dress code and insignia. Three of them were unhelmed, though likely not without head protection, but they all had the same dark clothing with hints of some form of armor underneath and, with one exception, all of them were clearly armed. *One trained in bare-handed fighting, perhaps, maybe even a God-Warrior candidate, or possibly just has a concealed weapon.*

There didn't seem to be any others, at least not to Ingram's quick glance around. That didn't, unfortunately, mean that they were unwatched.

"Hey, the boy's awake."

"Forget him," the deeper voice said, showing that it was the bare-headed, unarmed one talking for his group. "He's not the target."

What? I'm not? That makes no sense!

"The Coins are not absolutely clear on that," the tenor – this one holding a rune-covered staff, obviously the leader of the group Urelle had seen. "They're wavering."

The unarmed man, whose head was shaved so it shone, grimaced. "Eliane?"

One of the armored figures drew out a glittering golden coin – a full Shield, in fact, over an inch and a quarter across – with a golden thread attached to it. The woman let it drop to hang from the thread, and gestured over it, muttering an invocation too low to hear.

The Coin immediately swung away from the vertical, pointing in the direction of the bound captives. But it was not steady; it swung erratically across a noticeable arc, and occasionally even twirled around to point away from them by almost ninety degrees, although most of the time it stayed somewhere in the arc bounded by the three captives.

"Hmph. What's wrong with the Athena-cursed thing? It was behaving perfectly fine up until now." The bald one ran his hand over his head in a distracted gesture.

"Ours started having trouble earlier – around the time we approached that outlying estate I mentioned before," said the one with the staff. "It concerns me."

Ingram tried, despite the gag, to say "Who *are* you people and what do you want from us?" It of course came out as incomprehensible murmuring, but it *did* get some attention.

"Sorry, boy, but since we don't know your abilities, you stay that way," the woman named Eliane said, putting away the Coin.

The one with the staff sighed. "Look, arguing gets us nowhere. We both followed the Coins here, and even if they've decided to get confused *now*, that can't be argued. The girl's the one we want. The longer we wait, the more chance the *other* groups find us. Let's all just agree we both found her, and we can *all* get the reward."

"I don't like it," the bald man said, now rubbing his chin and glaring at the three captives. "Word is that the Ainax Stratei brought these straight from the hands of Ares himself. *Something* is messing with them, Takis."

"Pretty sure the girl's a mage of some kind," Takis said. "Maybe she was working on getting a protective spell going?"

"Let's just take all three," Eliane suggested.

There was a pause. "All right, you know, that's not a bad idea. There's *something* familiar about that boy, anyway. I can't place it, but I know I've seen him somewhere, so maybe he's important too."

"And the bug?"

"They said the target was a woman. Do *you* know how to tell what sex an Iriistiik is? 'Cause I sure don't. We'll take it, too."

"How do we work this, Panos?" Takis asked the bald-headed one. "The retrieval scrolls were meant to send back a prisoner and two guards."

Panos sighed. "Look, in the interests of getting us all out of here with a piece of the credit, I'll let you choose. We've got two scrolls, yours and mine. One of us takes the girl, sending two of theirs along, and the other gets the other two prisoners, but only sends one with them."

"And we both instruct both sides to support the fact that we were *both* in on the capture?"

"Agreed." Panos turned to the rest. "You all hear that? As far as anyone back home's concerned, all of us were in on the catch, we're all in on the reward. Got it?"

The others nodded, with a chorus of "yes."

Panos and Takis gripped hands. "Agreed," said Takis. "And for that, you get to take the girl, we'll take the other two."

"Done." Panos began to turn.

"You will release those children *immediately!*"

The high, clear, cold voice cut across the clearing like an arctic knife, freezing all eight of their captors for an instant.

Striding out of the shadows of the forest came a tall figure, clad in a long battle-coat of black and silver, hair matching the coat, eyes cold as the voice. Victoria Vantage locked gazes with the others as she came. She had no weapons visible, but her very movement was a warning of peril, every step unwavering, confident and icily furious.

"What the... this is none of your business, woman!" Takis said, and at his gesture the others were unsheathing their weapons.

"First, I am Zarathanton Guilded, young man, and that makes *any* instance where people are taken captive and their captors argue how to divide their spoils *my business*." The Adventurer's Patch gleamed high on one shoulder. "And second, that is *my niece* you have there, and that makes it utterly and inarguably *my business*." She had approached to within seventy feet of the group.

"Stop where you are," Panos said, matching her chill voice with his own stone-solid tones. "Or you're going to regret it, whoever you are."

While they spoke, Ingram noticed Eliane was silent, studying Victoria with a narrowing, worried gaze.

"On the contrary," Victoria Vantage said, and without so much as a movement, a gargantuan double-bitted axe, six feet from helve to head, was in her right hand, her left coming down to get a grip, "you will release my child and her friends now, or I assure you: not *one* of you will leave this place alive."

"Enough! Take her!" snapped Panos and Takis at once.

Seven of them started forward; Eliane gasped and suddenly shouted, "Ares' *Balls*! That's the Vantage V—"

The warning was far too late.

Victoria Vantage streaked forward to meet her assailants, and a single shout in *Artan* echoed with supernatural power through the clearing: "*Sharee-Ka-Hazi!*"

A ripping storm of silver-glinting light tore through the clearing, the titanic axe a blur that caught and shattered weapons, cleaved through armored torsos and exposed heads, a spinning, zig-zagging streak of death that ended with Victoria on the far side of the clearing.

All eight of their captors collapsed to the ground, blood fountaining everywhere.

Victoria sagged, her axe's handle her only support for several minutes as she slowly regained control of her breathing. "Honestly, I'm far too old for this."

Chapter 10
A Rescue and Decision

Quester's perceptions were, he knew, faster than any ordinary human's. Even so, he had not truly been able to follow Lady Vantage's lethal sprint across the clearing; it had been but a confusion of swings and impacts and spraying blood, with the woman herself following a deadly geometry that took her past each of the eight assailants in the time it took to draw a breath.

Their rescuer straightened after a moment, lifted her axe, and approached. "Hold still, all of you."

The axe came down and severed the bonds holding the three of them together; in an instant, the weapon vanished, and Lady Vantage took out a dagger and began cutting them free.

Urelle immediately flung her arms around her aunt, silently trembling for long moments as Victoria stroked her hair. "A little different from one's fancies, isn't it?" she said quietly.

Urelle's scent was filled with a mixture of fear, relief, excitement, and confusion. She pulled back enough to look up. "We... were ambushed," she said. "This wasn't one group, it was two." She shook her head. "And... no and yes. I mean, it *was* different, terrifying. But... I'm not sorry I came." Her face fell. "Just sorry we had to be rescued."

The tang of confusion became stronger. "But Auntie, how did you *find* us?"

"That group that was following you," Victoria answered, "was interested in fast pursuit, not in hiding their passage. I may be a bit out of practice, but theirs wasn't a terribly hard track to read." She looked at the other two. "Ingram? Quester? Are you both all right?"

"I... think so, Lady Vantage," Ingram said. "Headache from whatever they used to render us unconscious, but it's not like we haven't gone through *that* before." He grinned at Quester. "At least we weren't hanging up in shackles this time."

Quester buzzed his own amusement. "Yes, this was at the least a somewhat more comfortable imprisonment."

"I couldn't overhear most of their conversation," Victoria said, "but it sounded like they were going to take *all* of you. I had thought, young man, they were after you alone."

The sharp tang of guilt and confusion rose from his friend. "That's what *I* thought, too. They *were* Aegeian, too. Same accent I grew up with, no mistaking it. But their instructions apparently said they were after a female, not a male, target."

"So I heard. Tell me the whole story, then."

"Very well," Quester said. "I can also repeat their debate essentially verbatim. But be warned, we cannot linger long. One part of their discussion made it clear that there are other groups searching for... well, whatever or whoever their target is."

"Yeah, they mentioned 'all the others,' which implies... well, not just one or two, anyway," Ingram said.

Urelle had straightened herself, then walked resolutely over towards the bodies. Quester saw Victoria start an abortive gesture; the scent of worry, sadness, and pride overlay her movements.

Not to his surprise, Urelle had the smell of someone fighting very hard to keep her body from embarrassing her. But then, slowly, that odor faded, to be replaced by a calmer, meditative smell like the Great Road after a brief thunderstorm. Flickers of light danced around the girl's fingers, and two golden Coins floated up from the bodies. "I need these," she said.

"Their tracking Coins? What for?" Ingram asked.

"If I can get any kind of feel for the *kind* of enchantment on them, I can probably figure out how to negate it. Won't be quick, though, so you're right, we have to get moving."

"No point in leaving anything for our pursuers," Victoria said. "Everyone, search two of these bodies and take whatever seems valuable, dangerous, or interesting. We may learn more about them and their goals from whatever we find. *Then* we move."

"'We?'" repeated Urelle cautiously. "Aunt Victoria, I... well, I thought you..."

"...would be dragging you back home?" She gave a sad smile as she bent over the body of the unarmed warrior. "An Adventurer learns to have a sense of... well, the direction of fate, I suppose one could call it. I could certainly *make* you come back with me, but tell me, Urelle: do you feel that you have finished your work here?"

The black-haired girl looked up, her stormcloud-gray eyes surprised and, after a moment, worried. She paused, there amidst the carnage, and Quester could sense that calmness rise, peace and clean thought overriding the smell of blood and death.

She shook her head. "I still feel I need to be here. Not just because I *want* to help. I can't explain it, but –"

"No need, child. We – the Vantages – were Eyes of the Watchland in Evanwyl for a reason, and that sense is part of it. Not all of us have it… but enough. So yes. We. Unless you have an objection?" She looked sharply at Quester and Ingram.

"After you saved us from humiliation and likely worse, how *could* I object? Save to say I do not want to be the cause of more difficulty to you and yours," Ingram said.

"Auntie! You were working with Toron, and what about Kyri—"

"Taken care of. I'll explain later. Let us finish this most unpleasant task and begin moving before we talk more."

Urelle shuddered. "Shouldn't we… well, do something first? A prayer? We don't want revenants or—"

Victoria struck her forehead in chagrin. "What's wrong with me?"

"If you might allow me, Lady Vantage," Quester said, "These eight were taking someone you clearly think of as your own daughter. That might explain it."

Quester caught the cinnamon-and-pepper of shocked surprise, followed almost immediately by amusement and tenderness. "Why… yes, of course." She smiled down at Urelle, shaking her head in chagrin. "And now I distinctly remember myself saying they would release 'my child.'"

"Auntie!" Urelle gave her a huge hug.

Smiling, Ingram said, "Well, that aside, she was right. I'll say a quick prayer for them to Ares and Athena; they're caught in the Cycle as much as the rest of us, so it's my job to pay them their respects."

Ingram went to each body, sketching symbols in the air and murmuring prayers in a language Quester did not know. If he had wanted to intrude, of course, he could have lifted the meaning from the boy's mind, given that they were linked, but that would be intolerably rude; their link allowed them to speak at will, but

Ingram – like most without the Nest's gift – did not like uninvited contact. Quester *could* make out the symbols of the Shield and Spear, of Sword and Chariot, as would be expected.

Quester did, for a moment, sense... a distant presence or presences, as though a faraway mind had focused for a moment on this place, these people. He noticed, also, Urelle looking oddly at Ingram, and for an instant he thought he saw a faint glow about the boy's fingers. If so, it was but the briefest of moments, gone in the instant he thought it was perceived.

When Ingram finished, there was an undefinable difference in the clearing – a sense of quiet rather than disturbance. "There. Now the bodies are... just that. Their spirits have gone on," Ingram said, with the odd assurance that sometimes made him seem much older than he was. "If we were home, there would still be a burial or a pyre, but here... we do what we must, and leave."

It did not take long to strip the corpses of anything of interest – weapons, jewelry, any papers, other accoutrements. Even Ingram seemed reluctant to strip the bodies, but Victoria made sure it was done. "While I'm not going so far as to search the more uncomfortable areas," she said calmly, "you would be amazed as to what can be hidden beneath clothing."

"Which way should we go?" Victoria asked, once everyone was finished. "This is, after all, *your* adventure to start with, Ingram."

"We were headed south. This other group must have come from there. I figure that means there's at least a fair chance none of the others are due south, or they'd have run into each other. So, let's keep going south."

"Agreed. Lead the way, I'll follow," Victoria said. "I know some tricks for obliterating tracks. If we can keep that up for even a few hundred yards, it will make us that much harder to follow, especially once Urelle gets a chance to negate that spell." She gestured. "And you, Quester, stay near me and give me the whole story."

By the time he had finished telling everything there was to tell, Victoria had finished her efforts and was walking alongside him, her scent intense with thought.

"You were right, Ingram. It *is* a pretty mystery, though, as to why they would *not* be after you, but instead after, apparently, Urelle."

"Or myself," Quester said.

"*You?*" Ingram said, startled.

"Our captors were quite wise in that; while for various reasons it is appropriate for most purposes that I am referred to as male, in physical construction I am in fact female, as are most of the Iriiistiik. The ratio is somewhere around five hundred to one, although only the Mother produces children, usually with the assistance of one or more Brood-Kings."

"More than two years with you, and this is something I don't know?"

Quester gave the bob and scent that he knew his friend would interpret as a smile. "For me, it was not important or relevant, and the Queen Mother had told me that I was to think of myself as male for most purposes." He paused, feeling surprise. "Which is something I of course did not previously question – you do not question the Mother – but now I wonder if there was more reason behind it than I know."

"All right," Ingram said after a moment. "That... complicates matters. After my recall message, it was natural to assume the pursuers were after me; the message *tells* me I will be in danger. But if not... maybe I got lucky. Maybe the real targets were the people *with* me, and what my people wanted was for me to be able to find the targets." He looked at Urelle and Quester. "You. One or, I suppose just possibly, both of you."

"Why in the *world* would someone in Aegia want to capture *me*?" Urelle demanded, and Victoria's expression echoed the surprise. "I've spent my life in Evanwyl, until we came here, and I've never done anything to draw attention to myself." She looked at Quester. "You and Ingram, at least, have been out there Adventuring. Stands to reason you must have gotten in *someone's* way."

"Indeed," Quester said, thinking carefully about their past adventures. "And I can certainly think of a number of people and even organizations that might remember us with great hostility. However... none, that I can think of, have any connection with Aegeia, and none that would not have placed Ingram at least as high on their priorities."

"Perhaps we are looking too closely into the past," Victoria said. "If I recall some of our conversations, yours is not the only nest of the Iriiistiik recently destroyed."

He froze, then glanced down at Ingram. "The Sorter, at the Guild."

"Yeah." Ingram bit his lip thoughtfully. "Three, at least. Yours and two that the Sorter knew of. And I don't think there's *that* many Iriiistiik Nests, are there?"

"I do not know the number, but it would not be overly large, no," Quester answered, feeling an unpleasant, shivery sensation, as though he had entered a brood-chamber to find the eggs all dead and rotting. "Do you think this is related?"

"Maybe not... but given the circumstances, I have to at least *think* about it. Someone or something who wants your people dead, and might work with Ares or one of his subordinates?" Ingram frowned, then shook his head violently. "But no! That makes no sense! The Cycle's focused on *Aegeia*. The war isn't to be taken to the outside world; it's purely limited to the lands within Wisdom's Fortress. If there was a Nest inside the mountain range, well, maybe it would become of importance, but outside?"

Quester had been thinking back over the entire story, and now another fact finally crystallized. "I think we are still missing crucial facts," he said slowly. "You recall the dialogue of our captors, about the behavior of their tracing-Coins?"

"Yes. What've you thought of?" Ingram asked.

"Apparently, they were reliable until very recently. The first group said it became unreliable on the road to the estate; the second, apparently, hadn't noticed anything until they were asked to check after our capture. At that point it was erratic, pointing mostly towards us, but occasionally swinging ninety degrees, generally northward. That is... most suggestive, taken altogether."

He saw the others frowning, smelled thought and confusion. "Do you not see? The only thing that changed so recently is that Lady Vantage *left the estate*, leaving us behind. So—"

"By the *Balance*, yes, of course," Victoria breathed. "I would have been *behind* the first group, even as they approached the estate. And when you were held here—"

"—you were approaching from the north!" Urelle finished. "Auntie... Auntie, I think it's *us*."

"It would seem so," Ingram said, and the small face was graven in lines of worry that made it look years older. "The real question then is... *why?*"

And for that, Quester had no answers.

Chapter 11
Conversations and Secrets

Urelle studied Ingram out of the corner of her eye as they walked. He was *silent* when not talking, and his feet would glide over the forest floor, hardly displacing a single leaf, lifting up and over or around even the smallest branches without, as far as she could tell, even *looking* at them. Even walking next to him she had to strain to hear the faintest whisper of sound from his passage; she sounded like a blundering *ralangas* by comparison. She tried to imitate the motion, but despite the training she'd had from Lythos, it was much harder than it looked.

He noticed, and smiled. "Took me a long time to learn. Longer than my instructors liked."

"How long?"

"About... um, six months. But that was with a lot of other stuff. If that was the only thing I'd had to learn, I probably would have got it down in two months." He watched her for a moment. "You'll probably figure it out in one. You've got a touch for it."

"Really?" The question was accompanied by a particularly loud *snap!* from a twig beneath her feet. She grinned and raised a wry eyebrow. "I mean, *really?*"

Ingram's laugh was light and sunny. "You'll make *more* noise before you make less, I'll promise you. Not that it matters that much as long as we're talking."

"I noticed that sometimes when you and Quester were patrolling... you know, when we were coming to Zarathanton... you were so silent that I wouldn't have known *either* of you were there without looking, and then sometimes one or the other of you would just move over to meet the other, as though you had said something. But you hadn't."

He nodded, slowly. "I guess you would have, at that. Quester... he gave me a great honor, about a year ago, after I ended up getting hurt badly defending him. He accepted me as part of his Nest."

She glanced back at the tall, angular figure of the Iriistiik. "But his Nest was destroyed, right?" she said in low tones.

"Apparently the Mother told him that so long as he existed, so would the Nest. Anyway, it's more than a formality. He... well, we can *speak* now, mind-to-mind, when we want to."

"Wow." She thought about that. It was certainly a convenient talent, especially for two Adventurers who might need to stay dead-silent but still communicate... but linking one mind to another must also come with some risks. "You both must trust each other *a lot*."

"I would trust Quester if he told me I had to jump off a cliff without a second look," Ingram said bluntly. "And I'm pretty sure he'd do the same for me."

"Naturally," the Iriistiik said. "I can glide."

Ingram burst out laughing.

"But," Quester admitted, "I would also trust you if you said to leap into a raging torrent, and I have no particular ability to swim." He tilted his head.

Ingram's eyes went distant for a moment, then he shook his head. "We're companions all now," he said. "Ask aloud, if you have a question."

Quester clicked assent. "Then, yes, I have a question. There have been a few times in our association where you have mentioned... a reserve, a backup, a hidden card, so to speak. Yet I saw no such in the moment we were captured, nor afterwards."

Ingram gave an embarrassed smile. "Well... yeah. I have to *know* the danger I'm in, be able to focus on it, and it has to be pretty immediate. Plus, I don't know if I can call on... my backup, so to speak... more than once. Maybe I can, but I sure don't *want* to if I can avoid it." He looked around at all of them. "Sorry to sound mysterious, but it's a secret."

"I have heard of similar things," Victoria said. "Bargains made, debts owed by beings of power that can be repaid by a single service. Just do not fall into the most common trap of such weapons of extremity."

Ingram looked at her curiously. "And that is..."

She smiled. "Telling yourself that there could always be a *worse* extremity, so that you never dare use it at all."

Urelle saw a startled expression cross Ingram's face. Apparently, he'd never thought of it that way. "Auntie's seen a lot, and she's got a lot of good advice."

"She has, indeed." Ingram paused and turned so that he could bow deeply to Victoria. "Words of wisdom that I will heed... and should have remembered; my people called it the parable of the Always-Worse. Though of course, one doesn't wish to use such reserves too casually, either."

"As with all things, young Ingram, it is a matter of balance," Victoria said.

After a moment, Urelle looked back to the lavender-haired boy. "I think... Ingram, whatever's going on, it's *clearly* tangled up with Aegeia and your Cycle, right?"

"I don't see any way around that, no. How you outsiders connect to it, I don't know, but my recall, these people hunting us, it's pretty clear there's *some* kind of connection."

"Then can't you tell us something *about* Aegeia and its Cycle? I don't really know much about it at all, and from what Auntie has said, I don't think she knows much more than I do."

"No," admitted Victoria. "Aegeia is a strong ally of the State of the Dragon King, and by extension of Evanwyl, but she has always been a fairly private one. So yes, I too, would like to hear what you could tell, Ingram."

"As would I," Quester said. That startled Urelle; she'd assumed Quester already knew everything about Ingram and his people. "You have always been kind and generous with everything... except your past. You speak little of it, or of your people. You are clearly still *proud* to be of your Clan... yet you were also ashamed, as though you knew yourself to be unworthy. That... discussion you recounted to me explained some, but not nearly all."

Ingram was silent for so long that Urelle started to wonder if he was going to reply at all.

Finally, he sighed. "Yes. Yes, of course, you all deserve to know as much as I can tell you."

"First, understand that the Camp-Bels themselves are kind of outsiders. They entered into the middle of one of the Cycles some time back, when the Founder's ship had crashed and the survivors found themselves here. So the history I've been taught... well, it's through the lens of the Camp-Bel's experiences."

He reached into his pack, brought out the small, oblong object Urelle had seen him using on occasion during their travels. "This datapad holds a lot of records of... well, lots of things, including copies of some of the notes made by other Camp-Bels through the years, so with that, the public history, and what I've seen and heard, I've put together a lot of it.

"Way back… quite a few Chaoswars… the Aegei, the gods of Aegeia, had some kind of major discussion that almost culminated in direct conflict. The Highfather and Highmother together noticed something about the way their conflict and its reflection in their worshippers in Aegeia interacted with the powers of the world, and 'saw both great peril and great promise.' They studied and conferred, and they saw that when God and Mortal were associated in the same undertakings, in just the right way, it created…"

He hesitated, squinting at the screen. "Created a sort of resonance, a reinforcing power that not only supported the mortals and helped guide and strengthen them, but that within the area dominated by the gods – Wisdom's Fortress, as we call it today – the powers and memories and wisdom of the gods were *also* strengthened."

"In what way?" Victoria asked. "Not the mechanics – I'm sure that's not something the gods let someone write down – but what was the assistance granted?"

"For the worshippers and those around them? The best way to describe it is that it *clarified* things. If the gods played out their debates in a way that *involved* mortals, the mortals' worship and belief cycled back to help them learn the lessons and return them to the mortals as well. So, lessons of passion and justice, of courage and strategy, of heroism and compassion versus treachery and cruelty, these became *ingrained* in the population, and the increased focus and belief of the mortals strengthened the gods."

He looked around at them, then realized they'd stopped moving. "Come on, I know it's hard for me to discuss this while walking, but we can't stop yet." He looked back down at the faintly-glowing device. "For the gods, it's said that one of the *major* benefits was that it weakened the effect of the Chaoswars. That's why the Lady Herself is often consulted by even vastly more powerful gods, because she will know and remember things wiped from the minds of even the ancient and mighty."

Victoria's eyebrow rose. "Are you saying that the Lady knows what happened during all the Chaoswars since their Cycles began?"

"Not *everything*. But she will recall more, and more clearly, than the others. Apparently, nothing can fully overcome the effect of a Chaoswar – it is said that even the Wanderer himself is not entirely clear on the events that have passed two Chaoswars ago – but some can *mitigate* the effects, and that is what the Cycle does for the Aegei."

"Why Athena and Ares?" Urelle asked. "I admit I don't know details of your people's beliefs, but they're both war gods. Ares is the violent one who likes fighting and bloodshed, and Athena's the wise strategist, so I see there's a conflict there, but why not Aphrodite versus Athena or Ares or..." she trailed off, seeing Ingram's pained expression. "Sorry. Did I say something bad?"

Ingram bit his lip. "Not... *bad*. Just... uninformed? Ares *isn't* like that. Well, he *can* be – in some Cycles that's his persona – but really, he's more about *passion*. Sure, that can express as hatred and bloodlust, but it can also be courage, the burning desire to protect someone, the fierce determination to achieve a dream. Athena is about *wisdom*, about consideration, about analysis and strategy and tactics. But that can be destructive too – you can wisely and passionlessly decide that some course of action will work out best in the long run, and thus it's perfectly okay to, say, kill these five thousand people."

He put the datapad away. "So... my best guess – and it's just my guess, along with a few things I heard in Temples along the way – is that because Ares and Athena both touch on war and strife, but have such different approaches, that they made a perfect choice for a Cycle that could be constrained within Wisdom's Fortress and used to teach reinforcing lessons on balancing passion and calcuation, emotion and thought, all that kind of thing."

"But I've heard there's actual *wars* fought during your Cycles! I mean, *real* ones, with armies and people fighting on both sides and *dying* and all that! Every Cycle! How can the people believe in gods that use them for, what, moral plays?"

She was stunned when Ingram began laughing. "Hey! It's not funny! Fighting wars as object lessons, *killing* people—"

He held up a hand. "Please, hold on." He stopped laughing and his face became serious. "You know, of course, that death is not the end. Right?"

"Well... that's what we believe," Urelle said after a hesitation. "Myrionar has Its world beyond this one, where those who are Its true followers will live again, to be reborn here or to live forever in the realm of the god Itself. But... well, I don't know anyone who's *been* there and back."

"I have seen a few," Victoria said unexpectedly. "Those who had fallen and were given the chance to return to this world, to complete that which they had left behind. Yes, this life is not the only one."

"Then understand that those who fall – or even those merely *injured* – in the Godswar are honored beyond all others," Ingram said earnestly. "They are the teachers of the lessons of the gods, and the students as well, who give their pain and lives for the sake of all. Their souls are gathered – each to the realm of the god they serve – and rewarded greatly for such selfless service, even if they themselves did not understand it at the time. They will see their families and friends again – perhaps returned to this world when the Cycle has completed, or perhaps when their families and friends have themselves passed on to be re-united with their loved ones."

Urelle looked at his face, and the violet eyes that shone with a startling faith. "You really believe that."

"I do," he said, without hesitation. Then he *did* hesitate before speaking again. "I wanted to be a God-Warrior myself. I *really* wanted to. It was my childhood dream, the daydream I had every day. I trained as a Camp-Bel... but I also tried to train as though I'd be a God-Warrior, as though I might one day be good enough to be a vessel of the power of the Lady." He flushed with obvious embarrassment. "I knew it wasn't *possible*, of course, but I dreamed about it anyway."

"Why wasn't it possible?" Quester asked. "God-Warriors *are* trained mortals, are they not?"

"Well... yes, of course they are." He rolled his eyes. "But the *Lady*'s God-Warriors, the Spear and the Shield, they're, well, *women*. Not men. And I knew... I grew *up* with... one of the ones destined to be hers. Even when we were little children, we knew Berenike would *have* to be the Spear of Athena."

His face shone as he pronounced his childhood friend's name. Urelle felt a twinge at the sight, but couldn't quite identify it. "What about the other gods? Do they have God-Warriors? Do they get involved?"

"Oh, all of them have their own representatives and God-Warriors, yes – Hephaestus' Hammer and Anvil, Aphrodite's Mirror, Ares' Sword and Chariot, all of them. They take sides during each Cycle. *Usually* it's the same ones on each side, but that can change depending on the, um... *roles* that Ares and Athena play."

"So, you could have trained to be a God-Warrior for another god?"

"I *could*... but Athena's the Camp-Bel's patron, though we've worked well for people on all sides." He was quiet for a moment. "But this isn't about my childhood. Basically, what you need to know is that the country goes through this upheaval every several centuries, generally after all the cities of the gods have broken away from Aegis, Athena's city, and become independent. This leads to various conflicts that end up drawing Ares out, sometimes to try to resolve them, sometimes to take advantage of them to lead to conquest, whatever. Ultimately, Athena opposes him, there's lots of dramatic conflict, and Ares is defeated – often by Athena herself, but sometimes by the God-Warriors taking him on. A few times, Ares has surrendered, and in at least one Cycle *Athena* was the villain of the piece and Ares defeated her and ruled Aegis and the rest of Aegeia until the next Cycle."

Urelle shook her head. "It seems... a pretty crazy way to run a country to me, but if your people are okay with it, I guess I can't argue."

They walked in silence for a while.

"We're taking one of the more difficult routes," Victoria pointed out at last. "I understand your orders told you to avoid the more traveled, but it *will* take us considerable time to get there if we must walk through the wilderness."

"Can't be helped," Ingram said. "If we take any of the easier routes, not only will it be easier for our hunters to find us, but we'll also be more likely to put other people in danger. Imagine being on one of the ships going down the Great River and then having one or more of these groups ambushing us. I can't risk things like that."

He looked over at Urelle. "I'm hoping you really can do something about those Coins."

She looked down at the two glittering golden Shields in her hand. "So do I."

The complexities of Aegeia washed over her with the worry about these people coming perhaps from all directions, seeking them. She imagined Ingram's scenario, a battle on a ship as it drifted down the river, or what might happen if they traveled with a caravan down one of the Great Roads. But with those images, inspiration suddenly struck her. "You know what? I think I can." As the idea grew, became more detailed, she found herself laughing. "I'm *sure* I can! When we camp, I'll show you!"

Chapter 12
Enchantment of Misdirection

"This looks like a good spot to camp," Ingram said, studying the small, perfectly circular clearing. "Then Urelle can show us what she's come up with."

"Wait a moment, young man," Victoria said, keeping him from entering. Her sharp blue eyes darted about the grassy, flower-strewn meadow with a flat rock outcropping near the center. Ingram could see tension in her pose, her hand held so that she could summon that immense battleaxe in a moment. She muttered something that Ingram thought was a spell. He also thought she sniffed the air.

The tension released suddenly, and she nodded. "Yes, this will be ideal."

"What were you looking for, if I might inquire?" Quester asked. "I can understand that the circularity of the clearing might be suspicious, but by your scent you were able to allay those suspicions simply by looking."

"See these?" She tapped a set of stones. "Ordinary, yes, but the pattern is obvious to those who know what to look for. There's also a simple spell – I'll teach it to you – that will reveal the markings of the Wardens of the Forest. See those stones, in that pattern, with those markings? It's one of the safe havens they've made for travelers. They're spotted through all the forests, even the Forest Sea."

"You were also *smelling* for something," Ingram said.

"Excellent observation," she said with a smile. "Yes. There *are* a few creatures that can either mimic the setup – although they can't actually replicate the spell-markings, so that's usually sufficient proof. Still, I like to be *sure* that I'm not stepping into an *eyrgines* or into the trap of a *naluthaka*."

Ingram made a face. "*Eyrgines*, I've heard of them. Giant carnivorous plants?"

"Whose traps look like pretty, circular clearings, yes. That's what I checked by smell; they have a characteristic, very subtle perfume, it's a lure for various larger animals. Makes the area seem peaceful and inviting." She went on. "And the *naluthaka* you might better know as meadowmaws."

Both Quester and Urelle flinched at that. "They're *real?*" Urelle said, then looked embarrassed as the others looked at her. "Well, I'd only heard about them in *Seven Tales of Terian*, and you know that some of those are kind of made-up…"

"Perfectly correct," Victoria said, and ruffled her niece's hair. "*Plenty* of those collections of tales are nothing but rubbish. But the good ones often have a lot of truth to say within the rubbish, and I'm afraid that's one of the nastier truths."

"How did you make sure that this was not a meadowmaw's lair?" Quester asked.

She pointed along the edge of the clearing. "The *naluthaka* creates a huge trapdoor *out* of a clearing, cementing it together underneath so that it can be lifted in a flash and the meadowmaw be able to grab its prey. Try as they might, though, that *cannot* be done perfectly, so if you look very carefully around the edges, you will see a faint line showing the seam."

Ingram nodded. More and more, he was starting to appreciate how fortunate they all were in having Victoria Vantage with them. No matter how good they might be as young Adventurers – and even Urelle looked like she was going to be very, very good – there was no substitute for decades of experience in the job. "You've got a lot to teach us."

"I will do my best, I assure you." Her smile, quick and bright, added warmth to the response.

A little while later, Urelle gathered them near the campfire on the flat, clean stone. "It's a matter of energy flows and redirection," Urelle said, placing the two Coins in front of her.

Ingram studied the Shields. "How do you mean that? Is there energy flowing from us to these things?"

"Sort of. Not exactly." Urelle frowned, even as she began sketching mystical symbols onto the silver-tinted leather she'd laid on the ground. "How do I put it… Well, have you ever seen a crystal winged harp?"

"Attended a concert by Reiva Freyavalyn, in fact. Beautiful music from a beautiful instrument."

"*Reiva?* I thought she never left Thologondoreave."

Ingram grinned, warmed by her surprised and slightly envious look. "She doesn't."

Even Victoria looked startled. "You've *been* to Thologondoreave?"

"We have," Quester affirmed. "The circumstances were... unusual."

"I would think so," Victoria said, eyebrow still raised. "It took *me* six years to convince them to let *me* visit. But we're off the trail – Urelle?"

"What? Oh, yes. So, you must have seen her sing *to* the harp, and have it respond, right?"

Ingram remembered the play of gemlight through the *Odinsyrnen*'s coal-black hair, and a voice as pure as diamond singing one perfect note after another, and the harp responding with the same notes, even as she danced away from it. "Yes."

"Well, it's kind of like that. The harp will only sing back to *one* note for each specific crystal of the harp, its resonant pitch," Urelle said. She put one Shield carefully into each of two circles of symbols she'd scribed onto the leather. "And to make it respond, you have to sing out that note, sending those vibrations through the air to touch the crystal."

Ingram nodded, studying the symbols. He hadn't really learned much about magical symbology, so he couldn't tell much about it; it *was* clear that the two circles were different, and he *thought* that one of them was signified as the dominant. "So, the Coins are sending out magical vibrations, so to speak?"

"More the opposite. By our existence, we... well, vibrate the essence of the world. We're a particular *part* of the world, and our existence speaks to the world, resonates with it. These Coins are mystically designed to sense that vibration, as a magnet seeks the northern and southern reaches of the world when placed in a compass."

"But—"

"Oh, that's very simplified. Really, we're *masses* of these... vibrations, resonances, essential signatures, whatever you want to call them. Whoever made these Coins had something that was attuned to a particular characteristic that relates to me, or you, or Auntie – whatever it is they're really seeking – and it is drawn towards it, whenever enough power is placed into it to amplify the reaction."

Now her hands were weaving about the Coins; for a moment he thought he saw an almost invisible wavering, like heat-shimmers, tracing the same path as the girl's delicate fingers. "Now, to *negate* that entirely – to shield us from being traced – that's going to take time. But I think I *can* do something right now that should at least buy us that time."

She gestured for everyone to come closer. "Just like the singing, it *is* possible to reverse the process, if you can set up the right conditions. What I'm going to do is attune one of these even more to us – whichever of 'us' is really involved – and then invert the other's performance, focused through this connection I'm making."

Ingram scratched his head. "So, what... the second Coin will be calling to us instead of us calling to it?"

"Better. It will be... oh, *shouting*, I guess I could say, singing out as loudly as it can, the same vibrations that the other Coins respond to. And as long as we keep the first Coin with us, it'll keep channeling our... essence vibrations to the second Coin, which then keeps shouting them out."

"As long as we..." The idea suddenly solidified. "Ohh, Urelle, that's *brilliant!*" He found himself laughing at the thought. "But even if we leave the one behind, they'll figure out the trick as soon as they find that Coin."

"Could they use that against us?" Victoria asked. "I think it is a brilliant idea, Urelle, no doubt, but if I understand correctly this Coin will be connected to the other by *your* magic. Presumably a good mage could trace the 'shouting' as you put it, very easily. And perhaps strike directly at *you* through such a connection."

Urelle frowned, thinking. Ingram found himself just staring at Urelle despite the frown, forced himself to look away. *I have no right, nor do I have the time for... anything like that.*

"Yes and no, Auntie, in order. Yes, if one of our enemies who is also a magic user of talent, preferably a Shaper like me, got hold of the Coin, they could follow the trace to the Coin we keep with us. No doubt. But they can't use it *against* me, not unless they're either ridiculously powerful so that they can target magic miles and miles away, or were something... oh, like a Great Wolf, that could grab that connection and *pull* through it. I'm just maintaining the spell, not shoving my whole *self* into it. And even if something like that happened, I'll almost certainly feel something happening and I can just drop the spell." She turned back to the Coins.

"Ingram's other point still stands," Victoria said after a moment. "If we just drop the Coin somewhere, it will not be long before it is found."

Urelle grinned, a smile that said "watch." "That's why I'm not stopping *there*." Urelle muttered several phrases in what Ingram thought was *Artan*. "Now, everyone – put one finger on the first Coin. *Don't* touch the circle around it!"

Ingram carefully complied; the Shield was large enough – barely – for all four of them to get a finger (including a shining-chitin talon) on the golden surface. Urelle made another complicated gesture, then nodded. "Now, everyone lift your fingers... good."

She focused her attention on the second Coin and whispered several more phrases of magical import. "Now, something, anything small, from as far away as you can think of. Anyone?"

There was a pause, then Victoria reached into her pouch and brought out a small golden figurine. "This came from Elyvias; perhaps I've traveled farther, but I doubt it."

"*Perfect.*" A white smile flashed in the dim firelight. "Far, far to the east." She took the figurine and stood it atop the Coin, completed another ritual, and then gave it back to Victoria. Then she picked up the two Coins and tucked the first one into a small pouch at her waist, and threw the second one high into the air.

It arced up, glinting white-gold in a slanting beam of moonlight, and – just as it reached the apex of its arc – was suddenly snatched up by something perhaps the size of Ingram's arm that flew by on batlike wings. Whatever it was circled higher, and then flew off away from the remaining glow of sunset.

"It's now connected with Elyvias – wherever that figurine came from," Urelle said. "It *has* to make its way there, and it will. Animals will catch it and carry it for a while, it will be dropped on hillsides that face east and roll down them, be spotted by someone who is traveling east, whatever, and..."

"*Double* brilliant, by the Lady!" Ingram was amazed. "What you're saying is that our... vibrations will now be sent to *that* Coin... and the *other* Coins will follow *it*."

She grinned back. "Exactly."

Victoria was looking as proud as any woman could be of her child, something that sent a slight pang through Ingram's heart. He repressed that reaction; his own problems weren't hers.

"A most elegant solution," Quester said. "But surely an enchantment – even one Shaped – of that nature cannot last forever."

"No," she admitted. "I have to sustain it. As Aunt Victoria said, it's connected to me directly, my strength goes through the first Coin to the second. For now, it's very small, but the drain will increase with distance; at some point I'll have to drop the enchantment before all of my magical resources are bound up in it. But that should be several days, at least."

"If we keep pressing on while they're going in the wrong direction for several days, that will give us a lot of breathing room," Ingram said, feeling some of the weight of worry lifting. "Obviously you can't do that trick again, since we'll be left with only the one Coin. Will this give us enough time for you to figure out the way to suppress the magic entirely?"

Urelle frowned, staring down at the glittering Shield. "I... hope so. It's the best chance we've got, anyway."

Victoria nodded. "As you say, it is indeed the best chance. And I think your instincts are now vindicated; even had our two friends, somehow, dealt with the prior two groups of assailants, I see no way in which they could have thrown off the tracks of the others."

"Neither do I," Ingram agreed. While he felt less tense now, the urgency of his mission still nagged. "I wish we could set out now." At Victoria's raised eyebrow, he raised his hands as though to ward off a blow; she smiled thinly. "I know we can't," he said, "but I *want* to."

"What do you think we're going to find?" Urelle asked. "I mean... that message *has* been chasing you for a couple of years, right?"

"I don't know. That's the problem; my imagination can throw up all kinds of horrible possibilities."

"Well... what was Aegeia like before you left?" Victoria asked. "One must presume that whatever has passed since must have roots in what already was. Yes?"

"I suppose. Especially since they did, as you mentioned, send the recall no more than six months after I departed." Ingram busied himself setting up the cookpot and the fire while he thought back on things he hadn't allowed himself to remember for years. It was... surprisingly hard to do.

"Well... Ares had emerged, oh, maybe twenty years before I was born. The city-states have been drifting apart for decades, maybe the last century and a half, so it seemed about the right time. He manifested incarnate in General Aloysius, who'd broken an attack from Velos through pretty much nothing but his own force of personality and passion. Once Ares was fully manifest, of course, he ascended to the High Throne that he and Athena share through the Cycles."

He remembered what he'd been taught and what he'd seen, and waves of loss, fear, pride, hope, and disappointment crashed together and made him hesitate. To cover his discomfiture, he dug in his pack for ingredients to roast in the pot. "At first, he had his hands full fixing things at home. End of a Cycle, things just tend to fall apart. You couldn't have all of Aegeia breaking apart if people didn't start forgetting their direction, I guess. So there was all sorts of corruption in the *Ekprospos*, the enforcement of laws had become pretty lax, terrible crimes were common, all of that. It made him *furious* to see all the injustice in Aegis, and so he set about changing that."

"Is this... normal?"

He scratched his head. "*Normal?* Well... it's not unusual. Like I said before, Ares isn't a *villain*, at least not most of the time, and even when he is, he'll try to hide it."

"When you say law enforcement was lax and crimes were common...?"

"Corruption at the top, remember? So sure, if you robbed one of the Archons, something would get done, but not so much for the common person. There was a whole *series* of murders when I was a baby that..." he shook his head. "Never mind. That was an aberration anyway – not from corruption or anything.

"Anyway, that was the first thing he did. Took him several years before he was satisfied, since he had to get *people* to change their minds – the gods can't just come in and force people to obey. That doesn't really fix anything.

"Then he declared that we needed to also strengthen ourselves against the forces without and within. That also was pretty popular, especially since he'd fixed a lot of what was wrong with the city by then, and people still remembered Velos' attack – as well as one assault from an arm of the Maelwyrd Pirates, something we hadn't seen in, like, a century or two."

Quester buzzed and gave a scent that Ingram knew as derision and cynicism, something like oiled dirt with alcohol. "And then this extra strength made him consider bringing his enlightened... passionate rule to the other cities?"

"Yeah, you've already got the idea. A couple of them *had* already tried pushing their way in, of course, and they were also feuding amongst themselves, so again, it wasn't as bad an idea as it might sound."

Victoria fixed him with a narrow glare that made him want to crawl away and hide; Urelle's incredulous stare didn't help, and the shift in Quester's scent drove it home.

"Young man," Victoria said after a moment, "Conquest is *always* a bad idea."

"Well..." he swallowed. "Um. Yes, I guess. Yes. But what I meant..." he hesitated.

The cold stares thawed slightly. "I understand what you meant, Ingram. That it seemed... less bad an idea than it would if you just started conquering peaceful, harmless neighbors."

"Yeah." He thought a moment and cringed both inwardly and outwardly. "Wow, um, now that I think about it, I really said that pretty badly."

"I suspect you said it as your people *thought* it," Quester said gently. "After all, your god-ruler Ares could justify it. And he *is* a god of war."

Urelle scrunched her face up, then smiled. "You know, given what we already know about Aegeia... maybe Ingram's wording's closer to right."

"Pardon me?" Victoria looked both startled and shocked.

Ingram noticed that unlike himself, Urelle did *not* wilt beneath her aunt's gaze. "Think about it, Auntie, Quester; *both* their ruling gods are gods of war. They have a Cycle *based* on this conflict between them. In *that* context, war's pretty much *inevitable*, so even if the thought of war *not* being a bad idea sounds... well, insane to us, it's maybe not so crazy for them."

"Hmph." Victoria tilted her head, as though studying something she couldn't quite make out. After a moment, a trace of a smile appeared on her face. "You may be right. It seems a terrible way to run a country, but if Ingram's description is correct, it at least *works*, and has done so for a very long time." She nodded to Ingram, who finally let himself relax a bit. "My apologies, Ingram."

"No need to apologize." He gave a grin-and-shrug. "You're not the only ones who don't really get how Aegeia works." He thought back. "Now what was I... oh, right. So basically, when I left, the country was completing full-on preparations for war. Almost everyone fit to fight was volunteering, except the Clan."

"Why wouldn't the Camp-Bels volunteer?" Urelle asked. "You're citizens, right?"

"Oh, sure, very proud of it, too. But the Founder gave her loyalty first to Athena, and through her direction, to protecting the rulers of the city-states. Eventually that became sort of a general-purpose rule that we protect the legitimate rulers of a country. In the Cycle, we've become... well, sort of the insurance that assassination will rarely be used as a method of war. Not *never* – some Cycles are pretty brutal – but if you have to go through a Camp-Bel bodyguard or three to get to a ruler, you'll probably think two or three times before you do.

"So anyway, that means we've already all got jobs to do, and volunteering as soldiers isn't one of them." He tried to keep his voice light.

"What's wrong?" Urelle asked.

Spear and Shield, what's wrong *with me? I can't hide* anything *these days!* "Nothing."

"You can choose to *say* nothing," Victoria said, and her voice was gentle, "but I think none of us will believe that it *was* nothing." Her gaze sharpened. "And some of it goes back to that series of murders you mentioned."

He cursed inwardly again, but it was against pain, not anger. "I... all right." He drew in a breath.

"I... well, I knew I wasn't a real Camp-Bel all along, understand. That... moment that made me run away was more... well, a trigger, not a total surprise or anything. I was adopted when I was a baby because..." He paused, then forced himself to go on.

"That series of murders was the beginning. A little after the time I was born, they started. Someone or something was murdering children – most of them infants, though there were some victims as old as two or three. There were a few adult victims, but they were pretty clearly collateral damage – they got in the way of the killer, saw something they shouldn't.

"The first wave of murders, though, was in the lower city, and so there wasn't much investigation at first. That's part of what I meant about corruption, how far Aegeia can fall toward the end, or beginning, of a Cycle: it didn't affect the people at the top, so there wasn't much effort devoted to it."

Urelle's entire posture and gaze showed both disbelief and sympathy, and he realized that there was a certain frightening parallel between that set of events and the murder of Urelle's own family. "So... what about the Camp-Bels?" Urelle asked after a moment. "Couldn't they do something?"

"Remember what I said about how they're sort of separate? We can't just go randomly poking our noses into the business of Aegeia, we have to follow the commands of the rulers – or sometimes of Athena or her emissaries, if they send their own clear instructions. Anyway, *that* didn't happen until the killer struck one of the higher houses. *Then* it became a priority."

"Soul-reading? Resurrection magics? Were they able to find out..." Victoria trailed off as Ingram shook his head.

"Whatever it was was either destroying or at least badly damaging the souls of the murdered. That made the top suspects a *zarbalath*, a Great Wolf, or maybe one of the parasitic *thansaelasavi*, because even the cursory investigations indicated that the killer wasn't always the same size, or maybe even shape. So it was either a shapeshifter itself, or it was able to steal other people's shapes, maybe make them forget what happened while under control."

"Or had magic to change its shape," Urelle pointed out. "If a mage like me, or worse, a spirit-mage wanted to do those kinds of things, they could do it."

Ingram shuddered, looking at Urelle and suddenly envisioning the delicate-seeming Vantage girl with a cold, deadly smile. "Yeah, I suppose so." He looked down for a moment, stirred the pot in front of him. "So, the investigation finally started, but there didn't seem to be any *pattern* in it other than that young children were being targeted. At least, not until the Camp-Bels got involved. We have some really powerful... thinking machines, I guess you can call them, left from *Rhyme and Reason*, and some of the Captain's Crew are trained to use them."

"I could *hear* the capitals in that. What's the Captain's Crew?" Urelle asked.

"Oh, they're... the inner circle, is the best way to put it. They're handpicked by the Captain to take the traditional roles of the Crew of *Rhyme and Reason*, and they get access to the secret manuals and such to learn those roles, and how to operate all the remaining tech – much better than any of the rest of us. Which makes sense, there's not that much of it and a lot of it is pretty delicate." He frowned, rewound the conversation in his head.

"So anyway, no one outside of the Captain's Crew knew the actual details, but they somehow got the thinking machines to analyze all the information on the killer, his victims, and so on, and it suddenly told them what the pattern was, and where the killer would strike next, a house with twin babies, a boy and a girl. The Camp-Bels went to stake out the house, set up a perimeter... and found out a few seconds too late that the killer was already inside."

Despite nerving himself up for this story, he found he couldn't continue.

"I believe I see," Quester said. "One of the twins was killed. The other survived. And that was you."

He nodded, took a breath, forced himself to go on. "My twin sister was killed, and I would've been dead a split second later if... if my... if the people who raised me hadn't stopped my natural father from tearing me apart."

"Your *father* was the killer?"

"It was a *zarbalath*, one of the parasitic demons who lives on fear, pain, and the souls of the weak and young. It had been possessing people, passed from one to the other. And by then it was *very* strong. The house was destroyed, my natural mother was already dead, and my natural father died in the battle."

He managed a sour smile. "From the Camp-Bel point of view, it was hardly a victory at all. We'd had all the information, but had failed to secure the home properly. Now they had an orphaned child with no close relatives, one orphaned due to *their* errors. The fact that I would've been dead without their intervention was the only bright spot in it. So, they took me in, made me one of them, as the only apology they could give to the dead."

"Oh," Urelle said. "And that's why you've said you aren't a 'real' Camp-Bel."

"Right. I am not descended of those who first took the oath to the Lady, I'm not of the Starblooded – I mean, maybe there's some in me, maybe not, but no way to be sure. The point is that I couldn't match up to my brothers and sisters who were *really* part of the Clan. Berenike did her best to help me, but I knew I'd never measure up. So, I figured I could join the new army; I was better than their regular recruits, that was for sure.

"Father forbade it, and made me promise I wouldn't go behind his back. Got the Captain herself to come down and take my *oath* on it. I couldn't *believe* it!"

He felt the incredulous anger rising again. "I mean, sure, if they had some real *use* for me it'd have made sense, but they *didn't*! Even when every single person from my cohort got an assignment, they had *nothing* for me!" His voice was louder, sharper, almost shouting, even though he was *trying* to keep control. "They wouldn't even let me bodyguard some minor noble in Amoni Agapis, and no one even *thought* there'd be combat in *that* city."

Urelle's huge gray eyes looked at him, filled with sympathy, and he couldn't meet that gaze, not now, not with anger, pique, and shame filling him, so he looked down. "So, I was almost the only person *left* in the Clanhold my age. Except Berenike, but she had to spend most of her time training for her ascension. She'd stop by when she could, though, until…" He stopped. "Eh. That's enough."

Victoria was looking at him with an appraising glance. "That *is* upsetting. And, I will say, suggestive."

"Suggestive?" Of all the words she might have said, that wasn't one he'd have expected.

"Oh, *most* suggestive. Of what I am not sure, but I do, indeed, find it difficult to believe that they would prevent you from serving in *any* capacity. Unless your Clan is particularly arbitrary and unreasonable?"

"Not... *particularly*, I wouldn't think," he said after a moment's thought. "But—"

"No 'but,' I think. I have never met another Camp-Bel in person, so I cannot speak to how great the disparity between you and they might be. However, I cannot believe that one of your talents would not have been used for *some* purpose. The fact that they did not... suggests that they had some very strong reason for keeping you where you were."

"But *why?*" The question burst from him with a startling flare of desperate, tragic need. "*WHY?*"

Victoria spread her hands. "That... as of yet... I cannot say."

"But," Quester said, "we may well be on our way to find out. Perhaps that 'why' was exactly the reason your recall message has been following you for two years."

Ingram froze. The thought of... an *explanation*, a reason, of finding out from his mother and father that it *wasn't* just that he was a failure and embarrassment, just something kept from obligation and guilt... it filled him with a longing so intense that for an instant he could not breathe.

But he swallowed that longing, denied the desire. What he *wanted* didn't matter. What mattered was the truth.

So, all he *said* was "Perhaps."

Chapter 13
Ares, Not Ares

"Lord Ares!"

He turned towards the call, seeing one of the *Ekprospos* coming towards him. With an annoying effort, he recalled her name. *Artemisia Igemon*, that was it. "Lady Artemisia," he said, inclining his head. "How can I be of service?"

She smiled slightly up at him; General Aloysius, his incarnate form, was a man of heroic stature indeed, so even the fact that the night-haired woman topped six and a half feet left her nearly four inches below his height. "I wanted to say how your speech inspired my entire regiment. Some few of my men and women had been unsure of the need to march against Velos, but now there isn't a single word that fails to approve."

He returned her smile. "Most gratifying, Lady," he said. "It is, of course, a sad thing that it is necessary, but Velos has lost its way; despite their supposed patron, they have begun inroads into the great forests, untouched these centuries; they have forsaken much of their hunting and fishing, letting farmers supply their meat while they turn their skills of bow and sword to war; they worship less in the moonlight. We are not the only one of their neighbors that Velos has tested, but we are the one that can stop them, set them back on the course appointed to them."

She nodded. "I know, and you may believe that I am ready."

"Excellent." He smiled again as another thought struck him. "And take this command to the others: it is in my mind that *your* regiment will lead the way, for is there not perfect symmetry in that one who bears the name of my sister of the hunt should lead the forces that liberate her city-state and return them to her fold?"

Her eyes widened, and her arms rose up, first in an upright fist, then brought to her heart, in salute. "Lord Ares! It shall be as you say!"

"Then go now, and prepare. With the plans made, the people behind us, we must not delay, else Velos may learn of these plans and give us far more difficulty than we expect."

"Sir!" The tall woman turned and strode away, a proud bounce to her step at the new honor.

He maintained his usual thoughtful, pleasant expression with difficulty as he made his way up the hundreds of steps of the Aegeian Path, through the Temple of the Guardians, where he nodded at the statues and the worshippers, and then up the second staircase to the High Temple with the Throne in the center. There were fewer worshippers here, but still a few, so he restrained himself from a sardonic glance at the Statue of Athena – her glittering silver spear held in one hand, her great golden Shield raised in the other.

Finally, he entered the private quarters, sealed them, and allowed his face to relax; at the moment, that meant it held an expression somewhere between a grin and a sneer.

It really was *extraordinarily* difficult to maintain this act. But Ares' image was mostly that of a passionate hero – one who might turn to a dangerous fanatic, true, and thus eventually need to be brought down by his sister – but always one acting on his righteous passions. While he had already begun – starting a decade or two ago – setting the foundations for changing that, becoming an "Ares" much more to his own taste, it was not something he could hurry.

This was even more true with the more important people at the top, such as Lady – currently Undergeneral – Artemisia Igemon. They had grown up before he could have begun the changes; getting them to become the oppressors of his empire would take time, even with the godly aura to influence them.

On the positive side, the Lady of Wisdom had yet to manifest her God-Warriors; neither the Spear nor the Shield of Athena had appeared, which always brought a real smile to his face. The pre-emptive work done early paid many dividends indeed, and not having to hide his true nature from emissaries of Athena was a major benefit. One of her epithets, the Clear-Eyed, referred to how her agents were endowed with often-supernatural abilities to see through deception and disguises. While not even the goddess' power could pierce *his* disguise, he was much less sanguine about the ability to disguise deep and subtle plans from her sight, or that of her true agents.

He glanced towards the door. *Deimos is still not here.* That was... annoying. Yes, hunting a moving target was difficult, and with multiple teams searching there was the strong chance that it would be another team that captured the target, but once the target *was* found, Deimos would know, and would undoubtedly be the one to notify him.

Still, there was no great hurry; as long as this last obstacle *was* eliminated, it did not matter greatly if the elimination happened today, tomorrow, or three months from now.

But it *was* tiresome to have to remember names and faces and such. These beings thought they were so *important*, and treated even their lessers, children and poor and otherwise, as though *they* were important as well. He found this infuriating, and likely hypocritical. How could they be so stupid as to actually believe that? Still, the game must be played as it was, not as he might prefer it; his forebear had done so for thousands of years in a single role, so he truly could not complain about a few decades.

His extended senses tickled, warned of the approach of someone *far* more interesting. By the time they reached the door, he was already seated, sipping essence-laden tea. "Enter."

The figure closed the door behind it and stood for a moment, tall and slender and noble in countenance, a faint glow emanating from his golden hair and skin and the gold-and-silver armor he wore. His bow was also of gold, with a crystalline string, and arrows of diamond and auric leaf protruded from his quiver.

He bowed. "Lord Ares." When he rose from the bow, his expression was far less noble, much more akin to the knowing grin on his patron's face.

"I see you have progress to report."

"Much progress, my Lord," said Arquetani, the Sun of Apollo. "The Oracles within Lyra, Apollo's city, have been shifting their messages subtly for all this time. Now, for the first time, the messages are guiding them towards their own holy war, this one for the preservation and control of knowledge, since that's one domain of Apollo, and one that can conflict with Lady Athena's, as 'wisdom' of course requires much knowledge to be gathered."

"Excellent. There are no questions?"

"Few, my Lord. The groundwork has been laid for a long time, the increasing gathering of works from surrounding lands, the promotion of security around the Libraries, and so on. I believe they will be ready to become the next target – most likely, they will enter once Velos begins to totter, ostensibly to protect the city of Apollo's sister, but with the underlying motive of seizing their archives and secure the city for themselves."

"What of the other God-Warriors?"

"No word of either of Athena's – I would presume you would know that better than I." Arquetani's smile flickered with good news. "Geryotrin was able to insinuate himself into the mind and soul of the Anvil of Hephaestus, so we now have an agent in Amoni Agapis who is properly placed to start *that* city on its way."

He laughed. "You hid that card well, Arque. Any others?"

"Not yet. You already have Apollo's Sun – myself – and his Harp. But I'd expect that we'll see more soon. My main worry is that more gods may incarnate shortly. I admit to being *particularly* concerned about..." he nodded towards the exterior.

"My *dear* Athena? Not to worry." He smiled, and this time allowed his teeth to glitter like crystal blades. "She is *entirely* taken care of. There is only one path for her to manifest now... and that shall never happen."

Chapter 14
An Unwanted Encounter

Victoria saw the tension in Urelle's entire body vanish abruptly – a tension that Victoria had not consciously realized she had seen until it had disappeared. *Ah. Of course.* "The spell has reached your limits, then?"

"Auntie? How did you *know*?" Urelle stared at her; the other two looked back from their position a little ahead.

"An educated guess from observation," she answered with a smile. "I saw you relax. You'd been under tension, then relaxed without anything visible to cause it. Only one explanation for that occurred to me."

Urelle shook her head, smiling. "You're too sharp for me, Aunt Victoria. Yes, I just let go the spell."

"In truth?" Quester made a swift flutter of his wingcases and a dip of his antennae. "I had thought you would have dropped it long since. It has been two and a half weeks."

"You *really* just dropped it now? Sword and Spear, that's *impressive*." Ingram stared admiringly at Urelle.

Not at all to Victoria's surprise, the youngest Vantage's cheeks darkened and she smiled brilliantly at Ingram. "It's not *that* impressive," she said, "I just hung on as hard as I could because I knew the longer it ran, the better the chance we lost most or all of them."

"Have you any idea how far our wayward Coin traveled before you released the spell?" Victoria asked.

"Vaguely? A long way. I think... maybe a thousand miles?"

"A *thousand*..." Ingram and Quester both burst into laughter, the young boy's human chuckles overlaid with the cheerful buzzing of the Iriistiik. "By the *Founder*, what our pursuers must think! A thousand miles in less than three weeks? Over fifty miles a day!"

"And if they check now, they must reverse course," Quester said. "Most of them must be hopelessly far away from us, unless they have magical means of transport."

"I wouldn't discount that possibility too far," Victoria said after a moment. "Perhaps they cannot use such transport *regularly*, but the distribution of multiple bands at considerable separation, looking for one target, would strongly argue to me that whoever sent them could, at the least, send them to multiple places at once."

"I... guess," Urelle said slowly. "But... even so, they almost certainly can't have any long-range transportation magic, or powerful mounts, for the group as a whole. They wouldn't have been walking to the estate, not if catching... well, whoever they're really after was *that* important."

"Hmm. That is a good point. Some individuals in some of their groups may have such transport, but it won't aid them as a group. They *do* have transport to bring people back to their headquarters, wherever that is – presumably somewhere in Aegeia, based on what they said when debating who would take credit for your capture."

"Did you take those scrolls?" Ingram asked.

"Certainly," Victoria said, "but unless we want to attempt a preemptive assault on an adversary of which we know scarcely anything, they won't be much help to us at this point."

"No, I guess not." Ingram looked around, scanning as usual for dangers.

Victoria approved of his continual alertness. The deep green light of the Forest Sea made everything slightly indistinct, but also meant that the undergrowth here was minimal. As long as they could keep a clear sense of direction, they could travel reasonably well... as long as none of the many dangers of Zarathan's jungles didn't catch them unawares.

So far, they'd caught the dangers unawares – noticing the subtle fogginess about a certain part of the forest that she recognized as the trap of a wandermind, Ingram catching a forestfisher as it attempted a dropping ambush (and practically breaking the spidery thing in two), Quester surprising them by being able to speak to a small tribe of creatures who seemed to be mostly spines and mouths, convincing them to let the small party pass, Urelle unleashing controlled lightning against a cloakwolf pack and sending the nigh-invisible creatures fleeing. The Forest Sea was living up to its grim reputation, and her memory; every other day brought a new lethal threat into range.

But even Urelle was demonstrating that she was, indeed, a Vantage. She was young, she was new, but she was learning, and Victoria could not deny that having someone with true talent for magic along was a comfort. There really *were* some threats that needed a mage to deal with them well.

"We should, then, be safe from our pursuers for a while, yes?" asked Quester.

"I would think so," Urelle said. "While we've been heading this way for two weeks, they've all been going east. We didn't run into anyone in the last couple of weeks, so I *have* to guess that there's no one left ahead of us. And retracing their steps to catch up with us won't be easy. We've moved... how far?"

"Something over a hundred miles," Victoria answered.

"So, if we assume our enemies are as fast as we are, they've all gone at least a hundred miles in the wrong direction."

Ingram's face clouded. "Maybe I *should* have taken the river route. It's going to take a long time to get home."

"Perhaps," Victoria said. "But second-guesses are a waste of time, and you know it. You had what seemed sufficient reasons to avoid that path. We can hardly change it now." She pushed forward, following Ingram and Quester through thickening undergrowth. *A clearing ahead, most likely.*

"Although that *does* give me a worrisome thought," Quester said.

"What's that?" asked Ingram, then immediately shouted "Yow!" and fell backwards.

"What... Oh dear," Victoria said.

There *was* a clearing ahead... in the sense that the land *itself* was cleared away too. Ingram had fallen back and now was standing up scant feet from the edge of a precipice. Moving cautiously up, Victoria could see that the drop was over a hundred feet down, possibly twice that. A winding river below – probably an unmapped tributary of the World River that flowed from Heart of Water – had carved out a channel through the earth and stone that cut almost due west, across their path.

"Well, now, this is a pretty obstacle, isn't it?" she muttered under her breath.

"Easy enough for Quester and Urelle, I'd guess," Ingram said. "Looks like we've got climbing to do, though."

"I could probably float you to the bottom," Urelle said, "but I'm not sure about getting you to the top on the other side." She looked apologetic. "So many different spells to learn, and, well, I was focusing on ones I could use on my own…"

"Founder's Grace, you've got nothing to be sorry for," Ingram said with a laugh. "Plenty for us all to learn yet. It's not like even Lady Victoria knows how to do everything, right?"

"Quite right, Ingram," she said. "While we prepare ourselves, Quester, you said you had a worrisome thought?"

"Yes. It occurs to me that since our enemies did not, in fact, know where we were, they must have scattered themselves widely, and an obvious set of locations would be along the most-traveled routes such as the river. Yes?"

"Certainly." The implication struck her. "Oh, *Balance*. We're not much over a hundred miles east of the River." *And if they were following something moving east…*

Ingram shrugged. "It's *possible*, of course, but even then, they'd have to have been in just the right spot or they'll *still* be miles out of position to catch us." He glanced down at the cliff. "Still, maybe we *should* see if Urelle can give us a quicker way down."

"Perhaps we can be of assistance," said a calm, chill voice.

The group emerging into sight from the northwest was diverse – two armored *bilarel*, gray-skinned giants eight to nine feet high and heroically muscled; a cloaked figure she was fairly sure was a *mazakh* from the green-glinting scales on its hands; a pair of fluttering blade-faeries; a pale, delicate, pointed-eared woman with white-gold hair who almost had to be one of the *Rohila*; one Child of Odin whose black hide-wrapped hands indicated a master of the Way of the Hammerfist; and four humans. Despite all the differences, though, there was a similarity – and a familiarity – about the cut and symbolism of their armor and other accoutrements.

The one who had spoken was human, whipcord-thin and barely topping five and a half feet, with a narrow face and a shock of straw-colored hair. Despite his size, Victoria tensed; there was an air of utter lethality about him, perhaps partly because of the nearly colorless eyes that made his black pupils seem pits in the center of whiteness. He wore brief, stylized armor of red, black, and bronze – a cuirass, a helm that was more a crown than protection, gauntlets and engraved, ornate vambraces, and armored boots with greaves, leaving considerable areas apparently unprotected. At his side, not yet drawn, was a broad-bladed shortsword.

Ingram stepped forward and bowed; though his movements seemed relaxed, Victoria could see he was deathly pale. "Lord Deimos," he said.

The pale, deadly eyes flicked to Ingram's face, and the brows rose the breadth of a hair. "Is it... Why, yes, it is, the young Camp-Bel." He did not bow, but inclined his head; Victoria did *not* like the way his lips curved in the hint of a smile.

Still, the movement was one of acknowledgement, if not complete respect, and the threat in the eyes was a fraction lessened. "I had *heard* you had departed on an... extended mission." The colorless gaze flicked from Ingram to Victoria and Urelle; Quester, Victoria thought, was at least partially concealed by the brush behind them. One eyebrow rose again, and she saw a shadow of suspicion on his face.

He gestured to those behind him. The *Rohila* came to his side, and Victoria saw, with a sense of inevitable dread, the glitter of a Coin in her hand; the woman whispered something to Deimos. His eyes narrowed and his teeth were bared in a smile that held no trace of warmth. "How... interesting. *You*... or, I should say, one of those with you..." his gaze settled on Urelle, "...are the one we seek."

Ingram swallowed so hard that Victoria could hear it. But he reached back and touched the *anai-k'ota*'s shaft. "You may not touch her," he said. His voice shook, but he continued, "She is under my protection, as a Camp-Bel and as a Guild Adventurer."

Whatever this man is, he is something formidable indeed; Ingram is not easily frightened. Still... "Assuredly you may not," she said, and Twin-Edged Fate materialized in her hand.

Their opponents also drew weapons, but Deimos held up a hand. "There need be no bloodshed," he said. "We seek only one. And we shall not slay her. You could even accompany her, if you wished."

"For what purpose do you seek her?" Quester asked, stepping into full view.

There was a shift in Deimos' expression; it was too quick and distant to be certain, but Victoria thought he was *very* displeased to see the Iriistiik warrior. "That has not been revealed to me," he said after a moment. "But it is Lord Ares who commands it."

"Lord Ares does not command the Clan," Ingram said, and his voice was clearer – though the dread was still there. "Only our missions, our Founder, and, in the end, the Lady of Wisdom. You are none of these, Sword of Ares."

Sword of Ares? Victoria felt a spurt of fear that was purely her own. *By the Balance, this is a God-Warrior!*

This was a situation more dire than she had imagined. The previous hunting parties had not been harmless, but if even a *tenth* of the legends surrounding the God-Warriors were true, they were adversaries far more formidable than even the Justiciars of Myrionar... and Victoria would not have cared to test herself against any of them, either.

And if *half* the things said of them were true... they were directly empowered by their patron god, and far beyond the weapons of mere mortal Adventurers.

"I cannot gainsay you there, little Camp-Bel," Deimos said after a moment. "Yet I do not forbid you to journey with us. You may guard her all the way to the Throne of War itself, if you wish."

"I'm not going *anywhere* with you," Urelle said bluntly. "We've already *met* two groups of you Balance-wreckers."

"I am afraid you are quite wrong," Deimos said. "You *will* accompany us, young woman. It's only a question of *how*." He dropped his hand.

But Urelle acted even as his people moved. Lightning bloomed, a forest of crackling, roaring blue-white, knocking the blade-faeries from the air and scattering the others. Even Deimos flinched, the way a man might from an unexpected light.

Ingram moved in the moment the bolts faded. His first steps were unsteady, the shakiness of a man in terror forcing himself to move, but in three feet they firmed, the little Adventurer committing himself fully to the charge, towards the God-Warrior himself.

Victoria had the same idea, and in an instant, she was matching Ingram stride for stride. *Deimos is their leader. He is the strongest of them. Take him down and we may have a chance against the rest. Fail to do so...*

But Deimos, startled or not, had seen them coming, and his shield came up, caught both the *anai-k'ota* and her great Axe on it with such contemptuous strength that she felt she had sought to cleave a granite cliff in half. He *shoved* forward, and Victoria tumbled away. *Myrionar's Mercy, he threw me back like a child!*

Ingram had been flung even farther, and rolled to his feet between the *Rohila* and one of the human warriors. One of the huge *bilarel* was engaging Quester, and the Child of Odin had just reached Urelle. His arms lashed out to catch her.

Even as Victoria turned to face Deimos again, the Child of Odin's eyes widened as the delicate-seeming hands closed about his arms and *clamped* down. Little Urelle *yanked* the massive Child of Odin off the ground and then *threw* him into the next two attackers.

This time *both* of Deimos' eyebrows rose. "That... was unexpected."

The distraction had given Victoria a chance to focus, to recall to herself the discipline of the Eight Winds. "Shall we try again?" she asked, raising the immense Axe and channeling some of her *self* into it.

Deimos smiled, and an aura of blood-red rose about him. "By all means, my Lady."

"Not by herself, she won't!" Ingram said. His two other assailants were down already, and he tore his way across the ground towards Deimos.

Too late, Victoria saw the scaled arm of the *mazakh* rising, opened her mouth to call a warning, but light was already starting from the clawed hand—

In the last splintered second, Ingram sensed it – saw movement from the corner of his eye, noticed the direction and intensity of Victoria's gaze, or simply *felt* it with the gut instinct of a trained Adventurer – and whirled, interposing his weapon between himself and the *mazakh*.

But it was no single beam or bolt; a *column* of luminous power roared from the *mazakh* and hammered Ingram back ten feet, twenty, thirty—

And Ingram Camp-Bel tumbled over the edge of the cliff, a look of horror on his face as he disappeared from view.

From the distant sky there came a flash of auric light.

Chapter 15
Berenike

She rose from below the cliff in a glow like sunbeams on water, bronze curls tumbling across her shoulders, skin of olive-touched gold, a body as strong and tall as Urelle remembered her sister Kyri's, and cradled in her arms was Ingram, staring at the newcomer with such awe and joy and love that Urelle felt something constrict in her chest.

Then the girl laughed, and the sound *itself* was joy, a clarion cry of courage and triumph that dispelled thoughts of fear and defeat. "Never fear, Ingram," she said, and her voice was somehow bells and trumpets. "Always shall I be there, if I am needed."

This... This is his reserve, his backup, his final secret card, Urelle finally realized. Her senses tingled with the power near her; magical strength mixed with a touch of something else she had never felt before.

The newcomer placed Ingram down in the brush near the cliff's edge and rose. Now Urelle could see that the girl wore armor somehow akin to Deimos', but where his was red and black and bronze, hers was gold and green and silver, shining and bright and *bold* in the same way Deimos' was in some manner deadly, threatening, dark. Over her shoulder was a quiver of javelins or throwing spears.

She strode forward, still smiling, and Deimos had gone pale with rage or fear or utter disbelief beneath his dark skin. "*Berenike?!*" he said in a strangled voice. "Impossible."

"Sword of Ares," Berenike said, "by oath and by bond, Ingram Camp-Bel and those he calls allies and friends are under *my* protection. You raise your hand at your peril, for the Lady's Spear stands ready to strike you."

"*Ridiculous!*" he snapped. "I know not what kind of trick this is, but I know it must *be* a trick!" He gestured to his people, who had regrouped. "*Take her!*"

The entire group focused on Berenike – *except*, Urelle noticed, *Deimos himself. He's slowly backing up... is he planning to* retreat?

Berenike's laugh echoed through the clearing again. "*Storm of Spears!*" she shouted, and hurled one of her javelins.

The dark-metal spear transformed in the moment it left her hand, became a shard of pure golden light that *shattered* into a hundred hundred bolts of luminous force. They hammered into and then broke the spell-wall before the *mazakh*, impaled the *bilarel* in a dozen places each, pursued the Child of Odin and sent him careening into a tree, blew away a cloak of shadow around the *Rohila* woman, who arched in shock and agony and fell limply to the ground, struck the remainder with such force that they somersaulted backwards, weapons flying from their hands, bodies falling like stringless puppets.

Berenike shifted her stance the slightest bit and Deimos raised his arms, seeing that there was no escape.

It did him no good at all.

Without so much as a pause, Berenike was *there*, in front of Deimos, and her fist blazed like the sun come to earth as it smashed through the Sword of Ares' guard and came up, a meteor of light, to catch him on the point of his narrow chin. Brilliant energy flashed, a shockwave of energy that lanced around and through the God-Warrior, making his body convulse; Deimos arced upward, reaching sixty feet before plummeting back to earth like a stone.

Urelle thought that *must* have ended it, but to her utter amazement, Deimos was not dead. He rolled painfully to a sitting position as the Spear of Athena strode towards him. Deimos' face was white, streaked with red blood below the mouth and nose. His hand dove into a pouch at his side and dragged out a piece of paper. Even as Berenike drew back her hand, he gasped a single word—

—and disappeared, leaving but a few drops of blood behind.

Berenike stopped, frowning. "Lady's *Spear*, that's unfortunate. He'll have run back to Ares, no doubt." She shrugged. "Nothing to do about it *now*, though."

She turned to face them and smiled. "And you are Ingram's friends. It is good to meet you all at last." She gave a strange salute – bringing her two fists in to her chest so they met at an angle at the center, then rotating both so for a moment both her fists were vertical at her sides – and bowed. "I am Berenike, the Spear of Athena."

Quester gave his own bow. "I am called Quester," he said.

"Hold, now; my friend should be introducing you." She leapt lightly through the air and landed at Ingram's side. The boy had been simply *staring*, Urelle realized, unable to do anything other than gawk while the newcomer took care of the opposition in two moments.

"Now, Ingram, introduce me to your friends *properly*," she said.

Ingram blinked, and shook himself. Urelle also noticed that the *aura* seemed to envelop Ingram as well as Berenike, both of them seeming touched by the magic, or greater than magic, that had appeared along with the Spear of Athena.

"Um… sorry. Berenike, please allow me to make known to you Quester of the Iriistiik, Adventurer and partner to me in our Adventures; Lady Victoria Vantage of Evanwyl, herself of the Guild and a warrior of great deeds; and Lady Urelle Vantage, a mage who is young, but of impressive power already. They were our charges once, but they have followed me on my quest to be my protection, as well. My friends, this is Berenike of Aegis, my oldest and dearest friend in the world and, as you have just seen," his eyes shone up at Berenike again, "the living Spear of Athena."

"It is a pleasure to meet you," Victoria said. "And we are all certainly grateful for your intervention; I admit, I did not like our chances against Deimos."

Berenike grimaced. "Him *and* that group? No. It was fortunate that he was not prepared for me, and that his power is less…" she grinned, "…*direct* than mine. Oh, against most foes he's still beyond merely formidable, but Deimos was always more about breaking his opponents' wills and weakening their resolve than direct action – 'dread,' you know – while my job is, well, to hit the Lady's enemies as hard as I can until they stop."

Her head came up for a moment, and Urelle saw a tension on the olive-gold brow, a narrowing of the eyes as though she saw and heard something no one else could. "I would stay, but I cannot leave my duties for long, even for my oath-bound friend." She kissed Ingram on the forehead. "Until we meet again!"

She leapt into the air, smiling at Ingram as she rose up, seeming to fall away *upward*, until she turned away and disappeared in the same flash of gold light that had heralded her arrival. The sense of magic lingered about Ingram for a moment before also fading away.

"Well!" Victoria said after a moment. "That was… fortunate, if abrupt. Ingram, if you don't very much mind, I think we need to understand just who Berenike *is*, and how it is that she's coming to your aid."

Ingram turned his face back to them, and to Urelle's surprise, there were *tears* running down his face, even though he was smiling. But he wiped them away quickly. "Yes," he said. "Yes, I suppose you do. I just... I mean, I knew she'd come, but it had been so *long*..."

He trailed off, then snorted and smacked himself a couple of times. "Sorry, I need to focus. I was acting... embarrassingly silly there, wasn't I?"

"Yes, you were," Urelle said. It came out sharper than she'd intended, and she wondered why.

"She's... overwhelming," Victoria said after a moment. "It's not, perhaps, so surprising. Is that what she was like when you were young?"

Ingram laughed, sounding more natural. "Well, *sort* of. Not really. That... aura around her, that's from being a God-Warrior. You must have felt Deimos' aura? That... *pressure*, that dread of what *could* happen, of what *will* happen if you face him? Same kind of thing, but of course you were feeling what an *enemy* would get there, and what a *friend* gets from Berenike."

"Logical," Quester said. "So, his allies did not feel dread at all?"

"No. I haven't fought alongside Deimos myself, of course," Urelle saw a shadow of his shame at being kept out of action, "but from what I've heard, it's more the opposite – an absolute confidence that they carry terror *with* them, and their enemies will flee or be crushed. Berenike's not as, well, *dark* as that, but it's the same thing; if you're on the other side, you'll be seeing this bright, undefeatable warrior and know that you're facing something totally beyond you."

Victoria had been examining their fallen enemies; Urelle noticed that she looked a shade paler than normal. "What is it, Auntie?"

Victoria rose from next to one of the *bilarel*. "They are all dead. I had expected one or two survivors. A terrible blow she struck – and leaving not a trace of her weapon save the wounds." She looked down, shaking her head, at the bloody rents covering the gigantic body.

"You killed eight people in one quick motion," Ingram pointed out. "Okay, this is a few more, but still, not *that* much more frightening."

Victoria's lips curled in a wry smile. "Young man, you are superficially correct. I suspect, however, that you know perfectly well that there is a large difference here."

"Maybe *he* does," Urelle said, "but I'm not clear on it. You *did* do pretty much the same thing when you rescued us."

Her aunt chuckled. "I suppose it must have *looked* that way, yes. But first of all, to do that I had prepared myself ahead of time. By the time I announced my presence, I had already focused myself into the Eight Winds and I continued to prepare until I had to make my move.

"Then, please note, afterward I was exhausted. I could barely have raised my axe to *block* for a few moments following that passage at arms. Berenike immediately delivered another blow that was *utterly* out of my ability to perform, and did not seem at all winded by her efforts."

Victoria shook her head. "I do not think that even one of the Justiciars of Myrionar could have done anything like what she did. And finally, not only were there *more* of them, I would judge that group to have been *far* more formidable than the eight we first encountered. *They* had no *bilarel* with them, and if they had casters, they were not prepared for such an assault. If you watched closely, Berenike's attack destroyed – rather casually – at least two sets of magical defenses and *still* slew the ones behind those defenses."

Thinking about those points, Urelle felt a leaden chill in her gut. If Auntie was right – and she almost always was – that group had been *totally* out of their league, even leaving aside Deimos himself.

And this Berenike had killed them all with *one* attack.

"Auntie... I think we might be out of our depth in this," she said slowly.

"That's *why* I didn't want you following," Ingram said. He didn't sound angry or annoyed; more concerned, and, behind that concern, afraid. "I *have* to go. I can't choose anything else, not and be... well, who I *want* to be, who I've *claimed* to be, all my life."

"If they're after you like this—"

"They might be after *you*!" he shot back. "It doesn't make *sense*, but for some reason it really does look like they're chasing you... or maybe Quester." He shrugged and grinned weakly. "Or even you, Lady Victoria. But if you stayed in Zarathanton... you have friends at the Palace. They could..."

He trailed off at Victoria's expression. It had suddenly become dark, grim, mingled with one that Urelle had *rarely* seen on her aunt's face: chagrin.

"Young man," she said after a moment of silence. "The Sauran King himself has been assassinated, in his own castle. There is nowhere in all the *world* that I would have thought more safe from assault than *T'Teranahm Chendoron*, and yet the most ancient and powerful sovereign on Zarathan – save only the Archmage himself – was slain *in his own throne room*. Clearly, if someone seeks your, or our, ruin, there are ways to accomplish this, especially if your location be known."

Ingram nodded unwillingly.

Victoria took a breath, then continued slowly; her brow was furrowed now with concentration. "But there is more. Understand that I must now break a confidence. In my conference with Toron and his aides, it was clear already that such an act could not occur in isolation, and that in order to prevent panic and fear, we were to keep *all* news that seemed connected with such a plan to ourselves and to only discuss it with those in the Palace." She shook her head. "But it matters little now; surely the results of these events have already become frighteningly clear in Zarathanton, if nowhere else.

"I told you shortly after I rescued you that Lythos had taken a message to Kyri. But that... avoided telling you the details. When Lythos came to me at our home, he brought with him terrible news: the *Artan* of the Forest Sea have been wiped out nearly to a one, and the remainder have fled. The Suntree has fallen."

Urelle stared in disbelief at her aunt. "No... no, Auntie, that's impossible, the Suntree's stood for *Chaoswars* of time, it's..."

Victoria hugged her gently. "Lythos had *come* from the fighting, Urelle. He saw the Tree falling with his own eyes. He would have fought to the death, except he wanted to seek us out, make sure that we, at least, were alive. I gave him another task, sent him with a message to Kyri, so that she would know what was happening here." A tiny laugh. "It was not, perhaps, the most coherent of messages, but it will suffice... but more importantly, it gave Lythos something to do rather than meditate on the losses of his people."

She looked back at Ingram. "But again, something terrible is also happening in your home country. We are being hunted – which one of us is truly the target may not even, at this point, be relevant. The important point is this: I do not believe all of these things are unrelated."

Urelle found herself nodding; her own gut, tense as it was, agreed. "Yes. Assassination in one country, invasion in the one just to the north, and *something* terrible happening in one of our allies to the south, and... Auntie, our *own* troubles. The corruption of the Justiciars, our own God-Warriors in their own way."

Quester gave a buzz-growl and a sharp scent of lightning and musk. "And perhaps even the slaying of the Nests and Mothers. Ours was at the foot of the Ice Peaks, the northern point of the Forest Sea; another of which the Sorter told us was nigh to Aegeia, perhaps within its northern borders, and the third between the Gyrefell and the Nightsky River."

"Ares' *Balls*," Ingram murmured. "That's not all that far from Evanwyl or from Dalthunia, which fell, itself, not all that long ago. I think you're right, Victoria. By the *Lady*, I'm sure you're right. There's a *connection*."

Without warning his eyes widened and he gave a half-heard gasp, turning towards Victoria – and Urelle saw the same horrified expression on her aunt's face. An instant later, the hideous realization broke through to her as well.

"Oh, Myrionar's *Balance*, Auntie," she said at last, seeing Quester's antennae drooping in shock, "that's it, isn't it? It's started.

"This is the beginning of the next *Chaoswar*."

Chapter 16
A Cycle of Doom and a Mystery

Chaoswar.

The word echoed menacingly through Ingram's mind.

On its own it was a *silly* word. War was usually chaos. Putting the two together was near enough a redundancy. But as every living being on Zarathan knew, had been taught, had read in books or heard in legends or seen in ancient carvings, there was nothing whatsoever silly about it.

"Chaoswar" was only the translation, anyway, of a phrase in Ancient Sauran that meant something more like "the world plunged into war, that only chaos shall remain." The world grew, flourished, the shattered countries that had been healed their wounds and became mighty again, great heroes drove back monsters and abominations from the land, and all was well. And then... every few thousand years (how many, no one really knew)... *something* happened. The world went mad. Petty disagreements became violent arguments. Monsters became more cunning, devising longer-term plans to bypass defenses around the roads and cities. Those who dreamed of vengeance or conquest found it easier to gain followers, to raise armies and gold and the patronage of demons or gods.

The wars escalated, and in the end, the forces released... would somehow *resonate* throughout the world, so that even as the war and devastation reached a climax, the *knowledge of the world* faded. Even the gods, even the Great Dragons, could only recall very imperfectly what had gone before. And so, the world would slowly emerge from chaos and confusion, and begin to rebuild anew... knowing only that in the end, no matter their achievements, one day the world's madness would come again...

It was the prayer of every parent and every child that *they* would not be born into that era.

And now we are.

He wanted to ask if they were sure, but that, too, would be foolish. First, because of course they could not be sure. How much did any of them, even

Victoria, know of the world at large, of what passed not just in Evanwyl and the State of the Dragon King and Aegeia, but in distant Elyvias or Artania or the White Blade State or Skysand?

Second, because he did not need to ask. He *knew,* somehow, that he was right. The next Chaoswar was upon them.

"If that's what we're against... if that's what's really *happening*... Auntie, what can we *do*?" Urelle was as stunned as the rest of them by the thought, by the enormity of the idea that the terrible legend had become reality.

Victoria did not answer; Quester, too, was silent for a moment.

Ingram drew a breath. "We do," he said, trying to sound confident, courageous, and strong, and not sure he sounded at all like any of them, "exactly what we're already doing. There's only one country in all the world that's *ever* resisted the Chaoswars, and that's Aegeia. Whatever's going on there now... if it disrupts our Cycle, that protection will *end*. Whatever force is behind the Chaoswars *must* be always seeking to destroy that resistance."

"You believe there is a force behind them?" Victoria asked mildly.

"I think there *has* to be. Could it really be *natural* that this kind of thing happens, has been happening since the Fall, half a million years ago? I say no. Something is behind this constant return of utter destruction and obliteration of knowledge, and whatever the Aegei might know of it, they did at least set in motion something that opposes it. That's one of the reasons *why* the Founder swore her oath to Athena."

"Perhaps your recall to your clan is also connected," Quester mused.

"Probably." He noticed Urelle walking to the fallen corpses of their enemies. "What..."

She had stooped down next to the *Rohila*. "Got it!"

"Oh, right. Another Coin."

"Now we have two again." She rubbed the back of her neck pensively. "I *could* pull the same trick again. This time I'd think we've *got* to have gotten rid of everyone to the west of us. If I send it off to Elyvias a second time we should *really* pull people off course."

"It might not be a bad idea," Ingram said. Obviously, repeating the same trick *too* many times would end up failing, but twice? They'd probably think that the misleading enchantment had broken, which it had, and figure they had a lead on the real location. "Actually, it's a *great* idea to do it again. Unless someone can somehow see through it and find us directly, it'll be a help whether they're fooled or not."

Quester bobbed his antennae. "Yes. Yes, you are correct. If they believe the directions they receive, they will move away from us. If they do not... then they must mistrust *any* directions the Coins give, and at best they will be moving more slowly as they check and re-check their directions, or go to trying to locate us by other means entirely."

"And since they have very little idea of who we really are," Victoria finished, "any other means of divination will be hard-pressed to give them even a general direction. Yes, Urelle, when we camp—"

"—right now," Ingram said.

Victoria opened her mouth, paused, then nodded. "Ah. Of course."

"Of course *what*, Auntie?"

"Deimos. We do not know where he has gone exactly, but we *must* presume it was to warn his master. They could be preparing an assault force even as we speak. Deimos was clearly injured, but how badly we do not know; his power may have been the only thing keeping him alive, or he might be back on his feet in a few minutes."

"Myrionar's Sword, you're right!" Urelle's gray eyes flashed. "Everyone, sit down, I'll start the preparations."

Despite knowing the need to hurry, Ingram saw Urelle stop herself, close her eyes, and focus before beginning the preparations. *She knows that we can even less afford a mistake in this magical working.* He knew his own instructors would have been pleased by her presence of mind under pressure, though of course they still would have done their best to increase that pressure. It was the Camp-Bel way.

The young mage worked through the ritual more swiftly this time, having successfully done it once before, and having no need to explain the process. In a few minutes, she tossed one Coin into the air and it was snatched away by a large raven and borne aloft, sailing away to the east.

"We will take a quick look at the possessions of our fallen foes, but I do not want to linger long," Victoria said.

"Hold on." Urelle raised her hand. "Let me check over the area. They were defeated very suddenly, and you said she broke even magical protections, so I can probably tell if there's anything powerfully magical hidden on any of them."

"A good idea. Do not leave powerful magic for either our enemies to recover, or others to find if it turns out to be dangerous," Quester agreed. "As long as we can be sure none of *it* is easily traceable."

"I think we can prevent that, yes."

It did not take long with Urelle pointing out the right areas to search. Among other things, they recovered a beautiful crystalline sword that seemed to have been carven from a single gigantic sapphire and then chased with gold and silver runes, a collection of elixirs or potions, one of the transport or recall scrolls, a powerfully enchanted necklace of red and violet metals, and several other magical ornaments that would have otherwise passed unnoticed.

"I'll look over these later. For now, I'll just put a concealment enchantment over them – sort of practice for what I'll be doing on the last Coin in a couple weeks – and we'll stuff them in Ingram's neverfull pack."

"Good enough," Victoria said. "But let's get moving, please. I am becoming increasingly nervous. I would like many miles between ourselves and this location."

"Right. But have we figured out how to cross this gorge?"

"For now, let us just head west along the edge. Perhaps an opportunity will present itself," Quester said, antennae testing the air. "I scent the presence of water some distance off; if there is a stream entering the canyon, it may have cut its own, smaller, access into the chasm."

"Okay," Ingram said, as they began walking, "but why not just go down first? We were pretty sure we could make it to the bottom; it was just the climb back up on the other side."

"I suspect none of us would like to be boxed in by canyon walls if our pursuers locate us," Victoria answered. "But we can always begin the descent once we have an answer to the climbing problem. Perhaps, after we camp, we will find that one of our newly-acquired trinkets has the capability we require."

They walked in silence for a while, Ingram trying not to dwell on the worldshaking implications of the situation. *One thing at a time*, he told himself. *You can't stop a Chaoswar by yourself, but maybe you can help save Aegeia, as is a Camp-Bel's duty.*

But after a while, the silence became oppressive. He looked over to Urelle, who happened to glance at him at the same moment.

For some reason, that glance... *touched* him. Meeting Urelle's stormcloud-and-steel eyes sent a *frisson* through him that wasn't exactly excitement... but wasn't exactly *not* excitement, either. He didn't know what to make of it, except that he liked it.

However, it was also weird and made him cast about for something to say. "Um... Urelle, you know, I was wondering... I wasn't so surprised on our first journey to see your sister do some spectacular things – I mean, she's huge, for one thing. But you picked up that Child of Odin who probably outweighed you two-to-one and *threw* him like a sack of feed. How? Did you boost your strength or something?"

She opened her mouth, looking puzzled, then suddenly laughed. "Oh! You know, it's something everyone sort of took for granted back home, I forgot you never lived in Evanwyl."

"The Vantage strength," Victoria said with her own smile. "Those in the close family line have that strength. I have it, their mother had it, all three of the children have or had it. Why? No one knows for certain. Some say it's a blessing from some deed done centuries ago, others a touch of blood from something powerful in the line. But it's there, and as you saw, to this day it's nothing to laugh at."

"Indeed," hummed Quester. "I have seen strong grown men who would never have been able to do what Urelle did. That also explains how you can move your axe with such ease."

Victoria nodded. "We all have our talents, of course. Urelle's the first real mage in the family for quite a while. Oh, I know a few tricks, but nothing like her. You've got that mind-trick you can do with Ingram, plus of course your jumping and gliding."

Quester made a dismissive gesture. "Merely facets of being Iriistiik, nothing more."

"We could dismiss the strength – or indeed most other talents – in similar ways, young one."

Quester's antennae tilted, and Ingram smelled a waft of woodsmoke and pineweed; his friend was thinking on that.

"Can I ask you something, Ingram?" Urelle asked hesitantly.

"Of course."

"Why 'Ingram?' Your name doesn't sound *anything* like the names of other people we've heard of from Aegeia, at least so far."

The question triggered a wash of emotions, a roiling mess not easily sorted out. There was a moment of fond memory, a surge of guilt and anger, a touch of excitement and pride, more. "Well... no. It's one of the Clan Names." He paused, trying to isolate and understand his reactions. *I really am proud of my name. It's just the context of the Clan... despite the recall, I'm not over what happened. I still don't understand it.*

But he hadn't really explained. "Camp-Bel the Founder did not come from Zarathan at all. She came from up there, somewhere in the stars; some people say she came from the sister world, Zahralandar itself. Anyway, the Clan preserved a whole set of names from the Founder – most of them taken from her crew, we think, but some of them from important people in Camp-Bel's history or stories. Ingram is one of those; reading the remaining tales, he was something like a magician and a hero-thief, though the Camp-Bel claimed there was no magic on her homeworld."

"Oh. That makes sense. The names, I mean. I can't imagine a world with *no* magic."

"Neither can I." He tried to smile.

Apparently, that attempt was a failure, because Urelle looked at him with concern. "What's wrong, Ingram? I didn't mean to pry, I mean, if those were secrets..."

"No, no, it's not really secret. Clan tradition, but not like some of the *real* secrets of the Clan." He swallowed. "I... honestly? I don't *know* what's wrong, really. It just... upset me, somehow." He frowned. "I guess it's because I used to be *proud* of the name, and then as I got older, I got to be *ashamed* of it because I wasn't living up to it. I wasn't even good enough to be a *real* Camp-Bel, let alone one of the best of them."

"Young man," Victoria said with quiet conviction, "I admit to knowing little about the Camp-Bels personally – I have met no other – but I assure you, there is no clan of warriors or defenders of *any* stripe who would find you less than an ornament to its name. I do not know why or how they convinced you so completely of your inferiority, but I *am* absolutely certain that it was utter rot. And the fact that they recalled you as they did shows that *they know it.*"

Ingram felt a shock of tingling cold in his gut, a burst of fear and hope and confusion. *No, that's not true! I was* never *that good! They wouldn't even have had any* reason *to lie to me that way, to trick me... even if I could imagine how they could have done it...*

But on the other hand, he was equally unable to imagine that Victoria Vantage was either so poor in judgment, or so willing to mislead him, that what she said could be dismissed.

Could it be true? Could I have been... good enough? Better *than good enough?*

But if I was... then why? Why convince me I wasn't? Why...

He reached into his neverfull pouch and withdrew the box, opened it, touched the Insignia. He was barely aware he was walking; everything was concentrated on that golden symbol.

If you wish to know why, came Quester's thought-voice, *then think of what it accomplished* for them *to do it. What was the effect, the result that would have been different had they treated you as you must have deserved?* Ingram heard the buzzing of Quester's voice, realized that his friend had also spoken aloud, so that their other friends could understand.

"That's... a really good point." Ingram took a breath, put the Insignia away, and concentrated. *All right. Take it that Lady Victoria is correct.* Even as a *theory* the idea that he wasn't a disappointment, that he was *fully* worthy of his name, felt almost blasphemous, as though he were dismissing the Clan's fitness to judge him. But if it *were* true? If he was at least as fit as any of his relatives within the Clan...

Slowly, understanding came. "...I was not *seen*," he breathed. "I stayed within the Clan grounds almost all the time. I had to *sneak out* if I wanted to go elsewhere, unless I was traveling with Mother or Father or others of the Clan. I wasn't sent on patrols, or given apprentice assignments – guard duty in safer locations, escort duty with veterans, that kind of thing. I just stayed in, studied, trained, played only with people on the grounds."

"Indeed," Victoria said. "An interesting train of thought, is it not?"

"*Very* interesting," Ingram said. His gut was churning now, a mix of hope and fear and anger, and he increased his strides.

When I get home... I will demand *these answers!*

Chapter 17
A Mother's Advice

"Of course I want you to succeed, my son," said his mother. "But there is only so much I can do for you without making my King and husband doubt that it is *your* success, and not *mine*, that he sees."

He nodded, unwillingly, in acquiescence. Having Mother's whole-hearted support in his endeavors would make everything vastly easier, of course, but she was right; then there would be – would *always* be – the question as to whether any of the credit belonged to him, rather than to the Queen and Mother of all. "I understand, Mother."

"Oh, look not so downcast, Raiaga. Still there will be many things I can do to ease your way – not so much as to make the King misdoubt your power, but sufficient to be of much use. I *do* want to see you recognized, have him acknowledge you and let you take your place among the true Elders, even though your years are so tender." She laid a hand on his shoulder and squeezed gently.

It was... strange, to find that comforting, especially as Mother wore a human form, as was her wont and custom in her home. Beautiful, of course, with long dark hair and an unusual paleness of complexion, the only hint of her inhuman nature visible in her eyes, one violet as twilight cloud, one yellow as gold.

But it *was* Mother, after all – the only one who he trusted. He was her own grand experiment, one that the King had permitted but never approved – which by itself showed her power and influence. None other of the true people would dare such a thing without both permission *and* approval.

"Would you be able to assist me in the design – if not the performance – of the ritual to seal off Aegeia?"

"That I can certainly do, Raiaga. But does not the power of Ares give you the knowledge and capability? He has done it before, yes?"

He growled deep in his throat. "Apparently not; it was *Athena's* doing in all the Cycles I can discern. It would seem that she does it when she is ready to begin the work of taking back the country from her brother." He smiled grimly. "I, of course, want to do it in order to isolate the country and prevent any possible meddling from outside, at least until my control is complete and absolute. And since Athena is *not* going to manifest, I can't even try to trick her into doing it for me."

"Well, worry not. So long as you have Ares' power for me to work with, I am sure I can design such a ritual that will serve your needs." She seated herself and leaned back in the chair, which reclined to exactly the angle she preferred. "But I would caution you, my little darling, to never be so certain where the gods are concerned. There is *always* a way for one such as Athena to manifest."

"Hmph." He looked down, frowned, then shrugged and forced a smile. "Of course you are right, Mother. But the only path to her manifestation *now* is to reach the main temple and claim her spear — and you know how very restricted is the set of beings who could claim it and survive to become the Goddess Incarnate."

"Indeed, and you are in all likelihood correct, Raiaga." She smiled slowly. "But tell me... does anyone *else* know this? That you have found a way to prevent her incarnation by any but the most improbable means?"

He thought; that smile meant that Mother was planning something, and she would need accurate information. "A very few of my inner circle. Who have their own reasons to keep it quiet, and over whom I have certain... leverage, as you know."

"Well, then, Raiaga, your mother has some advice for you, if you would hear it."

He smiled back; it was a *different* smile, one he could feel, as he could never truly feel a smile towards any other being. "Always, Mother. You are wiser than I, and I am no fool."

"Best that you are not, my son, or my King will surely end you. Would have already for your ambition, save that you are my special child." She waved that away. "But attend. You have yourself said that only Athena uses the barrier you contemplate, yes?"

"True."

"Then here is my suggestion."

It was a short enough description — an outline of a plan that both awed him with its simple beauty and made him want to stab himself for not thinking of it himself. With difficulty, he controlled that impulse; Mother did not like to see him so seized by rage, and rightly so. Instead, he focused on the lovely *symmetry* of the plan. "I am awed and humbled, Mother. I should have thought of that, and yet it is only right that you do so."

She ruffled his hair. "Oh, Raiaga, you know how to speak well to your mother. Then if you follow this path, I can promise that I will ensure the seal will be enacted as required. This does not endanger anything in your main plan, I trust?"

"Oh, no, no." As he fit the new idea in, he felt his own smile broaden. "No, far from it, Mother, I believe it will make the entire plan even stronger. You perceived weakness and turned it to strength."

"Well enough, then." Her face was suddenly cold. "But this shall be the only such favor I will do you, Raiagamor. As my King and the Father of our people has said, this must be *your* test, and weakness is the thing he will abide least of all in one who wishes to be seen before him. A few other small services I may provide, but I, too, am limited by his decree, even though I be your mother; and in truth, Raiaga, if you wish to become one of his favored and, in time, supplant him? You must provide your enemies not the slightest vulnerability."

He bowed his head. "Yet you believe I may succeed?"

"Oh, my strange and wonderful child, you may, if you control the nature you gained from your true father, if you master yourself as you master others. If you do not... you will die."

"I can only die in one way, Mother, and," he gestured, "I have guarded well against that."

"*Two* ways, Riaga. Be not so arrogant. Yes, you are harder by far to destroy than any of my other children, but do not doubt for a moment that the King, or any of his Elders, could rend your soul asunder – and so he shall, if you fail."

A distant, echoed noise reached his ears. A chime? No, a banging... as on a door...

Fang and Claw, this had best be important! It was a matter of great preparation and effort to arrange these meetings with his mother, meetings that aided him in maintaining his focus and control, and once canceled it would be some time before another meeting could be had.

But the banging renewed, with the sense of a distant voice calling. *No choice, then.* "Mother, my apologies – I must go now."

As she nodded her understanding, he waved his hand over the crystal set in the bracelet on his left wrist, and without so much as an instant's hesitation his mother's castle vanished, replaced by his bedchamber – and the door, which rattled in its frame as someone *hammered* on it again. "Lord Ares! *Lord Ares!*"

"I come! Stop that racket, Phobos!"

He yanked open the door – then froze.

Phobos stood there, uniform spattered with blood, supporting the figure of Deimos, who seemed unable to stand on his own.

"What happened?" he asked, gesturing for Phobos to bring Deimos in.

"I do not know. He arrived in the recall chamber and collapsed. I could barely *sense* his mind calling to my own."

"That is... distressing indeed," he murmured. "Who else knows of this?"

"No one, Lord," Phobos said after a thoughtful pause. "There were none in the chamber when he arrived, and I brought him here straightaway. No witnesses as far as I know."

"Clean up any traces. I want no one to get a hint of this." He bent his perceptions towards Deimos – and cursed with shock.

"My Lord... what is wrong?"

"What was he *fighting*?" The words were forced out from between teeth gritted tight in rage... or even, just possibly, fear.

The wounds on Deimos' body were terrible, yes; they would have killed any ordinary being outright. But one such as Deimos should not have been struck down by them.

To Ares-Raiagamor's vision, Deimos' *soul* had the look of a curtain slashed to ribbons by a berserk hand. No, it was more something rotted or pierced by innumerable tiny holes – the *shape* was retained, but there was barely anything actually holding it together.

Phobos' eyes widened as he, too, gained a sense of what had happened to his brother-warrior.

In that moment, Deimos' eyes opened. For an instant they stared, blankly furious and fearful of something beyond the room in which they stood, but then they focused, and with a groan of pain he reached out and grasped Ares' arm. "Fading," he whispered.

"I know," Ares said quietly, as he still studied the wounds on body and soul. *It's as though he was struck by a storm of missiles that pierced his essence as well as his body*. "Phobos, fetch a new body for Deimos. We must transfer as much as may survive, as fast as possible."

"*Wait!*" Deimos gasped. "Phobos... *there is a survivor*."

The other God-Warrior's face went so pale it looked greenish for a moment, and something tense and alien moved within it. "You are certain?"

"Yes."

"Did this 'survivor' do this to you?" Ares asked. "And survivor of *what*?"

"No," Deimos said, raising his eyes to meet that of his Lord, and they were already clouding towards death. "It... was... *Berenike*," he forced out, and then his hand unclenched; Deimos slid to the floor, life nearly gone.

Riagamor felt as though someone had rammed a silver dagger into his heart; his hand actually came up to touch the armor encasing his chest, verifying that the pain was merely shock. "Berenike?" he repeated, even as Phobos stared at him with pale, gaping features mirroring his own disbelief. "But... that's *impossible*."

He *knew* it was impossible. Berenike had died over two *years* ago. He'd *arranged* that death, the final removal – or so he'd thought – of a threat he'd believed dealt with a *decade* ago. He'd been to the *funeral*. He'd seen the body – *smelled* it, known that scent and known she was dead and gone.

And even if she were *alive, how...* "How," he said, speaking urgently to the dying man, "how could *she* have done this to *you*?"

With a final effort, Deimos answered, and though all his remaining strength was in those words, still Ares had to bend near indeed to hear:

"She is already... the Spear of Athena."

Chapter 18
An Unexpected Refuge

"Ingram," Victoria said, "How are certain are you that we are still on the proper course?"

"About a hundred per cent," Ingram said. "Why?" Quester caught a hint of amusement from his friend.

"Because I haven't noticed you stopping to take bearings much, if at all, in our travels. And there are so many ways to get lost in the Forest Sea. I've been through this general area before, and to make sure we were on the straight course meant one of us had to ascend to the canopy and check sun and any other landmarks... rather frequently."

"Another advantage of the Camp-Bel legacy." Ingram displayed a peculiar object, oblong, with most of its front surface taken up by what seemed to be a window; however, what was currently visible through this window was some sort of self-illuminated diagram with arrows and some other symbols on it. There were colored studs on the front beneath this window, and faint lines on the sides showed that there might be hidden small compartments or holes there. Quester had seen the device before, but even now he didn't understand details of its operation.

"And this is...?"

Quester saw Urelle gesture, then blink, shaking her head. "There's no magic on that thing. Some on you, but none on it."

"No, of course not. This is technology. It's way beyond what most of us think of as technology, but the Founder and her crew didn't *know* anything about magic when they crashed here. In fact, according to the stories they didn't believe magic *existed* until their new hosts made it pretty hard to maintain their disbelief." Ingram glanced down at his viewer, then put it back in the pouch at his side, continuing to lead them onward.

Quester could see Urelle trying to grasp the idea of people who literally did not believe in magic at all. He remembered how hard that concept had been for him to understand. But there were other things to discuss. "You say you have been through this part of the Forest Sea before, Lady Victoria?" Quester asked.

"Years ago, of course. But yes."

"Anything you could tell us about that might be of importance here?"

"Hm." She was quiet for a few moments as they continued to walk. "I am not sure, to be honest. The Forest Sea changes, as you must know. Except in places where some species or group has managed to heavily entrench themselves, the dominant creatures may change from year to year. The land *itself* may be changed by conflicts between powerful beings; I have seen a valley that was later a flat plain, and, of course, we all know how the Fallenstone Hills came to be."

Quester nodded in human fashion. One of the few tales to survive all the Chaoswars was that one – the story of the Fall of the Saurans, centered around the Great Dragon Syrcal, whose nascent envy of his more powerful and spectacular brethren had been fanned to virulent evil by agents of Kerlamion Blackstar, until Syrcal had performed a ritual of the King of Hell's design that made the Dragon vastly more powerful... and, it seemed, utterly corrupt, and under the direction of Kerlamion. In his battle against Elbon Nomicon, Syrcal had been thrown down and the impact of his fall had created the Fallenstone Hills.

"Still..." Victoria said, "If that viewer of Ingram's is as accurate as he says, I would expect to come across a small lake soon. There are a few rivers that flow down from Wisdom's Fortress and never make it to the larger river – they come out somewhere along the coast between Shipton and Aegeia. One flows through this area and into a lake, which has an outlet for the river to leave to the south.

"*If* all that hasn't changed, there will be an old... fortress, small castle, something of that nature, on the near shore to us. It's the only reasonably intact structure in a set of ruins; there used to be a town of some sort there, and one that lasted for some time; you don't get such massive stone buildings in a new town."

"Intact? Would it be defensible? Suitable to stay a few nights in?" He asked the question quietly, so as not to be heard by Ingram or Urelle, who were walking together and discussing the viewer and technology in general.

Victoria glanced in their direction and arched an eyebrow at him. "Assuming nothing has happened to it in the interim, yes, it would be quite serviceable for a stay of a few days," she replied in the same low tones. "Might I ask why?"

He verified what he had sensed earlier, testing the air with his antennae as the breeze blew it towards him from the others. "Urelle is near the end of her strength.

I believe she has been driving herself to keep the diversion spell going as long as possible, and I can scent the stress and exhaustion in her — even though it is not, I admit, visible."

Victoria's eyes rolled heavenward and she sketched the symbol of the Balance before her. "Stubborn as all my relatives," she said, her gaze softening as it lingered on Urelle. "It *has* been noticeably longer than the first time. If I am correct, that also means she is far less capable of wielding her magic at this point?"

"That is what she said, and the enervation I can sense would certainly imply that this is true."

"Should I simply tell her to let it go now?"

Quester passed more air over his antennae, then gave a deliberate shrug. "She is not in *severe* danger as of now, and if she can make it to the ruins, it would not hurt to have the diversion continue as long as possible. It is, of course, up to you; she is your responsibility, after all."

The tall woman studied her niece for several minutes, then nodded. "If we sight the castle before the end of the day, well enough. Otherwise, I'll tell her to let go whether she wants to or not."

The occasional rays of sun were slanting very low when Quester, currently in the lead, broke through into a clearer area, to see a broad sheet of blue-green water stretching off into the distance — perhaps two or three miles across, and likely several times that long. On the near shore were ruins, as Victoria had described them — a collection of stone structures, large and small, in various states of collapse, vines and other overgrowth slowly taking them over. He could trace the town's outline in his mind, see where there had been docks, hints of roads, piles of rubble that had been warehouses, and so on. This had been a prosperous settlement once, and not small, perhaps as many as ten thousand people living and working in this now-ruined city.

Quester could see that the encroachment of the jungle was weakened greatly the nearer one got to the center of the town; presumably this was due to the slowly-fading verminwards around the settlement and its buildings.

Dominating the shoreline was the castle or fortress — a massive stone edifice perhaps a hundred feet in height at the peaks of the two towers at each end of the structure, and at least thirty or forty feet high along even the lowest portions of the structure. From what Quester could see in the setting sunlight, it was constructed mostly of a lighter-colored stone – granite was his guess – and, at least from this distance, appeared to be entirely intact, unlike any of the surrounding buildings.

However, what made Quester pause and study the entire area more intently was that the jungle *stopped* at a distance of perhaps a hundred yards from the castle; even the ruins near the castle were clear of overgrowth. He glanced over at Victoria, seeing her mouth tightened and eyes narrowed. "It was not so clean when last you saw it?"

"No. It appears someone has claimed the fortress for themselves. Or did in recent years, at any rate."

"Balance, Auntie," Urelle said, coming up to the two of them. "I didn't expect the castle you mentioned to be in such good repair."

"That is precisely what we are discussing," Victoria answered. "It was not so pristine twenty years ago."

"Well, this wasn't done in a day or three," Ingram said, "unless whoever's in there is *really* powerful. Probably – almost certainly – not our pursuers. They wouldn't really have much reason to settle down and clean out an old fortress."

"I cannot argue there," Victoria said, still studying the distant towers.

"Let us continue," Quester said. "If the residents are not hostile, we will have a more comfortable resting place tonight, even if all they offer is a floor."

"And if they *are* hostile?" Ingram asked.

Victoria shrugged. "It is unlikely they will be so hostile as to engage us in combat, Ingram. They may well wish few visitors, of course – choosing to set up one's household so far from any others is something of a statement of intent – but in my experience, even such people won't begrudge a few Adventurers a space to sleep, if no more. The few that do…" her scent was suddenly sharp and deadly, "…well, they're often ones that Adventurers are needed *for*."

"Onward it is," Ingram said with a grin.

A broken stone road, encountered after half a mile of hiking, made their progress swifter, and before the last rays of sun had left the upper third of the towers, the four of them were standing before the main doors of the castle. Quester – and, he was sure, the others – had noted the additional signs of occupancy; within the ten-foot wall surrounding the building, there were no weeds, the paving-stones were unbroken and in place, and there were small gardens spaced around the perimeter – at least as far as they could see, and presumably all around the castle. The gates had been half-open, but the faint tingle across his body told Quester that there were active and well-maintained verminwards.

The doors were mostly of a wood Quester had never seen, of startling hues ranging from deep red to yellow; the effect was of a curtain of flame within a grate, the metal binding the door providing the grate portion. Only one thing marred the artistic impression; a white or cream rectangle about five feet from the landing before the doors.

"Well, that's interesting. A *note* on the doors," Ingram said.

Quester stepped up and read:

Travelers are welcome within, as long as you can pass the wards at the threshold. Please leave all as you found it. Take what you need, as long as you leave something of equal value in its place.

"A courteous mystery, I must say," Victoria mused after a moment. "No signature, no indication of their own identity, but a clear statement of hospitality that expects equal consideration. I have no dispute with these conditions."

"Nor do I," Ingram said. "Quester? Urelle?"

"They seem perfectly reasonable," Urelle said.

"I agree," Quester said. "As long as the wards mentioned are not against Iriistiik."

Victoria chuckled. "I doubt we are dealing with so precise a protection."

Ingram shrugged. "It could just be a trap, of course. Lure us in and get us comfortable. Then *bang!*"

"Certainly, it could. I doubt it in this case, for various reasons, but we will keep an eye out. And choose adjoining rooms and ward them ourselves."

She touched the doors, and before she could even push, they began to swing inwards. Lightglobes glowed to life, illuminating a wide hallway paneled in a gold-colored wood, with deep blue carpeting.

The four of them stepped across the threshold; Quester noted another tingle – similar but in no way identical to that he had felt at the verminwards – and saw the others blink or twitch. It appeared, however, that whatever the wards protected against didn't include Iriiistiik, lavender-haired boys, or women named Vantage.

"My word," Victoria murmured, looking around at the spotlessly clean sweep of the two staircases curving to the second floor, and the subtle but noteworthy accents of gold and silver around the room. "Hardly the drafty and gloomy castles of your favorite tales, eh, Urelle?"

Urelle smiled. "I don't think I'll complain. As I've started to find out, the Wanderer's words are very true: 'adventures get a lot less fun the more nights you spend away from a really decent bed.'"

Ingram laughed loudly, the sound echoing up the stairs. "Wisdom I can't argue! But it looks like decent beds might really be in our future tonight!"

Chapter 19
A Midnight Encounter

Urelle looked at the wide, soft bed with its black-and-green patterned coverlet longingly, but sighed. *Can't go to sleep right now.*

She had, with relief, let go of the enchantment on the distant Coin once Auntie had brought it up. She *had* been pushing herself very hard, and it *had* been time to release it, but – being entirely honest – she didn't think it had been *too* hard. The effort involved had felt... well, like a good workout with Lythos. Pushing herself, stretching her capabilities as a wizard in a *good* way. There had been the *edge* of pain forming, but not quite being reached.

Still, releasing it had meant that her magical strength had flowed back, slowly returning to its full power, and with it she'd found a somewhat annoying alertness. Her body was still tired, but her mind wasn't nearly ready to rest, even though a glance at the stars from her window showed that it must be approaching midnight.

Have to work up the countercharm. Maybe I should work on that for a while.

If this castle had a magical workshop, or even a meditation room, one with the appropriate wards to prevent spiritual intrusion, that would be ideal. Much better than trying to improvise a circle in the wilderness. She threw her cloak on, picked up her pack, and slipped quietly into the hallway, gesturing to ensure the wards around their rooms remained intact. By now she was pretty sure that this wasn't a trap, but might as well leave them up.

She paused, then hit her forehead as a reminder that she was being stupid. Maybe she didn't want to wake them up, but she needed to make sure that if someone else woke up, they'd know she hadn't been kidnapped out of her room or anything. She scribbled a quick note and stuck it to the door with a simple adhesion spell.

The four of them had chosen rooms on the second floor of the right-hand tower; a spiral staircase in the center of the tower led up to each floor, which had a circular hallway connected to the staircase. Each door around the hallway let into a small suite of rooms, each laid out for the use of one person, so they'd each taken one. Hers was between Ingram's on one side and Victoria's on the other; the staircase entrance was just a little farther down the hall, across from Quester's rooms.

Workshops tended to be either very high up, or very far down. This did seem to be a residence tower, however, so Urelle guessed that any such rooms would be below, in the basement; Quester had found a staircase that led downward, but aside from making sure the door to it was closed, they had not bothered with it. Securing their own rooms, getting dinner, and resting had been the priorities – with her dealing with the trace being something for tomorrow.

The stairs downward were broad, flat, and smooth, with patterns etched or engraved into the gray stone that gave shoes a good purchase, ensuring no slipping down the stairwell. Descending, Urelle felt the faintly cooler air she expected underground, and sniffed. There was no noticeable trace of mold or other decay, which encouraged her to think that the basement was also as well-kept as the rest of the castle.

As she approached the bottom, she noticed that there was light coming from below. That made her pause; so far, the one constant they'd noted about the house was that things like the lightglobes were dark until someone needed them on, and she had not yet come close enough to activate them. At least, not based on what she *did* know so far.

There was no movement below, however, and the welcoming note had given no warnings about avoiding particular locations, so she dismissed her concerns and continued down.

The stair ended in a room that was something of an echo of the entryway above, with two hallways leading out of it on either hand, and a door directly ahead of her.

Hmm. Well, I'm in the far rear of the castle, near or at the center of the long axis. If I was making an enchanting or spiritual circle, I'd put it at the very center – the symmetry couldn't help but support any working you made, especially if there's any mystical sources nearby.

That meant, if she was right, that she should go through the door directly across, so she did.

A hallway ahead had another door on each side, and one more ending it. Still following her tenuous logic, Urelle proceeded to the end and opened the door.

Ha! I was right!

A broad, circular room – nearly a hundred feet across – lay in front of her. In the center, a full fifty feet in diameter, was one of the most complex ritual circles she had ever seen or heard of, a circle with multiple geometric figures inscribed within it – a triangle, a square, a five-pointed star, and more. Elaborate, carefully traced symbols followed every line and curve. Studying the ones nearer her, she could see multiple symbologies involved – Ancient Sauran and *Artan*, runes she thought were connected with the Children of Odin, some that looked more like picture-symbols, and more; at least a couple looked like they were Toadish.

Once more, Urelle hesitated. Whoever had placed that circle there had meant it for mighty works indeed, powers that, if channeled wrongly, could probably split the castle above like a tineroot by an axe.

On the other hand, she couldn't have *imagined* a better place to do her practice and finish her research. Stepping farther into the room, she saw there were bookshelves on the walls, a dozen of them, filled to overflowing with books ranging from slim pamphlets to immense tomes so thick and heavy she wasn't sure an ordinary person could lift them. Other sets of shelves held powders and crystals and samples of other materials. Massive, solid worktables were spaced at intervals, some covered with intricate alchemical apparatus, others with more esoteric materials that she wasn't sure she recognized.

For a moment she considered the possibility that she *had* imagined this place. That either she had just gone to sleep and was dreaming in a far too realistic fashion about the work she *should* be doing now, or that the castle itself was one of those mystical locations – usually turning out to be diabolical traps – where what you thought of needing would be provided.

But no, she was *sure* she hadn't gone to sleep yet. She couldn't entirely rule out the second possibility, of course, but… it just didn't feel like that. The symbology of the circles seemed universally positive – even the darker symbols were placed so that they were negated, cleansing them from any works within.

Looking more closely, she saw that the circle shimmered with magic of a sort she associated with… well, *housekeeping*. Dusting, moving vases and such aside, preserving food, things like that. A simple, utilitarian magic she hadn't expected. *Now why would…*

Oh, that would be clever. She studied the different geometric forms, and realized that their elements could be moved so as to make any or all of them active or inactive – with a gesture. *I was right. Whoever did this made it so that they could have* any *of a dozen or more magical matrices available without having to draw and redraw them.* The additional enchantments prevented silver from tarnishing, materials used to anoint portions of the array from spoiling, and so on. *A lot of foresight went into this. Or maybe just a lot of experience and cursing at the way they* should *have done something.*

With full understanding of the array – or, being more honest with herself, with enough understanding of its basic workings – Urelle took a breath and walked to the center of the geometric figures. A few gestures realigned it to be a pure warding circle, ideal for walling out any extraneous influences, shielding her from even the most malevolent interference, as she studied the Coin to see if she could tease out the last clue to breaking its enchantment.

The frustrating part was that she was *so close*. She could *see* the way the magic twined about the Coin, how it vibrated in sympathy with her presence, and those vibrations were, in turn, echoed by its sibling Coins. The magic swirled around it like a symmetrical, beautiful knot. But there was *something* else involved, because she couldn't, to continue the metaphor, quite get her fingers to grasp the threads and tug any of the strands free. It *looked* like it should be straightforward to unravel, but none of her tentative approaches had shown any promise.

But within the pristine and protected perfection of this circle, just maybe she could grasp what she was missing.

She let her awareness reach out and inward, once more outlining the spell in moving, geometric lines, a rosette of energy in motion about the unmoving, yellow-cold core of the Coin. It was the same as it had been before…

No.

In this environment – perfectly still, quiet, with even the ambient magic of the world silenced – she could see something else.

It was almost invisible – a phantom shimmer, almost like a glaze of polish upon the strands of enchantment. It took all her concentration to see it, but she was sure it was there. And it was clear, now, that this was the true barrier between her and dispelling the enchantment. It was as though the knot she envisioned had been spread with glue, permeating every turn and curve of the magical string and fixing it together immovably.

The question was… what *was* this? It wasn't any magic she'd seen before…

Abruptly, her concentration was shattered as she saw movement across from her; the door was opening.

At first, she thought it was one of her companions – Ingram, perhaps, for the figure looked fairly short. But as it emerged into the light of the workroom, she could see that it was someone in a dark travel cloak, hood drawn up so the face was hooded in shadow, leaning on a knob-headed cane. She thought, by the slow and cautious way it moved, that it was an older man; white or gray hair trailed from beneath the hood.

The man did not glance in her direction, and it struck her that the dark stone, her being seated and slight figure, covered with her own dark cloak, must make her hard to see. And with the circle still complete, he would not be getting a hint of her presence in any other fashion.

He turned and moved towards one of the worktables with weary deliberation. He stopped, facing the table, his back to her. That back was *tense*; just his pose showed that he was in great pain or great inner turmoil.

Then she had to bite back a gasp, for the figure *expanded* without warning, rising up until the man must have been six feet or a bit taller, straighter; she was somehow certain that the man must be younger now. The cane, too, expanded, widening and drastically lengthening, becoming an elaborate staff of dark wood bound with silvery-shining metal, a faintly-glowing crystal crowning the staff.

And then the taller figure sagged down onto a bench before the worktable, and she heard a gasp of... pain? Perhaps, but she thought it was also *fear*. She heard a single quiet, desperately controlled sob of someone who was terrified, but still sought to keep hold of their rationality. It was the sound of a man who rarely cried for any reason, who found himself unable to *stop* himself from crying, and the sound was heart-rending. The last time she'd heard that was when she'd heard her brother Rion crying alone, in the quiet of night... a few weeks before he was murdered. She had hesitated, chosen not to intrude on his pain.

She couldn't ignore that kind of pain now.

"What's wrong?" she said, standing slowly. "What are you afraid of?"

The man jerked upright and half turned, catching one foot on the bench, and fell sprawling onto the floor, the great staff skittering away across the smooth stone until it nearly reached the edge of the ritual circle.

She gestured and opened the circle, running to the man's side. "Oh, Balance, I'm sorry, I didn't mean to startle you that bad! Are you all right?"

"Ow! I broke my nose!" The man's voice was thick, both with unshed tears and the damage done to his nose – and she saw with a wince of guilt and sympathy that there was, indeed, blood streaming from the man's nose.

"I'm *so* sorry! I've got a healing draught somewhere, hold on—"

The man was getting to his feet and she heard, surprisingly, a pained chuckle, though still with more than a hint of tears, a chuckle that turned into a full, deep laugh that echoed around the room. "HA HA ha ha... ohh, god, that hurts, but it *is* funny, jeez, that must have looked *ridiculous,* the way I fell…"

He chuckled again, and gestured; and the staff flew back to him; he caught it gracefully, whirled it around once, and planted it on the ground next to him, the metal-spiked end striking a flash of sparks from the stone. He waved away the bottle she had finally extracted from her pack. "No, don't worry, it's already fixing itself – see?"

She stared. Indeed, the man's nose was straightening, blood no longer flowing, incipient swelling going down.

The sight was somewhat unsettling, so she shifted her gaze and surveyed the staff as the healing continued. It was of a thick, straight piece of dark-brown wood, with silver and gold symbols inlaid in between reinforcing strips of a metal that gleamed with a silky, silver texture different from anything she'd ever seen. At the top of each section were two symbols; one appeared to be an elemental or power symbol, while the one below each of these was a strange set of lines and curves; the three elemental symbols she could see were some sort of starburst – a brilliant, silver-white dot with almost flower-petal wavering rays radiating from it - a stylized wave, and a red-gold flame.

A faintly-glowing crystal, clear as water, topped the staff, bound into place by the same metal bands that reinforced the wood, while the heel was a point, a long spike of the same silky-silvery metal. *Something about this… it's almost* familiar. *As though I know it.* Somehow, she knew that the other two faces of the staff – those she could not see – bore a thundercloud and a mountain, topped by a pair of scales. A chill went down her body, even though she couldn't quite understand why.

In a few moments there was no sign the man's nose had ever been injured, and he muttered a swift cleaning spell that made the blood instantly vanish from his face and clothes.

"Well!" The man seated himself again on the bench, this time facing Urelle, the hood of the cloak once more shadowing his face. "My apologies for intruding; I guess you must have been using my circles, there?"

"I was, yes, but no need to apologize. This *is* your workshop, then? You are our host?"

"It is, and I am." The smile had faded from his face, and she could see more than a shadow of the pain and fear she had heard before.

She bit her lip, then repeated her earlier questions. "So, sir, what *is* wrong? What are you afraid of?"

The momentary smile was wry. "Tenacious, you are," he murmured, in a voice higher and rougher, which then returned to its prior baritone. "Why do you ask?"

"Because... because I don't like seeing someone in pain. No matter who they are." *And because of what happened the last time I ignored it.*

"A good answer, I think," he conceded. "I don't like it, either." He sighed. "What is wrong? I find myself in a trap with neither sides nor doors, so it cannot be evaded nor escaped. And I've evaded a *lot* of traps of all kinds before, so that's what scares me. I *know* I'm not avoiding this one."

"A... trap?"

He smiled, a flash of white from within the hood that vanished almost the instant it appeared. "Call it... destiny. Something's going to happen to me... sometime soon. I don't know the details yet, but when it happens, it's going to be very bad, and I have to..." his voice shook for a moment, then firmed, "...I have to prepare. Have to make sure some of my legacy isn't lost, that contingencies are set up, my own backup plans in motion. But I never thought... about this particular issue so much before. And not knowing exactly *when*... I know I have to do some of it very fast, just in case."

There was *something* about the way he spoke that teased at her, touching that same chilled-spine feeling that the tall, glittering staff had called forth. It wasn't... quite the way anyone else she knew talked. Yet, somehow, parts of it were *familiar*...

But his problem wasn't familiar. It *was* frightening. The thought of *knowing* something terrible was going to happen to you, and being unable to know exactly when... "Is there anything I could do to help? I know you don't know me, but you *are* our host..."

He glanced from her to the circle and back. "Well, now. You're a mage of some sort, so... perhaps. What is your specialty?"

"I do a little of several things, sir. But mostly, I'm a Shaper."

"A *Shaper*! Really? That's not common. Few people really have the focus and determination to be a good Shaper, to grab the very fabric of reality and bend it to their will, rather than being a summoner, or channeler, or whatever."

She flashed him her own smile. "I like the idea of *fully* controlling the magic, of understanding how it works. Of being able to make reality change under my direction, I guess, though by *Myrionar* that sounds awfully arrogant of me, doesn't it?"

Another small chuckle. "Perhaps... but that's not uncommon for those of us who are Shapers, and I'm more Shaper than anything else." He studied her closely, half-seen eyes narrowing within the cloak. "Something about you is familiar, child. What is your name?"

She felt the word *child* was going a bit far, but then chided herself for the thought; if this man was the builder of that circle, he was likely far, far older than he looked. "Urelle Vantage of Evanwyl, sir."

"Urelle *Vantage*," the man repeated, in the tones of someone presented the solution to a mystery. "Sister to Kyri Vantage, I presume?"

"What? You know who I am... who *she* is?" The chill was back again, stronger than ever. "Who... who *are* you?"

For answer, he slowly rose and threw back the hood, cast back the cloak.

Hair the color of sunlight crowned a young man's face, a face that was not dark, paler than almost anyone she had ever heard of, save only perhaps the Watchland himself, who also had that nearly unheard-of hair. Dark brows set off eyes that were brilliantly blue, a rare and spectacular color, as well – nearly as rare as Ingram's lavender. With the cloak cast back, she could see beneath a tailored travel-robe of black and silver... and beneath it, faint, squarish shapes of an armor she had only seen on one other person – her friend Ingram, who said it had come from the Founder's own world.

Her gaze flicked to the Staff again, and now she knew why gooseflesh had sprung out across her arms, her whole body. "The Wanderer," she breathed.

He inclined his head.

Urelle had *thought* she was ready for anything... but she'd daydreamed about meeting the legends in her books, and now a daydream stood before her, a daydream in pain she had never imagined during her own fantasies. "You've met Kyri? How is she?"

"I haven't had the pleasure of meeting her *yet*," the Wanderer answered. "But I will. I expect our paths to cross fairly soon. I do know *about* her, and your family – my sympathies and condolences on that, by the way. And yes, I know about the Justiciars."

"If you *know*, then why haven't you done anything?" she snapped, then clapped her hands over her mouth. *Did I say that to the* Wanderer?

A wan, sad smile crossed the young face – a face she now knew was old, old, older than any human she had ever met. "Because I dare not. The events happening in Evanwyl are *much* darker than you know, and even I can't tamper with them."

"But wait, Wanderer – it was always said you were *immune* to destiny, that you couldn't be held by the bonds of such things. I know that's in *all* the tales. How can you—"

"It's not nearly so simple, Urelle." The Wanderer seated himself heavily, with an air of exhaustion; with a gesture, he caused another chair to slide over before her. "To explain would take quite a while. I would rather ask you what you seek to do *here*."

She wanted to pursue the first question; how could he *not* interfere, how was it that the Wanderer, one of the legendary heroes, could know of the evil of the Justiciars and do *nothing*?

But his tone was firm, and she remembered that one of the greatest mistakes of Adventurers was failing to take advantage of what they were offered, because they were too busy focusing on something else. The Wanderer was *asking* what she was doing; he was clearly interested, if for no other reason than to distract himself from his own distress. What sort of an idiot would she be to not find out what he might say about her problem?

She pulled out the Coin. "This Coin resonates with... well, I think it's me and my Aunt Victoria, but maybe also Quester or Ingram. Anyway, there's a lot of these Coins being carried by people from Aegeia who are hunting us. Sent by Ares. We don't know exactly why, but it's not for any friendly reason, that's for sure."

"Have you analyzed the enchantment?"

"I've tried. First, I sort of diverted it – used a resonance between two of the Coins to make them track the other Coin instead?" She detailed the procedure she'd used, and the Wanderer (*the WANDERER!*) nodded and smiled.

"A clever stopgap trick to give you time, yes. Nicely done. Costs you to maintain, though."

"Right. I just let it go the second time this evening, so they'll be starting to get back on the right path now. I *have* to break this enchantment. I thought I'd gotten it figured out, but it just wouldn't *budge*. But in your circle, I finally saw... well, *something*." She described the impossibly subtle, transparent magical effect to the Wanderer.

He extended his hand, and she placed the Coin in it. He gripped what she now knew was the legendary Staff of Stars and concentrated; light flared from the crystal atop the Staff, light pure and white and yet, somehow, touched with every color of the rainbow. The light concentrated on the Coin and sparkled for a moment, before fading away.

"I see what you mean," the Wanderer said after a moment. "But that's... a subtle thing indeed." His gaze was speculative, analytical. "You can *see* that using the standard analysis and detection enchantments?"

"Only in your circle, sir."

One eyebrow rose. "Fascinating."

"Is there something unusual about that enchantment, sir?"

"Quite. I would venture to say that the vast majority of magicians of any stripe would be hard-put to detect it, even *with* the aid of my circle and far more powerful analysis spells. Still, given your... family connections..." his voice suddenly had the air of someone gifted with a revelation. "Yes, given that, it makes sense that you could see it."

"Can you break it, sir? The enchantment, I mean? Make it so that Ares' people can't follow us anymore?"

"*Could* I? I daresay so. While I may not *quite* be the most badass mage on this planet – there's at least five or six others I know of who outclass me – I'm pretty darn good." He grinned at her, and this time the fear she'd seen had grown more distant. "But I think it'd be much better if *you* broke it."

"But I don't know *how*, sir!"

He waved that off. "Of course you don't, *now*. But you *will* know how, once I've finished *showing* you how."

"You... you'd *teach* me how, sir?"

"Yes, I think I will. If your most formidable Aunt Victoria doesn't object, that is."

"*Object?*"

"You would be astonished the number of people who might object to their children having anything to do with me." He smiled down at her. "But I would very much like to teach you what I can, in the time I have left. Because," he said, his voice suddenly soft and pensive, "I think that's one of the things I *have* to do."

Chapter 20
Revelation of a Legend

"The Wanderer." Victoria's voice was level, with just a *hint* of the doubt she felt.

At that, she couldn't deny that she felt a certain *frisson* of awe at the figure before her. A bit shorter than she had expected, perhaps, but in other particulars, he matched the myths well enough. And from the way the man stood, the faint traces of power she could sense, her long experience told her that he was a very formidable being, indeed.

"Isn't it *amazing*, Auntie?" Urelle said, her gray eyes sparkling in the lights of the dining room, where they had all met – and where the purported Wanderer had caused a feast to appear from nowhere. "He says he'll teach me how to break the enchantment on the Coins, and maybe other things, too!"

Ingram was silent, staring at the legend-come-to-life in front of him. Quester, too, was silent, though if Victoria understood his body language correctly, he was not quite as shocked, or trusting, as his friend. *Well, at least two of us are not taking everything at face value.*

"If true, yes," Quester buzzed, confirming her guess.

"If... true? What do you mean?"

"He means," Victoria said, not taking her eyes from the brilliant blue ones across from her, "that it is all very well and good to *claim* to be one of the greatest Adventurers, but it's something else to be *certain*. And someone who would dare pretend to *that* role would be undoubtedly powerful and dangerous in the extreme."

The Wanderer – if that was truly who he was – grinned widely. "Aunt you might be, but I hear a mother's caution," he said. "And I'm glad at least a couple of you don't take my word for who I am." He looked at both Urelle and Ingram. "Your aunt and your friend Quester are very wise *not* to trust. Urelle has, perhaps, a bit more reason to, because she caught me unawares – unless I played a part even better than one might expect. But understand, Urelle," he looked directly at the young girl, "I *could* have played out that scene exactly as you saw, down to breaking my own nose if necessary. Trust... but *verify*."

"In that case, can you prove your identity, sir?" Victoria asked. "I cannot deny that I'd be extremely gratified to have the Wanderer to assist us in any way, but I *do* need some confirmation of who you are."

The Wanderer looked thoughtful. "*Prove* is always hard. But perhaps. Certainly, I can first give evidence that we are, at least, of the same profession." He pulled the cloak back from his shoulder, to reveal an Adventurer's symbol.

Victoria squinted at it as she stepped forward. The background – a high cliff with a blue and green waterfall flanking one of red - was not immediately familiar, but it responded with the same white flash and chime as any other Adventurer's patch at the touch of her verification wand.

She nodded. "Well, that relieves me to a small degree. Still, yours is an extraordinary claim."

"Which requires extraordinary evidence. I can certainly prove my power to you, but while that might be entertaining, it's hardly evidence of my identity. Hmm." He stood, thinking, for a moment, and then he raised a brow again. "Now, there's a thought. One moment."

He turned away from them. Victoria sensed a faint touch of magic, and perhaps another power, and realized that he was now surrounded by a sheath of silence; the sounds of the room were deadened when they passed near him.

A few moments later, the young-looking man turned back, expression serious. "Have you still faith in Myrionar, Victoria Vantage?"

She thought for a moment. "Yes. Yes, I do. I still pray to It for guidance, and I know It swore a mighty oath, indeed, to Kyri, one that no god would make lightly."

"Then pray to Myrionar, and ask if It can verify who I am."

She raised her own eyebrow in turn. "Indeed? Kyri was the only one, save perhaps Arbiter Kelsley, whom I have known who has *spoken* with the Balanced Sword. You believe that I will be answered?"

"I am *certain* you will be answered – and that you will know it is the true voice of Myrionar."

"I see." She thought for a moment. "I will, if you pardon me, go outside of your castle for this."

"As you wish."

She walked out, through the front doors, then well outside of the walls, into the ruins; this was not merely a moment for privacy, but one in which she should be some distance from the center of power of the one she was questioning.

In the partial shelter of one half-collapsed building, surrounded by vines and fallen stones and the scent of ancient earth, Victoria closed her eyes. *Myrionar, I call upon your Balance, on the Mercy, Justice, and Vengeance that are yours, to cut through any falsehoods, to gift me with the truth, and tell me for certain who this man is, he who claims to be a legend.*

For an instant, there was nothing. And then she felt the power that always surrounded the Altar of the Balanced Sword, but ten, no, a *hundred* times stronger, the distilled *essence* of every service she had attended, the absolute knowledge of a presence that watched over her and defended her, and there came a voice:

I hear your call, Victoria Vantage, and in this moment, you do indeed require and deserve an answer. The one you have met is the Wanderer, he who came from Beyond all other things. Trust in his advice and counsel, for the short while it is offered; few indeed are those given this chance.

The impact of that soundless voice was tremendous; it echoed silently through her head, with absolute conviction and undeniable surety, and she knew, beyond any possibility of doubt, that it spoke truth.

But even more than that vast and overwhelming *presence*, it was the voice *itself* that struck her speechless, left her pale and stunned, grasping for a way to make sense of what she had just heard.

For she *knew that voice*. She had last heard it when her oldest niece had bidden her farewell on a quest that might end in her death.

Slowly she raised her eyes, and found she was staring directly into the Wanderer's; the wizard had appeared before her in that moment. And she saw the same knowledge reflected in his gaze. "What... what does this *mean*?" she demanded in a hushed voice.

"You must guess what it means," he said quietly. "Here, you are so far from her quest, from the destiny she follows, and your own path set so that you shall not meet for years yet, that it makes no difference. You cannot affect what is to come; in a sense, it has already happened, even though it is still well in your future."

Victoria took a breath, controlled the chaos in her mind, brought her suddenly-panicked breathing and heart to heel. "You imply magics more potent than I have ever heard of – at least, outside of ancient tales."

"We play in the realms of the gods – as do you, now." The Wanderer's voice was calmly certain. "You're getting ready to butt heads with *Ares*. This will *be* one of the ancient tales, a thousand years from now. You haven't really grasped that, not in your heart, have you? This isn't just magic, it's magic of the *foundation* of reality, the power of the gods, and we're playing a game against powers that could squash even *me* like a bug if I make a mistake."

He looked up at the sky past the broken walls. "And greater forces are at work than those of just Ares. Everything connects. Kyri and those who will join her are one part; you and Urelle and Ingram and Quester are on a different quest, yet one that is part of the greater war; so are five people from my own world; and there are others." His tone grew pensive. "The stories like to make their characters the focus of the world, but if you really read them all, you know that there are *many* adventures happening, all at once, and it takes a constant supply of heroes to keep the world protected."

A flash of insight. "And it is not *magic* that binds you, that brought on the terror my niece saw in you, is it? It's *knowledge*. Someone, somehow, has come from the future and told you what is to come... in a manner that prevents you from avoiding that same future."

His smile was cold, stiff, mirthless. "You're sharp as a razor, Lady Vantage. Exactly. Oh, I *can* avoid it. I am, after all, the Wanderer, and the very existence of the knowledge gives me a loophole. But at the same time, I *can't* avoid it because the only way for me to do so will... well, cause an even worse disaster. All I can do is try to make sure that the consequences are as small as possible. Set up plans that will minimize the disaster, provide for some way out later."

He took a breath and she could hear it shake. He was doing the same thing she had, bringing himself under control. "And *one* of those things that has to be done is to give you four the best possible chance to survive your own destiny."

"Are you saying we cannot turn aside, either?"

He shrugged. "*Cannot* is a pretty absolute word. I'd say more *will not*. Can you imagine getting Ingram to set aside his current goal? Quester abandoning his friend? You and Urelle leaving him to his fate alone?"

She shook her head. "No. I do not see that happening."

"Then it's as near *cannot* as it gets, and still leaves everyone free will."

"If you know the future," she said after a moment, "then you know whether we will succeed or not, yes?"

A shake of the head. "Not only are there some powers that cloud the direction of the future, but my personal foreknowledge ends well before your quest's conclusion. I know that you have a *chance*, and that it is not merely the enemy manipulating events."

"You, for instance."

"Heh. Certainly me. I've been meddling since I arrived on Zarathan, and it's my job description by now. Though there's others playing what they call the Great Game a lot better than me. I'm just the wild card that sometimes messes up the board, to use a really mixed metaphor that still kinda fits."

She turned and began walking back to the castle. "And is that what you're doing here? Messing up the board?"

"Pretty much," he agreed cheerfully; then he grew solemn again. "Which is why I have to ask you to leave Urelle with me while you go on."

"*What?*" She stopped and put her hands on her hips. "And why should I do that?"

"Because she needs instruction, and you will have precious little chance to get her any once you leave here. At the same time, you will have no chance to convince Ingram to stay here for a week or three."

She had to agree there. Ingram had admitted that even waiting to write her a note had technically violated his oaths, and while he had made obvious efforts to appear patient, his single driving focus was to get back to his home and find out what had caused his Clan to send for him, and assassins to be sent after either him, or his companions. "I admit that is true. But he and Quester could continue on their own."

"And you would stay here, accomplishing... what?" the Wanderer said, striding onward. "I suppose you could practice your own arts, but aside from that?"

"We are pursued by the forces of a god, as you yourself pointed out," Victoria said, nettled. "I should leave my niece alone? What if they're seeking *her* rather than myself, or Quester, or Ingram?"

"Then they would have to get to her through *me*." The voice had shifted; it held none of the lightness, the strangely playful tone that seemed omnipresent even when he was being serious. This was a voice of iron. "And in one of my own strongholds? Even the God-Warriors would be well-advised not to try it. I assure you, there are very, very few places in the entire *world* where Urelle will be safer. You have my word on that."

Knowing that he was who he claimed, Victoria found herself accepting his promise. It was certainly true that he had survived literal ages, against an array of enemies who were also legends. "*You* could come with *us*, instead. Train Urelle in the evenings. We would undoubtedly all be safer then, would we not?"

"There is a world of difference from an hour or two in the evenings, and entire days spent in hard tutelage, as you must know very well. I have little enough time to teach her, and you will be facing God-Warriors, assassins, others who wield magic, or *ki*, or even psionic power. The most talented and focused of would-be heroes still can't learn everything in a day, even if the tales might compress three months of learning into a few paragraphs." He smiled that odd smile again. "The Power of Montage still takes time."

"I have no real idea of what that *means*."

"Don't worry, hardly anyone does. I have to amuse myself sometimes, even if no one else gets the joke. But you get the point, yes?"

They passed through the gate as she thought. Reluctantly, she found herself agreeing with the Wanderer. Urelle was clearly very talented, but she was reaching the limits of her own self-instruction and the limited resources she had brought from Evanwyl. If they were to continue at all, Urelle *needed* to understand how to expand her gifts.

Victoria recalled all too well how many, many long, bone-weary, brutal hours of practice and sparring and exercise it had taken to bring her to mastery of the Way of the Eight Winds. And, more to the point, how there had been times that nothing less than a living teacher, with new advice and new resources, had been needed to help her move on when she had taught herself all she could. Magic could hardly be any less demanding, even if likely somewhat less bruising, to study.

And if Quester and Ingram continued on, she admitted, they would need all the help they could get if Deimos, or any of their other enemies, caught up. Yes, perhaps Berenike would show up to save the day again... but perhaps not, especially if Ingram were struck down swiftly enough that he could not activate whatever bond lay between them.

Still, there were other issues. "And what about when you have finished this instruction, then? How would she find us? She's hardly ready to wander the Forest Sea on her own!"

"Can't argue that," the Wanderer conceded. "I'll trek around alone, but even I rather *prefer* having people to help watch my back in places like that. But trust me, I can find you when we're done, and if you can't come get her, I'll bring her to you. That much I can do."

Victoria sighed. "Very well, then. I will leave it up to Urelle."

She entered side-by-side with a legend.

Chapter 21
Finding a Loose End

He stood over the open grave with his fists clenched, such venom boiling in his veins that there were *claws* starting to cut their way into his palms. Gritting teeth that had gone pointed, he took hold of his anger and forced it, immaterial step by immaterial step, back into the cage he had forged over the millennia to hold it. There were times to let it free... but not now, not here, where his transformation into something inhuman would betray far too much.

The grave was *empty*.

Just seeing that, *thinking* that, again was enough to cause the incandescent rage to wrench against its confines, nearly break free. There should have been a corpse there, one moldering to bones by now, after two years and more.

With control that he thought his mother would be proud of, he raised an eyebrow and looked to Phobos. "There appears to be something missing."

Phobos snarled, *his* rage uncontained, and kicked the memorial so hard that the enchanted stone chipped. "How? *How?* We were both *there*, we *saw* her corpse!"

A gesture quieted Phobos. He glanced over, saw the reborn Deimos staring with knitted brows at the empty hole. *He has only very tattered memories of his prior incarnation; the damage done to him was extreme. We were fortunate to salvage any of it.*

And fortunate was only the truth; having to *create* another "Deimos" from power, will, and word would have been a tremendous undertaking at this point, especially since as Aloysius-Ares he had to be visible frequently throughout every day. Even the tattered fragments of the prior Deimos had sufficed as a structure to be placed in another of the waiting bodies, a template that could be built upon once that body was properly converted.

"It matters not *how*," he said finally, his voice fully controlled. "There are any number of ways. A subtle magical duplicate, a truly powerful illusion – since we were not *watching* for such deception – or perhaps some technological trick of the

Camp-bels. We saw a body buried, we believed it was Berenike's. It seems we were wrong." *Even the scent could be faked in more than one way. Since it was dead, there was no soul to be detected.*

"Someone dug here before us," Deimos said.

"Are you certain?"

"Yes." The new Deimos' voice still held a hint of an inhuman timbre, which was one reason he'd been kept out of the public eye thus far. "The layers of earth, the compaction, other factors I can smell and sense. The grave was opened at least once before, quite a long time ago."

"Hm." There was an obvious reason to un-bury a corpse – two of them, really. The first would be if it *wasn't* a corpse, which certainly would make sense. It would have been difficult to hide signs of life in an apparently-dead body, especially from a soul-sense... but not impossible, given that he hadn't suspected subterfuge, and therefore had not looked for it.

The other reason would be to have the body ready for a resurrection. Raiaga rather doubted that possibility; while it certainly *happened* on occasion, it was extremely rare, and most spirits that had gone on really did not want to return – nor did the powers that ruled the afterworlds generally like releasing their charges back to the world that had destroyed them. Though, admittedly, Berenike was certainly the sort of spirit that *would* choose to return, given the chance.

But as he had said, the details did not matter. What *did* matter was that this was as close to proof of the detestable girl's survival as he was likely to get. Berenike was alive, and if he put any credence in Deimos' words, she was the Spear of Athena already.

Damn the Cards anyway. They had given him just enough hints, but not quite enough knowledge to ensure that his actions had succeeded. Then again, the King had warned him that this was their way.

And they had been absolutely right on several points. Most telling right now was the threat that this single human girl posed to his entire plan. If she *appeared* in Aegis – if she declared herself the Spear before the citizens, and challenged Ares' power – it would divert the entire course of the war. He hadn't finished half the campaigns he had planned out, and all of them had to be finished before he could prepare to declare his final victory.

Berenike must be kept out of Aegeia. She must *not* be allowed to return, or if she was already here, she must be drawn out and, if not killed, at least somehow prevented from making her move here – and she would do so soon, of that he was sure, if he couldn't stop her.

He turned away. "Fill it back in," he said to the semi-human figures who waited respectfully a short distance away. "Make it so that none can tell it was ever opened." He strode out of the graveyard, pulling a veil of deific power over himself and his two companions as they left.

Once they were well away and in a deserted side street of Aegis, he transported all three to the High Temple. Most powers could not teleport up the Aegeian Path – not far up it, anyway – but as he *was* Ares, he could do so easily.

Sure, they were now safe from any possibility of observation, he looked at Phobos. "You had something else to report?"

"One request, and one thing to report, yes. You will not like it, Lord."

"I have not liked a great deal of recent news. Consider me warned."

"Your Coins have proven inadequate."

He blinked in startlement. "How?"

The question resonated with puzzlement and shock, and honestly so. He had used the *Cards* to forge that enchantment. They *had* to work. Even the King would agree with that.

"They *seemed* to work at first," Phobos said, glancing at a crystal that projected alien symbols into the air; Raiagamor had never bothered to learn to read his allies' script, but he was starting to think he probably should. "But they have twice, now, shown a sudden shift of the target towards the east, in the direction of Elyvias. After the first such shift, which lasted approximately two weeks, the Coins abruptly turned back to the west and south. The next shift occurred within a day, and indicated, once more, that east was the direction of movement. This lasted more than two weeks, and has just recently ceased. The current indications from most parties are that the direction is to the south and east again."

Raiagamor frowned, then snarled. "Someone was *redirecting* the spell."

"It would seem the most likely possibility."

"That would *not* be a trivial effort. Depending on how it was done, it might require more ingenuity... or more power. Perhaps even a touch of godspower, to be sure it worked." He thought. *Something causes a shift to the east; dropped for a short time, then re-established; lasted for two weeks, dropped...*

Ahhhh. "I believe I see. Clever, indeed. A mage, almost certainly, one who used their personal power as a relay, to transmit the localization signal onward to one of the Coins as it moved; presumably some form of enchantment to make the selected Coin continue moving in the chosen direction." He bared his teeth in an appreciative, but still furious, smile. "But that stretches their reserves, so they can only hold it a short while. A week, two weeks at the most."

He paused. "How many of your search parties have *failed* to report in?"

"Four, sir. Do you wish to see where on the map?"

"Yes."

Four sparks of light appeared on a phantom map of the main continent. Raiagamor immediately leaned closer. One of the dots was an outlier, not far from Salandaras; they'd probably met some of the dull but formidable inhabitants and, well, that had been that.

But the other three...

Two sparks glowed close by Zarathanton, just to the south of the great city. The third, farther south, deep in the Forest Sea's southernmost extension.

"These two first, yes? And then this one..." another thought struck him. "This one, in the Forest Sea; that's Deimos' group?"

"Exactly, sir."

"But he was originally following the river..." his finger traced the path from the river; yes, if he'd been moving due east, the distance would fit someone like Deimos and his forces moving for two weeks. "Interesting. Interesting."

He decided to wait a few moments before deciding how to proceed. "You said you had a request?"

"Yes, sir. You recall that Deimos spoke of 'a survivor?'"

"And indicated, to be blunt about it, that it was not precisely my business. Are you about to tell me he was wrong?"

"Not... precisely, My Lord. Although it *does* concern a project you were... involved in."

He tilted his head, then realization struck him. "You mean a survivor of the *Nests*?"

"That is the only thing he could have meant. He spoke to me, not you. It is our people who are concerned with the Iriistiik; we are fully aware that you helped us for your own purposes."

"True, true. But still... those annoying insects are inherently against the sort of country I'm going to create. And I *did* pledge to aid you in their extermination. So not only was Berenike there, but also there was at least one of them?" He looked back towards the map.

A slow, sinister smile began to grow on his face. He reached up, touched the first pair of dots, trailed his finger down, passing through the third, and continuing on. "Oh. Oh, yes. My friend Phobos, I believe I have a *most* enjoyable mission for you."

Phobos' eyes glittered, with a hint of inhuman light within those brown orbs. "Yes, My Lord?"

"I need to be assured that Berenike is *not* in the country. You need to find and destroy any survivors of the Iriistiik – and that interest lies with my own, as well. We have no need of a species that is led by such powerful beings as the Mothers."

He pointed at the map. "To do what our adversary did, they needed *two* Coins. One to serve as the diversion, one to be the focus and... transmitter, one could say. Of course, once they dropped their concentration, the first Coin was far, far away.

"So how, then, could they have done that trick a *first* time, let alone a second?"

His fingernail – lengthened to a glittering claw – stabbed into the phantom map, where two sparks flickered. "*Here* is where they were. They were caught, but somehow defeated two parties of searchers – and gained two Coins. Then," the finger moved south, "they traveled for two weeks, diverting the search parties in the wrong direction. But when they dropped it, or shortly thereafter, the searchers who had been west of them were now in their path: Deimos' group."

"Ah. It is clear, My Lord. By defeating Deimos' group, they gained another Coin, and thus were able to repeat the trick."

"Precisely." A fanged grin. "And so, if we assume they continue their movements, then after two more weeks in the Forest Sea, they will be... here." The finger indicated a small blue dot, marking a suspected lake. "They are heading south. They intend to make their way into Aegeia by rounding the base of Wisdom's Fortress."

Phobos looked at him attentively.

"Send your people *here*," he indicated the points south of the lake. "Here they will find your enemy, as well as mine, and if Berenike is not with them, she will be forced to come to their aid if you press them. She aided them once; I cannot doubt she will aid them again."

"What makes you so sure?" Phobos asked, an inhuman timbre in his voice.

"She is the Spear of Athena," Raiagamor answered, smiling a lethal smile. "She must know something about that group, if she is not with them – something vitally important. Otherwise, why did she appear there, so far from Aegeia? Yes, she will come."

"Do I lead them, then?"

"No. You will *follow* them, but do not expose yourself, as did Deimos. I want you to watch, and when Berenike appears," he handed Phobos a small, red crystal, "you will break that crystal. That will tell me that Berenike is *outside* of Aegeia... and I will take care of the rest."

Phobos nodded. "As you command. Should I bring our other ally?"

Raiagamor considered. That "other ally" was extremely powerful and dangerous... but also a secret weapon. And the point of this action was not really to *kill* Berenike – though it would be a fine, fine thing if that were to happen.

Best to save *that* resource for later, he decided. A secret weapon was best saved for moments when your opponents seemed unstoppable by your not-secret weapons.

"Not for this mission, no. Take as many of your people as you think will be needed."

Phobos studied him, and then smiled – a smile which showed little trace of humanity. "I am the only one required to survive."

"Exactly. I will not object to you having a complete victory over all your opponents, of course... but all I require is you to witness what is necessary and ensure I have word of it."

With a bow, Phobos turned and swept from the room. Deimos blinked slowly, then followed after.

Not quite recovered to his role yet, Raiagamor mused. *But soon.*

He smiled again, a grin of blades and death. *And soon, as well, will be the failure of Berenike!*

Chapter 22
Looks to the Future and the Past

Ingram turned and gave a last wave; he saw Urelle do the same, just before they turned a corner and passed out of sight of the Wanderer's gateway. The little sad jolt he felt as he accepted that it would be weeks before he saw her again echoed down to his guts and then finally up to his head. He found himself trying to smile and frown simultaneously.

What bothers you, my friend?

Quester's mindvoice was, as always, calmly sympathetic, comforting. Ingram felt his expression settle into a sad smile. *Oh, just finally accepting something, that's all.*

Accepting what? If I may ask my Nest-Brother?

I... guess. Not sure I want to say it to Lady Vantage, and she's the only other person here to talk to. He took a deep breath. *I think... I really, really like Urelle. I mean... I don't know if I love her. How long does it take to be sure of that? But I know I'm going to miss her* terribly, *every day, just... seeing her. Talking with her. Knowing she's there.*

Soundless, fond laughter echoed in his mind. *We have both noticed this, Lady Vantage and I. Neither of us are blind. It seems the two of you notice less than we. According to my knowledge of human behavior, this is... not surprising.*

The two of us? You mean she...? The flash of startlement and hope and joy was unexpected, intense... yet, strangely, touched with... guilt? He couldn't sort it all out.

I believe so; her scent and yours agree on such things, and your reaction to her fascination with the Wanderer fairly closely echoes hers towards Berenike's appearance.

"Towards *Berenike's*...?" It was a moment before he realized he'd spoken aloud; Victoria Vantage's eyebrow rose.

"What was that, Ingram?"

"Um... sorry. I was having a private talk with Quester and he startled me." At the same time, it dawned on him that Quester's comment had touched something much deeper... the source of the guilt and confusion.

Maybe Urelle *did* have a reason to regard his reaction to Berenike with the same unease he did her constant, awed regard for the Wanderer. More reason than he had, in fact, since Urelle hadn't spent her childhood with the Wanderer, and he *had* spent his with Berenike, or wishing he *could* spend it with her.

Quester, I have to figure myself out someday.

My friend, we all have parts of ourselves we have never fully understood. I still need answers to my own existence.

Maybe, but you didn't make your existence that way. That's your Mother's doing. He grinned. *This is all my problem.*

But not a terrible problem, I think.

"I must say," Victoria said, "that must be an extremely convenient ability to have – this mental connection you share – but it is somewhat disconcerting to know people are carrying on conversations in front of you and see it only by shifts of expression. Or scent and posture, in Quester's case."

Ingram laughed. "What you're saying is that it's a little rude."

"Perhaps only that I *feel* that way," Victoria said with a deprecating smile. "After all, if you have something private to discuss, there is no reason you should not, and this bond of yours allows you to do so while not separating us." She smiled, the expression making her look many years younger and emphasizing how she was very much related to both Kyri and Urelle. "Possibly, I'm just jealous."

A waft of creosote and flowers from Quester. "Lady Vantage, it is not *impossible* that you and Urelle may be given the same bond. It is just..." he trailed off.

She held up her hands, chagrin on her face. "Oh, dear, Quester, no. I was not trying to pressure you into anything of that nature. I understand that bond represents your very specific closeness to Ingram. Yes?"

"Thank you," Quester said emphatically, and his scent became much more relaxed. "Yes, it is... very important. We have journeyed together for two years now, shared all triumphs and pains and fears and joys that comrades – that *Nestmates* – might do." His great faceted eyes focused on her own. "And I say, quite honestly, that if we continue to travel together as we have, that it may well be that such a bond will follow in time. But it is not given to a non-Iriistiik lightly, and it was only about six or seven months ago that I offered this bond, and that Ingram accepted."

"Understood. Might I inquire as to the range of this link? It may have some very practical applications."

"Oh," Ingram assured her, thinking back on a particular time he'd let himself get captured, "it *does*. Quester said he *thought* it was about two or three miles, right? Not that we've ever really tested it."

"That is my guess. Between normal Nest members, a few miles is the limit. Mothers can speak with each other across the entirety of the world, or possibly beyond, it is said. Certainly, I could hear the voice of our Mother at many, many miles distant. But I am no Mother, so I must assume I cannot maintain the link at great distance."

Victoria nodded. "Still impressive, and I can see many ways in which it must be useful."

By now, the three of them were passing beyond the main borders of the town and starting to skirt the edge of the lake in order to continue their southward journey. White clouds floated high above, occasionally veiling the hot sun and giving a few cooler moments. The lake lapped at the shore with little waves, and Ingram saw tiny forms scuttling back and forth in the wet sand and gravel – lakefleas and pygmy shore crabs, for the most part. Birds of spectacular colors occasionally flew up from the green jungle, and in the distance, a small, bat-winged shape rose and fell; one of the Least Dragons was on the hunt.

He sensed Lady Victoria's gaze on him. "What is it, Lady Vantage?"

"You mentioned Berenike in your unintended outburst, and it reminded me that there were some questions about her that I never got answers to."

"Go ahead. Though there's lots of things about her I wouldn't know – especially anything about her being a God-Warrior."

"Why did Deimos say that it was 'impossible' for her to be there?"

"Oh. Yes. Yes, that would be hard to understand without an explanation." Ingram felt his hands tighten into fists, forced them to relax. *I really don't want to think about... that time. But she does need to understand.*

He swallowed, finding that he couldn't speak for a moment. "It's... well, hard to talk about. In the end, that's what led to me running away. But... okay." A breath, another, relaxing as they walked along the shore.

"Berenike was always my friend, since I was very little. We played together because she was one of the only kids near my age in the compound." He smiled briefly at the memory; a smile touched with melancholy and amusement in equal parts. "I thought she was a year older than me – everyone did – and it wasn't until I was, like, twelve that we happened to be talking and found out we were actually the same age. Her... clan? Tribe? Whatever, they counted years from the time they *started*, so you were one – in your first year – the moment you were born, while most of the rest of us counted it from the time you *ended* a year.

"Anyway, she stuck with me even though I *was* such a hopeless case, took time to practice pretty much *everything* with me at one point or another. She was one of the reasons I *stayed* a Camp-Bel, even if not much of one. Or so I thought, anyway, if you're right about me not being a disappointment."

He paused, his perception of the past suddenly wrenching around into a completely different path. "I guess... if you're right about that... she was there to *push* me to be even *better*." A hesitant sense of wonder slowly trickled into his thoughts, and he saw Berenike's glances, her comments, other actions, in a completely different light. *Could she be right? Could I have been being* prepared *for something* more?

He shook himself. "Well, anyway, we'll go with what I thought at the time. Usually, I was stuck in the Clan compounds, but every so often Berenike and I would find a way to sneak out. Mostly that was a chance for her to see how well I'd learned my lessons in a real setting, and for her to teach me new tricks outside of the Clan, but we'd do other things – explore the hills outside of Aegis, things like that." For a moment Ingram paused, and Quester could feel that his nest-brother's thoughts were in the past, perhaps drawing strength for what was to come.

Continue when you are ready, he thought. *Victoria and I will wait.*

He smiled quickly at Quester and sent a pulse of *Thanks* to him. "Okay. Ummm... Right. So, I don't want to brag about anything, but this next part's important. On one of those trips, we were trying to cross the Syvia – a stream, you might call it the Chillrush, I guess. It's a big stream or small river that comes down from somewhere in Wisdom's Fortress and through some of the hills, all the way to near Aegis.

"Anyway, Berenike slipped – a bunch of the stones shifted just as she was stepping on them, and even she couldn't quite keep her balance and went down.

The water's *really* fast there, and it sent her down the stream, so fast I could barely keep up with her sprinting down the shore. And then she went over the edge and down into the Hungry Pool." He shuddered, remembering the moment that it had happened, the terror he'd felt echoing back into the present.

"The Hungry Pool?"

"It's a deep pool overhung by rocks, where the currents flow around and into it so that it drags things under – whirlpools appear and disappear regularly in it." A chill went down his arms, making the fine hairs stand up. "One man who drowned there, his body didn't wash out for more than a week."

"Merciful Balance," Victoria murmured. "There are trap-pools like that in Evanwyl. What did you do?"

"The only thing I could think *to* do," he answered, taking a deep breath as though preparing to dive, remembering. "I whipped the *anai-k'ota*'s cable out to its maximum length, hooked the one end around a tree at the edge, and dove in." The memory took over, and it was as though he was there again…

***

The Syvia's waters tore at him, a thousand icy hands towing him into the depths with a force that strained his arms, made the weapon's cable sing with tension. The current lashed and swung about, turning him around and over despite his skill at swimming. The darkness below the stones was that of a cave, impenetrable, and the churning froth of bubbles made the normally-clear water misty and distorting.

A shape loomed up before him, and he thought he saw hair wavering in a glint above the shape, reached out desperately, but his fingers brushed only solid granite, foundation of the earth, not his friend, as his lungs began to burn, his throat tighten against the need for air. He pulled at the cable, twisted the mechanism; even with its help, he barely returned above water, refilled his lungs with cool, precious breath. *She can hold hers longer… but not much!*

A second dive into the chaotic maelstrom, this time bashing him into rocks, pinching the *anai-k'ota*'s cable between them, leading to a frantic struggle to free it before he, too, drowned. His heart hammered even faster, tears blurring his eyes even when he broke the water. *No time! She's running out of time!*

He imagined Berenike trapped in the darkness, eyes wide, hair tangled in the rocks, unable to break free, her mouth opening at the end, when she could no longer keep from breathing…

No!

A third time, he plunged into the waters, driving as hard as he could for the blackness below the largest boulder, hand stretching out, searching...

And his fingers snagged on a leather strap – soft but strong tooled leather, a pattern he could recognize, one of Berenike's backpack fastenings.

He gripped that strap with all the strength left in his arm, kicked out as he triggered the *anai-k'ota*'s retraction one final time.

It wasn't enough. The additional weight of Berenike – *for it had to be Berenike, it had to be* – and the savage grip of the water was too much even for the weapon's powerful magical mechanism to overcome.

No! he thought again. *Not this close! I will not lose her! I will not die!*

The current hammered them down, but his feet landed on the rocks below, and he *pushed* upward against it, felt his weapon take in that few feet of slack, anchor him again, give him a chance to push off *another* rock. His lungs were filled with spears of agony, his two arms screaming with strain as one held Berenike and the other maintained a deathgrip on the shaft of the *anai-k'ota*, but he refused to let go, locked his throat tight.

Another leap off a rock, and the current... was it weakening, becoming erratic? A trickle of air escaped, momentarily fooling his body into thinking he was starting to breathe, easing the tension for an infinitesimal moment as he arched his body, stretching out his legs, down, *there*, stone, bending and springing forward as hard as he could—

—and the current *was* weakening, and the cable began to retract, finally, dragging him up as his vision was graying out, almost unable to cling to consciousness...

Abruptly, his head broke the surface of the water and he gasped, pulling in fresh air with unbelieving relief and triumph – triumph he immediately stifled in fear, for the form he dragged with him was not moving.

Somehow, he pulled Berenike up on shore, still gasping, bringing in air to make up for the unknown eon of time he had spent in that dark chaos. Her body lay limp, sprawled, unconscious or worse on the stony ground.

She was not breathing, and his fingers could find no sure evidence of a pulse.

He dropped his weapon, tore the backpack from her and rolled her over. *Remember the lessons, the teachings of the Founder and her people. Hold the head* so;

clear the mouth... nothing there... make sure the airway is clear... Now push *on the chest, thirty times, tilt head* so, *two breaths, by the* Lady *her lips are cold, like death,* no, *compress the chest,* please Athena...

A minute, two went by, and he was barely conscious, his aching arms almost unable to continue, his own lungs unable to provide *him* with enough air, but he refused, continuing, praying...

Without warning, Berenike's form contracted and she coughed, shoving Ingram back so he nearly fell into the water again. A gasp, inhaling, and then coughing again, expelling water that had made its way into her lungs, a spasm of coughs that racked her entire body, and she fell back, gasping, but alive.

Alive.

***

He saw the others staring at him, Victoria's eyes wide and sympathetic; Quester's scent, and his mind-touch, were also comforting. "By the Balance, Ingram, you did well."

He felt his cheeks heat slightly. "I did what any friend would do."

"So that, then, is why she feels such a debt to you," Quester said.

"That, and I insisted that we tell the story the other way around."

"What?" Victoria was startled. "Why?"

"She was in training to be a God-Warrior," Ingram said. When the others looked at him without comprehension, he went on, "Her falling into that situation and not getting herself *out*? Having to be rescued by a second-rate Camp-Bel who wasn't even a candidate for the training himself? That would be... shameful. Maybe she'd have kept her position as a trainee – I'd have hoped they wouldn't be so stupid as to kick her out – but maybe not. There's a *lot* of pride and tradition surrounding the God-Warriors, and especially those of Athena and Ares, since they're the ones that the whole Cycle tends to focus on.

"So, from her point of view I didn't just save her life, I saved her honor and reputation. And it didn't matter to me that she got the credit; she was alive, and I knew I'd finally done something that *mattered*, so that was good enough for me."

He looked up into the sky. "So. That was why she decided to really teach me everything she could about her *own* training – the God-Warrior training – hoping that it would help me past my own limitations." He frowned. "Or more than that, if your guesses are right.

"In any case, every so often we'd go off and train on our own. And then one day…"

Chapter 23
Island of Joy and Loss

"To *Kyriarcnis*?" Ingram repeated, his voice wavering in shock. The thought was... impossible. Frightening. Dangerous.

Everything he'd dreamed of.

"Shh!" Berenike put her hand gently over his mouth, looked around, listening, to see if anyone else in the house had heard. After a moment, she withdrew her hand. "Yes, Kyriarcnis, the Island of Mastery."

"Where the God-Warriors *train*," he whispered. "I'm not a trainee! I'm just a…"

"You're my *friend*, and not 'just' anything," she said with finality. "I've been teaching you a lot of things – and you've been a very good student—"

"Well, as good as I *could* be when I'm—"

"A *very good student*," she said, overriding him. "And the one who traded *his* honor for *mine*. Stop worrying about what *you* owe *me* and let me worry about what debt *I* owe. No, Ingram, I won't let you argue about that, now or ever. Accept it."

Seeing the smiling iron determination on her face, he finally laughed quietly and spread his hands in surrender. "As you wish, Lady Berenike."

"Don't you *dare*."

"Ow! Don't poke me like that! All right, all right. But Berenike, how?"

"I've got a little sailing boat. It'll get us there and back. You can *see* Kyriarcnis from the harbor, after all, so it's not like either of us could get lost. You *do* know how to sail, right?"

"Of *course* I do!"

"Ha! Don't be so defensive. I still had to ask, you know. Wasn't one of the things I taught you."

"So, you *can* get us there, but… why?"

"Because," she said, golden eyes glinting mischeviously at him, "there's training and testing that can *only* be done there. And the Masters already know about you, anyway."

"What? No, Berenike, the secrets—"

"Ingram, Ingram, I took *oaths* with the Masters. I had to tell them if I was ever going to mention the secrets. They consulted the Lady and allowed it."

"*Really?*" He was stunned. Lady Athena had *spoken* to the Masters of Kyriarcnis of *him*?

"Really. My *guess* is that *She* knows what you did, even if no one else does. And even the people who *think* you're not good enough – and I think you *are*, so shut up – even those people have never said you don't have honor, or can't keep a secret, so the Masters knew if you were sworn to secrecy, it would be all right."

"Well... if you're sure it's going to be okay..."

She hugged him. "Of *course,* it will. It will be a few of the absolutely *worst* days you've ever had!"

He made a face. "Yours, too?"

"Oh, by the gods, Ingram, yes. I know, I don't complain much, but that's because the Masters don't put *up* with whining candidates. But there were some days I *really* wondered if I shouldn't just give up and go get a bodyguard slot with someone maybe over in Amoni."

Wisdom and War, I'm not sure I'm looking forward to something like that, he thought. At the same time, though, he *was*. Even if he *failed* the tests, as long as he failed them *well*, he'd have nothing to be ashamed of. He, after all, wasn't a Candidate for God-Warrior. The few Camp-Bels he knew of who'd gone to Kyriarcnis hadn't passed all the tests, but they'd still impressed the Masters. If he could manage not to embarrass himself...

"Then when?"

"Tomorrow. Get all your equipment together, clean your weapons, all that. You have to be at your best, and *look* your best, when we meet the Masters!"

"Tomorrow!" It was already part-way through the afternoon. "Great Wisdom, I've got to start getting ready *now!*"

She laughed again. "Yes, you'd better! I'll see you tomorrow morning, at the side gate. Make sure your parents don't know!"

"I'll... I'll tell them I'm off for a few days for meditation and practice. I do that enough, and it's not like I have many other responsibilities." He tried very hard to keep bitterness out of his voice at the last.

"Good idea. See you half an hour after sunrise, then!"

He hugged her, feeling the warmth of her affection supporting and lifting him, as well as her arms, which were, as usual, hugging with their accustomed exuberance. "Tomorrow!"

***

Kyriarcnis rose from the early-morning fog, towering cliffs a hundred- and fifty-feet high fading at the bottom, making the Island of Mastery look like a mountain floating in the sky, heights of blue and gray stone crowned with greenery and an occasional flash of white or pink or gold marble.

Ingram felt tension and hope squirming in his stomach, like two snakes fighting it out, and tried to meditate, to calm himself. Breathe *in*, cool blue of peace, blow *out* red of fear or anger or doubt, breathe *in*...

After a few minutes the snakes were more like small worms; uncomfortable but under control. He looked up, to see that they were turning, heading into a narrow gap in the barrier cliffs. They passed the entrance, stone rearing high above them, barely a stone's easy cast to either side, and into a circular harbor. Ahead, Ingram could see three wooden docks projecting out into the water.

Something seemed odd about the wooden structures, and after a moment he had it. "They're floating; is the harbor that steep, that there are no pilings long enough?"

"Is it that steep?" Berenike laughed, her voice echoing cheerfully from the cliffs around them. "See how the shore stands straight? So it goes below the water! There is no beach, no gentle slope. Those cliffs are as tall below as they are above. If you look, you can see that the landing area from whence the docks reach was carved out from the rock itself."

As they approached, Ingram could see that his friend was right; the flat stone beyond the docks corresponded with a semicircular divot cut from the living rock above. That was, by itself, impressive; carving out a landing a few hundred feet across from a hundred-fifty-foot cliff must have been a mighty undertaking, even with some magical help. Unless the gods had done the work, but he doubted it.

All the legends surrounding Kyriarcnis emphasized how much people had to do for themselves.

Ingram leapt out of the little sailboat and secured her to the dock as soon as Berenike brought her in, earning another smile from the bronze-haired girl. "Good. We're finally here. How do you feel?"

"Nervous," he answered. "Excited. Scared, a bit. Maybe a little queasy."

"Some exercise will help settle *that* down," she said, grinning.

"Maybe." He looked around, but aside from a few stacks of crates, the docking area was empty. "Where are the Masters?"

She pointed upward. "There."

He blinked, then looked around again. The area *was* empty other than the crates, the docks themselves, and the two of them. And their boat.

There were no stairs. There was no sign of a cable-lift or anything like it. Well, that wasn't *entirely* true, now that he was looking. There was a pulley arrangement and guide bars – spaced about twenty, twenty-five feet apart up the cliff.

But there were no ropes or cables *on* the pulleys or supports. No steps. Not even a ladder.

He looked back at Berenike, to see her grinning even more widely. "Well, what are you waiting for?" she asked.

"How...?"

She shook her head. "I'm disappointed in you. Didn't you come here to take the Tests, to meet the Masters?"

"Of course I did!"

She pointed up again. "Then realize the first test's already started."

Before he could react, she sprinted to one of the stacks of crates, leapt to the top, and bounded straight up, to catch a handhold ten feet up, then flipped herself up and around, grabbing hold of one of the cargo lift guides, yanking herself up, and then jumping a full fifteen, twenty feet to catch the next support...

"Ares' *Balls*," he muttered.

There was no way he was going to match her speed. He couldn't clear a fifteen- or twenty-foot jump, that was just ridiculous. But the rock wall wasn't *perfectly* sheer. In fact, there were projections and indentations all over it at various points.

The cliffs were *scalable*. Maybe not the *outer* cliffs, but at least this one wasn't impassable.

He clambered up the crates and began climbing. As he looked up, gauging his approach, he saw Berenike reach the top and wave.

Hades and Persephone! She's already there! I'm going to fail the first test before I even meet the Masters!

He lunged upward, stretching, barely snagged a higher handhold, and then found himself dangling in air, held only by three fingertips.

Or maybe I'll just die because I'm stupid! Controlling his movements *very* carefully, Ingram felt around, found a foothold, another handhold. Then he methodically released his right hand, let it rest a moment, and then made his way to the first lift support.

"*Survival* is the goal," he murmured to himself, quoting one of the most basic Camp-Bel truths. "'If there is no survival, there can be no one to judge, for good or ill.'"

He *would* reach the top. And he would *not* rush simply because his friend – the actual Candidate for God-Warrior – was so much faster than he. *I'll go as fast as I really think I can – and no faster.*

With his mind focused and purpose clear, he ascended.

Sometime later, he hauled himself over the edge of the cliff and sprawled there, breathing hard, luxuriating in the comfort of *not* having to grip something, *not* having to balance precariously on narrow pieces of steel or rock. He flexed his hands and arms slowly, to keep them from stiffening, but otherwise lay still for a few moments. Then he pushed himself to his knees – and realized he was not alone.

Berenike was there, of course – but she was standing *behind* five other people.

The Masters of Kyriarcnis.

Only one of them *looked* like Ingram's imagined vision of an old master: skin like seamed onyx, bright black eyes glinting, along with the hint of a smile within a flowing white beard, white hair trailing to the shoulders, wearing a white and blue chiton.

The others were of startling variety. Scarcely coming up to the old master's shoulder was a gold-skinned woman, older than Berenike, reed-thin, in bronze armor, with a sword at her side and three javelins carried on her back. On the other side of the old man was a massive Toad, four feet from nose to rump, wearing a harness covered with tubes and pouches and slots for crystals and other odd devices.

Next to the Toad loomed a *bilarel* woman, in the gold and silver robes of a Priestess of Athena, and on the other side of the tiny gold-skinned woman was a human man in a flamboyant outfit, black and red and gold and brilliant green interwoven from the fancy shirt and its beautifully lace-trimmed sleeves, to the polished boots and elaborate and gem-inlaid hilt of a long rapier at his side, all topped with a hat with a long plume of radiant-bird feathers. His face was narrow but filled with good humor, and one eye twinkled green while the other sparkled bright blue.

Ingram forced himself upright and bowed as low as he could, despite the trembling in his limbs.

"Prettily done," the well-dressed man said. "But please, young one, sit down and rest. A climb and a half you've had, one I'd rather not assay myself."

Ingram remained standing, looking at the others uncertainly.

"Oh, go on," the Toad said. "You've passed your first test, you're allowed a little rest before we put you through the others. And you should be introduced." He gave a bounce-bow of his own, as Ingram slowly sank back to the ground. "Shockhand Circlebane at your service."

"Garnet Pyritane," the little gold woman said with a nod. Ingram realized she was a *Tholosyrnen*, an offshoot or relative of the more commonly seen *Odinsyrnen*, explaining her stature despite her age, which appeared to be well into her thirties.

The old man waved cheerfully. "Potami Omous," he said.

"Elgakniti." The *bilarel*'s nod was barely perceptible.

"And I, laggard and last, am Rishard of the Silver Blade." This was accompanied by a vastly elaborate bow in keeping with his clothing. "Each of us is a master of a different field of conflict. Mine is the battlefield of diplomacy, persuasion, and honor, where words hold as much sway as blades. My opposite number, of course, is the lovely Garnet, who trains one to be a master of all armament. Old Potami, how to best others without weapons at all, while our favorite Toad instructs in the defense against, or use of, the mystical powers... and the mighty Elgakniti, the understanding of the higher powers."

Elgakniti snorted. "And already Rishard seeks to confuse you. His instruction is not in being a pompous popinjay, no matter his appearance; it is in *intrigue*."

Ingram felt that he had recovered enough to stand again during the introductions, so he did, and bowed quickly. "I am honored to meet you all. I hope it is no great bother – I know I was slow to arrive."

He saw the five exchange glances. For a moment, oddly, he thought they *also* glanced to Berenike, as though awaiting a sign or word from her.

"Not so slow as to be hopeless," Potami said after a moment. "Not so slow, at all. I have seen worse first climbs by those who later did well, indeed. So, calm your mind on that score. Berenike would not have brought you before us if she thought you laggard in your studies or your skills."

"Still," Garnet said, dark bronze eyes surveying him from his own height, "to be tested by us, so swiftly, will be no small or simple thing. The next days will task your limits in all ways – your skill at arms, your speed and strength, your knowledge, and above all, your focus, your discipline, your will."

"What she means," the Toad continued, "is that this is some dangerous stuff we'll be doing here. Are you sure you're ready for it? No shame in saying no, when I tell you that the climb, there, was the simplest part of the testing. Say no, and you just go down and sail home. Say yes, and you won't leave until all five of us have tested you – and maybe you won't go home at all, or go home badly hurt."

Ingram swallowed. He knew God-Warrior candidates were pushed beyond human limits. And some of them died during the training.

But Berenike had brought him here. *She* believed in him. He didn't see *why* she did, but he just couldn't disappoint his best friend. His heart beating faster, he took a deep breath and then deliberately met the eyes of each of the Masters. "I'll... I'll stay. No matter what."

"Excellent!" Rishard said. "Berenike, because he has never been here before, or faced our tests, or even our instruction, you are allowed to accompany him. You may not directly assist him, of course, but you may explain things that are unclear, help guide him to the proper path..." and here, he smiled brilliantly, "...and simply be there to assure that he is not alone."

Berenike came and stood beside him; her hand gripped his, and he felt a hint of confidence rising within him at that warm touch.

Garnet nodded. "Then we shall begin."

***

"Ares, Hephaestus, and lost *Zeus*," Ingram groaned. "I've never hurt this much in the morning, Berenike!"

"And that's just the first day," she said with a frighteningly cheerful expression, laying out a breakfast on the stone table in the hut they had been given, situated in its own clearing, only a mile from the harbor. "Eat up, you'll need your strength! It's Master Rishard next."

"Lady's *Wisdom*," he muttered. "After the disasters yesterday, they're still testing me?"

"Not *entirely* a disaster." There was an odd glint in Berenike's eyes as she spoke. "You *did* manage to cut Master Garnet, and that one strike on Master Potami must have stung!"

He shook his head. "She probably just wasn't used to the *anai-k'ota* – it is a pretty rare weapon – and I just got lucky with Potami. Both of them then thrashed me pretty much unopposed."

"Shockhand wouldn't say that about *his* test."

He managed a smile – though even *that* hurt! "I guess I did pretty well at getting through the magical dangers. Though being a Camp-Bel, I have some special tricks I can play."

"All God-Warriors have their own tricks, so that's all right. And the Masters aren't scary at all, are they?"

He *did* laugh at that. "No, I was wrong to be afraid. They're *tough*, and I'd bet they'd be real scary to *fight*, but they're... actually pretty nice."

"See? I told you. They want us to be our best, not our *scaredest*."

"That's not even a word, Berenike."

"It is *now*. And you know what I mean."

He did some cautious stretches as she finished setting up breakfast – which was a welcome change, since he usually did the breakfasts when they were out on their occasional excursions. "Yes, I do."

He was just taking a bite of biscuit when a dull *whoom* sound echoed outside.

The two of them were up immediately, Berenike out the door just a fraction before him.

Rising from the forest about a mile and a half distant was a column of black smoke. "Athena's *Name*, what's happening?" Berenike whispered. "That's near the main training camp!"

Two more explosions shook the forest, both nearer than the first; Ingram saw red-orange fireballs rise and become black billows of smoke. He hesitated, and saw Berenike, too, momentarily paralyzed by indecision. Should they wait? Should they go towards the trouble and see if they could help?

Or should we flee? Ingram thought, knowing that *that* choice would never occur to Berenike.

Five figures burst from the trees only a hundred yards away, four of them running flat-out with the fifth being carried by the largest of the others. "Berenike!" roared Elgakniti, Garnet's blood-soaked form clinging to her. "Ingram! *Run*! Get to the harbor and go, *now*!"

"What? No, Masters, let us help! What's happening?"

"Black treachery and blacker magic!" Rishard snarled. "Something subverted the wards around Kyriarcnis, *all* of the wards!"

Shockhand spun and hurled a sphere of sparking energy behind them; lightning burst outward from it and poured in a torrent through the trees. "Don't think that will hold them long! We have to go!"

"But the others—"

"Dead," Potami said, his accustomed smile gone, tears visible as the Masters reached them.

Berenike's eyes went wide with horror. "All... *All* of them?"

"The first sign we *had* of the attack was the utter devastation of the Candidate Encampment," Elgakniti growled, and she shoved Berenike forward. "If you hadn't been here with Ingram, you'd be dead now, too! *Run*, Hades take you! Run!"

They ran then, but even so, Ingram had to stare. "But you're the Masters, can't you—"

"These dung-eaters know what they're doing," Garnet answered painfully. "I don't know how much they have in reserve, how many more of those attacks they can manage, but—"

A wet, meaty *thokk* sound cut her words off short, and Elgakniti pitched forward, a spear of stone eight feet long entirely through her chest and Garnet's body. Blood sprayed everywhere, and Ingram heard himself screaming in tandem with Berenike.

The other Masters hesitated only a moment; it was clear both were dead, and there was neither time nor point in trying to carry their friends' bodies. The Toad sent a storm of magical arrows humming, vicious and true, through the air, but the line of figures now advancing – surrounded by an aura of shadow – slowed only fractionally.

"Go!" Rishard said, and his glittering rapier cut a shockwave through the air. "I shall hold them here! Get the children to safety, Shockhand, Potami!"

They didn't argue; Shockhand instead bounded alongside Ingram and Berenike, intoning spells and summoning power, and Ingram felt defenses materializing and thickening about them, most strongly on himself and his friend. "We can't leave him alone!"

"We have our *duty*," Potami panted, breath coming harder as they kept running. "The others are dead, but one Candidate and one other child remain in our care, and we will – we *must* – die before allowing them to be slain. This is our oath and our duty."

As they sped along the path towards the harbor, dark figures appeared in the woods at either side, almost even with them. "Gods, they've almost caught us," Ingram heard himself say with a shamefully terrified squeak.

Potami glanced at Shockhand, and then stopped.

Instantly, the dark figures – figures which moved with a sharp, inhumanly liquid grace – shifted to focus on him.

A detonation of pure white cast the figures back, screeching and burning, and Potami turned, running heavily to catch up, with more shapes in pursuit – though at least some yards farther distant.

"They are... vulnerable to light and the spirit..." he gasped.

"Oh? Well, that's a good thing!" Shockhand said. "I've got just the—"

This time it was a slender black-crystal arrow, piercing and shattering the Toad's mystical defenses as though they were paper and glass, transfixing him between the eyes so he tumbled, limp and unseeing, to the ground. Two more arrows slashed out, one ripping entirely through Ingram's left arm.

"*Shockhand, no!*" Potami's cry of anguish echoed through the forest. "Oh, by the Spirit..."

His gaze fixed on Berenike. "Child, you are... the last. You are the best of our children. The light... is with you. The *Lady* is with you. Get... your friend... to safety. You must."

"No, please, Master—"

"Go! I will give you the time!"

And now they were alone, and for an instant the early-morning twilight turned to the dawn of a white sun that spanned half the island, and there were screams and snarls of hatred and pain.

Ingram was gasping for breath himself now, his sides aching almost as much as his legs, his arm burning and wet with blood, but he knew that to stop, to even *slow*, would be death. Berenike ran alongside him, sobbing with loss and rage and fear, but still so fleet that she had to slow her steps to keep alongside him.

"Ingram," she said, "You have to survive."

"What? We *both* have to—"

"I *brought* you here. I have to get you home safe."

To his astonishment, she swallowed and suddenly smiled, tears still glittering on her face but her expression now the invincible confidence she had shown him so many times before. "I *will* make sure you get home safe," she said. "My oath on it, as I told you."

A faint glow shimmered about her – Shockhand's protections? Something else? And without warning, she caught him up.

He felt her accelerate, even *carrying* him, and the path blurred by, the figures of their enemies receded for a few precious moments until Berenike stopped as swiftly as she had fled.

They were on the edge of the cliff, the harbor far below, and nowhere to run.

Berenike looked into his eyes, then kissed him on the forehead, hugging him close. "Be safe," she said.

And then she flung him out into space.

The world seemed to shift then; as though *he* stood still, and *Berenike* was the one falling, falling *up* with one hand stretched towards him in farewell, curving up and away with that certain and triumphant smile carrying her confidence and blessing.

Then she turned and the world reoriented, and Ingram screamed as he plummeted towards the water... and Berenike turned to face the dark shapes behind.

Chapter 24
Answers Yield Questions

His friend's scent had echoed his story as he became more and more immersed in it. There had been tangs of fear, aromas of fondness and pleasure, sharp miasmas of anger and hopelessness and self-doubt. But... "She *threw* you off a hundred-and-fifty-foot cliff?"

A chuckle. "Does sound like it's backwards for the idea of saving my life, but not really. There's ways to dive into deep water from high up and survive, and she knew I knew those methods. I oriented myself and basically turned myself into a spike when I hit the water."

"I did something similar in my youth," Victoria said. "Though only from about seventy feet, not twice that. Not an experience I would like to repeat, given the choice."

"No, I wouldn't want to do that jump again, myself."

"And Berenike?"

"Everyone *thought* she was dead." He shuddered and drew his travel cloak tighter about him. "Those were... the worst days. I think our pursuers thought *I* had to have died in the fall, at least long enough. I was picked up by a Camp-Bel cutter that had been sent out to respond to a partial alarm – I guess one of the Masters had managed to send out some kind of signal, and the cutter had gotten there first. With what we know now... I guess that must have been real lucky. Any other ship might have been connected to the enemy.

"Anyway, I'd survived but I was pretty bad hurt; I hadn't been able to keep exact control when I hit the water, and I'd been bleeding already, so I ended up at the healers and in bed for a while. And for a couple of days, I didn't think I *wanted* to survive. Berenike was dead, and somehow, I felt it was my fault."

Quester nodded. "And then?"

"A couple nights later, Berenike showed up in my room. She was all banged up, no surprise, but she was alive." A flash of echoed joy, flowers and rainstorms and a touch of fruit wine. "*Alive*. I just cried for about five minutes when I realized she was really there.

"She said we'd keep it a secret, just the two of us. You see, we realized that the attack had been meant *for her*. She would've been sleeping in the Candidates' Hall any other time, and the wreckage showed the hit took place on the north side of the Hall – right where her sleeping pad was."

"How did she survive an attack that killed the Masters?"

Ingram grinned. "She became a God-Warrior that night. Athena blessed her as the sole survivor. Also, the Masters had already taken some toll on the attackers. Unfortunately, even she couldn't *beat* them all, but it gave her enough power to let it look like they killed her; she swapped clothes with one of the human members of the attacking group and made it look like her; that's what got buried in her tomb."

Ingram frowned. "She really regretted that. Having to run away, I mean. That meant that the treacherous filth was able to clean up their traces. No one found any bodies or clear traces of who was responsible, so it ended up being unsolved." His fists tightened. "But now we know who it was, don't we?"

"In all probability, yes," Victoria said. "Ares must have been behind it."

"And now that Berenike's shown herself," Ingram went on, "he'll know he failed to kill her before. She'll be a target again."

"This may work in our favor to some extent," Quester said. "She spends most of her time elsewhere, and I presume she will start working to undermine his efforts, now that she no longer has to conceal her existence."

Ingram blinked. "Huh. I never thought of that. But yeah. Yeah, that makes sense. She can start interfering in his work, looking into what's really driving him – why he's hunting us, for that matter – and that will mean he can't just focus on us." He nodded sharply. "Yes, that's good." His voice shifted to anticipatory amusement. "And she's a *lot* stronger than she was."

"I suppose she must be," Victoria said. "Thank you for sharing this tale with us, Ingram. It does... clarify a number of things for me."

"I wish you had shared it with me earlier," Quester said; he allowed just a trace of reproach in his words and scent.

"Well... I know. Sorry, Quester. But parts of it I couldn't have told so well until you'd met Berenike, and we never *quite* got to that point in our prior adventures."

Quester buzzed his own laugh. "Not quite, true, but I think we have been very close a few times – not the least being our test to become Adventurers, yes?"

"Oh, yeah. I *did* think about that more than once, especially once I saw the Darkness That Devours, but knowing the circumstances, I wasn't sure she *could* reach us there."

Victoria's stride paused. "The Darkness That Devours?" she repeated. "*That* was the portion of our adventure that old Bridgebreaker threw you into? By the Balance, what was he *thinking*?"

"That we'd asked for the fast track and we'd better prove we had what it takes," Ingram said seriously.

She pursed her lips tightly, disapproval visible in the green light of the forest. "Still, there *are* limits. Those creatures, the Xiilistiin, who took others' powers and knowledge were bad enough, but the Darkness... it was perhaps worse than all of them. How did you defeat it?"

Ingram dug into a pouch, pulled out a ridged cylinder with some sort of key or pin on top, and tossed it to Victoria; stenciled across the cylinder were the letters ELF. "Extreme Luminance Flare," he said. "Basically, a short-lived sun in a can. It did *not* like it at all; I wouldn't be surprised if it died from that." He paused. "Well, *would* have died from it if it were real. Stayed real. Argh! How do you *talk* about the Arch's sort-of-real worlds?"

"Fortunately, one doesn't have to talk about such things often. But I know what you mean." Victoria studied the flare, which Quester knew weighed about five pounds, and then handed it back to Ingram. "Fascinating. Technological – from your Founder, then?"

"Some of the tech left from the ship itself, yes. So how did *your* group deal with the Darkness?"

"I'm afraid there's details I can't discuss," Victoria said after a pause, "but I will say ours took more effort and was less elegant than having a sun at our fingertips. I like to think, however, that ours was thorough enough to ensure its demise."

"Lady's Blessing on *that*. I don't know where that shapeless horror came from, and I don't ever want to see anything like it again." Ingram looked at his viewer and nodded. "This way, we were drifting a little."

Quester turned in the direction indicated, and the little party moved onward.

***

"An interesting tale Ingram told us today," Victoria said quietly, glancing at the sleeping form of the lavender-haired boy.

"Very. Yet..." Quester hesitated, but saw the raised eyebrow, smelled amusement mingled with concern. "...yet there was something... how do I put it... *off*."

"Exactly," Victoria said. "Yet, being entirely honest, I cannot for the life of me say *what* was off about it. Something about his tone? Some details that didn't quite mesh? I am not sure."

"To me, it was the story entire. Parts of it – even most of it – I am sure are true. But I had the feeling of hearing... oh, almost a human children's tale, where certain elements of the tale were changed to make it fit what your sensibilities believe is appropriate for children."

"So, you think he was hiding something from us?" Victoria looked pensively at the sleeping figure. "If so, it was a masterful performance, I will say. And as I trust his basic good-will, I am also at a loss as to say *why* he would be hiding something in that story."

Quester riffled his wingcases and let his second-hands gesture a confused circle. "No more can I." He thought back over the story as Ingram had told it, carefully. "No. He was hiding nothing, at least not deliberately. Your people are excellent at concealing gesture and expression and word at need, but hiding your *scent* is much harder, and while Ingram's scent changed many times during the story, never did I smell the sharp tang of duplicity. Whatever is... off, so to speak, it is not something he did deliberately."

"So, he told the tale as he believes and knows it?"

"I am certain of it. Whatever bothers the two of us..." He hesitated, then went on, struck by a new idea. "It may be that it is because we lack so much context. Ingram has just started to open up about his past. We still have much to learn."

Victoria shrugged. "That is certainly possible. Aegeia is an odd country, and his Clan Camp-Bel odder in some ways. So... taking the story as it is, have you any thoughts?"

"I think there is much implied in it – perhaps things that Ingram himself does not see."

"Yes, there is. Berenike had trained on the island for at least a couple of years, and all five Masters of the Island turn up to test her friend?" Victoria snorted sharply. "That goes *far* beyond what would be expected for a favored student bringing in a second-class friend."

Quester thought about it, then felt his body stiffen. "They *told her* to teach Ingram. And they thought that both Berenike *and* Ingram might be the targets of the attack."

"It makes sense. And Berenike herself..." Victoria trailed off, then continued, "...if Ingram described truly, I think Berenike was *certain* they were after him. Why that would be, I don't know."

Quester smelled the burnt-lemon of frustrated puzzlement. "I don't know, either. But at least we know the mysteries we need to look for."

"Hmph. Mysteries abound, young Quester. I prefer answers, myself." She looked into the darkness around the camp. "Because mysteries, left too long, tend to become deadly."

Chapter 25
Lessons of Magic

"Look deeply into the Coin," the Wanderer said. "Find that overlay, that faintest shimmer that you saw before."

Urelle obeyed. She and the Wanderer stood in the center of the great circle of power; he had set it, this time, to an eight-pointed star, and the lines and symbols blazed blue-white around them.

The twining brilliance of the spell's lines slowly came into focus again, the symmetric beauty that resonated with her, or perhaps others of her party, that called to others of its kind, as well. But once more, within the silence of the enchanted circle, she found she could just descry that faint-glimmering hint of supernatural substance enclosing the spell in its protective, adhesive sheath.

"Excellent," the Wanderer breathed. "You see it already, I bet? A tiny glitter, a shimmer that's almost as transparent as air?"

"Yes. It looks like it surrounds the Coin *just* a bit outside the substance of the Coin itself – like a layer of perfect glass, no thicker than my fingernail."

"Very good. Very good." The Wanderer nodded, though she could only see it out of the corner of her eye; she had to maintain focus on the Coin and its enchantment. "Now, consider; what is it *doing* there?"

"I thought it was... *sealing* the spell. Protecting it, making it hard to break or undo. Like I said before, like painting a layer of glue onto the threads."

"Hm. Yes, that *is* a good description. *However...*" he paused. "However, I think that's only part of it – an incidental part, even, of the work of this particular feature of the spell."

"Incidental?"

"Well, no, it's not just a happy accident, so to speak. It's intended. But the *primary* purpose of that layer is very different. Examine it more closely. Examine what it *feels* like, to put it a different way."

She extended her senses again, though she wasn't sure what the Wanderer meant. Finally, she visualized herself touching it – not the Coin itself, but the nearly-invisible layer around the object. In her visualization, she stretched a finger out and gently stroked the surface...

With a gasp she drew back. "*Balance!*"

"What did you feel?"

"I felt... I felt like someone's finger was *touching* mine, following it!"

"Ahhh." He was silent, the slightest trace of a smile dancing on his lips.

After a moment it suddenly came to her. "It... it was *my* finger. My touch."

"And if it was...?"

"Well, that makes sense. It resonates with me. Or maybe more than me. So, it's echoing me when I try to touch it."

He nodded. "True enough. But consider *how* that might be accomplished. It is obvious that this is not something derived from a simple seeming, yes?"

"No. I mean, yes, it isn't that simple." She frowned, thinking. "In fact... sir, I don't see any way it *can* be accomplished. Not the way it was, anyway. If the people had *access* to us, they could have gotten a sense of our true selves, our souls or spirits, our personas, and built the spell from that. But if they could get that close, they wouldn't have *needed* the spell. They'd know who we were and where we were and all that."

"Yet it *was* accomplished," the Wanderer said. "Clearly you are missing something."

And as a teacher you don't want to tell me, you want me to at least try to determine what that something is on my own, she thought. Which was only the correct way to go about it; her teachers had *all* emphasized that while they would give her the *tools* to understanding, the best grasp of magic, or anything else really, could only come from oneself.

All right, so we have an apparent impossibility. Something that resonates perfectly with at least one person, but that had to have been made without any direct knowledge of the person. And it couldn't be just random chance; someone had based their entire *strategy* on this; they'd never do that if their spell would just happen to target one in millions of people.

For a few moments she just sat there, gazing stupidly at the Coin. There just didn't seem to be any way to grasp this problem – any more than the spell allowed her to grasp its essence and unravel it.

But the Wanderer was *trying* to be a teacher. She had to assume that meant that, first, there *was* an answer (which there obviously was) and second, that he thought she had a chance of figuring it out.

So. The object wasn't giving her any clues. What about the *creators* of the object? That would be Ares, or his subordinates, and that meant...

"Wanderer... can I think out loud to you? And have you check me, a little?"

He nodded, that tiny smile still playing about his mouth. "Of course."

"They're seeking a person, or people, that they don't actually know. They don't know what they look like, where they are, what their profession is."

"This seems to be the case."

"But they *do* know they're looking for a female – even though maybe they don't know the *species*."

"Implied by their conversation, yes."

"So... they know of the existence, and a few hints of the nature, of their target. Who apparently, aside maybe from Ingram, didn't know anything about *them*."

"All right so far," the Wanderer said.

"By the *Balance*," she said, with sudden annoyance and enlightenment. "It's a *prophecy*. Just like yours!"

"Not *just* like mine, perhaps. But I would bet on it. Chaoswars have all the powers heavily intertwined in them; foretelling, prophecy, scrying the future, whatever you want to call it, people will be desperately trying to use whatever they can to get an advantage."

She looked back down at the Coin. "So somehow they constructed a link to a *concept* that linked to *us*?" She shook her head, and then froze. "I see... two possibilities. Neither of them good."

"Ah. Tell me."

"The first is that it's not just prophecy, it's *destiny*. The events are preordained and unchangeable, so once they had the prophecy, they could... Ugh, I don't have the words... somehow link to the prophecy?"

"I'd phrase it as they could channel their magic to the fate they had already determined, yes. But, if it helps, *destiny* is really, really rare. Most events, even ones that *seem* inescapable, aren't; there's no cosmic order waiting to enforce them, or if it is..." he grinned, with the air of a man enjoying his own private jest, "...if it is, the cosmic order's being *directed* to enforce it."

"Then the only other thing I can think of is... we're dealing with Ares. Can the *gods* do something like that? Link prophecy with reality, so that the prediction is in alignment with the spell, which is in alignment with the target?"

He nodded gravely. "They can, especially with the right tools. And one can generally assume a god to have the requisite tools – living and otherwise – to hand."

"Then this is *godspower*. The energy of the cosmos itself, the foundation of the world. *That's* why I can't touch it."

Finally, she saw him look down. He knelt, and studied the Coin carefully.

"So it is," he said. "Godspower, that is. Though, to be fair, there is more than one kind of god, and more than one kind of power they wield. However, in your sense, yes, that's exactly what this is." His strange blue eyes, similar to, yet different than, those of Aunt Victoria or the Watchland, held her gaze. "But have you yet looked upon *yourself*?"

"Myself...?"

"It is often said that self-knowledge is the most difficult, yet most important, goal," the Wanderer said. "So, mage... look to thyself."

She blinked, then looked down, focusing her attention not on the Coin, but on the hand that held it.

Slowly she became aware that there was *light* playing about her hand, *within* her hand, moving and flowing. She moved her hand, tensed it, but the flow was uninterrupted. Then she thought of summoning light, casting a spell through her hand and will... and the luminescence coalesced, directed itself, concentrated within the faint tracery of flesh that it now almost completely obscured... and then flowed away, returned to slow and rippling flickers as she shifted her will elsewhere.

It was... beautiful. Rivulets of liquid, shimmering fire of all colors, infinitely divided as they circulated through her like blood of the sun. And gradually, she became aware that there were *boundaries* to the flow, but not the boundaries of her flesh; the energies played about her, flaring up, dying down, sometimes within, sometimes without... but always constrained, never going beyond a certain point that might waver like ripples on a shore but always remained, as did the shore itself.

And there! At that insubstantial edge, the faintest of glints, a shine of glassy perfection...

"I... I have *godspower*?"

"In a sense, we all do," the Wanderer said, quietly. "Look closer."

The malleable shell of power was almost invisible. But she focused more upon it, *willing* it to be more visible. *That is part of me. I can see it – I* will *see it!*

The veriest *touch* of mist rose, making the ephemeral just a breath more *real*, and now there were glints, sparks as distant as the faintest stars, twinkling gold and silver and blue... "Those... those are the colors of *Myrionar*!"

"And whence, then, the power of the gods?" the Wanderer said. "From those who believe in them, who hold them up, who give them their faith. Thus, the most powerful of all wizards are those who can reach in and turn to their own hands the power of the soul itself, for *that* is the essence of godspower. You are of Evanwyl, a faithful child of the God of Justice and Vengeance, and Myrionar's mark is upon you. You are *connected* to Myrionar, in ways you do not even know."

She slowly raised her head to stare at him incredulously. "We all... have godspower?"

"The gods have *more* power. They have the faith, the worship, the *will* of their believers. But the power of the soul is the very foundation of all power – and a soul that is a true mage's? There is nothing truly beyond anyone like *that*, if they understand what they are doing, what needs to be done." He gestured, and she saw more clearly the Coin and the shell of power about it, a structure she had not before perceived. "Look at it. Look at yourself. And then remember that you are a *wizard*, and choose the way in which the world will walk."

She swallowed hard, but turned her attention to that structure.

It was a brilliant design, she saw at once – a matrix of power that reinforced itself, that would direct its strength against any pressure. Pushed on all sides, the very force of the push would be brought against the one seeking to crush it.

By comparison, her own soul's manifestation was chaotic, bubbling and frothing and moving constantly, so that its best defense was that it moved out of the way and returned; to fight it was like fighting water, while to fight the Coin's enchantment was to attempt to crush a diamond without flaw. Perhaps it might be worn away over the ages, but she didn't *have* forever. For all she knew, Auntie and Ingram and Quester were already being stalked.

Without flaw?

She realized that this was the key. If the structure of the spell was truly without flaw, it would be nearly impossible to break. But surely nothing could be perfect. There must be some faint difference, an irregularity, tiny as a mote of dust perhaps, but *something*, the place where the crystal had finally come together, the stitch that connected one side to the other, *something*.

She called on her own power, and saw both spirit and magic congealing, becoming ordered, a swirling vortex of glassy fire. And there; about the Coin, the merest *hint* of a pattern within the matrix, a swirl. It was there. She knew it *had* to be there... so it was. She muttered words only half-remembered, half-known, but she felt her will *catch*, snag on the fabric of magic and power that lay about her, and she *willed* that flaw larger, visible, a seam, a nigh-invisible plane along which it might – just might – be breached.

Her heart was beating fast, and distantly she was aware she was gasping for breath, sweat trickling down her face, as she attempted to dissipate energies she had never imagined before. But that was far away, irrelevant, for she could *see* it now, and she *wrenched* at reality once more and focused her energies, called for a blade and struck the enchantment once, twice—

There was a detonation that threw her half across the room. Stinging of something on both cheeks and above her brow, and she lay, stunned and exhausted, on the cold, polished stone. Slowly she raised her eyes.

Where the Coin had been was the sparkle of dust, sifting back to earth.

"Well done," the Wanderer said.

***

"Well, you *are* a Shaper, sure enough, and a strong one, too," the Wanderer said a few moments later, as he caused the remnants to disperse and opened the circle. "The enchantment is broken; the remaining Coins will just be regular coins now."

"You say that as though you're surprised," Urelle said.

"Because I am. Oh, pretty much *every* kind of magic-slinger does *some* Shaping, some tampering with the basic laws of the universe, but it's *hard* to do. Takes willpower, takes a certain strength and resilience of spirit, takes having a lot of... *connection* with the essential forces of the universe. Inborn talent for magic, one might say. Ultimately, most mages end up being only a *little* bit Shaper and mostly something else."

"How do you mean that?" Urelle knew some of the theory, but having the Wanderer explain it would probably clarify things – or at least give her perspective on how *he* viewed magic.

"Summoners use their little Shaping to open the ways and contact things to be summoned, to bind or reward, stuff like that," the Wanderer said. "Elementalists, to seek out, trigger, and direct the elemental forces. Symbolists use it to connect with the underlying reservoir of mortal faith – tapping directly the stuff that feeds the gods, in a way – based on what symbols mean to themselves and others."

He gestured, brought a cup from a nearby bench to his hand, drank a bit before he resumed. "Spirit Mages and Necromancers cheat by using the energy of souls or spirits directly. Channelers call on higher, or lower, powers and their Shaping is mostly just to resist the damage of becoming someone else's pipeline to power. Alchemists use it to call forth the essence of material substances and collect and combine it. And so on."

He studied her. "A *true* Shaper, they're really rare. Someone who gets their effects by directly revising the operation of the Universe? Believe me, that's not just rare, it means you're someone with a hell of a lot of will." He grinned. "Really, how much gall does it take to basically tell *the entire universe* 'no, I don't like the way you operate, change it for my convenience?'"

She laughed. The Wanderer wasn't anything like she'd imagined, and she was always finding herself being balanced between disappointment and amazement with him. "So, what you're telling me is that I'm one of the most egotistical people in the universe?"

His blue eyes twinkled. "When you need to be, anyway."

"Is it good that I'm a Shaper? I mean, for what you were talking about before?"

He nodded slowly, smile fading. "It's... crucial. Understand, I *am* unique in this world. In all worlds, so to speak. There are elements of who and what I am that I literally *cannot* pass to anyone else, no matter how hard I try. But for those I *can*, well, I am a Shaper. In some ways, I am *the* Shaper – there's tricks I can pull off that even Idinus can't manage, and he's been at this game a *hell* of a lot longer than I have. Only a Shaper can learn the really useful tricks I have to pass on, and there's not many I can trust." He nodded slowly. "You, I can trust."

"Why? I mean... it would be wonderful to have a chance to learn what you can teach, but you've known me only a few days."

"I know your *family*, though. Remember how old I am, though I'm pretty good at hiding it. The Vantages have been trustworthy for generations. And you – sister of Kyri? I can't explain it all yet, that'll be for you and her later on. But I can trust you with it... with some of the secrets, with some of what's to come."

He looked down at the table before them. It glowed like a sheet of glass illuminated from below, and the Wanderer had shown that he could make notations on it with finger, staff, or even just his own focused will, notations that might remain for days, or be erased at a gesture. Currently, it was covered with the wizard's cryptic notes about her own work and capabilities.

"You've already started to get a good handle on what I call *mobility* magics – letting yourself travel faster or in different ways. This kind of magic is conceptually similar even if its effects – flight, running faster, or even teleportation – are very different, indeed. Of course, you can approach some of them from completely different conceptual angles and derive quite divergent spell designs for them. For instance, teleportation can also be derived from attempts to control the... hmm... nature of distance and/or time."

"You can *do* that?"

"Oh, certainly. Other spells can be done that way, too. For instance, let's take your Airwing. That's basically, in my own home parlance, a magical emulation of a powered hang glider. You've got a force construct that essentially rides the air, and a bit more of your power that sort of pushes it along, so you can guide yourself and stay in the air.

"Now, much better would be a real flight spell. One way to do that would be to refine the Airwing – make your supporting force construct a better, more streamlined wing, and then make the equivalent of a jet engine to propel it along." At her puzzled glance, he went on, "Oh, yeah. Jet engine. Easiest way to describe it is that it takes in air and channels it through a narrow orifice, using something to compress the air and make it go very fast as it leaves. For a mechanical version, you use fire – I'll leave the details for way later, if you're really curious – and for a magical version you could do it several ways.

"Anyway, the fancier way of doing flight would be to manipulate distance directly; you make an enchantment that controls your distance from the ground reference, and that shortens or extends your distance from targets along your line of flight."

Urelle blinked. "But that's *impossible*. Distance is distance. If I'm a mile away from something, I can't make myself half a mile from it unless I actually *go* there."

"Ahh, with magic there is *so* very little that is actually impossible. Here's my favorite analogy." He pulled out a flat sheet of something she thought was rubber. "Here," he said, gesturing and putting a blue dot and a silver dot on the sheet. "How far apart are these dots?"

She studied them. "About three inches?"

"More or less." His hands grabbed the sheet, gripped, and pulled, stretching it to more than three times its former size. "How far apart are the dots?"

"They're... about nine or ten inches apart. But that's not the same as changing distance!"

"It's *exactly* the same, when you realize that what we call distance and existence is predicated on... well, a *foundation* that may not be as *material* as my little sheet here, but is very much as *real*. Space – the phenomenon that allows stuff to exist – has its own structure, and it can be manipulated, too. That's one of the basic keys of being a Shaper; you can manipulate not just things *in* our space, but the nature of the very space we exist in."

The concept was... difficult to grasp. But it made sense, in a way. Just as you couldn't make a painting without a canvas, there must be some underlying reality that would act as the canvas of all substance. "You can really do that?"

He bowed – and suddenly he was all the way across the broad extent of the laboratory. Then he was next to her, and without so much as a breath he was again on the far side of the room, and once more appeared standing before her in his original position. "Yes," he said.

She stared. "How? Teleportation's suppressed! And... that wasn't the explanation I had heard for teleportation, anyway."

"*Long-range* is certainly dangerous – in several ways. It's *much* harder to interfere with short-range teleportation. And yes, there's other common methods – making some kind of a resonance link between *here* and *there* so that you can choose being either place. But those *particular* little jumps were space-warps." He took the rubber sheet up again, bent the sheet until the silver and blue dots touched. "Like this."

She stared for a moment. "Can you teach me *that*?"

"That and more, yes. Movement, swift and unstoppable. Defenses, nigh-impenetrable; attacks to give even the most powerful opponents pause; spells to mend and destroy, ways to analyze the nature of matter and even change it to your need. I'll give you the essence of all of these, and enough to help you continue your exploration of magic on your own."

He grinned again and winked. "Of course, you're not going to match *me* for a while, but hey, that'll give you a target to aspire to. You *have* learned some of the basics already, and you're used to pitting your will against the stubbornness of the universe. That's really going to help."

The young face – that still managed, somehow, to look very old on occasion – became grave. "And honestly? You're going to need it. I don't know exactly *what* is going on in Aegeia, but if Ares has somehow gone rogue... that's really, really bad. You'll need every advantage you can get."

"Can't you... well, help us? Directly, I mean."

To her surprise, he didn't immediately refuse. Instead, he bit his lip, looking into the distance, and twirled the Staff of Stars absently for several long moments. Finally, he sighed. "I don't know."

"You don't *know* if you could help us?"

"Really, no, I don't."

"That... prophecy-thing again?"

"Yes." He looked hard at her; she had a feeling he was analyzing her down to the last hair. For a long time, he was silent.

At last, he nodded – to himself, she thought – and spoke. "Here's the situation – as much as I can tell you. Something *very* bad is going to happen to me, and not all that long from now. What happens after that isn't going to be good at all, but it'll be worse if I can't set up ways to counter it – to at least make a provision that it *can* be countered someday."

That *was about as clear as solid rock*, she thought, but didn't say anything.

He sighed. "At the same time, I *know* I have other things that I have to accomplish – things I *will* do, after that – which aren't possible if that bad thing happens."

She chewed on that. "So, you're saying the prophecy says *both* that this terrible thing will happen to you – the one you're preparing for – and that at the same time, you'll also be just fine?"

"Near as I can make out from the information I'm given, yes. The bad thing happens, takes me out of the picture, basically... but at the same time, there's two other events I'm going to *have* to be present for. And maybe a couple others – it's vague at points. See, if you time-travel, you have to be *really* sure that you're telling people only what they're *supposed* to know – what will properly close the time-loop – and no more, because the last thing you want to do is cause things to divert from your known history."

"Um... explain that?"

He sighed. "I'll try. Imagine... imagine that I'm living in a future where a big bad god's taken over Zarathan. But I can time-travel back, and I know that if I tell someone, say my younger self, about how it happened, that he can then *stop* the big bad god from taking over. Okay?"

She nodded. "Okay, yes. I understand that. You go back and tell yourself, maybe, some vulnerability of the bad god, so you or someone can kill him before he gets too strong."

"Exactly. But now what happens? There's no conquest by the big bad god, so everything's fine. But then I don't have a reason to go warn myself, because it never happened. But then if I *don't* warn myself, past-me won't know about the vulnerability, so the big bad god *will* take over, so then I *do* have a reason to warn myself..." he looked at her and grinned.

Urelle knew her face was wrinkled with painful concentration. "*Ugh*! It's like the conquest *has* to happen, and *can't* happen, at once!"

"That's called a time paradox, and they can give you a real headache. Anyway, the solution is that, since the past-me who was given the information about the bad god knows how he got it, and knows what happens if he *didn't* get it, when past-me gets to the right part of his timeline, *he* goes back in time and tells his past-self *exactly* the same thing that he was told. It has to be *exact* because if he says anything different, there's a chance that his past-self will do or think something different."

She considered that. "All right. So, what you're saying is that your... source, the one telling you parts of your future, is telling you only, and exactly, what it knows you *were* told... from their point of view in the future."

"Perfect! And you're mastering the twistiness of time-travel pretty well. So, yes. They *can't* tell me certain things. Apparently, I have to figure out this paradox on my own."

"Well... could you time-travel forward, do the things you're supposed to do afterward *before* the bad thing happens, even if they're after? If... that makes any sense?"

He crossed his eyes and made a ridiculous face; she couldn't help laughing. "It does make sense, actually. But... I don't like it. Messing with time is *always* dangerous. Even prophecy, which is just *seeing* through time, and often only to *possibilities*, not certainties, is treacherous and often self-fulfilling. Actually, traveling into the future to make sure the future happens... that's even worse than doing the travel-into-the-past loop thing."

He flipped out his hand; a sheaf of paper appeared there. "Study those while I think about this."

"Those" turned out to be some pretty complex magical concepts – discussing things like how to protect, or how to influence, other people's minds. The "protect" part was appealing, but the idea of directly... well, changing the way people thought? That felt *wrong*. But, she supposed, understanding how it was done probably helped in defending against it.

And by the Balance, this was diving into the understanding deep. "Disrupting or confusing immediate, surface thoughts is, of course the easiest of the mind-affecting approaches... delusions and hallucinations can be produced, though the latter are very difficult to tailor to a specific appearance and effect; if such control is needed, exterior illusions are preferred... temporary loss or changing of memory is relatively straightforward, if the precise nature and boundaries of the target memories are known and there is sufficient access to the subject's mind... While in combat, quick-and-dirty memory modification can cause the subject to lose track of key players... if simple actions are required, it is often easier to take direct control of the motor functions rather than attempt to overwhelm the subject's will and direct their mind... long-term memory loss or modification is extremely challenging... the soul retains all memories... tend to return under appropriate stress...

"She realized, sometime later, that her eyes were grainy and she had re-read the same passage three times. Looking up, she saw the clock just above her worktable showing two hours past nightfall. *Myrionar's Balance, I've been studying for almost six hours?*

She got up, and her stiffness told her that she had, indeed, been sitting there that long. After the initial pain, though, it felt good to stride down the hallway and up the stairs to the small dining room and kitchen that the Wanderer was using for the two of them.

As she came in, she saw he was there, brooding over the remains of his own meal. He raised his head, and she suddenly shivered as she saw the drawn, pale face with its unnaturally blue eyes, eyes whose gaze now locked onto hers.

"I think I have found the answer," he said, with echoes of fear that set her own heart racing. "And I will need your help to achieve the impossible."

Chapter 26
Sacrificing a Hero

"Where are you taking me, General?" Artemisia Igemon asked curiously, her arm still comfortably through his.

"Ah, my love," he said with a smile, "let it be a surprise."

In the past few weeks, the relationship between the great General Aloysius and Lady Artemisia had gone from rumors to actuality. Raiagamor was mildly amused by how easy it had been; apparently, he was playing Aloysius very convincingly as a still-human Ares, and that was attractive to a number of people – not the least being his skilled, powerful, and ambitious right-hand sub-general.

Playing a lover was, of course, tedious and dangerous work, as hitting all the right emotional notes when one did not feel them in the slightest – and when some were, indeed, antithetical to one's actual self – was taxing in the extreme, and it was far too easy to make a single tell-tale slip. "Love" was not a word generally in the vocabulary of the Great Wolves, and there, Raiagamor and his half-brethren were very similar. He supposed he loved his mother in some fashion, and she him, but that was an emotion far, far removed from the cloying and intensely *altruistic* emotion that humans often meant by the term.

Fortunately, the time for that pretense was nearly over. They had passed through one of the concealed doors in the high temple and were descending into tunnels hewn from the living rock of the hill. Artimisia Igemon had a role to play of her own... but he very, very much doubted she would do it of her own will.

That was, of course, the reason they were approaching the Swarm-Heart. The *Xiilistiin* could solve *this* problem very neatly. "Free will" was merely a minor challenge for them to surmount, after all.

"Now, close your eyes a moment," he said as Aloysius. "Keep them closed until I say, all right?"

"As long as it isn't some juvenile prank," she answered, but closed her long-lashed eyes anyway, smiling faintly.

"I assure you, no prank. I believe you'll be... astounded." It was a great effort *not* to smile, *not* to let a trace of irony, sarcasm, or eagerness beyond that of a kind and affectionate man for his beloved taint his words.

"All right."

A few more steps brought them to the great door, which opened at his touch.

Before them stretched an immense chamber, a hundred fifty yards across. In the center was a... structure, an interwoven, organic-crystalline webwork that reached from the floor to the ceiling, sixty feet up, that flickered and glowed and pulsed with green and yellow and orange light, chasing up and down the numberless strands and then bursting into the ovoid shape in the center of the web. Some strands stretched most of the way across the entire chamber. This was the Nexus, the Swarm-Heart of a Xiilistiin Swarm.

But most of the chamber was given to the Xiilistiin themselves.

A few of the creatures were very human or humanoid in appearance, those who had taken the shape and knowledge of a target human. But they were in the vast minority, as most of those with a human shape had had theirs refined to meet even the most exacting examination and then set to work undermining Aegeia according to the grand plan.

The rest wore their true forms; viciously slender shapes with triangular, large-eyed heads, with a stabbing chitinous beak above a ripping mouth, mantis-like arms curled up, ready to strike, smaller, claw-fingered arms folded beneath the first, rounded abdomens trailing slightly behind and supported by two legs that were bent in readiness to spring. Vestigial, useless wings sat high up on the shoulders of the creatures.

Several stood near the doorway, in readiness; Deimos was with them, his gaze sharper, more focused, than it had been but a short time ago, and a deadly smile played about his lips.

Raiaga prepared to shift his grip to a come-along. "Now you can open—"

Artimisia's arm twisted, her body swayed sideways and back, and he suddenly found himself spun about into the wall. He grunted and turned—

AGONY!

Something ripped through his side, transfixing him from left to right, passing directly through his heart. His chest burned; he let out a coughing snarl of pain, even as power flared nearby and the air hissed with the sound of a hundred arrows.

Vision clouding, he felt himself caught up, hurled back through the air; he tumbled across the stone and heard the heavy door swing to, a mutter of magical phrases that he recognized as an efficient sealing spell. Finally, he blinked his vision clear against the searing pain (*by the King, there's* silver *in whatever this is!*) and managed to see where he was.

He lay on the floor of the hallway, the door to the Swarm-Heart closed and sealed. Artemisia stood over him, her olive face a shade paler and grim, with her bow drawn and aimed at his head.

He wasn't sure whether to snarl or laugh; it seemed that his pretense had not, after all, been good enough.

"I *knew* there was something wrong with you, Ares, but... what *is* that place? What are those *things*? You might as well tell me, before you die."

"D... die?" He spoke the word as though forcing it out past pain and the approach of death; in truth, while it was not *lethal*, it was terribly painful, and there was little effort in the act.

"As soon as you began implying a romantic opportunity, I became suspicious. I was able to deliver secret messages to Amoni Agapis, and the Hammer of Hephaestus delivered me a god-slaying arrow."

We corrupted the wrong God-Warrior of Hephaestus first, I suppose. And she tells naught but truth; the King-damned thing is *trying to rip my essence apart. If she knew what I* actually *was, she would have succeeded in killing me!*

"Well... played," he said, in the pained voice of the General. He needed time – time to deal with this arrow, time for the Xiilistiin to break the enchantment and open the door, or for Deimos to do it himself. He didn't think Artemisia had anything worse to attack him with... but then, he hadn't thought she'd had any intention of attacking him at all. "I had... no suspicion—"

"Talk quickly!" She glanced at the door. "I have no doubt they'll be through fairly soon, though that's a powerful seal I've made."

Inwardly he shrugged. Telling her would take at least a bit of time, and it wasn't as though he had any intention of letting her get away to talk. "The creatures... are called *Xiilistiin*. They are an," he took a pained breath, "exceedingly *useful* species. Functional in and of themselves, but... with a particular talent to take the essence of another being and make use of it. Even, with assistance, to become a perfect duplicate of the original."

While he spoke, he concentrated his power on the Arrow of Hephaestus. *A deadly work indeed, God-Warrior, and against what you thought I was... it would have worked. Would have slain anything not-god, and severely injured and banished Ares himself to his own realm.*

But against the Hunger of our people? Insufficient. Methodically and swiftly, his power began to unmake and consume the Arrow.

Artemisia's face was twisted with revulsion. "And you? You are one of them, a false Ares?"

He chuckled, and felt the Arrow's power break in the same instant. "A false Ares, yes. One of *them*?" He rose to his feet, ripping the Arrow's shaft from his body. "Far, far worse than that, Sub-General."

She saw the transformation beginning, and – to her credit – spent not an instant gaping in disbelief, horror, or shock. Instead, the arrow she had held ready ripped into his chest and she sprinted like the wind itself back up the corridor, hurling a handful of fire-caltrops behind to slow pursuit.

She knows her only hope is to reach a public place, where she can denounce me, and I cannot kill her without effectively confirming her claims. The thought was filled with a frisson of amusement and hunger.

At his full height now, he lunged after her, neither arrow nor flames nor mystic-steel spikes slowing him in the least; she had gone less than a hundred and fifty yards before he streaked past her and stopped, arms spread wide with glittering claws barring her way.

Again, she showed why General Artimisia Igemon was one of the most feared and deadly warriors in all Aegeia; without so much as a beat of wasted emotion or movement at his horrific speed and appearance, she dropped into a slide, going *beneath* him and cutting upward simultaneously, driving her sword straight into his groin.

It *was* painful, he admitted, for there was *silver* in that blade, and the fact that it couldn't kill him did not in any way reduce the burning, hateful agony. But he kept his smile and shifted front-to-back, catching her even as she tried to roll to her feet. "A brilliant and most devastating blow, my General," he said, and struck the sword from her hand with a negligible expenditure of force. "But your intelligence was, alas, faulty, and your weapons of no use against me."

A *third* time she did the right thing; wrenched one arm from his grip (since he was not, after all, trying to kill her, he couldn't hold so tightly as he might) and in a single motion ripped a javelin from the quiver on her back and drove it straight into his left eye.

He laughed, for *this* weapon was neither god-killer nor silvered doom, merely highly enchanted. "How very ungrateful," he said, and threw her back down the corridor – to be caught by a dozen of the Xiilistiin and Deimos, who had just unsealed the door.

"Un*grateful?*" she snarled – anger failing to mask her rising terror. "What would there be to be *grateful* for?" She struggled mightily against the insectoid creatures, but each was nearly as strong as she; a dozen of them held her easily, and two of them began to extrude strings of resin which would bind her. Deimos released her once it became clear she could no longer free herself.

He raised an eyebrow in mock surprise. "Why, your imminent promotion, Artemisia," he said, smiling broadly while casting aside the javelin, his eye unmarked, undimmed.

"What 'promotion?'"

"You," he said, following the group as they moved towards the glowing, pulsing Swarm-Heart, "are about to become the Lady of Wisdom incarnate."

Now, at last, horror conquered confidence and anger and hate, and he restrained a shiver of pleasure at seeing the warrior breaking, at *tasting* her realization of not merely helplessness, but a doom worse than she had imagined. "What... how?"

"Not the *true* Athena, naturally," he said, and touched her cheek with one long, sparkling claw, drawing out the smallest, headiest fragments of spiritual dread, tasting each as carefully and with the same focused pleasure as any connoisseur. "I have no use for her, and indeed I've done everything in my power to make sure she will never acquire a new vessel. But I *did* slay Ares and take *his* power."

Now she broke in truth, for his words were a stroke against the foundation of their faith – the eternity of the Gods and Cycle. "No. No, you couldn't—"

"Oh, I could and did, little mortal warrior," he said, mirth echoing through every word. "In his very chambers, I slew him, and he had the same stupid shock on his face as *you* do, now. He couldn't believe it, couldn't *understand* how he had been so outmaneuvered." The giggle that escaped him at the memory was filled with malice and glee – and perhaps, he might have admitted, a touch of madness. "Ares is *gone*, unless another be created out of whole belief and focus – but so long as I exist, any worship of 'Ares' must pass to *me*."

She fell silent, eyes wide with defeat and dismay and loathing.

"And so, you understand, after my allies have taken all you are and were, then I will complete the transformation with some of Ares' own power, make the new 'you' a god in seeming well enough to fool even the other gods, if they come not too close, study you overmuch." His smile widened, the Nexus' light reflecting green-touched rainbow from his crystal teeth to her sweating, stunned face.

With a supreme effort, she ripped one arm free of the twining, not yet hardened resin and the clinging arms that had, just slightly, relaxed their grip; her hand came up holding a razor-edged dagger – and drove it straight towards her own eye.

Had he not sensed the peak of her resolve in the very instant it was formed, Artemisia Igemon would have succeeded. As it was, the dagger's tip *did* plunge into her eye before he caught her arm and stopped the sharp steel blade from continuing straight into her brain. She gave a cry of double agony, the loss of her eye the less compared with the knowledge of her final failure.

"Marvelous," he breathed. "Oh, Artemisia, your spirit will be *strong* within the Xiilistiin, and you will play a *magnificent* Athena!"

The last he saw of Artemisia was the look of incandescent hatred and nauseating loss as she was dragged into the glowing heart of the nexus.

Chapter 27
How to Fight Your Evil Twin

"You are going to trust *me* to erase your memories?" she said, fear and incredulity equal in her heart.

The Wanderer bowed his head. "I have... little choice."

"Little *choice*?! You know... *everyone!* Or at least everyone knows *of* you! You could have Idinus himself do it, or Phantasm of the Crystal Tower, or Calladan, the head of the Adventurer's Academy, or—"

He shook his head. "No. Or rather, yes, I *could* ask those, or others, to do the work. But some of them... some I dare not allow a look into my head, even if I know they are essentially benevolent. There are things I know that such practitioners simply *could not miss* if they could be allowed such free access to my mind, even a duplicate. Others would insist on knowing too much about the whys and wherefores. Almost *all* of them, though, *cannot* know the one key thing they'd *have* to know in order to do the job correctly."

Urelle bit her lip. "You mean... that there *is* a duplicate."

"Exactly. If... what I suspect is to happen... happens, there must not be the *slightest* suspicion that I've made prior arrangements, let alone that there is a fully-capable duplicate of myself in existence, even for a short time. My... current course is known to a few people, and suspected by a few more. If even the smallest hint were visible, if there were the slightest suspicion that I'd visited any such people *now* without a very, very clear necessity, I'd be able to tell that I'd diverted *somehow* from my normal behavior."

She thought that through – especially the last sentence – and a slow, dawning horror oozed into her thoughts. "You're... you're saying that *you* are the enemy you're trying to fight?"

He froze, then lowered his face into both palms. "Oh, dear *God*, I did blow the secret there, didn't I?" he muttered, voice muffled but still understandable through his hands. The Wanderer sat there a few moments, unmoving.

Finally, he dropped his hands and sat up straight. "Well, now, I guess I can stop tapdancing and get straight to the point. Maybe that was my subconscious telling me I didn't have time for that Khoros-like bullshit. He was always better than all of us at it; I shouldn't try so hard.

"Yes, that's *exactly* what I was saying," he said firmly. "Something – I don't know what exactly, or how – is going to hit me in a way that will... rrgh, how to put it... *invert* me. Maybe it'll bring out all my most repressed subconscious desires, or somehow flip my moral compass or whatever, but the ultimate result is going to be that the Wanderer is going to be a very, very bad guy for a while. And how long 'a while' is, I don't know."

The very thought terrified her. In the two weeks she'd been there, she'd gained some vague idea of what the Wanderer was capable of – and it seemed every bit as much as legends and books claimed, though he often tried to downplay his capabilities.

The thought of that power turned *against* the world... "Can't you just prevent it? Go somewhere else that this event can't happen?"

"Time-paradox is a dangerous thing. If I evade this, there's any number of disasters that could come out of it, some of them possibly worse than having mirror-universe Me running around, even if I *would* look terrible in a goatee." She let the opaque reference – so common in his conversation – pass by; she thought she could get the basic sense of it.

He was looking at her expectantly. Accordingly, she thought about not just the current conversation but everything that had led up to it, and slowly she started to make real sense out of what he was doing. "This... duplicate. *That's* the one that's going to be turning."

"Right."

She thought about what he'd said about the other, more powerful people. "I won't be able to know *what* other things to look for in your head," she said finally. "So, I *might* come across something I shouldn't know, but I'll have less chance of having the context to make that knowledge dangerous to you, or me."

"Right. To an extent, the very... unlikeliness of the idea that I would have someone so young do something so delicate will protect you from having anyone even suspect you had the chance to learn any of the big secrets."

She thought she had the idea now. "So, you're going to build a... a *vulnerability* into the duplicate. So that when that-you breaks, the other-you can beat him easily, and…"

Urelle trailed off as she saw him shaking his head. "Not that simple, unfortunately. Whichever *me* exists, unless I make actual changes to the *personality*, he'll be careful to check himself for any off-market modifications, so to speak. I don't dare try changing the personality; that's *far* too complex to even attempt without a few dozen years to work on it, so I'll have to be *way* more subtle than that.

"And you should note that in neither case am I going to be stupid; whenever it happens, the bad-guy Wanderer isn't going to suddenly glow with black power, grow an evil-looking beard, and start laughing like a cheap play villain – even if he thinks it would look kinda cool. He'll keep *acting* like the original until he can go somewhere else and start contemplating how to address the world with his... new perspective. So, he's not an *immediate* threat, even to, say, people traveling with him. They may not even notice a change."

"So, what *is* the point of the duplicate?"

"You're right in that I want to give the real-me an advantage – but it has to be a very low-key one. I can't give him, oh, an expiration date. My source – coy as it is – made it fairly clear that the bad-me is going to stick around until someone – which may somehow be me, but can't be me at the same time, *thank you so much cloudy oracles* – manages to arrange his destruction."

He looked broodingly at his Staff. "So, the only solution I can see is to modify what I know *subtly*. Remove a few key pieces of knowledge wholesale, make edits in really specific areas of memory, and so on. That includes modifying his memory of exactly what *we* did here to fit with what I've been teaching you, minus this rather important bit of work. Basically, I want to remove a few *really* devastating weapons from his arsenal – ones I haven't used, so they're not hooked into events that have lots of background that can't be hidden, and most importantly, remove any memory that *I knew he was coming*. If he suspects I knew, well, he'll know – none better! – what I'd have done, and then that'll be that."

"But he still couldn't remember what you hid from him, right?"

The Wanderer wobbled his hand side to side. "One wouldn't think so. But the problem is that memories aren't just etched into your brain; they're engraved into your *soul*. Editing a soul? That's not just hard, that's *crazy*-hard work. Konstantin

Khoros could do it. Idinus, probably. Me and you? What we're going to have to do is... well, *fog* the soul's impressions. They can't be completely eradicated, especially since... well, *I* – the good guy – have to retain the memories."

"But won't you be separate?" This was steadily getting more confusing, but Urelle wasn't going to give up. The Wanderer had a real, true plan that somehow involved *her*, and there was no way, not by the Balance itself, that she was going to fail him.

The shrug of the shoulders was eloquent. He beckoned for her to follow, as he led her out of the laboratory. "We really *can't* be separate, not on the level of the soul. That's one of the big, tricky parts of this – on which I'll be doing the heavy lifting, don't you worry! My *nature* – the one that makes me immune from almost all destinies, or at least with a way out of them – has to do with exactly who and what I am, and that goes all the way down to the uniqueness of my soul. So, my duplicate and I will have to share a soul; some of mine will have to be incorporated into his."

She looked at him narrowly. "I can't imagine that he couldn't detect that if he wanted."

"Of *course* he could. Which is why it's deadly important that he never thinks to *look*, at least not for, oh, a year or three. After that, it won't matter."

"I thought you didn't know how long he—"

"I don't. But what I *do* know is what events the current-me has to be involved in after his creation. Once those are *done*, fine, he can find out the truth. He won't be able to affect what I've done, what *had* to happen, once we're past that point."

"I'm still confused, though. Why do you need *me* – or anyone, really – to help you? You're going to have this separate 'you' that you're doing the work on, surely that's the safest of all? *You* do the erasing, *you* already know everything, so you aren't even *possibly* a, what, security risk? So—"

The Wanderer nodded and gave an explosive sigh. "Naturally, that *does* make sense. Except that I'm... too close to the problem, so to speak. I'm *directly* connected to any part of my own soul, and he'll have to have a pretty darn big chunk if he's going to act like me and think he *is* me without finding internal limits right away that will trip off all *kinds* of warning bells. It's like... like..." He paused, brow furrowed deeply in thought.

After a few moments, he nodded and went on. "It's like you're trying to mold clay in absolute, lifelike detail, while you hold the big, heavy chunk of clay in your other hand. Your fingers holding it make impressions. Every vibration of *either* hand changes the angle or heaviness of every stroke of a tool or press of a finger.

"But if you put the clay on a sturdy, stable surface, suddenly it's a hundred times easier. The clay can be turned, shaped, carved while staying always in the same position. What you do only affects the clay when you *want* it to."

Urelle pursed her lips, then nodded unwillingly. "You're so connected to your own soul that you'd be disrupting your own very delicate attempts to... edit your memories, implant new ones, and such. And memories being so delicate to begin with..."

"...even a very *tiny* mistake by me would be magnified into something that he really couldn't *help* but notice," the Wanderer finished, tension in every syllable. "So, I can *direct* you. I can give you instructions and procedures and knowledge and all of that. But the actual *work* cannot be done by me, because I'll ruin it by the very *nature* of the work."

She stared at him for a moment. The young-looking face was still drawn, his eyes circled. "This... this really is a terrible plan, you know that?"

"Oh, Urelle, I know." His voice was suddenly very low, and shook. "I know how terrible it is. And how it's still really the only choice I have. I... I *chose* this path, Urelle. I wanted," he paused, and a faint, wondering, sad smile hovered on his lips, "I wanted... to be a hero. To be the Adventurer. And this is where that dream led me. If that means I have to risk the entirety of my *self* against the possibility of my becoming the villain of the piece? Then that's what I have to do. You already understand that, I think. You and Ingram and your aunt and Quester."

She closed her eyes and swallowed hard. "Yes. And I understand... you'll have to erase *my* memory, too."

A sad, sympathetic smile. "Yes. So that you haven't an inkling that there's more than one of me, nor be able to guess, or even know you *should* guess, which 'me' you may encounter later."

She looked at the feast laid out on the table as they entered. "I'm not that hungry," she said after a moment.

"Can't blame you. But I can promise you one thing; helping me on this will make you the most formidable young mage possible... and *that* you won't forget, though obviously the *way* you remember it all will be... different. I appreciate you worrying about *me*, but you should be a lot more worried about your own mission."

"I'm not afraid of *that*!" Which was, all things considered, true; compared to the nearly-cosmic threat they'd been talking about, the dangers of Aegeia seemed distant and harmless.

The Wanderer's smile twisted slightly. "You will be," he said, and his voice was oddly higher, cracking slightly like an old man's. "You *will* be."

Chapter 28
The Takers of Nests

"What *can* be keeping her?" Victoria muttered.

"Studies, I presume," Ingram answered, making her jump.

"I hadn't realized... yes, I suppose I *did* speak that aloud," she said, with some chagrin. *You've had six decades to learn to hold your tongue when necessary, Victoria, and now it runs on its own?* "My apologies."

"I'm worried about her, too," Ingram said. "No need to say you're sorry about it. I mean, I'm sure the Wanderer's treating her well, but if she's pushing what she can do, who knows what might happen?"

She glanced up and around, as usual surveying their surroundings to ensure there were no threats. Quester was ahead and above, using his flight and leaping abilities to scout ahead and hopefully prevent any unpleasant surprises. "She had little choice," she admitted. "If we're to be at odds with Ares and his people, we will need all the advantages we can get, and then some. And Urelle will be *most* formidable once she has enough skill; I've seen enough wizards-in-training to recognize a prodigy when I see one."

"While I agree, are you *sure* you're not a little biased?"

A short, swift smile. "I am very much biased in how much I *care* for her, but I would like to think that I am capable of separating that from an evaluation of her *capability*."

"Spoken like a Camp-Bel, by the Wisdom!" Ingram grinned at her and did a walking bow. "But I admit, I'm wondering what's going on. It's been four *weeks*."

"None too much for imparting someone knowledge gained over centuries, I suppose." Victoria knew she was reassuring herself as much as Ingram.

A swish and buzz of wings warned them as Quester dropped from above. "We may be in danger," he said, even as his clawed feet dug into the ground upon landing. "There are significant forces ahead, strung out across our path, no more than a half-mile or so distant. I had to maintain distance, so at the moment I can say little about their nature, but there were scouts spread wide; I have no idea how far their net is flung, but it would appear to me that we are nearly in its center."

"We could back up and try to go around," Ingram suggested.

"Possible," Victoria said, but even as she did, she felt tension rising, her body preparing for a battle she hadn't even decided upon. "But we do not know *how* this group has found us. If they have more of those damnable Coins, they will be able to see us diverting from the path, and know they are discovered."

"The Wanderer and Urelle surely made breaking *that* spell a priority," Ingram replied.

"Certainly," Victoria agreed, "but priority does not mean success. We cannot *assume* they succeeded."

"Given the presence of this force," Quester said, "I would suspect they had not. Or did not do so right away, thus giving our enemies a chance to find us."

"You say they're about a half-mile away?"

"And closing in."

Victoria sighed. "We must at least attempt to divert. If Urelle *has* broken the spell, we may well avoid confrontation."

"Quiet and careful, then," Ingram said.

Quester ascended into the trees again – where his coloration and skill would make him difficult to detect – while Victoria and Ingram began heading to the west, trying to leave as little trace as possible. *Half a mile... in this terrain, that will take some large fraction of an hour for them to cover, if they are truly searching. Perhaps longer. If we can get out of the range of their scouts...*

That would give them an excellent chance of avoiding the group entirely. Even if their pursuers happened across their last camp, they would do so already most of a day behind, and would be very hard put to catch up – and without the Coins to lead them, their pursuers could not know exactly what line they took, and thus would swiftly pass their ability to cover enough of the jungle to matter.

Victoria focused once more on the Eight Winds, and especially on the Guiding Wind, the Wind of Spring as described by the Northern Masters, gentle and dependable, as delicate as the tread of a leafhopper on a blade of grass and true as the flight of a dragon. Her feet glided noiselessly across the leaf-strewn ground, shuffling when necessary in a pattern that would sound, not like a woman walking, but a small animal, scuttling about its business from one safe spot to the next.

She noted that Ingram was similarly silent. *I must give credit to his clan's trainers, if not to their proper care of his spirit. They have surely given him much skill, especially for one so young. A shame they found it necessary to undermine the very confidence that would have strengthened him most.*

As always, that subject led her to wonder what *had* driven his clan to such a strange, apparently self-defeating course. What had they known or suspected? What about Ingram, or perhaps about the forces that now threatened Aegeia, had made their treatment of him seem sensible?

Ingram froze, and she mirrored him, squinting in the direction of his gaze.

Something moved — something whose coloration and motion blended so well with the background of trees and bushes and leaves that Victoria was not at all sure she would have seen it on her own, without warning. It appeared to be a cloaked, bipedal figure, stalking carefully along in just as silent and cautious a manner as their own. *Advance scout. Sword and Balance, they've constructed an arc ahead.*

The scout had not spotted them yet, however. Its movement would take it *past* them at perhaps thirty yards distance. With the intervening brush, and both of them staying utterly still, it was possible they might still be undiscovered. Victoria willed steadiness and stillness throughout her being, thought of being merely an immobile bush, nothing of consequence. Ingram was so still he seemed not to even be breathing.

The creature moved forward another meter. Two. Ten, and it was coming abreast of them, making its closest approach. Victoria *did* hold her breath then, *willing* it to keep going, to see nothing unusual whatsoever.

It stepped forward. Then another step. Two more, and it was beginning to draw away from them now. *A few dozen yards and we will be well behind it. We will be able to move and open the distance — and then we will be past their scout line—*

She realized *another* form was passing by, this one about twenty-five yards away on the other side. *Another scout. Their line is close-spaced, indeed, for a sweep. Or they have far greater numbers than I would have guessed.*

But that figure, too, was slowly passing them. Ingram remained still as a stone, with her frozen in place a few scant yards away.

And then the first figure stopped. Its head turned, tilted, and it was only then that Victoria realized that the faint breeze of the forest was blowing precisely towards the creature from their direction.

It's forty yards distant. Let it be unsure, let the smell be not enough to—

It let out a keening, trilling shriek, utterly inhuman, piercing, echoing far through the woods with a low-buzzing undertone.

"Ares' *Balls*," Ingram said casually, and without a pause the lavender-haired boy launched himself at the one giving the alarm.

Muttering her own curse, Victoria sprinted for the other nearby figure.

It whirled, quick as light on water, but the thin blade it drew failed instantly before the edge of Victoria's massive axe. The impact drove the creature flat to the ground and the backswing tore the cloak, revealing a triangular, insect-like face with a piercing beak – something she remembered with a chill from decades before. *Great Balance... Xiilistiin!*

And then the forest echoed with a thousand answering trills of hatred and fury.

"Quester, we need somewhere to run!" she shouted to the trees above.

The Iriistiik's answering voice was unsteady, and she understood why; these were his people's constant enemy. "I know. By the *Mother*, who would have expected..." A moment of silence. "I see a possible refuge, or at least a place where we might stand off many times our number! I am showing it to Ingram!"

That link of theirs. Well, that will be useful; not having to describe in words, but show directly, something your partner must know.

Ingram had downed his opponent as swiftly as Victoria; he stood still a moment, as the cries of the other Xiilistiin began to approach, and then nodded sharply. "Follow me, Lady Victoria!"

She ran after the boy, who still managed to keep ahead of her despite her far longer legs. *Either I truly am getting old, or he is just astonishingly good. Or, I suppose, both could be true.*

Ingram dove and rolled, and she barely saw the reason in time to repeat the maneuver – a Huntsman's Doom, a plant that attacked anything taller than a child with harpoon-like vines. *Well, that may momentarily impede any pursuit.*

They drove through a thick patch of brush and Victoria found herself stumbling over tumbled pavement blocks. Before them were more ruins of the sort that were found throughout the Forest Sea. The most important point of *these* ruins, however, was that there was a massive, half-sunken building ahead, its one visible entrance between two narrowly-spaced walls.

"A fine place for a stand," she said, somewhat out of breath as she reached the dimly-lit entrance, "but I hope there is some way out of it behind us, otherwise I do not like our chances."

"That depends on the number and quality of our enemies," Quester said. "But what I heard... does not make me confident." The Iriistiik's antennae were quivering with obvious fear.

"They're not going to get us," Ingram said. "You hear me, Quester? We beat a mob of these things for our qualification test; we can do it here."

Victoria reached into her neverfull pack and withdrew a great indigo-wood bow with a string of woven crystal, and a quiver of arrows. "If you have any weapons with range, let us use those first."

"Naturally." Ingram pulled out a boxy contraption that, after a moment, she identified as a crossbow or other projectile-thrower with some form of ammunition storage incorporated into it. *I remember little Endrei using something like that. My, that was a long time ago.*

Quester, of course, had his throwing spears, though obviously they wouldn't last long if he couldn't recover them. "Here," Ingram said. "Use mine."

"But then what will you—"

"Like Lady Victoria said, we need to know if there's another exit from here, and that means someone has to look. I'm the best for that, with my special equipment and the fact I can fit into smaller places easier."

Victoria exchanged glances with Quester, but she could tell that he had no effective arguments. "Very well, then," she said, "get going. But do not take long."

She spun and released an arrow in a single movement; the Xiilistiin that had just emerged from the forest pitched to the ground without a sound. "Because once they begin a rush, it will be a matter of minutes before they reach us."

"I know." He slid his special goggles over his eyes and darted off into the gloom.

A hiss-buzz combined with a sharp *crack!* noise, and another of the buglike creatures spun and fell, head cut nearly in two; Victoria had been just able to see that the weapon Ingram had given Quester fired thin, sharp spinning discs. "That's quite nasty."

"The *hedri'at*, as Ingram calls it, is, indeed, a vicious weapon." He turned a small crank set in the side of the thing. "As long as tension is maintained in its motive spring, it can fire these discs with great speed and accuracy. One can also do some interesting tricks with it."

"Such as?"

Quester glanced up, where one of their enemies had concealed themselves at the far end of the wall. "This."

He tilted the weapon slightly and fired at an angle away from the wall; a pair of silvery blurs spat out... and *curved around*, to vanish behind the far end of the wall; there was an accompanying high-pitched, buzzing scream.

Victoria felt both of her eyebrows rise. "Shooting around corners? A useful trick, indeed. I cannot say my bow can match that."

There were three... four... six... now many more forms just visible beneath the trees. "Massing for a charge, I think."

Quester shivered. "Yes. Warning: do not allow them to capture you."

"I am familiar with their vile habits, yes. Recall that I was present for the origin of the Adventure on which you were tested."

"Yes, of course."

She squinted, then raised her bow and loosed twice, murmuring the appropriate command. Her arrows kindled into white fire and exploded, scattering several of their adversaries and leaving some of them sprawled and still.

"It appears your bow has its own advantages," Quester said dryly.

"One *does* acquire various useful items over the years," she agreed. "Alas that I cannot do that *all* of the time. My own magical strength is nothing like that of my niece, and that's what's required for that trick."

The deliberately casual banter helped her stay steady, even as the woods began to crawl with Xiilistiin. She had no idea now how many there were. Dozens? A hundred or more? Only the narrowness of the approach to the doorway would reduce the rush. And that assumed none of them could climb up – although the high and still bare dome of polished stone above would make that chancy even for such creatures. Still, if they could run along the top of the walls, that would allow more of them to mob the entrance. None seemed to have thought of that... yet.

"If you can do it a few more times, it will at least keep them back for a bit," Quester said.

"Oh, I can manage several more. But not nearly forever, or even for hours. As Bolthawk would have said," she felt a combination of lost fondness, sadness, and anger at the name of the Justiciar, "it will come down to axe-work soon enough."

"Save a stroke for me," the Iriistiik said, his buzzing voice grim.

"If it comes to that, I shall. But I hope it shall not."

Another screeching trill keened out, and the Xiilistiin paused in their advance. A larger figure stalked into view, broader and taller, its armored body darker, in shades of purple and crimson.

A dismayed hum and odor of a sewer came from Quester. "A Swarmfather."

"Ah. I had never had the pleasure of seeing one before," she said dryly. She had studied enough of the semi-parasitic Xiilistiin to know the implications; a Swarmfather was created by feeding several strong beings to a specific Xiilistiin during some kind of ritual; the result did not become a duplicate of a single being, but instead a single Xiilistiin with vastly increased capabilities, and at least some of the particular talents of each of its... donors. As a rule, they were extremely formidable and highly intelligent – much smarter than their smaller brothers and sisters.

The Swarmfather hummed, and then spoke, in a surprisingly human voice. "Information to those pursued: two of you are not of interest to us. Send out the Iriistiik and we shall depart content."

Well, that's a surprise. Obviously, the Xiilistiin would be interested in destroying any of their ancient enemies, but she had thought that the Xiilistiin were working with their Aegeian enemies, and all indications there were that more than one of their party was the target.

Of course, it could just be lying. If we were willing to sacrifice Quester, we'd have weakened our group drastically, and be that much easier to kill. Since we are not, of course, the question is moot.

She aimed and fired twice, once more muttering the command words, and the Swarmfather vanished momentarily in a double detonation of sun-flame, reappearing as an angular shape tumbling away, trailing smoke. "I believe that makes our position adequately clear," she said, pitching her voice to carry.

The Xiilistiin gave a collective screaming trill of fury and surged out of the woods.

Quester looked at her, head tilted, the cinnamon-cedar smell of startlement clear. "You are most... *direct*, Lady Victoria," he said, unleashing a series of edged discs into the oncoming mob.

"In these situations, it's the best approach. The longer we spoke," she fired another two, normal, arrows and two more of the bug-like people fell, "the more they could take time to consider approaches. They will find their proper strategy, and likely earlier than late, but I would rather it be later. Thus, infuriate them."

"This may result in them overcoming us through no tactics other than sheer numbers." He hid behind the side of the doorway, then popped out to send a storm of edged metal at their opponents.

"Don't despair *yet*, young man," she said, withdrawing one of five little spheres tucked in one of her pouches. "I haven't been an Adventurer for this many decades without collecting quite a few surprises."

She stepped out and pitched the glittering crystal sphere – glowing from within with a ruby-red light – high and straight. It came down within the heart of the mob, and instantly flame blossomed, expanding to a forty-foot sphere of red-gold incandescence, casting aside Xiilistiin like toys, leaving dozens, perhaps a hundred, on the ground, unmoving.

That shocked the Xiilistiin into reconsidering the wisdom of a massed charge; a few stragglers continued the charge – to be mowed down by Victoria's and Quester's withering barrage of sharp steel and pointed arrows – but most withdrew.

"That *did* cost them, Lady Vantage."

"It did, but there are far more of them than I had hoped. It appears they have hundreds, while we are three – and one of our number not immediately available."

"Ingram reports that he has found passages that may lead to an exit. If such is the case, we may wish to collapse this entrance behind us. Do you believe this can be achieved?"

"Without triggering the rest of it to fall on *us*, you mean," she said. "Keep them off while I study the structure, please."

There are the supports for this archway. The wall is also load-bearing, but there are cracks... columns farther back look sturdy enough, so if we were to—

Sound beyond sound lifted Victoria from the floor, threw her twenty feet back; only her long training, and armored clothing, kept the impact from being bone-breaking. As it was, she knew the dull-yet-knifelike pain of crushed or torn muscles. *Concussion blast... have they a mage of some sort? Unfortunately, too likely...*

Quester was picking himself up slowly, but Victoria could already see shadows approaching the doorway through the cloud of dust the blast had created. Ignoring the screaming pain across her back, she drew and fired two more flaming arrows into the mass of figures, saw with a touch of relief that they withdrew. *Myrionar's Sword, we won't survive many more of those, though. Especially in this enclosed space.*

She risked another of the powerful firespheres, throwing it low but fast; it went just far enough so that the raging flame was not channeled into their own doorway. *That should hold them a moment.* "Quester, are you all right?"

Immediately she knew that speaking was useless; she could *feel* her own speech, but nothing but a dull ringing in her ears and very vague impressions of other sounds. Quester had risen but looked unsteady, leaning against the wall. She waved for his attention, pointed to his harness. He nodded and unfastened one of the vials there, drank, as she did the same from one of hers.

Her hearing cleared, though there was still an odd undertone to sound, and most of the pain in her muscles went away. *Magic and alchemy certainly help one recover... if you survive the immediate event.* "Where did that come from?"

"The Swarmfather. Not dead, just injured, and I suspect he has been healed by now."

"Balance's Sword *impale* him," she muttered. She risked a glance out the door; the taller, broadly angular figure of the Swarmfather was just visible in the clearing smoke – and he was just beginning a sequence of gestures. *Now!*

A single arrow hummed outward and caught the Swarmfather in the middle of his invocation. Mystic energies exploded and knotted around him and he gave a piercing shriek of fear, rage, and pain.

"*That* will make him more cautious about casting spells in eyeshot of us," she said with satisfaction.

"So, he will find a better vantage point."

"Likely, but that will take at least a few more minutes. What of Ingram?"

"He is levering open what he believes to be a – *Mother preserve us!*"

"What? *What is it?*"

The Iriistiik's voice was heavy with tension and fear. "The Xiilistiin were waiting just outside! Ingram is fleeing back this way, trying to collapse things behind him, but they are close!"

Another complex set of trills from outside, and she heard and saw the swarm beginning to move. "And they know about it; they must be spread about the entire area." A deep chill was forming in her heart. They were trapped.

And then, from deeper within the building, there was a detonation of golden light that seemed to penetrate the stone itself.

Chapter 29
Amnesia on Demand

Urelle felt gooseflesh marching across her entire body, like an army of ice-coated ants, as she stared down at the still, unconscious face of the Wanderer... and looked up at the alert face of the Wanderer with his narrow half-smile. "He's... really you. I mean... I knew you *said* you would do it, but..."

"I know, it kinda creeps me out, too."

"He doesn't hear us?"

"Nope. I created him and then locked him down into a sleeping stasis, so to speak, and made sure he was temporarily blind and deaf so that he couldn't get accidental input that might interfere. There'll be a little bit of external input from the other senses, but I'm pretty sure it won't be significant as long as the environmental control around him stays comfy." His blue eyes looked sad and worried. "Boy, I hope this works."

"*You* hope it works? If it doesn't work, what's going to happen to *me*?"

"True. You *are* taking a big risk. But I am really pretty confident you can do this. You edited my memory perfectly yesterday."

"That was a *tiny* memory – I just made you think we'd had those things you call BLTs instead of egg-bread and sausages this morning. And you had *told* me to do it, so you were willing and cooperative – I didn't have to fight you over them. And then you remembered the real stuff afterwards!"

"Doesn't *seem* like much, no, but believe me, it was an excellent test. Maybe the most important part of it is, quote, 'the things you call BLTs.' I gave you descriptions and images and sense-inputs, all that kind of thing, and you *gave* me that memory. Perfectly. I remembered the toasted bread, and what kind of bread it *was*, and the bacon – which was thick pepper bacon – and really good tomatoes, which most people on Zarathan haven't even *heard* of. You've never eaten a BLT, but you created a perfect *experience* of it. That's the trickiest part of implanting the memory. Sure, the mind will sort of build its own interpretations on top of its recorded memories, but the record itself has to be really, really good and convincing, or the interpretation will be 'off,' so to speak."

He held up a hand before she could speak. "And to your other points, true, I wasn't resisting, but I don't expect Dupli-Me to resist, either. He's sleeping and unaware, and I've dismantled the built-in defenses. That much I could do on my own. And yes, I remembered the truth afterwards, because we weren't trying to drill it too hard into my soul and you *told* me when it was a false memory, so I could dredge it back up pretty easily. But I still *had to work* to do so. If you hadn't given me a hint that it was there, I wouldn't ever have suspected we didn't eat BLTs for breakfast. Well, not unless I started thinking about it and said 'hey, wait, where would I have gotten those awesome tomatoes?' which, admittedly, I probably would have the next morning when I started thinking I would like to have another BLT."

Urelle understood the point. "Which is why you've worked hard on detailing exactly what goes into each of the replacement memories – so it'll fit exactly with what that version of you still knows, so he'll never think to *ask* the question 'what's wrong here?' Right?"

"Right. So, are you ready?"

She shivered. "I don't know if I'm *ever* going to be really ready for this." She took a sip of juice from her cup, then nodded. "But I guess I'm as ready as I'm going to be."

"Then good luck. I will be outside the circle, so I have the least possible chance of interfering." He carefully picked his way across the complex mystical figure, not stepping on any lines, and closed it fully with a gesture of flame once he was out.

Urelle turned to the sleeping body and began her focus meditation, drawn both from her magical training and the Eight Winds training Lythos had given her. She arranged her notes and cues and gemstones of recorded images and sensations into the five major divisions.

Five divisions. Five separate sets of memories she would need to remove and hide away forever. There was a sixth, but that would come after all the others were done, once the Wanderer assured himself the main work had been finished.

She drew in a deep breath, and then began muttering the words, focusing her will, reaching out, reaching out for the mind before her…

***

It was a confused, echoing mass of sound, light, heat, cold, falling, flying, scent, pain, and pleasure, a cacophony of every sense. *It's worse than any of the other times I practiced!*

At the same time, it was *similar* to the prior practices the Wanderer had given her; so she gritted teeth that she knew were mere figments of her own self-perception and focused again, sought a filter that would provide coherence to the memories, sensations, thoughts, that filled the mind she had entered.

She focused first on sight; make of memory order, of order light, of light a vision that represented the memory she sought. Slowly, slowly, the same vision she had seen that morning coalesced before her. Not a library or a temple, but a huge, rambling mansion, with scrolls and books and pictures and sculptures scattered about the entrance hall, some being slowly moved around by indistinct entities that seemed composed of wisps of violet cloud. The various items, and even the mansion itself, sparkled with a rippling rainbow luminance, both as solid as mountains and evanescent as mist.

This is my... perceptual construct, the Wanderer said, *that represents his mind. You can't see a mind or a soul, but we mostly think of things in visual terms, so when I'm here* inside *his mind, I make it something I can understand.*

Briefly, she wondered how someone who had been blind from birth, or creatures naturally without sight, might envision a mind; a structure of sound, resonances and pitches and amplitudes varying in a vast network of harmony, perhaps?

But that didn't matter; she had to find what she had come for.

She advanced up a set of steps, those also strewn with notes and books and sometimes odder items, like flat pieces of glass that somehow displayed moving images. The Wanderer had given her... a *sense* of the memories she was to remove, though not the details. "The more you've seen them and thought on them, the harder they're going to be to *remove* from you afterward," he'd pointed out. "If you follow the clues I've given, you'll find them, no fear."

No fear? Easy for you *to say, Wanderer! You're not the one who has to worry about backlash from your own soul!*

Because this *was* dangerous. She was no more physical than this vision of a mansion; this was her *self*, projected into the Wanderer's own, her soul stealthily creeping through the memories of another - and that other was a being which, if awakened and threatened, could wipe her from existence quite literally with a thought.

Aside from that, there were still other potential threats; subconscious defenses that might notice the alien among them, memories that she found sufficiently of interest that she was distracted and lost her way, and others. She had to avoid them as much as possible, and not just because she was at risk. The more disturbance she created, the more likely the duplicate Wanderer would retain a subconscious impression of something wrong – which would cause this elaborate, fragile plan to unravel swiftly.

She passed through a set of elaborate double doors, to find herself in a long hallway set with more doors, each labeled with some kind of coded symbol. The hallway began to curve away and branch in the distance, and *those* branches also branched. "His memories... the whole lot of them," she murmured.

For a moment she could *almost* envision the nigh-infinite tangle of mental hallways; not a library or an archive or a vault, though undoubtedly there were some of all of those, but an immense, tangled, interlocking network like the tree-roots of an ancient, ancient forest, so intertwined and extensive that it would be folly to even imagine separating one set from another. She shuddered and shook her head. *Without hints I would get lost here.*

Focus on the first set of hints. A silver rose; an abstracted image of a golden city; a handsome man with slightly-slanted eyes, dressed in black, emerging from a slash of blue light; pages of a book flickering endlessly by, each one showing nothing but a different view of the night sky. She had no idea what these *meant*, but that wasn't important; what was important was that these ideas meant something to the *Wanderer*, and that all of them together should guide her to the right location.

One of the wispy violet haze-things drifted nearer as she concentrated on the hints, the images the Wanderer had given her. It flickered, then spread out, enveloping her and—

—with a tremendous *wrench* she was somewhere else. It was a large room constructed out of massive blocks of stone, a fireplace on one side sending out cheerful flickers of light, deep rugs scattered across the floor, large and comfortable chairs placed near the fire; through the archways where one might expect more of the house or castle where such a room existed, though, were mists and flickers of pages and stars.

The Wanderer stood before her, facing another man – a tremendously tall man, over seven feet, wearing a peculiar, five-sided hat with strange symbols on each of the sides, and holding an elaborately-crowned staff. This man spoke.

"Nowhere else are you found, Wanderer. I have stridden through every shade I could reach. It is not merely that you can *evade* destiny; you have almost no imprint on destiny. There are no shades of myself, of course, but you know the reason for this – a reason that in no way should pertain to you."

The Wanderer's eyebrow had raised. "You know, I come from Earth, not this place. It's possible none of my parallels came here."

A deep, resonant chuckle. "Do not think I neglected that possibility; I have sought echoes of you there, as well. Nothing. Only you."

The Wanderer's gaze dropped after a moment. "All right. Yes. There is a reason. But I can't explain it."

For an instant – an instant that stretched on and on and on – Urelle saw the Wanderer *fragment*. She saw the Wanderer, now a younger man barely older than she was, standing in a city so huge and strange she could barely grasp it, looking up at a building and comparing a number on it to one in his hand; she saw him caught by people she knew to be guardsmen of this world and thrown into a car; the young Wanderer stood behind a counter, keeping a store that sold dice and cards and strange-looking books; he was hunched over a desk with one of those flat-mirror things, glowing words streaming from it as he moved his hands across some sort of panel covered with symbols; he sat shivering against a wall, clothes in tatters, a sign begging for food or money next to him; he stood in front of a vast audience, a look of amazement and awe on his face as he held up a strange trophy, a spindle-shaped cylinder with three fins projecting from the base.

And there were more: the young Wanderer lay behind a ridge of earth, aiming a long, slender sticklike weapon that gave a crack of thunder and fire; he was in a house, tending a baby with dark hair but something of his looks in its rounded face, the Wanderer's own face tired and sad; his blond head was bent over a person on a flat, white bed in a room lit by brilliant lights, and there was a blade in his hand; he was on a horse, wearing a black round helmet and some sort of uniform, jumping gates at speed, face shining with excitement.

And there were more and more, and she almost closed her eyes and shouted against the infinite babel of him, the innocent, the vicious, the lazy, the energetic, the happy, the despairing.

The instant of allternity passed and she wavered, her concentration near to breaking. But now she could see the *connections*, that this memory, this *concept* of his somehow infinite self was directly connected to something else. She followed that sense, seeing a sparkling shimmer that echoed the images the Wanderer had given her, and she stepped through an archway...

...to see a weapon, similar to the one she had seen him firing, but far larger, mounted to a carriage like a catapult; as she looked closer, she realized that the weapon sparkled and moved and hummed with every one of the infinite images of those other Wanderers.

She recognized it, suddenly. This was... this was the dream-shape, the mind-formula, for a spell. A spell that somehow drew on the infinite... alternatives, possibilities that had in some manner become the singular being called the Wanderer. The shape also told her that this spell was a weapon, a *terrible* weapon, and she understood. *This* was her first target – a monstrously deadly weapon that must be removed from the hands of one who might misuse it.

Urelle prepared her own magic now, a faint golden-white haze, so thin that even the violet cloud-beings seemed as solid and hard-edged as rocks before it. Slowly, slowly she wove the magic about the shape of the weapon-spell, around and above and below, gradually – oh, so very gradually – thickening the mist and shifting its color, making it seem a part of the archway's background, just another part of the wall.

At the same time, she could not help but get a stronger *impression* of the spell – of how it could draw out the potential of the wielder's own soul and focus it into a bolt so powerful that the power of lightning and fire paled. A part of her wanted to stop, study it, see if somehow, she, Urelle, might be able to—

No! I didn't come here to learn his secrets. I came here to *hide* them. They're to be erased. I'll just make it worse if I try.

But it was terribly tempting... and horribly painful to see it beginning to fade, to take on the pearlescent golden sheen of the mist, becoming indistinct, sinking farther and farther into the depths of an infinite sea of fog and dreams. She clenched her jaw and continued, weaving the mist of time and forgetfulness thicker and thicker until it weighed down upon the invisible memory, pressing it down into the past until there was nothing left save the wisps of thought that *led* to this thought, this construct.

Those, too, had to be erased, a step and a branch at a time, until she saw it – the point at which *this* concept had come into being, the event in the very conversation between the tall man – *Konstantin Khoros*, she suddenly realized, his name being such an essential part of the memory that she could not help but hear it – and the Wanderer.

This is the place, where I have to edit the conversation, remove a branch and replace it. Now that she was here, now that she understood what she was removing, she knew what she was listening for, and how and when to replace the conversational memory with another that *could* have happened, but hadn't.

The Wanderer had been right; knowing what memory she was *inserting*, as well as what she had seen, she recognized the correct moment – a point where the conversation had paused, and the Wanderer, already thinking of that element of his existence, began to form the concept of using it in a more formidable way than he had ever done before.

She fogged to invisibility that pause, that branch in thought, and brought the continuation of the conversation closer, bridging it with a mundane inquiry about refreshment. This tiny change was sufficient, and she saw the mists she had already shaped shimmer, become more solid, take on the rainbow sparkle of the Wanderer's own thoughts.

"It *worked!*" she said in amazed gratification, and laughed. "It really *worked!* His mind's accepting the—"

A flicker, and abruptly there was a shadow across the luminance, something casting darkness before it like a cloud passing over the Sun.

Balance take me! I spoke, I focused on my *thoughts, I thought of him separately!*

A vast, dim *Something* moved, a Something that had the shape of the Wanderer but less of his awareness – a Shadow terrible and grim. *One of his subconscious defenses! It's tracking me. I have to hide!*

But how? How could she hide in someone else's *mind*, literally enveloped in their soul?

She pulled open a door, found herself in one of the endless hallways, ran, casting her mind-mist about. But the Shadow of the Wanderer was tracking her, looming above, around, *through* the halls of the mind. She ducked around a violet cloud-thing, but it, too, seemed to now suspect she did not belong; the edges of the cloud snared her, slowed her down. Her own mist released its grip, but not before the slightest bit of the Shadow brushed her.

Agony burst through her soul, burning fire and acid and crushing pain and the torment of suffocation. She felt herself on the edge of dissolution in the instant, forced herself to stumble onwards, moving, always moving. Slowly the horrific sensation faded, her mind recovered, but the Shadow was still following. *How can I hide within his own mind? It can recognize what belongs, what does not!*

But she *had* to hide, had to quiet the Shadow, make his defenses settle, so that there was not the slightest hint that something was odd and wrong. *But how? If it knows—*

She turned then and focused, focused with all her might on images, of a night in the laboratory and an old man becoming the younger Wanderer and his pain, and a question asked...

The violet mists hesitated, but she focused more, remembering every flicker of candlelight, the sound of quiet feet, the echo of a repressed sob, even as the sensation of the approaching Shadow filled her with fear.

The purple cloud swirled abruptly, and she was caught up, conveyed in an instant to that moment, when she had first met the Wanderer.

The great Shadow still towered over her; *it must loom across the entirety of his mind*, she thought, and then caught herself, focused entirely on her memory of that moment, of *herself*, of her surprise and fear and awe.

The Wanderer's Shadow bent over her... then, very gradually, straightened. The light began to brighten, the dimness to retreat, until at last the light and shadow of the memory was as she recalled.

Urelle wove the mists about her again and gave a shaky, if nonphysical, sigh. *I survived. I managed to quiet its suspicions; let it see only its own memories of me.*

She let herself gather her courage for a few moments – but only a few. *Time is not my friend here. I succeeded with the first – but there's a lot of work yet. Four more to go.*

And then... then I will also forget...

Chapter 30
A Moment of Desperation

Quester felt his connection to Ingram dim – but not before he saw the gold-armored figure appearing in that dazzling light. He turned back to Victoria. "Berenike! She has arrived to protect Ingram!"

"Excellent timing!" She glanced around the edge of the doorway. "Then all we need to do is get this arch down; we'll go out that way. You've seen it, of course—"

There was no time to warn her, no time to *act* at all. A Xiilistiin swung *down* from above the doorway and struck in a single motion, both of its murderous arms piercing through Victoria's armored coat and *yanking* her back – where the creature's vicious rostrum drove down into her body.

Victoria gave a piercing scream of shock and agony.

Quester did not remember moving, but the Xiilistiin was writhing on the ground in its death-throes, two javelins pinning it to the stony floor. He lunged out and swung the *hedri'at* up, unleashing edged death through the five monsters that had scaled the walls and dome. He sprayed the remainder of the weapon's ammunition down the narrow path, causing another retreat of their enemies, and ducked back inside.

Victoria was sprawled face-down on the stone, and there was a slowly-widening pool of blood beneath her.

No. No, no, I cannot allow this! Urelle and Ingram will be heartbroken, and we will have failed in the mission!

Turning her over, he saw with a thrill of ozone-and-flame-scented horror that she was still conscious, but unable to speak. Her throat had been punctured and only rasping, bubbling sounds escaped. Her blue eyes locked on his own faceted ones, desperate and pleading, *demanding* he do something. Her arms, too, were nearly useless, the shoulders and chest having been savaged terribly.

What do I do? What is she asking? Kill her before they reach us? No point – she will not live long enough for them to use her, not like this. She has perhaps minutes only, and she cannot take a healing draught like this – even if I had one strong enough, which I do not!

With a coughing hiss, Victoria Vantage forced one arm up, gripping Quester's so tightly he felt his armored carapace bending. Her expression was controlled – fearful, in pain, yes, but she was trying to *tell* him something!

If only I had had the courage to bond with them! If I had accepted, they were truly of my Nest – and why would they not be? Ingram has shown his heart's belief in them, what more should I want?

But there was no time to bond. That was a work of peace, of focus, of two minds coming at last to find each other and be well content with never being fully apart. He desperately wanted to know what Victoria wanted, but he couldn't—

Quester, the archway! Take the archway down!

For a moment he froze. He *heard* Victoria's voice, yet she could not have spoken; her mouth was not even *open*.

And then it dawned on him, and he felt a chill of wonder even within the terror of the moment, smelled jewelflower and ocean. *I hear her voice! I hear it in my mind, though we are not bonded!*

Well, that's a surprise, but a welcome one, and by the Balance *we can speak of it later!*

He still sat, unable to move from the impossibility of the thing. *But this cannot happen! I—*

Quester, Guild Adventurer, stop wasting the little time we have here! I won't be conscious much longer! That archway has to come down now!

The urgency and his duty overcame even the shock of the inconceivable. *Of course. But how?*

Firespheres. He *saw* it, suddenly – the pouch with the spheres, and then the two points where they must be placed, and a flash of a javelin or the sharp-edged discs of the *hedri'at* before it all dissolved in flame. *Quickly! Before they charge!*

He could already see the movement outside. He dipped his second-hand into the pouch, pulled out three remaining spheres. *I only need two for this.*

The third he hurled out the doorway. The massive explosion would surely buy him a few precious moments.

One sphere here in this crack. The other... He pulled out a dagger, dug between the stones desperately until he could *just* wedge the faintly-glowing marble into the right position.

He leapt back, caught up Victoria under her arms, and dragged her back through another doorway, deeper inside, and laid her down, behind the wall. Then he stood, hefted one more throwing spear, and threw, ducking back behind the edge of the doorway, as dark silhouettes loomed up in the entrance beyond.

The world evaporated in red heat and stunning pressure. Within the explosion, Quester thought he heard more shrieks of the Nest-Takers, their vangard enveloped in twin spheres of flame. Even behind the stone the concussion was stupendous, and a gout of orange and white sparks blasted from the doorway and filled the room with stinging pain.

But before the fire had completely died away, there was a grumble that rose to a deep, crackling roar. The light vanished, plunging Quester into blackness as deep as any cavern.

The doorway was sealed. His antennae and vibrational senses told him, through scent of thick dust and trickling of smaller stones and dirt, that more than half of the room beyond had completely fallen in. It would be the work of days to clear it.

He reached into another pouch, brought out one of the light-sticks he and Ingram made sure to always carry, and activated it, then gripped it in one second-hand as he used his main arms to lift Victoria again. *She still lives, but she fades quickly. Great Mothers of All, what do I do? She cannot die! But I cannot heal her!*

Somewhere far ahead, down many corridors, he sensed a shout, a clash, and – just perhaps – the faintest, dimmest trace of golden light.

Berenike. She is an emissary of Athena. Perhaps... just perhaps... she has the power to heal, as well.

Antennae spread wide, Quester began to move as swiftly as he could down the ancient corridors. His great, wide-set, faceted eyes picked up traces of ancient carvings, esoteric and mysterious, on the walls. Traces of water and crystallized remnants of long-past leaks drew streaks down the stone, and the air was cool and damp, filled with the scent of mold and earth.

Then, too, his antennae detected other scents, living and breathing, some hungry and predatory; other things lived in these catacombs, digging through the dirt for food, others lurking in wait for dirt-diggers or unwary explorers. But even the boldest of these, with a vinegar-sharp tang of venom as well as the musk of a large and hungry beast, had retreated from the straight ways, knowing the roar of flame and clash of weapon and not caring to test themselves against Adventurers or their adversaries. *For that I can be grateful; I am in no position to fight now.*

Victoria's breathing was becoming more shallow, and he could sense that death was not far behind. His own heart pulsed swiftly in empathy and terror of loss, the thought of facing Ingram or – so much worse – Urelle with that failure making his mandibles vibrate; he locked his jaws shut, but knew he could not hide his scent, and was once more grateful that no other was there to smell it and know.

And there was still the other impossible mystery: how had she spoken to his mind? *Perhaps* she *is a psionic? They are rare, but not at all unheard of among humans. Even if her power was weak, telepathy at short range, still, it would be a fine hidden reserve, a resource to speak not of until it was needed.*

Yet... No. Her own mindvoice – and mindvoices could not lie, not so easily, not with such forthright and simple thoughts – had spoken of her surprise. He had felt, hidden behind her straightforward words, her pain and terror and knowledge of approaching death, but her thoughts had been clear, without confusion. She *had not known* how she could speak to his mind, how he could hear her, but – true to all he had seen of her – had not allowed that to divert her from the path that needed to be followed.

Only the Mothers of my people can speak mind-to-mind without a bond. Have I, perhaps, been making a bond with them, without conscious decision? It is... perhaps not utterly impossible, though I have no understanding of how it might be done.

He squeezed them past a narrow point, where part of the corridor had sagged sideways, making the passage a tall triangle. *Now* the sounds of battle were clearer, and he saw a flash of that light, momentarily gilding the stones of the walls and the dirt of the passageway with auric fire. Xiilistiin screeched and snarled, and there were sounds of weapons and an explosion of some sort of magic.

He hastened forward, for what he *didn't* hear was the sound of Ingram's weapons, his cries of battle. There was still a *sense* of him there, but it was vague and muffled.

Around a corner, and the sounds were sharp and close. "Give back and give up, foul things!" said that clarion voice. "Threescore and ten of you have fallen, do you wish to make the tale an even hundred? You face the *Spear of Athena*!"

The light rippled gold and silver, and she came into sight, a sparkling jet of insubstantial yet lethal bolts of bimetallic energy spraying into the mass of creatures before her, sending them tumbling away, broken, unmoving.

But there were more, surging in from a gap in the wall nearly fifteen feet across, and he saw with an instinctive tightening of arms and mandibles that they were not all ordinary Xiilistiin; no Swarmfathers, no, but some with less-insectile, more-human shapes that meant they had absorbed some promising creature, taken their skills and powers. A jet of fire from one, barely parried by a shimmering golden shield, showed that at least one of them had skills of magic to draw upon.

Berenike's copper-green eyes flicked backwards at Quester's motion, and suddenly grew wide. "*Lady Vantage!*" she shouted in horror.

Quester's sense of Ingram suddenly strengthened, and he saw his friend's hand appear from behind a piece of rubble, pull him upright; Ingram stumbled painfully towards them. But in that moment, Berenike was carried backwards by the lunge of no fewer than *three* of the Xiilistiin, the distraction of Quester's arrival giving them the opening. Red blood sprayed across Berenike's armor, and she gave a snarled scream through gritted teeth.

But it was not enough to stop her – at least, not yet – for electric-blue light danced over her armor and her assailants convulsed, smoking from the power of lightning. Still bleeding, Berenike shoved the three twitching figures into the next wave of assailants and unleashed a detonation of power that shook the entire structure, casting back the attackers; Ingram tripped and went to both knees, before crawling on.

"Put her down! Quick, Quester, then help Berenike!"

He lowered the now-limp body to the ground and drew his blades. But the smell of death was hovering close about Victoria, and even if he and the Spear of Athena could somehow contrive to hold off the oncoming waves of the Takers of Nests, he was very much afraid that Victoria Vantage would not live to see it.

Chapter 31
Seal of a False God

Raiagamor bent low over the map, carefully modifying the outlines with the precision of his diamond claws. *The more precise the map, the more powerful and enduring the magic,* he reminded himself.

His mother, the Queen, nodded. "You found better sources since we first carved the matrix, I see."

"I sent a number of my allies to survey the boundaries that seemed less than perfectly known," he said. "The changes are small – the original matrix would, I think, have served us well enough, since Aegeia has long since mapped most of itself – but for what we seek to do, I would approach perfection as near as we might."

"A wise and proper sentiment, my son," she said. "And you have given me sufficient of your stolen godspower for me to work well with. I hope you have not weakened yourself overmuch, however, for you have much left before you."

A chuckle, some of it lying below the limits of human hearing, vibrating crystals about his hidden sanctum. "I have husbanded it well, Mother. More than enough remains for me to grow, to cultivate with other power so that it can become greater. I have been doing this for centuries, and what I have given you is not the greatest portion of what I have to my hand." He stood, having completed the refinements of the shape of Aegeia engraved in the matrix.

"*Wise* indeed, my son. I begin to have high hopes, which pleases me." He could see the delicate twining of godspower with magic and the Queen's own darkly-subtle power being re-engraved about the boundaries of the matrix. "You expect the time to be soon?"

"*Very* soon, Mother. Indeed, that is why I must do this only a few strokes at a time; the matrix must not be in a state of transition when the time comes, and Phobos' forces must be close, close indeed to intercepting the travelers, if my guesses are at all in alignment with the truth. When he breaks his crystal, it will shatter the one carried now by Artemisia, and trigger both his return here, and her transformation into a semblance of Athena."

"Then I will complete this, and we shall be in readiness."

He moved some distance away, to ensure that he would not interfere with her work, and touched a half-ring he carried, the other half borne by Artemisia – or rather, the Xiilistiin which had become Artemisia. His claws scribed a circle in the air and he held up the half-ring, investing the circle with its resonance, a resonance echoing to its distant twin and mate.

Instantly, light sparkled around the immaterial circle and he could see Artemisia Igemon, leading her forces against those of Lyre; Artemisia had succeeded in "liberating" Velos, the city of her namesake, but Apollo's city did not in any way favor this; they wished to "rescue" the archives and knowledge of Artemis' Library from the "conquerors." This rescue, naturally, took the form of their own army of liberation.

It was amusing how armies of liberation and armies of conquest looked so very similar.

"And how much of your power was invested in the charm for Artemisia?"

"Nearly as much as I have given you, Mother. She must, after all, be completely convincing, and while you and I have our own power to deceive, this is much less true of even the best of the Xiilistiin."

The Queen nodded, human fingers finishing the supremely complex gestures that sealed the matrix into its final state. "And you are certain of your control of these creatures?"

He smiled blades at her. "I have learned enough from you and the King to repudiate the idea of *certainty*, Mother. But I have told them half-truths for the most part, and trusted them with no more than they need know. Deimos and Phobos know more, but they are also more bound than they know. I have done what I could to—"

From his vision, silver-gold light blazed, illuminating his own chambers with their intensity, and as the light faded, he saw a gold-armored figure standing where Artemisia had been an instant before. At the same instant, Phobos appeared at the far side of the room, a sparkle of broken crystal still sifting from his fingers.

"Time is come, Mother! The crystal has broken, and our false Athena has appeared upon the field! She will make her speech, and then decree her Seal upon the realm!"

Her dark-haired head inclined. "Then we shall ensure her words are naught but truth, indeed. Across from me, if you please."

He took the position, his hands – now in human form – holding the matrix on either side of Aegis, his mother touching the apex of Wisdom's Fortress.

"The power and binding will cycle through both of us," she reminded him. "You must maintain that vision, of the energy, the *wall*, flowing about the country like an unending river."

"But…" he studied the matrix. "There must be a… point at which the power is placed into the matrix and thus the wall, where flow begins and must then be tied together. Will that not be a flaw?"

"Ah, child, you see clearly. Yet your studies did not range far enough, or – perhaps – my sources are somewhat more comprehensive than yours." As she paused for her own amused effect, he reflected that it was most likely the latter; she was only slightly younger than the King Himself, after all, and had delved into arcane knowledge of all kinds for literal ages longer than any other. "In truth, there has *always* been such a flaw. Very small, very distant, as far from any who might seek to enter or leave as it may be, but there."

He frowned, then nodded. "But one now held by a fortress that owes allegiance to none save itself."

"Indeed. It is, thus, a small enough flaw, for they shall know the Seal is up, and that none may pass; without reason, will they seek to find the passage, so small and hidden from normal eyes as it is? I believe there is little chance of it. Now attend; your pawn begins her declaration, and our timing must be precise."

Raiagamor gave over his thoughts and focused entirely on Mother, allowing her to act, following her guidance exactly; only once would she provide him such aid, so he would not risk the slightest chance of its failure.

In moments, he *felt* the power streaming about the perimeter of the matrix – and thus, by association and will, circling all of Aegia. It flowed through him, from one arm to the other, a river of ice and flame and thunder that both strained and invigorated him. He had to enforce iron control to not truly *taste* this stream of power, draw its nigh-limitless energy into himself. It would be a mighty boost to his powers, true… but then there would be no Seal, and the entirety of his plan would be at risk, for then Berenike would be free to act.

No, he must not give in to impulse. He must not shirk duty or focus. He must be everything his mother believed he was, and all that the King believed he was not.

He must – he *would* – prevail over all; his enemies, his half-brothers, the King, and most of all over *himself*, for he knew his greatest enemy was within his mirror and his heart.

The energy sped on, circling, a perfect and unbreaking flow, until Mother cried "Enough!" and they withdrew their hands in the same instant from the matrix.

A shimmering wall of light gleamed from every point of the boundaries of Aegeia – save, he supposed, for some incredibly tiny interval at the far north. But otherwise, it was flawless... and impenetrable.

"It is done, and well, my son," the Queen said, and her smile also held a hint of diamond blades. "Your country is now truly yours; for not blades nor spells nor even the gods will traverse that barrier. If there were a threat beyond those borders... it will trouble you no more."

He threw back his head and laughed, as in the circle of his vision two armies knelt before a golden goddess.

Chapter 32
Training Complete?

Urelle shivered, her eyes not entirely able to focus on the young-seeming man in front of her. "We have to do this... soon."

"Yes. The longer the memories stay, the more you *think* on them, the harder they are to hide, especially as you are conscious, and aware that they are to be erased."

She saw the visions that had passed before her... the hints of things too vast, too strange, too *alien*, and others so human that they could break her heart. "Everything I saw... is it... *real*? Are you... are you *really*..."

"I am what you saw... but whether your *interpretation* of what you saw is right, that I'm not touching with a forty-foot pole. What you removed were mostly keys to weapons that I would *not* want my dark self to have access to. Obviously, it's not impossible for him to eventually think of the same things and go down the same research path, but for each of those tricks... well, he'll have to spend months, years, maybe centuries to get them back, assuming he thinks of them. He might not; each idea one has is triggered by a thousand little things coming together, and he may never encounter the same triggers." He looked pensive. "Though he'll probably think of something new and horrid on his own."

"And I erased all the knowledge that led up to this," she murmured. "The prophecy, our discussions, all that." She took a breath. "Was that *Zahralandar* I saw?"

"You mean, the images of a huge city, flying machines and tens of thousands of moving metal vehicles? Yes, that was Earth, as we call it. I was born there. I came here."

"Do you ever miss it?"

He laughed. "Of course I do. Even today, I'll sometimes think of something I miss – a favorite food that's really hard to replicate here, a game, a book, or, of course, my parents, my brother..." He shrugged, his smile momentarily sad before brightening. "But what I have here? It's ten thousand times more than I could have dreamed, than I *had* dreamed, when I was a child. I've lived a dozen dozen lives, I've mastered a thousand skills, learned secrets not even the Archmage Idinus knows... I may *miss* my old home, but I would never go back if I had to give up who I've become."

"I guess that's as good as a life can get," Urelle said after a moment's thought. "I just wish I didn't have to forget."

"I understand. I wouldn't want to, either. On the bright side, you won't know you forgot anything; you'll wake up with a complete and detailed knowledge of what we were working on together for the past few weeks, and with some really quite impressive improvements in your magical abilities. Fortunately, our work here has... how can I put it... exercised, *trained* your spirit in the way necessary to let you put such new skills to use, even if the memories you have of the training are artificial. You learned what I had to teach and learned it well; that training is not wasted."

"Will I..." she trailed off, then took a breath and started again. "Will I ever remember what was erased?"

"*Ever?*" The blue eyes gazed off into unguessable distance. "Normally I would say no. But you *are* a Shaper, and you are a Vantage, and you're going to play in the game of the gods. Your soul is more resilient, more powerful than you know or will suspect. More powerful than *mine*, in a way. So... yes, I rather think you will, someday." He glanced towards his bedroom, where his duplicate was already sleeping. "Hopefully not before that problem is resolved, though."

"What will I have learned, in place of what I learned... well, for real?"

He grinned. "*Sore wa... himitsu desu!*" he said, with a look she knew meant another of those obscure references. "Why mix up that knowledge with the knowledge I'm erasing?"

He reached out and touched her shoulder. "Seriously, Urelle... thank you. For helping, for understanding... for having the courage to do what has to be done."

She felt a gentle touch of power, relaxing her. "You're... welcome, Wanderer."

As her eyes closed, she thought... *.and goodbye.*

It is not goodbye, his voice answered from within her own mind. *It is* au revoir *– "until later." You and I – the true Wanderer – will meet again one day. I promise.*

Holding that promise in her heart, she let the warm and caring darkness wash over her.

***

The crystal near her bed started singing some kind of *really annoying* song that featured musical instruments she couldn't identify. *Well, it's sure effective at waking me up.*

After her usual morning routine, she returned most of her clothes and equipment to her neverfull pack. *Always be prepared to leave, if you're an Adventurer. Aunt Victoria said that, and the Wanderer's said it at least twice since I've been here.*

"Good morning, Urelle!" the Wanderer said as she entered the little room they had been using for breakfast. He gestured, and an assortment of trays and dishes appeared on the table.

"You didn't teach me *that* spell." Then she paused and thought about the gesture, the *feeling* she'd gotten, the almost subliminal mutter she'd heard from him. "Wait, that wasn't... creation. That was summoning... no, *transporting*. You had the food made up before, and just brought it here!"

"Ha! See, that's why a magician never reveals his tricks to anyone; they're so much less awesome once you can figure out how they're done."

"But..." She checked the various dishes. "These are all *fresh*. The eggs are like they just came off the pan, the fruit like it was cut just a minute ago, this pan-sausage just finished searing... You can't have done it all at the same time, and even if you did, it should have cooled off or changed just a bit. You *can't* have timed it all perfectly."

"Can't I?" He grinned and sat down, helping himself to eggs and browned bread slices. "If I couldn't have done that, then how?"

She frowned in thought as she served herself some thin slices of fried roast along with fruit, eggs, and a juice she didn't recognize but liked. "Well... I can think of a few ways. Ranging from fairly simple to ridiculous."

"And thus, I still have a few tricks you can't figure out."

"You probably have a *thousand* tricks I can't figure out. You're the one who's the legend, not me."

"Fair enough." They ate for a moment in peaceful quiet, then the Wanderer sighed.

"I think, Urelle, that we've reached the point of diminishing returns. You're astonishingly quick, so you've learned a lot – some spatial tricks that will come in very handy, some defenses, some combat, some general enhancement and utility spells and overall magical concepts. But even with my advantages in teaching this kind of stuff and your talent..." He shook his head. "To make significant headway at this point will take a lot more time. If you feel comfortable spending another month—"

"No!" That was sharper than she'd intended. "I mean... I don't think I can afford that. I don't have any idea what my friends are doing now. For all I know, they really *need* me to help."

"I can't argue with that assessment. And I, too, have things I have to get to. Not that I won't help you out here and there."

"You don't have to—"

"I kind of do, actually," he said. "First, what's going on in Aegeia is definitely the kind of thing I'm *supposed* to help with. What's the point of being a legendary Adventuring wizard if you don't, you know, go out on legendary Adventures?" He nodded at her laugh. "Right? And second, you're my apprentice now. Been a long time since I taught anyone, but when you take an apprentice, they're your responsibility. Sure, you have to go do a lot of this on your own, but unlike the gods, *I* don't have to stay completely hands-off."

"Well, if *you* help, this should be easy!" Urelle said, but inside she felt... let down? *Why?* After a moment she traced it to a feeling that she'd be totally overshadowed by the Wanderer, and castigated herself for it. *Really, Urelle? You would rather go into a godswar with just Ingram, Aunt Victoria, and Quester, so that you can be the Hero? More like we'll all get killed!*

"Whoa, slow down. I can help *some*, but I've got other responsibilities. Plus the... info I have on what's going on there indicates that you guys are going to have to solve a lot of it on your own. I can help *some*, and I'll give you a way to call me, but most of it..."

He paused, then gave a wry grin. "Zarathan is a nexus of a lot of things, including choices, possibilities, even *reality*. Practically speaking, that means there's always something important, *lots* of somethings important, going on, at all levels from 'threatens this village' to 'threatens all existence.' Obviously, the bigger and more important someone is in the overall scheme of things, the more they get drawn into the bigger picture. And even if they want to help with the smaller picture, there's always something else demanding their personal attention."

He held up a hand. "Now, that's *good* in a lot of ways. After all, you wouldn't want, say, Zaoshiss of the Mazolishta to be dropping in to ruin every single town someone built in mountains he could influence. He generally doesn't, of course, because the *other* gods keep his attention.

"Same unfortunately holds true for people like me. I can pop in and out and give you help at some key points, but most of the work's going to be up to you. You're involved. There's some kind of prophecy at work, and that *by itself* warns me that there's only so much meddling I get to do."

Urelle finished her last bite of roast and thought on that. "How so? I mean, how does the existence of whatever prophecy or divination that's leading our enemies constrain you?"

"Simple, really. The prophecy clearly told Ares that one or more of your group is the key to their victory or defeat. That means that I *can't* just walk in and try to solve the problem myself. That would put me in *direct conflict* with whatever powers made the prophecy in the first place."

"But you're immune to destiny. Right?"

He laughed. "Er... yes and no. The best way to put it is that destiny has no *absolute* hold on me. That is... oh, to use an example from one of my favorite stories, let's say there's a prophecy about this bad guy that no man may defeat them. You could get around that prophecy yourself, or course, because you aren't a man, but I am, so normally that would mean I couldn't defeat this guy. But in fact, I *would* have a chance to defeat them.

"However, note that that's *a chance*, not a certainty. All that 'immunity' of mine amounts to is that you can't use absolutes against me. So yes, I *could* in theory also be the one to make Ares' plans go down the crapper, but there's no guarantee I'll figure out the right *way* to do that. Nor is there any guarantee that I wouldn't cause something worse to happen by intervening in such a ham-handed manner; maybe the power that made the prophecy would react very violently to my personally screwing things up."

He spread his hands before him, looking pensively at them. "And that would be neglecting other jobs I have. There are about five or six of us... meddlers who try to put out the absolute worst fires, or, more commonly, send the right people to be firefighters for us, while we go look for the next fire and try to deal with *that*. Upshot being, you'll be able to call on me once in a while, but I can't fix the major problems; I can get you past specific challenges, but the big ones? Those will be up to you."

"That's terrifying, you know? Ares is a *god*. We're just mortals."

The blue eyes sparkled at her with humor. "True. But it is mortals who support the gods. Sometimes, the mortals even *become* the gods. Trust me; if that prophecy says one of you could be a threat, that tells me that if you all pull together... well, Ares will be outmatched."

He stood, and after making sure she didn't want any more, banished the dishes and remaining food. "We should get you packed, then."

"You know where they are? I mean, how will I rejoin them?"

"Remember? I promised your aunt that I'd bring you there myself, and I will. I don't know where they are, exactly... but I know how to *get* where they are, and that's pretty much all that matters, right?"

"You are immune to the teleportation interference, too?"

"Heh. More I know how to *trick* the interference. If there's one thing I've practiced a lot, it's messing with people's assumptions, and there's *always* assumptions in blanket interferences like that. And the gods long ago decided they would prefer I didn't get up in their faces, so they won't be personally trying to interfere."

Trust that he knows what he's doing, Urelle! she told herself. *If he wasn't pretty good at what he does, he wouldn't be a legend.*

"I'm actually packed. If you give me a chance to run upstairs, anyway."

"Good. Go ahead, it's not *that* much of a rush."

She took the steps two at a time, realizing as she entered her room and grabbed her traveling cloak and neverfull pack that it was *Ingram* she was most looking forward to seeing. *Not Aunt Victoria? I... wow.*

That was so distracting a thought that it was a few moments before she realized she was standing, staring blankly like a fool at the wall. She shook herself and turned, running back down the stairs.

The Wanderer was now in his own traveling clothes, that strange blocky armor – so like Ingram's – visible beneath his tough blue shirt, black cape thrown over his shoulders and clasped with a glittering brooch, the Staff of Stars leaning against the wall nearby.

"There you are," he said, and handed her a small book; it was surprisingly heavy, the covers having the unique coolness of cloth over metal. "That will give you guidance as you continue to learn your control over magic. Not quite as good as having me there to help, but much more convenient, and it will take you very far, indeed."

She stared at the book, then took it, and bowed deeply. "Thank you very, *very* much, Wanderer."

"The least I can give... my young apprentice." The last three words were said in a somewhat disquieting tone, but then he laughed. "Never mind, another of my stupid jokes. Really, you'll need all the help you can get. And *this*," he held up a glittering lenticular gem, about the size of her fingernail, "is how you can call me."

She took it in her hand and looked at it; the gem sparkled like a diamond in rainbow hues. "How do I use it?"

His smile hinted at yet another private amusement. "Just hold it up and say 'Arisia.' I will know."

"And how many times—"

"No hard-and-fast rule here. Probably more than once, that much I'll say. But don't lose it; it won't be replaced."

She immediately tucked it into her neverfull pack, focusing on keeping it in her mind as she did so, so that it could be called forth again with a similar focus. "I won't!"

"Good." He extended his hand. "Then, shall we?"

She gripped his hand tightly, and the Wanderer brought his staff down in a flare of green and gold.

Chapter 33
Urelle's Fury

I'm losing her!

That was the thought foremost in Ingram's mind – a mind that seemed strangely fogged, unclear, as though the shock of Victoria's hideous wounds had rendered him unable to think. His hands fumbled with the healing kit that he'd used for years, almost dropping it.

Meanwhile, he was aware of the battle going on scant yards away, and hearing not just Quester's, but *Berenike*'s curses, as though she herself were hitting some unrealized limits.

But he *had* to focus. *She's bleeding multiple places. That hole in her throat... Athena preserve me, I think it's probably poisoned, too.*

Victoria's pulse was quick and faint, her skin far too pale, her respiration growing shallower. *What do I do? What do I do? I don't have anything for a transfusion! I could try to stitch the wounds together, but I don't think there's time, even if that Hades-cursed Xiilistiin didn't inject something with its beak that's destroying her from the inside! Founder, what do I do?*

"I shall never yield, monsters!" came another shout from nearby; Berenike's voice, no less ringing, but with more pain and less absolute certainty to it. That *terrified* Ingram. If *Berenike* could fail...

He sat, frozen with terror and indecision, mind fogged and confused in a way he did not understand, and guilt and fear tore at him with talons as sharp as any the monsters outside could have had.

There was a blaze of green and gold that lit the ruins with daylight and emerald. The Xiilistiin shrank back, uncertain, and Ingram sensed Quester had also turned to see the sources of this light.

The luminance faded, and not six feet from Ingram stood Urelle... and the Wanderer.

Her gaze found him and the great gray eyes lit with pleasure... and then went dark with shock and fear as she realized who he knelt above. "*Auntie!*"

"I... I don't know what to *do*!" Ingram said, voice shaking with the tears going down his face. "We can't use healing draughts, and she's bleeding so much and her pulse is almost gone and she's barely *breathing* and I think she's been poisoned and I can't *think*—"

Urelle's face was tight with horror, eyes wide, mouth opening and closing without any sound, her hands shaking as they reached towards her aunt, touched hands already cool and clammy and unresponsive. He could see shock and helplessness already reaching out to claim her, too.

Berenike flew past them, hurled backwards by a concussion of darkness and sound, and her impact with the wall was enough to shake the ground. The Xiilistiin gave a trill of triumph, and Ingram realized with another jolt of terror that the only thing standing between them and the insectoid monsters was Quester.

At that sound, Urelle's face shifted; the eyes of soft cloud gray became hard, the glint of storm-light on unsheathed steel, her mouth tightened and twisted in a silent snarl, and she shot to her feet.

"Wanderer." Her warm voice had gone colder than the peaks of distant mountains. "Save her."

"If it can be done, I shall." The tall, blond figure knelt beside Victoria Vantage, gesturing for Ingram to move back. Unable to help, with his mind only starting to clear, Ingram withdrew, and saw Urelle Vantage striding towards the battle, directly into the path of the Xiilistiin, who were on the verge of overcoming Quester as well, despite his friend's lightning-fast moves and deadly blades.

"*Get away from my friends.*"

Urelle seemed to have barely raised her voice; it was not a scream, nor a shout; yet those words *carried*, cutting across the cries and clamor of battle like a fanfare of execution. Pearl and aqua light limned Urelle's figure, and her hair flared out, lifting up within the aura of power that had just appeared.

A lunge, a slash of two bladed limbs – and the Xiilistiin *exploded* in fire and ice, cast aside, broken and burning by a gesture and word. Her forehead wrinkled with concentration and she murmured something below her breath, then curled fingers away from her palm and thrust forward.

A hurricane of force *plowed* into the Xiilistiin, blowing half of them back through the doorway by which they had entered. Ingram forced himself to his feet, drew the *anai-k'ota*, and leapt forward to aid her.

Though as she moved forward, her face drawn in the tension of anger and contempt and hidden fear and loss, he thought she was less in need of help than anyone he had ever met. It terrified him... and at the same time, he thought she was more frighteningly beautiful than he had ever imagined.

"How *dare* you hurt my *Auntie*?"

She showed the Vantage strength again, catching one clawed arm, moving with it in an arc that she accelerated, and then with a wood-and-glass splintering sound that sent a shiver through Ingram, she tore the Xiilistiin's arm *completely off*. The creature barely had time to scream before its own bladed arm impaled it through the chest.

Athena's Mercy! Ingram shuddered. He wanted to tell Urelle that was enough, more than enough... but then he remembered the graying face of Victoria Vantage, and thought that maybe it wasn't enough, after all.

The doorway was clear, Quester dispatching the last of the things in the chamber, but now Ingram could see clearly past Urelle – see that there was an *ocean* of Xiilistiin there. *A whole* swarm *of the monsters! Berenike killed more than a hundred of them, and there's more than that* out *there – and more coming in!*

Urelle halted in the doorway, and her gaze swept from one side of the massed enemy to the other, and then locked on a figure just emerging from the jungle; a Swarmfather.

It gave a warbling screech and swept its arm forward; the swarm, having withdrawn at the unexpected resistance, started towards them again.

Urelle did not shrink back; muttering more words under her breath, the light glowed brighter around her, and she stretched both arms out as though to embrace the oncoming monstrosities... then brought them down, and with a gesture sudden as a sword-stroke thrust both arms skyward.

The earth heaved, knocking Ingram to his knees; but that was the merest side-effect, as most of the clearing before them – a semicircle eighty feet or more across – *detonated*, a blast of force and shattered stone sending uncounted bodies hurtling skyward, to plummet limply down in a gruesome rain of death; one of those bodies, larger than the others, was the Swarmfather.

Dust billowed in obscuring clouds across the landscape like smoke from a hundred bonfires of green wood; slowly, slowly it dissipated, showing the remaining Xiilistiin fleeing into the woods, vibrating shrieks of terror echoing behind them with the dying reverberations of that cataclysmic assault.

Ingram saw her begin to raise her arm again, caught it. "It's enough, Urelle."

"*Enough?*" She whirled on him, then froze as she realized that she had brought up her other arm as though to strike him. She stayed immobile for several moments, then let both her arms drop; only then, he thought, did she really *see* the hideous scene before her, and stepped back with an expression of revulsion and dawning self-horror. She swayed on her feet, and Ingram caught her elbow, supported her so she did not fall.

In the room behind them, they heard the Wanderer's voice. "I can't *work* with monsters trying to sneak up behind me. Begone."

For an instant, Ingram's ears felt as though someone had rammed red-hot needles through them, pressure having peaked so swiftly he could not adjust. The pressure wave moved *past* him, going into the ruins, funneling a stupendous blast of wind through the tunnels, confined somehow from blowing back through the entrance where they stood, and Ingram heard Xiilistiin shrieks of pain and consternation and a distant *boom*, as of something giving way, a howl of a wind through a dozen passages... and then silence.

Lady's Mercy. The Wanderer just... casually... disposed of whatever forces were coming up behind us. Forces I did not even think could be there.

Ingram was starting to feel that his pride in being a Camp-Bel was nothing but childish posturing. *I can't possibly match these people.* It didn't help that he still had that sense of being wrapped in a fog, only halfway there, unfocused.

But seeing the nausea and guilt on Urelle's face, he realized he might not *want* to match them. Instead, he touched Urelle's shoulder and squeezed, gently, letting her know he was there. She turned and looked at him with incomprehending eyes. "I... I just... was so *angry*...", she said, and gripped his arms, as though she might embrace him... or was afraid he would run from her.

"Blame not yourself, or think this action was too extreme," Berenike said, emerging battered but upright from the doorway. "Yon monsters would surely never have stopped, save by a demonstration of vast power. It was in my mind to do just such a thing once I had won through, but some of my opponents had been given far greater strength and power than their exterior appearance warranted, and thus I was... interrupted, shall we say."

She looked about carefully. "But this battle, at least, is ended – and I must go, swiftly. I fear there is something subtle and dangerous afoot in our land." She pecked Ingram on the cheek, and then waved, falling away into the sky before turning and vanishing in a glint of gold.

Urelle pulled free and ran, unsteadily, back into the ruins. "Auntie? Wanderer, is she...?"

"Not yet," the Wanderer replied. "But now that I won't be *rudely* interrupted..."

Ingram could not quite follow what the Wanderer did – and by the wrinkles of concentration on Urelle's face, he thought she couldn't manage it, either. First, he removed a ring that he must have put on her earlier, placing it on his own finger, and then touched Victoria, tracing patterns across her body that fit diagrams of key bodily systems Ingram had seen in the ancient writings; the Wanderer gestured and a foul, green-and-red, puslike fluid poured from the wounds and across the stone, to be swallowed up in the earth nearby. He made criss-crossing gestures with his fingers, and the wounds began to seal... and then, finally, he reached towards her hands.

Ingram noticed that only then did the Wanderer hesitate. It was a fractional thing, a wince, but it was there, a moment before the Wanderer steeled himself to complete the task and grasped both of Victoria Vantage's hands.

Instantly, a gold and green glow rose up from the older woman and enveloped the Wanderer; black and bruise-blue and decay-green oozed up through that aura and flowed *into* the Wanderer, whose face tightened. Sweat broke out on his face and he went white as chalk, his breath coming faster in obvious agony. He choked for a moment, seemingly unable to breathe, but though Ingram thought he could see real fear in those blue eyes, he did not relax his grip.

Slowly, color returned to the Wanderer's face, though he remained paler even than his usual startlingly light hue and a sheen of sweat still beaded his face. At last, he released Victoria's hands and sat heavily back.

"She'll recover," he said, his voice far weaker than usual.

"Thank you, Wanderer! Thank you so much!" Urelle embraced him tightly, and Ingram heard himself adding his own thanks, his chest finally loosening. He realized his own face wasn't dry. *I was... crying. Afraid for Victoria, and Urelle, if something happened to her aunt.*

The Wanderer chuckled, a sound barely perceptible, and waved his hands ineffectually. "No, no, it's part of my job. I couldn't drop you off and leave you here with your favorite aunt dying, could I?"

"She is still unconscious," Quester said. "Though her scent is far better, and I hear heart and lungs working well. When should we expect her to awaken?"

"A day or so. That was... one of the worst things I've had to heal in a very long time. The Xiilistiin share several traits with regular hemipterans – bugs – and one of those is that they inject a necrotizing digestive liquid through their rostrums. It was basically melting her at the same time as she was bleeding out."

"And you..." Urelle said slowly. "You took her injuries onto *yourself*."

"Very observant. Yes."

"But then, *you* should be dying!"

"I should, indeed. But I've a trick or three that death really hates me for." His voice was getting somewhat stronger. "After all, in the normal way of things, I'd have died quite some few thousands of years ago." He stood slowly, but already looking better. "You'll find your own tricks, Urelle. Believe me, you'll be a Shaper to be reckoned with."

His gaze sharpened, and he was there suddenly to help catch Urelle as she sagged towards the floor. "You look poorly as well, apprentice," he said, and Ingram could see the glint of real concern in his eyes. Leaving Ingram to watch Urelle, the Wanderer stepped to the opening, gaze flicking around the scene.

He paused, staring out, for several moments. "Holy Jebus on a pogo stick," Ingram heard him mutter, and the blond head shook slowly in disbelief. He looked back, and though there was still worry on his face, there was also a dangerous smile as he crossed back and knelt next to Urelle, who was trembling with reaction and an exhaustion that Ingram could somehow sense.

"That," the Wanderer said, "was one of the *stupidest* things you could possibly have done, Urelle." The smile, however, did not waver. "You're barely to the point where you can twist reality to that level – if I get what you did right."

"I reached out... to the ground," Urelle said, her voice shaky. "Felt the... the *essences* within, the power that responds to calls for the elements?" At his nod, she went on, "and I... I released it. I imagined all the power of stone and soil, the *essence* of it, released skyward in a single moment, and... well, that's what I did."

"Yeah." The Wanderer continued to grin with obvious disbelief. "Urelle, releasing *all* the essence of an elemental source... you *destroyed* it. The stones and dirt out there have been reduced to pulverized dust, barely an atom left sticking to another in some places, because the essence of solidity, strength, power was stripped from them completely. I've known mages three times your age and four times your experience who'd never have *dared* try such a Shaping. Shaping the essence of the elements... you're literally ripping matter apart to make use of its power, changing reality to say 'that stone? It never existed.'

"I've got a spell for something *like* that," the Wanderer went on, "but it only releases a *part* of the essence across the area. I've never dared try releasing it *all*."

"But you showed me how to do it!" she protested. "The spell you called 'grenade.'"

"On *ONE ROCK!*" he said, smile suddenly gone. "*ONE!* Here's your assignment, apprentice – how many rocks the size of your fist *are* there in an area more than eighty feet across and maybe two or three feet deep?"

Ingram blanched; with that foggy feeling somehow lifted from his mind, he could make a rough guess at the number well enough, and it was... huge.

Urelle's eyes widened as she followed the numbers on her own. "Oh."

"'Oh,' my ass! Your Myrionar *must* have been watching over you on that one, because you came *this* close," he held his fingers about a hair's width apart, "to tearing your soul in half!"

"That... she could *do* that?" Ingram whispered in horror. If someone's soul was ripped in half... they were dead. So dead that even the *gods* might not be able to recover them.

"Damn *straight* she could," the Wanderer answered, and his face was once more a mixture of anger and pride. "That's the price a Shaper pays, that's the danger we play with every day. We're taking the burden of changing the way the world works, and the more we change it, the more of the world rests on our souls. And like muscles, souls have limits, and they can be strained, sprained, or even torn apart." He sat down on a stone nearby. "That's what kills most young Shapers, in fact. They get *too* confident with their power, get in over their heads, and then..."

"Is she hurt?" That was Quester, asking the question on all their minds.

"Not as bad as her aunt," the Wanderer answered.

Looking at the drawn, shades paler, and still unconscious form of Victoria Vantage, Ingram shuddered. He saw Urelle close her eyes and shiver as well. "How... how bad is it?" she asked finally. She looked so frightened now that Ingram couldn't help but reach out, touch her shoulder again. Her hand came up, her fingers gripped his tightly, and even in the midst of his worry, somehow the warmth of her hand seemed to spread through all of him.

The Wanderer held up his hands in a triangle and peered through them, studying Urelle. After a few moments he dropped his arms and sighed. "Bad enough. Consider it the equivalent of a bad sprain, maybe with a slightly torn muscle. You're going to have to go *very* carefully with your magic for a while – but you still need to work it every day, to make sure your soul is strengthened rather than permanently scarred by what you did. It's going to hurt."

"Hurt? I feel... tired, kind of dizzy, but I don't feel any pain."

"Oh, believe you me, you will. This is... well, it's like those times you go out and do something really strenuous after not having done much work for a while. You feel pretty good, maybe a little achy, but it's not bad. Then you go to bed, and the next morning it hurts so bad you can barely get up. That's coming, Urelle. It will not be a fun time."

"Then... why were you smiling before?"

The grin flashed back onto his face. "Because *damn*, Urelle, you are going to be one *scary* mage, better than anyone I've taught since..." He stared into the distance, then shook his head. "Since a long, long time, anyway. *If*," he went on, looking serious, "and I mean *if*, you take it easy and work your way back up to strength slowly."

"And you'd better," he said, and looked towards the east, where Aegeia waited. "Because I'll guarantee, you're going to need every bit of power by the time it's all over."

Chapter 34
A Departure and a Pause for Thought

"Are you certain the Nest-Takers will not return?" Quester did his best to sound merely professional, but he could tell that his scent betrayed his fear.

"*Certain* is always a trap," the Wanderer said quietly, looking back at the entrance to the ruins and the fire that glowed within, keeping the other three warm as they slept. "But I'd bet a lot of pretty much anything on it. There were two Swarmfathers with that gang, both of them are dead, and your group accounted for, oh, must be something like three hundred of the nasties, maybe more. Even if they had twice those numbers, seeing what Urelle did? They have *no* way to know she couldn't keep on doing that. No, they'll run back to their Swarm-Heart and regroup."

"Good." His second-hands wrung themselves nervously. "They are hunting *me*."

"And that worries you. Can't blame you there; Xiilistiin are some of the nastiest things Zarathan has to offer, at least on the level of 'entire species of trouble.' Still…" he looked at Quester, then shook his head. "There's something more behind this. Even if we assume they *did* kill your Nest and the others that disappeared recently, why hunt down one warrior-scout?"

"That disturbs me as well, yes. Could it be tied to the same forces that are hunting the others?"

"Ares' people, you mean? Hmm." The Wanderer looked up at the sky, and stood there quietly for several minutes, the gentle wind stirring his long blond hair into aimless waves.

Finally, he looked back at Quester. "My first instinct would be to say 'no,' mainly because even in his worst incarnations in the Cycles I've seen, Ares simply would *not* work with things like the Xiilistiin."

"That you've…" Quester felt his antennae droop, knew he smelled of highpine and earth. "Ah. It is a difficult thing, to truly grasp that you are *that* old. You have personal *knowledge* of Aegeia, of Ares and Athena, then?"

"Met both of them a few times, passed through Aegeia on its Cycles more than once. The thing to remember about Ares is that even the cruelest versions are *earnest*. He may get into all sorts of stupidly macho posturing and survival-of-the-fittest, or whatever idea hits him at the start of the Cycle, but his *purpose* is to be driven by his *passion*, and it's ultimately a passion for the world, for people, for challenge and triumph and all the motivations that might drive one to wage a war – which is why he can be a really good guy, or a really rotten one, but he's not..."

The Wanderer paused, seeking the right phrase. "Not... cold. He's not stupid, but he doesn't work from intellectual analysis. It's all about drama and glory and passion. It's *Athena* who's about rationality and tactics and balanced response and all that. But what all that means is that allying yourself with body and soul-stealing parasites is just completely *not* something Ares would do. Or Athena, either, but usually she's not the adversary, and from everything I've heard thus far, Ares is your problem, not Athena."

He grinned. "Of course, that's their... *Cycle* faces, too. The parts they play as the heart of the Cycle. Off-stage, so to speak, Ares is just a slightly ridiculous sweetheart of a god, and Athena's his more-together sister."

Quester tried to process all of this rationally, but it was difficult. He was speaking with someone who was, themselves, legendary... and he was discussing the gods of Ingram's land the way one would speak of... well, common party acquaintances. "I see." He paused, thinking back on the conversation. "But when you answered me, you said 'my first instinct' was to say there was no connection. But second...?"

The smile faded away and the lips pursed out in an expression like a man tasting an unexpected lemon. "Yeah. Second. Truth? I don't like coincidences, and I like them about a thousand times less on Zarathan, because coincidence is just Zarathan's way of shoving you into the plot."

"Plot?"

A snort of laughter. "The story. The Adventure. Whatever your destiny is. Anyway, that means that the idea there's *two* big bad somethings searching for a member or members of your party *really* rubs me the wrong way. Which means that, somehow, these guys *are* working with, or directed by, Ares."

"But you say Ares wouldn't work with the Xiilistiin."

"Yes." A sideways glance and a hint of a smile that was in no way comforting. "An interesting paradox. And unfortunately, I can't unravel it for you." He straightened. "I've got to get moving. A Chaoswar's on. If I'm going to try to minimize the fallout, I've got *so* many things to do."

"You will leave *now*?"

"I think so." He looked back where Urelle and the others were sleeping. "I've already said my goodbye to my newest apprentice, given her what I can. Victoria won't be up for a while. Ingram needs his sleep too, and there's not much more I can tell any of you at this point."

Quester bowed, then extended his first-hand in the human way. "It was an honor and a pleasure to have met you, Wanderer."

"Likewise, Quester." He gripped Quester's hand with just enough pressure to be sincere, then released it. "We may meet again. Probably will, when you least expect it and, hopefully, most need it."

"That is, after all, your duty as a legend," Quester said.

"Ha! Indeed!" He gave a sweeping bow, brushed his black cape over his shoulder, and set off into the night... vanishing into a mist of earthborne stars. Quester gave a buzzing sigh. *We are once more... united and alone.* It was, to be perfectly honest with oneself, a sobering thought. Strange though the Wanderer was, his power was undoubted and his knowledge vast. Now they were on their own, against opponents they still did not truly know.

Letting his mind wander, he busied himself with searching the shattered clearing and verge of the trees for anything of value. Urelle's mighty spell of elemental devastation had left little intact, but among the splinters of dismembered Nest-Takers and churned, dusty earth there were occasional glints of valuable metals or an undamaged gem. It allowed him time to think.

His presence and motion also kept smaller scavengers at a distance; the many corpses were undoubtedly an attractant, although in such small pieces they would likely prove unworthy of a larger predator's attention.

Quester found there were still things that *bothered* him about this last Adventure. Perhaps the one that stood out the most was Berenike. She had *destroyed* Deimos when they encountered him, obliterated his group and struck down the God-Warrior almost contemptuously. But in *this* battle, she had had trouble. Now, certainly the Nest-Takers were not to be dismissed as opponents, but the ones he had fought himself in this combat were surely no worse, and he suspected on average were notably weaker, than the members of Deimos' party. With the mouth of the ruin to keep them unable to attack her in large groups, should not a God-Warrior of Athena have had little difficulty in holding them at bay, even if for some reason she could not strike out against their massed numbers?

And Ingram, too; he had seemed... *off*, was perhaps the best way to put it. As though his attention were not fully on the job at hand, which was ridiculous; if there was anything Ingram could do extraordinarily well, it was focus on his task.

Nonetheless, the impression remained, and strongly so.

He paused in the midst of picking up another twisted piece of jeweled metal. *Both of them are of Aegeia. Both connected.*

And our adversaries, *if my conversation with the Wanderer holds, are all from, or directed by, Aegeia.*

It would not be at all surprising, would it, if such enemies devised very specific tricks to weaken the ones most likely to oppose them? Namely, Ares would use his power through his servants to weaken those of Athena. It was not an honorable or noble method, no, but if the Wanderer's instinct could be trusted at all, it *was* exactly the sort of thing that their current opponent would do.

That *would* explain the problem: if there was some enchantment, or psychic dampening, or even deific interference, with those that shared a bond with Athena and her specific guardians, the Camp-Bels... why then, it would only interfere with Ingram and his childhood friend. He, Victoria, and Urelle were entirely separate.

"If so, we need to figure out a defense for them," he buzzed to himself. "Because such a countermeasure will almost certainly get stronger the closer we get to Ares."

He looked back at the doorway, assuring himself that things remained peaceful. He could sense, very faintly, Ingram's sleeping presence... and for an instant, he thought he sensed Victoria as well.

That was another mystery. It should not be possible. Yet it had happened. Those had not been his thoughts that had directed his desperate actions to get himself and the mortally-wounded woman safely away from the Xiilistiin. Somehow, he had *heard* her thoughts, she had sent them directly to him, clearly and precisely, carrying all the meaning needed. With *Ingram* that would have been utterly unsurprising, but Victoria Vantage and he did not share any such bond.

But he had heard her. And for a moment, he sensed her again.

Was it some subconscious attempt to bond with Victoria? They had surely shared some adventures, and the human woman had shown many of the most admirable traits. Urelle, too, was a fine person, and Ingram was clearly drawn to her in the way of his people.

Yet it was still early days for such a commitment – and he did not know if *they* would want that connection. It had taken Ingram some soul-searching days to decide he would take what was, to him, a risk. Quester admitted that he had not fully understood Ingram's reluctance until they had completed the bond, and he could *feel* Ingram's thoughts and the images that accompanied them. Now that he *did* understand why human beings were afraid of such intimate mental connections, he knew it was not something to be done without much discussion and honest thought on both parts.

Still... he *had* heard her. And desperate though the contact had been, there had been not a hint of discomfort, of the connection being forced.

He sighed. "It seems I will have more than one thing to discuss in the morning!"

Chapter 35
The Show Goes On

Ares stood immobile at the base of the Aegeian Path, shield half-raised, other hand on the hilt of his sword.

Athena strode towards him, the armor of Artemisia Igemon transfigured into golden mail and plate that mirrored closely the statue far above them. She, too, held a shield, and her Spear glinted with silver.

Below them, filling the Grand Platea, were the crowds — the citizens of Aegis, the soldiers of three armies — watching to see which direction the Cycle would take, what the word of the Gods Incarnate would be.

She halted perhaps ten paces away, and inclined her head. "Brother."

He nodded his own. *The play must be performed to perfection.* "Sister," he said, nodding precisely, as had she.

"Your course of conquest is clear to my eyes," she said. "I would have it that you cease."

"That *I* cease? Dearest sister, you have but arrived. You, whose eyes see so clearly, have still had not the time to grasp all that there is to see. *My* course will unify Aegeia and rebuild her. What other course would you choose?"

She kept her distance, but paced slowly around him, circling. "Unification sounds like a fine goal, Ares. But the words I have heard elsewhere sound far less like a plan of *cooperation* and much more that of *subjugation*."

"You wound me, sister. In every step I have been the very soul of reason."

"Reason?" Her smile was cold. "For the god of Passion? This itself makes me fear something is terribly amiss."

Ares smiled more warmly. "My *dearest* Athena, I am desolate that you can see something so fearsome in my willingness to let my head sometimes function." He looked down at the crowd. "But come, would you trade blades with me this day, or would you speak with me more seriously? I stand ready to accommodate you in either, but if we are not to give the people the spectacle of two gods at war, let us at least spare them the disappointment of two gods arguing."

The nearest in the crowd might have seen her lip twitch in amusement. She shook her head at last, and this time a laugh did escape her. "Very well, brother. Truce and safe conduct?"

"Truce for this day, and safe conduct for you and all your men if you choose to leave. I so swear."

"Very well. *Men!*" she shouted down, and the armies below stiffened into alertness. "Lord Ares and I go to discuss what is to come – be it war or peace. We are given safe conduct. Be at liberty for this day, and gather again tomorrow. *Lochias*, you're still responsible for your men's conduct – I want no reports of trouble! Dismissed!"

She turned and extended her hand. "Lord Ares?"

He took it, and in an instant, they were in his chambers far above.

"And now *that* step is taken," he said, allowing his expression to relax to a contemptuous sneer for the people. "They will talk and drink and argue about what is to come."

Artemisia-Athena picked up a bowl filled with a dark-brown, mealy substance and began to eat; by itself that showed she was not human, because a human eating that particular product of Xiilistiin biology would die in some peculiarly frightening ways. In Artemisia's case, of course, it supported her and helped her maintain her shape and power. "What *is* to come? Have you decided?"

"We will actually discuss that today, at some point," he said. "There are two paths – which lead in the end to the same destination, of course – and I am unsure as to which I should follow."

"Why not discuss it now?"

"Because *now*, I wish to check on other events – ones that have not yet become public knowledge, but that will be."

He drew out a deep red crystal and regarded it, then called forth his power and energized the connection that crystal had with another. "Deimos, have you a report?"

"If you wait but moments, I will give one to you in person," Deimos' voice answered from the crystal. "Even now, I approach your chambers." The voice was... irritated, though not, Raiagamor thought, with *him*, and tired. However, it was also a *focused* voice; Deimos was fully recovered to himself, which was well. *I have many Xiilistiin, but only Phobos and Deimos for demonic assistance.*

The fact that Deimos was *here* was a bit of a surprise, and not necessarily a good one. "We await you," he answered, and cut off the enchantment.

In moments, the door opened and Deimos entered; his stylized armor was battered, there were traces of blood just able to be scented, and... was that a strand of *seaweed*?

The narrow face was even tighter with restrained anger that Raiagamor could sense despite the false God-Warrior's control. *This does not bode well*, he thought, and caged his own anger. "Was there... difficulty?"

"'Difficulty.'" Deimos repeated, looking with momentarily slitted eyes at his master. "Yes. That is an excellent word, Lord Ares."

"Are the Camp-Bels neutralized or not?"

"I cannot say."

Raiagamor paused, mouth half-open. That had *not* been one of the responses he had expected. "How is it that you cannot say?"

Deimos spat on the floor and threw himself into one of the chairs, face contorted in frustration. "Because I *do not know what happened to them*."

With immense difficulty, Raiagamor restrained himself and waited for Deimos to continue; Artemisia-Athena looked as though she was tempted to laugh; if so, she wisely restrained the impulse.

After a few brooding moments, Deimos sighed, then stood and bowed. "My apologies, My Lord. I will tell you all."

"I should hope you would. Go on."

He glanced at Artemisia, saw Raiagamor nod. "Well, as you know but the Lady may not, because of certain information received, we determined that the Camp-Bels had outlived any usefulness they might have for our regime. I was given a strong contingent of our allies, and summoned some few of my own, and prepared to descend upon their compound. Their patterns of behavior are well-known, and while it is difficult to get details of the *interior* of the secure areas, we know enough for a reasonable assault."

Artemisia nodded her understanding, and Deimos went on. "Except when we made our move, we found that most of the Clan had *already left*. It was only through good fortune that one of my aerial brethren spotted motion in the harbor and that we had much material closely connected to the Clan so that a quick divination told us that many, if not all, of the missing Camp-Bels were aboard the vessels we saw."

Raiagamor gritted his teeth and snarled softly. "They *escaped*?"

"Not so easily, and not completely, My Lord!"

Deimos looked half-offended, half-fearful at the thought of having failed his deadly master *that* badly; the expression gave Raiagamor a small measure of pleasure that helped him regain his calm. "Go on, then."

"Immediately, of course, we proceeded to the harbor, commandeered the three fastest vessels we could, and gave chase. They were sailing swiftly towards the west – I presume towards Shipton, and perhaps thence to the Twin Cities and Zarathanton itself. Maybe they planned to put some plea before the Sauran King."

At that, both Deimos and Raiagamor paused in momentary amusement; they knew that no help would be forthcoming from *that* quarter. Then Deimos resumed his story.

"Whatever their plans, of course, we could not allow them to escape, and with my forces' magicians we were able to overhaul them after about ten hours of sailing or so. We engaged them at long range, and then my two faster ships flanked them, while my vessel closed from the rear."

He gave a narrow glance to both Raiagamor and Artemisia. "However, due to your own actions, My Lord, My Lady, I was never able to complete the battle."

Raiagamor stared at him for a moment. Neither he nor Lady Artemisia had been anywhere near that battle – which, from the timing and the speed at which he knew such vessels traveled, would have been near the edge of Aegeia's waters. That would have been a few days ago at least, at which time...

"By my Father's *Claws*," he found himself swearing in disbelief. "You can't mean—"

"The Seal became active in the very *moment* the ships were crossing it," Deimos said with a hard-edged smile. "My own vessel lost its entire bow and went down so fast that I suspect not five other crewmembers survived, and I cannot say of my own knowledge that any did; I had to swim *eight miles* to shore, and after *that* I had to make my way *here*. Since I do not know the thickness of the Seal, I do not know whether any of the other vessels were caught in it and destroyed, or whether my other forces finished the Camp-Bels, or whether the Camp-Bels were victorious."

Raiagamor sat for a moment, torn between laughter and rage, before reason finally caught up. "They are all gone from the compound?"

"A few had been left behind to maintain the fiction that the compound was still inhabited; those are dead or in the hands of our allies for conversion. We may learn something from those, although it is my belief that they would be wise enough to leave only those who do not know the key secrets. The rest, we presume are either dead at sea, or still on their way to... whatever destination they chose."

Raiagamor rolled his head slowly around, letting the tension in his neck release, as he considered this. "So, insofar as *Aegeia* is concerned, the Camp-Bels are gone. Yes?"

"Yes. The forces I left behind completed clean-up. Any who investigate will simply find a mystery – the compound empty, as though everyone had disappeared, or had packed up and left in a single night. The latter is close enough to the truth, but I believe the important point, My Lord, is that no one will be able to tell *why* they disappeared, nor will it appear they were killed."

"Yes. Yes." As the incandescent fury slowly banked its fire, the situation became clearer, and he found it within himself to smile once more. *Oh, my, yes.*

"I believe this serves well enough," he said, letting the smile broaden. "The Seal is in place. They have left, but they cannot return, no matter what aid they might gather, no matter what they know. Even if by some mad chance they actually know about me and what I am – and I do not believe there is even the *slightest* possibility of that – it will profit them nothing. They cannot reach us, they can neither do nor say anything that will affect even a single person in Aegeia. No one even knows *why* they left. They will be a mystery, but not one that matters to us."

He rose and clapped Deimos on the back. "Worry not, Deimos; all is well. Perhaps it was not *precisely* according to our plan," he admitted, smile still in place, teeth glittering sharply, "but howsoever it came about, the Camp-Bels' part in Aegeia's history is over!"

Chapter 36
Discovery on the Seashore

"A defense *specifically* against those of Athena or her supporters?" Urelle could see Ingram's forehead wrinkling under its fringe of lavender hair. "Is that possible? And if possible, would it be actually *practical*?"

His glance had directed the question to her. For a moment, she thought *why ask me? I don't know anything about these things!*, but then she realized that when it came to *magic*, she did, in fact, know more than anyone else here about "these things." She held up a hand, saying in effect *hold on, let me think*.

After Quester had told them of his suspicions, Ingram had put the question nicely. There were two parts to the problem: the first being whether a mage or an entity wielding similar powers *could* find a way to inhibit a specific group of adversaries in such a manner, and the second being whether it *made sense* to do so – that is, was there an advantage to doing it exactly that way rather than making a general "inhibit everything that isn't me" spell.

Well, doing the latter *would be a really broad-application spell, effectively targeting everyone and everything within, well, whatever radius of the person or object with the inhibition enchantment.* That would tend to take a lot more power, or if it was a person-maintained enchantment, a lot of constant focus, since there would inevitably be more targets and they could be coming in and out of the radius during any reasonable battle or other activity. Definitely a point in favor of doing the more limited version, if you could manage it.

So, could you do that? And specifically, could you do it with the Camp-Bels and someone like Berenike?

"Ingram, when the Camp-Bels swore their oath, was it to the *rulers* of Aegeia, or was it to the goddess *Athena*?"

"To the goddess first, then to the rightful and just rulers second," Ingram answered promptly. "Once the Founder accepted that there really were gods, it made sense to swear to the power that was the source of the country's continuity first, and the current leaders and their heirs and assigns afterward. The 'rightful and just' bit also gives the Camp-Bels the right of judgment in case something went wrong with the existing leadership." The answer had the air of something learned in childhood and recited many times.

She nodded and continued thinking. *Okay, that* does *work, I think. Both Berenike and the Camp-Bels are directly, by oath, linked to Athena. If your spell... or godspower-based command, whatever... could be explicitly linked to that connection, then you wouldn't even* have *to concentrate. Anything with that metaphysical connection would be targeted.*

"I think the answer is *yes*, Ingram," she said finally. "I'd have to know a lot more about those kinds of powers to *do* it myself, but both the God-Warriors and the Camp-Bels have a specific and easily defined connection to Athena. That would make it *easy* to do, if you knew the right approaches. Might require godspower to really make it work, but we know our enemy is Ares, so..."

"That *is* disturbing," Aunt Victoria said in her most disapproving tone. "That means that if this enchantment can be carried by any of our adversaries, neither Ingram nor his friend and ally in extremity will be nearly as effective as they have been."

Quester buzzed a sigh, with a hint of both smoke and cinnamon and sharp burnspice. "Yet I do not see that it makes a difference in what we must do. Regardless of the impediments in your way, you must continue forward, yes, Ingram?"

"Yes," Ingram answered. "But..." he looked around, "again, it doesn't mean *you* all have to."

"You don't actually think *any* of us would leave you, do you?" Urelle heard her own voice, sharper and more pained than she had intended.

He flinched the slightest bit, then shook his head and laughed sadly. "No. I know you won't. Even though it'd make me feel better to know you were somewhere else safe."

"But it'd make *us* feel *worse* knowing you were doing it all alone!" Urelle said. "So, don't you ever bring up that stupid idea again!"

"Indeed. I am not in the habit of allowing foolish young men to get themselves killed over misguided concern or pride." Victoria flicked a glance to Quester. "On another subject, I believe the two of us have another mystery yet to be unraveled."

Quester's antennae flapped in acknowledgement. "I have not yet found an answer. You are not capable of telepathy yourself, correct?"

"Quite correct. I've known a few such before, and they all assured me that I had no more potential in that area than the usual human. But in the tales, I had heard of the Gray Warriors of the Iriistiik, such powers seemed more likely."

"'Gray Warrior?'"

She gestured to his carapace, which was deep black on the rear but shaded on the chest and more forward areas of the arms and legs to a smoky gray. "So the rare ones of your people have been called by Adventurers in the records I have read."

Urelle also vaguely remembered that name being mentioned in one of her books – *Cloudrider and Bladesong*, she thought.

Quester paused, then his antennae bobbed again, and a quick smell of flowers touched her nose. "It is not a bad appellation, and Mothers' Memory tells me now that such a name was not unknown." He paused. "It is both interesting and frustrating that only when something is called properly to my attention can I access the Mothers' Memory. Only now do I remember that there are and have been others such as myself, that you call the Gray Warriors. But whether the others had such abilities, I have very little, save to establish the bond such as Ingram and I share."

"Do other Iriistiik have psionic abilities?" Urelle asked.

"All of the Mothers, the Queens, do. On occasion a Thinker will. Rarely a Warrior. Perhaps one of the Tenders. Never that I can recall one of the Runners, the Keepers, or the Growers."

"Yet, quite clearly, you *did* hear my thoughts," Victoria said. "I was unable to speak at all, so our conversation could be nothing else. Unless you or I cast some sort of mindspeaking enchantment."

"I know nothing of magic, save what facts I see in the Queen's memories, or what I have learned on Adventure. Certainly, I know nothing of how to perform magic."

"I've never shown much aptitude for it, myself. Still... I can manage a few small spells, and under great duress as we were, perhaps it is possible."

Once more the glance was at Urelle. It was... gratifying, actually, to know that she really was the closest they had to an authority on something. "It's not impossible, Auntie. Pretty much *everyone* has at least a tiny bit of magical potential in them, and subconscious magic is a well-established phenomenon. In that situation, where you were absolutely focused on the need for Quester to understand you... yes, it could happen."

A scent of camphor and vinegar. "Possible. But I know the *feel* of a true mind-touch, and this was as clear and true as the voice of the Queen-Mother." A wriggle of the arms that Urelle thought was a shrug. "We must think of this more, but I suppose answers may be long in coming."

"I am simply grateful that it happened, however it did," Victoria said. "We are both alive because of it."

A buzz of amusement. "On that, we all can agree."

Since they were all walking together, they all had to keep alert. Urelle called up her power as she had... was it now a few *months* ago?... when she'd eavesdropped on a party of Ares' people at the gates of the Vantage estate.

Her eyesight became vastly sharper and touched on ranges of light beyond those of ordinary human vision, and she could hear the sound of a leaf striking the ground a hundred yards away. Even this simple magic was a notable strain – not dangerous, not even close to her current limit, no, but *noticeable*, as it would not have been a few days ago, before she'd wiped away every living thing in a clearing more than eighty feet across.

She shuddered inwardly at that thought. *That rage frightens me. I didn't care what I did, I didn't care what it did to me, all that mattered was I destroyed those who hurt Auntie. That's horror. I did it, and I didn't care.*

Urelle had made herself look at the whole clearing again, before they left, made herself *see* what she had done; enemies or not, she had *shattered* bodies with a contemptuous power, torn one asunder with her bare hands, obliterated tons of stone into impalpable powder by tearing from it the very essence of *existence*, just to vent her fury.

She wasn't sure if she would ever *stop* seeing that clearing in her dreams... and in a way, she hoped she never did. *Maybe it was necessary. Maybe something like it will be necessary in the future. But if I ever think to do that kind of thing again, by Myrionar's Mercy, I pray that I will do it without hatred and fury making the decision for me.*

With a shake of her whole body, she cast off the memory and focused on the present. Her enhanced senses followed her gaze as she swept her attention in a full circle.

Wait – what was that sound?

A hissing, crashing sound, then a fainter hiss, with an underlying rattle, followed by another hissing, booming crash, and the same faint hiss following...

At first, she thought it might be some kind of creature, walking or scraping its way along, but...

No, that hiss and rattle sounds... sounds like... like a stream running over unstable gravel. Like water.

"The sea!" she shouted suddenly. "Up ahead! I think I'm hearing *waves*!"

Ingram's head came up, and he took out his little instrument, glanced at it. "I think you're right!"

They hastened their pace, and in a few minutes, they pushed through thick, broad-leaved brush and emerged into a dazzling blaze of light.

Above, the sun shone brilliantly in a nearly cloudless sky of pure blue. Equally brilliant white-gold sand spread before them, the beach starting a few tens of feet from the edge of the forest, dotted with occasional dark rocks. Urelle inhaled deeply, smelling a scent she had never encountered in her life – a touch of fish, the freshness of the breeze that blew along the sand, the smell of salt, and tang of lands beyond.

Too, she stared at the heaving, emerald and aquamarine sea, great curved ridges of water charging endlessly towards the sparkling beach and rising, higher and higher, to be crowned with ivory-bubbling foam before crashing down into a chaos of sand-churned white and gray, to withdraw before the approach of the next teal-tinted titan.

"It's... amazing," she managed finally.

"Indeed," her aunt said, with a tone of wonder and satisfaction. "It has been so many years... one forgets that it is, indeed, so beautiful."

Ingram was staring out at the ocean with a smile so broad that it must be hurting his cheeks, and she saw the glint of a tear in his eye. "Yes. Yes, it is. Oh, *Athena*, I'm close to home now!"

He looked eastward, and they could see the dim shadows of mountains in the distance, mountains that came down to the sea. "Wisdom's Fortress. Quester, Urelle, Victoria – in a day or two we'll *be* there, Aegeia is *there*!"

A burst of cinnamon and fresh-turned earth. "I am happy for you, Ingram. Though we also will be approaching danger more closely, as well."

His delicate face tightened, but Ingram nodded; Urelle watched as his stance shifted, returned to the watchful Camp-Bel Guardian that he tried so hard to be. "Right."

"That doesn't mean you can't be happy about returning," Urelle found herself saying, then threw a quick glare at the tall Iriistiik. "Quester, really, did you have to bring that up *immediately*?"

The insectoid tilted his head and then his antennae drooped; she smelled contrition and a touch of shame. "My apologies. You are correct. There is no reason for my friend to reject the joy of coming home. I... merely worry for him, and so I remind him of danger. It was not well done."

Ingram gave his friend a quick hug. "It's forgiven. I can hear your caring and your happiness for me inside, anyway." He looked over to Urelle. "But thanks." His smile seemed brighter than the beach's dazzling reflection, and she felt warmer inside.

"Pardon me, all of you," Victoria said slowly. "But what do you make of *that*?"

She was pointing west, opposite to the direction they had intended to go. Squinting, for now the sun was starting to go down and was much more in her eyes, Urelle could make out several dark shapes against the water, quite some distance away – perhaps a mile or more. "I believe they are ships," Quester said. "Or, to judge from their position and some anomalies of outline, they *were* ships."

Ingram nodded. "Several shipwrecks – got too close to the shore for some reason, maybe blown there in a storm recently."

"Why recently?" Urelle asked.

"They're still mostly intact," Ingram said. "Even from here, you can see the one farthest out is twitching a little; wind and tide will tear ships apart when they're stuck in the shallows like that. They've been there days or weeks, almost certainly not months, and definitely not years."

"I hope the crew got to safety," Victoria murmured.

"Hard to say if they could have. If it was a storm, they'd have needed some good magic on hand to safely abandon ship and get to shore. If it was just an accident in decent weather, not too hard to abandon ship safely. Still..." Ingram frowned. "*One* ship isn't hard to believe, but that's four, maybe five or six."

Urelle brought up her enhanced senses again and focused on the shipwrecks. She could hear the creak and moan of stressed timbers, the whine and snap of wind in tattered sails and still-taut lines. The ships themselves sprang into far sharper focus, as though she stood only a hundred feet or so distant.

What she saw made her stiffen, and she heard her aunt say, "Urelle? What is wrong?"

"Looking closer at the ships," she said slowly, "there's scorch marks across several of the decks. I think I see arrows or something stuck in the decking and cabins. Parts have been smashed in by some kind of great force."

"A *battle*?" Ingram said incredulously. "Who was fighting who here? Are these the losers, the victors, or both? Can you tell?"

She concentrated, swept her vision up carefully, studying the masts. Tattered cloth fluttered at the peak of two of the vessels, and she felt a chill go down her spine. The flag was only half-visible, but the black was sprinkled with stars and she saw an open book, to the side of something curved and shining. On one of the other vessels, another torn flag, but this one's partial image was that of a chariot crossed with a sword and a torch.

"Myrionar's Mercy," she said. "Ingram, it looks like it was ships of Ares against the Camp-Bels!"

Chapter 37
The Trail of the Clan

Ingram sprinted up the verge, where the jungle's last traces firmed the sand just enough, his heart pulsing twice as fast as the effort demanded. *No! It can't be too late! I can't have come all this way, can't have gone through so much with all my friends, just for it to have ended* here!

The others followed, but only Quester truly kept pace, for Ingram wasn't holding back now. His friend's grasshopper leaps just managed to keep up with his lightning-fast strides. Finally, words penetrated his furious, terrified consciousness, words both spoken and thought to him.

"Ingram. *Ingram!* Slow down, my friend, pause just a moment!"

"I can't—"

Quester landed in front of him. "You *can* and you must, my friend and Nest-brother."

Almost he shoved past in his desperate haste, but he could *feel* empathy radiating through their link, *knew* that Quester understood absolutely and completely, and nonetheless felt that Ingram must pause in his headlong rush.

With a huge effort, he slowed, stumbled to a halt before the tall, angular figure. "Why?"

"If there is no battle," the Iriistiik said calmly, "then there is no hurry; it is over in one way or the other. If there *is* a battle, it lies over a mile distant; even with your training, a mile of such speed will have you weary indeed, and how well will you then fight?" He gestured behind them, where two other figures were drawing nearer. "And in a battle that may have gone poorly for two or more *ships* of Camp-Bels, how wise would it be to hurl yourself into the fray without all of your allies at your side?"

Breathing hard, Ingram forced himself to *think*, to cast aside the panic and long-held guilt and anger, and knew that — as pretty much always — his friend Quester saw the truth far more clearly. "Sorry."

"I should... think you would be," panted Victoria as she and Urelle arrived. "We understand your impulse, but I *expect* a Guild Adventurer to think more clearly."

He bowed his head. "You're right, you're all right, I'm sorry. But... can we move now?"

"Of course we can," Urelle said breathlessly. She didn't show any other sign of the fast dash up the beach, just started moving forward.

Now that he was thinking more clearly, he felt even more embarrassed. *My teachers would all have been disappointed.* But that wasn't going to help him either. The important point was to think clearly *now*.

"Is there any sign of a continuing battle or pursuit?" he asked. "Check the jungle near the wrecks."

"Brush is badly torn up opposite the wrecks," Urelle said a few moments later; his own far-seer verified this, and he thought he saw signs of powers at use. "Looks recent, but I can't tell *how* recent."

"Let's move as fast as we can and stick together," Ingram said. The others hastened their steps to a jog. *It will take us a few minutes to get there. I just hope it's not the few minutes that matter.*

They reached the area, saw that there was, indeed, tremendous disruption of the jungle, showing a running conflict heading north-northwest. "One group chasing another," Quester said after examining tracks, "as we would expect. But which is the pursuer, and which the pursued, is unclear."

"Myrionar and Chromaias," Victoria murmured as they pushed through another wall of tattered leaves.

Before them, a thirty-foot-wide stretch of the jungle had been *erased*, reduced to drifting, powdery ash along a hundred-fifty-foot path. He saw Urelle wince. "Incinerating barrier," she said in a low tone. "I've seen notes on that, but I've never tried to make anything like it."

"Presumably one side trying to stop the other," Quester said.

A form half-obscured by leaves caught Ingram's attention; he stepped over and pushed the branches out of the way... and then fell on his knees, feeling as though fire and ice were raging within his chest, as he stared at the body lying limp on the ground, blood staining the usually impeccable uniform. "Oh, *Athena*... it's *Kerridan*."

The Mask of Ares

"Who was Kerridan?" Victoria asked, eyes continuing her survey of the area.

"One of the Captain's Guardians." He reached out and with shaking fingers removed the gold bars from the uniform collar, bars imprinted with a tiny duplicate of the Camp-Bel symbol, and the two other pins, those of the Captain's Crew. "Given the Lieutenant's bars. Third from the top. If he was here... the *Captain* was here." He bowed his head for an instant. "Thanks in service, Kerridan. *Rhyme and Reason* will remember its Crew."

"And now we know the Camp-Bels were in all likelihood the pursued, not the pursuers," Quester said. "Those are heirlooms of your Founder, yes? They would not have left them behind, even had they found it necessary to leave the body, unless they were pursued close indeed."

"You're right." He straightened, gave both the sign of Athena and that of the Clan. "Rest now, Lieutenant Kerridan. The duty passes." He clenched his fist around the little pieces of metal and turned towards the blackened, ripped pathway. "He's still warm, the blood hasn't fully dried. Maybe..."

And then in the distance he heard it: a chattering, ripping sound, the war-cry of one of the inherited weapons, and above it the booming voice of the Captain: "The Clan! The Clan! For *Rhyme and Reason!*"

Now he sprinted, tearing his way through the remnants of the jungle, and he neither heeded nor cared for the cries of his friends, because *that* was the call he had feared and hoped for all his life, the call of the Captain to all the Clan to come, to rally to him, and Ingram Camp-Bel *would* answer that call.

Low-slanting sunlight filled a clearing before him, and dozens of struggling figures leapt and fired and parried and screamed and cursed. Not fifty feet distant, a huge form watched the battle, inhumanly tall, spidery in its thinness, with iron-edged wings springing from a narrow, armored back, gripping a huge maul in one hand and a black stone shield in the other; it was surrounded by a small guard of other figures, some human, some otherwise.

And all of them wore, on arm or hauberk or on spread-edged wing, the symbol of the sword and torch and chariot.

"*For the FOUNDER!*" he shouted, and charged.

Chapter 38
Ingram's Victory

Victoria focused as she ran, trying to keep up with the desperate boy as he answered that hopeless, clarion cry for aid. *Speed of East, Guidance of Spring, Light of South,* she thought, remembering the lessons Lythos had taught her as a young girl, the lessons drilled into her in the five decades since. *Circle of Summer, Wisdom of West, Flow of Fall, Hardness of North, Cleansing of Winter,* she completed the meditation, and felt the Eight Winds rising, unifying within the Ninth Wind of the Spirit and lending her all the aspects of every one of the True Winds.

Her body was lighter, her great axe sharper, the forest brighter and clearer, and she could hear the sounds of battle now, not merely the strange chattering, tearing sound of what must be Camp-Bel technological heirlooms, but the clang and rattle of weapons and armor, the shouts and curses, the hiss and sharp, loud snap and blast of magical spells and shields clashing.

And then they were through the verge and she could see the crews of the wrecked ships fighting for their lives – and the ominous group of figures watching the battle, as though for a particular moment or target.

Myrionar's Balance. *That's a Scutuzhak!* She hadn't seen one of the murderous things – demons usually serving either Erherveria or Voorith – for twenty years, and she would have been perfectly fine not seeing one for another twenty.

And Ingram Camp-Bel was sprinting straight for it, shouting his own battle-cry, his staff-like weapon with its twin half-moon blades held before him like a lance.

The creature whirled with blurring speed, as did its retinue, and stared for a startled instant at the tiny, lone human charging it; then its huge, cross-pupilled red eyes spotted the three others of their little party. It gave forth its own cry, a hiss and grinding rattle of rust-edged challenge from an unnaturally long and gaunt face, and gestured its guardians towards Ingram, whipping around one edged wing as it did so.

Steel-glinting shards of something streaked towards Ingram, but not one hit its mark; the *anai-k'ota* deflected them all in a sweeping parry that was so precisely guided that it looked casual.

And finally, Victoria saw the proof of what they had suspected all along.

There were eight or nine between Ingram and the Scutuzhak, three human, one bilarel, a scorpion ten feet long with a vicious intelligence in its multiple eyes, and several Xiilistiin. One of the humans was a mage, weaving a spell even as the lavender-haired boy approached, and the others had spread into a crescent, to surround and down the boy in moments.

They never had a chance.

Ingram Camp-Bel tore into the ranks of his opponents. The jet of flame from the wizard split harmlessly against the edge of the *anai-k'ota*, and then Ingram dropped to the ground, skidding between the legs of the bilarel with the blade raised; armor parted and blood fountained.

Ingram's face was set in a mask of cold fury; the doubts, the hesitations, the self-questioning were gone, and there was only the focus of the mission, his oath, his *life*, in one single moment.

The bilarel had barely begun to fall before Ingram was up, and the *anai-k'ota* broke apart, one crescent blade streaking out, trailing a chain that wrapped about the tail of the monstrous scorpion, a chain that then retracted, bringing Ingram atop the monster. It struck at him with a stinger a foot long, a move so fast that it flickered like lightning, but Ingram was faster still, twisting aside and pulling down, and then the boy was flung away into the air as the scorpion convulsed into death, its own sting buried deep between its eyes.

But Ingram was not done; he had *timed* that strike, somehow, Victoria knew, *calculated* the death-spasm's force and angle, and the twin chain-crescents preceded him, one catching the neck of the magic-wielding man and the other entangling the striking claw of a Xiilistiin. He sped past them through the air and then jack-knifed his body, imparting a vicious yank to both ends of the *anai-k'ota*; even from her position fifty feet back, Victoria could hear the green-wood *snap* of a man's neck breaking, and the sharper *crack* as the Xiilistiin lost its entire arm.

Ingram landed at the same time the bilarel's body actually finished falling to the ground, and spun about, his weapon back to being a double-bladed staff that caught another Xiilistiin blow and then rammed through the insectoid creature's face, whipped back to hammer one of the other humans so hard in the head that despite his helm, the man dropped instantly. The boy ducked and tumbled away from the remaining enemies, then lunged as one charged, severing one leg, and then there were only two left, and then one, and Ingram was turning away, the last Xiilistiin leaping for him—

—and brought down by Quester, whose final leap had carried him precisely behind his friend.

For an instant, the tall, angular demon froze, staring in what seemed disbelief, and even the rest of the battle was momentarily quieter.

And this is the boy who thought he could not be good enough. That he would always be, not merely second-best, but below ranking, never worthy to be a warrior and protector. Victoria smiled grimly, even as she moved forward. *Whatever else they may have told him, surely they must answer for those lies.*

"Who are you?" the Scutuzhak demanded finally, in a voice of screams and buzzes.

Ingram did not answer, but sped directly for the demon.

The black-stone shield parried the charge, and the maul swept down with a speed that forced Ingram to tumble aside, and then dodge again, and *again* as the blade-edged wings slashed out, cutting stone as easily as air. The *anai-k'ota* proved much less fragile, turning another wing-cut aside, but the momentum of Ingram's charge was broken. The demon's skeletal tail arched up and blocked Quester's sudden strike, as well.

This monster will take at least two or three of us. Victoria remembered all too well the price in pain and blood the last time she and her friends had faced one of the blade-demons. *And one working with other creatures? That tells me Ares has demons as allies, and strong ones at that, to call up a Scutuzhak!*

Words in *Artan* and Ancient Sauran from behind her, and a sparkling barrier arched out, curved around, almost enclosing the demon, keeping any possible allies from reaching it. Glancing back, Victoria saw Urelle wobble momentarily, knew the girl was nowhere near recovered. *This and one or two more spells and she will be done for the day. We'll have to carry this ourselves.*

But she had had time, she had maintained focus. She let the Speed of the East Wind combine with the Hardness of the North, and *flew* towards the demon, Twin-Edged Fate cutting the air itself in a deadly arc.

Even the lightning speed of the demon could not completely save it; it threw itself backwards, but the tail trailed behind, and her Axe severed it three feet from the end.

An unoiled-gate screech and a curse in a demonic tongue was its response, as yellow and gray fluid spurted from the stump. Both wings flicked a hail of blades outward, but they rebounded from Victoria's armored coat and Quester's exoskeleton; Ingram merely dove under the line of fire and came up in a lunge, one barely deflected by the Scutuzhak's right arm.

The long, gray, gaunt face stretched even farther, the mouth gaping six inches, a foot, more, and Victoria only had an instant to breathe deep before a blast of gray-green vapor enveloped them all.

Quester leapt high and wide, trailing shadowy traces of the gas but landing well clear of it; even so, his breathing whistled raggedly through his spiracles and he staggered as he landed. Victoria charged, instead, and to her surprise found Ingram next to her, his breathing halted like her own to prevent any chance of breathing that lethal fog. *But we can fight for only a few moments without breathing...*

The blade demon snarled as they pressed it. Ingram's staff cut and blocked and slashed and feinted, a whirling circle of edged death that its wings and arms barely blocked, and every time Victoria swung, it was forced to give back a step as it parried the great axe.

But its tail was already healing, extending slowly to its old length. They had surprised it, but they had not wounded it badly. *I can increase my weapon's power enough to do so,* she thought, *but it will take* time *that we do not have!* Ingram's face was growing red with the effort of fighting without breathing, and Victoria could already feel her lungs fighting her for air. The demon's gaunt face began to smile.

The atmosphere about her twitched, and then a powerful blast of wind screamed past them, dispersing the deadly cloud like dawn mist.

"Well done, Urelle!" Quester cried as he leapt back into the fray.

"Hold it!" Urelle shouted back. "Find some way to make it stay *still*, just for a few seconds!"

Victoria had no idea what she had in mind, but she caught Ingram's eye and nodded.

Once more, Ingram's unique weapon spun and the blade-ended chain flashed out; but the demon was yet faster, and had stepped back *just* far enough.

Fortunately, the demon hadn't really been the target.

The *anai-k'ota*'s blade wrapped tightly around the haft of Twin-Edged Fate, just below the monster axe's head, and Victoria was already in motion, speeding around the Scutuzhak. It saw what she intended, but Quester was above it and coming down, and it was forced to parry a smash of his longmace. Ingram was sprinting towards her, still holding his weapon, and then slid *under* the chain as she passed him, and the chain went taut – entwined entirely around the demon.

It heaved against the restraint, dragging both of them sideways, but then Quester landed, grabbed on to anchor Ingram, and for a few instants, the Scutuzhak struggled vainly, trying to find purchase on the thick dirt and failing.

Seven sparks of light flew from Urelle and landed, burning, around the demon; lines flickered and solidified, and abruptly there was a seven-pointed star enclosing the Scutuzhak, burning pure white in the earth. "He's sealed! Let go, just don't drag anything on the ground!"

Ingram, not Victoria, released his hold, letting her use her full Vantage strength to whip the chain free. The demon tried to stop it, but was pulled sideways and smashed into the side of the septacle, air flaring into blue impenetrability for a moment; the impact forced him to release the chain and it flew free, clearing the lines by a foot and a half.

"I can hold him," Urelle said, kneeling but face certain, her gray eyes steady. "I'll send him back to the Hells! Go help the others!"

"Thank you, Urelle!" The rage on Ingram's face had momentarily faded, and he smiled at her niece for just an instant before his face hardened and he spun around, catching the *anai-k'ota* as Victoria tossed it back to him.

Below the little ridge, a small knot of defenders struggled against far more attackers, and the defenders were the ones wearing the symbol of the Clan. Quester leapt up, taking aim, and one of his vicious javelins took a Xiilistiin directly through its chest.

Now the attackers had a problem; they could not ignore the three sweeping down on them from the rear, but diverting their attention from the desperate and trapped Camp-Bels might give them a chance. The leader of the attack, Victoria could see, was another demon – a thing of flame and stone, a spider of lava and death. It ground out orders in a bubbling, low-toned voice, and a knot of its people peeled off from the rest, turned to intercept the three of them; meanwhile, the demon moved forward, taking an active and immediate interest in finishing the few remaining survivors.

"Go on, Ingram, Quester! I have these!" Victoria said, and reinforced her focus. *It will leave me useless for a while... but Myrionar grant this will be enough.*

She reached through the swirl of the Eight Winds to the center of her soul, the Ninth Wind, that she could not yet control but could, for a brief moment, *touch*, as she had those months before. "*Sharee-Ka-Hazi!*"

And for one instant, the force before them, all ten attackers – human, Xiilistiin, hulking mass of mobile greenery, armored reptilian monster – froze, to her perceptions, to crystal immobility.

She sped forward, Twin-Edged Fate momentarily light as a baton in her hand, and she had time, all of a lifetime, to judge her path, the path that would take her past each and every one of them at the right angle and distance for a perfect strike. It was dreamlike, that speed, as headlong as a runaway cart and as smooth and certain as a dance, velocity and perception fused to a single transcendent moment of absolute knowledge and control of the laws of motion, of life and death.

The huge axe flickered out, seeming to move of its own accord, without effort, even as she was also conscious of the pure force of her motions, her hips and arms and legs and waist all coordinated to deliver the most devastating blows she could imagine, one after another, and she could not even see the results of one strike before the other was done, she had passed three, seven, all ten were behind her, and as the pressure of age and exhaustion and mortality reclaimed her, blood and ichor fountained in her wake as ten bodies in twenty pieces tumbled to the ground.

Breathing heavily, leaning on her axe, she stared down the hill, and saw her other companions smashing deep into the ranks of Ares' troops. Ingram's weapon was a blur, invisible save for the terrible blows it struck, and Quester leapt back and forth, clearing away any who thought they could close in behind the Camp-Bel child.

The demon pulsed a rumble of anger that vibrated stones in the ground, and lunged into the mass of defenders, taking strikes on all sides and bleeding flame and dirt, but catching a figure before it, bringing it down.

The figure made a movement as it disappeared below the flaming demon, and a concussion rocked the hill, sending Victoria sprawling.

Chunks of burning stone rained down around her and she saw, as she covered her head to protect it, that a great smoking hole marked where the demon had been. At the same time, she heard Urelle's voice raised loudly enough to echo across the field, and blue-white light flared up. She could *sense* the disappearance of the malevolent Scutuzhak.

As if that had been a signal, the attackers broke, fleeing as if with one will to the different points of the compass.

The battle was over, Victoria knew, and drew a deep breath in preparation for facing the question that remained: had they come just a few minutes too late?

Chapter 39
Clan Camp-Bel

Ingram stared at the knot of people remaining, most of them so covered with dirt, blood, and whatever fluids their adversaries had shed that he couldn't immediately recognize them. *But they're not* all *dead. Not all of them.*

Panting, he straightened to his full, if diminutive, height. "Clan Camp-Bel," he said, as firmly and loudly as his aching lungs and body would allow, "Ingram Camp-Bel reporting, by command of the Captain." He felt a sad smile on his face. "Sorry it took me so long."

"As... are we," came a faint voice.

Ingram's gaze snapped to the side and down, and he felt both awe and horror rising within him.

The form on the ground, within the still-fuming crater, should have been not merely dead but obliterated; Ingram had recognized that detonation. But though the green and white armor was cracked and blood trickled from most of it, the shape was still that of a man, a small, compact man whose face was rigid with pain and control. His helmet, too, had cracked and fallen away.

"Captain," Ingram said with disbelief. Then, "*Captain!*"

"Such... concern I do not deserve, Ingram." The brown eyes, a shade lighter than the skin around them, might have held a touch of humor. "As I have failed you twice, now."

"Failed... *me?*" Ingram shook his head slowly, unable to grasp that the Captain – *the Captain!* – could say such things to him. "No, sir, *I* failed the *Clan*! I ran away, I stole from the Clan, and when you called it took so long to find me that..." he gestured with a trembling hand at the bodies strewn about.

"Failed you, indeed," the Captain said; it seemed a faint mist came from his mouth as he did. His body did not move, but his gaze shifted. "I see... you brought allies. Strong allies, that saved the few of us left."

"Would that we could have arrived sooner," Victoria said. "But do not speak. Let us tend you, and those others of your Clan who require it."

The slightest movement of the head. "No healing... will suffice now, unless one of you be priests or healers of truly mighty gods." He glanced down, and Ingram saw there were two black puncture wounds that had penetrated the armor – armor that looked *melted* around the edges.

Victoria saw it too. "Myrionar's *Sword*. It bit you."

"And the *delipyrga* is already working through me." He grinned suddenly, showing white teeth like a cheerful snarl. "But I fed it a Mark IV grenade at the same moment. Its own body shielded me a bit." He winced, and Ingram saw another puff of vapor... or smoke.

Mother of All preserve him. His friend's thoughts were filled with a shuddering empathy. *Demon's venom. We have nothing strong enough for that. He will soon begin to burn.*

"No!" Ingram shouted. "Athena's *Spear*, no! There must be... must be *something*! I've come all this way, I have your *summons*, I have the *Insignia*, I have to know *why*!"

The Captain managed a nod. "Not much time." He glanced at the others.

Ingram shook his head. "They're my friends. I trust them. Tell me!"

A sigh with a hint of blue mist, a faint scent of cooking that sent a pang of nausea along with horror through Ingram. "As... you will. You were... to be hidden. Being hunted by forces..." The Captain winced again and could not restrain a moan. "...forces we now know were Ares. Killed Berenike..."

"I know!" This wasn't the time to tell him Berenike wasn't dead, though it'd probably make him feel better. "But *why*?"

"You... foretold to stop him. Do not know... exactly how."

"Me? Stop *Ares*?"

"Had to hide you. Keep anyone from seeing you. From thinking... you were worth noticing." Smoke was now constant, and the *smell*...

The Captain gasped, a puff of blue mist, then reached towards him. "No time... your parents know more..." Fingers that were starting to darken scrabbled within the broken armor, came out holding the Insignia that had been on his chest. The Captain pressed it into his fingers. "Still in... Aegeia. Have to find a way there. Talk to them."

"We're almost there, sir! I'll—"

"It's sealed off, Ingram," said another voice. He looked up, saw the Second Lieutenant, Pennon, kneeling now beside the Captain. "Cut one of the pursuing ships in half when the seal came down."

"*What?*"

"Must... find a way!" The Captain made one last supreme effort. "You are... not what you believe... not what we *made* you... you..."

Flame burst from his mouth.

Ingram felt himself yanked backwards, by who he could not say, as the Captain began to *glow*, first a dull, sullen red, then brighter, the color of the reddest sunrise, then orange, ascending to yellow, then white, and as he and the others stumbled back it blazed to a blue-white fury that scorched his skin at fifty feet... and then so bright that they all cried out, shielding their eyes. For an instant, Ingram realized he could *see* the bones of his arm through the flesh, so terribly brilliant was the light... and then it was gone.

Flames licked up from a pool of swiftly-cooling lava. Of the Captain, and even his armor, there was not a trace.

Everyone was silent for a moment. Then Ingram, ignoring the pain prickling his skin, rose and faced that boiling pool. The other Camp-Bels followed, even those with broken limbs forcing themselves upright. Ingram bowed, and gave three salutes, knowing the rest did so as well. Then he turned, and trying to keep his voice under control, extended the Insignia. "The Captain is dead. Command passes. Pennon, you are Captain, now."

Pennon looked down and swallowed, her usually round and cheerful face suddenly looking ten years older. But she took the Insignia, removed her Lieutenant's mark, and replaced it with the Insignia. "I assume Command of the Ship and the Clan," she said slowly. "In the name of the Founder, I pray I shall lead you wisely."

"The Clan salutes the Captain!"

As Pennon opened her mouth again, another chill swept over Ingram. For a moment he thought a cloud had passed over the sun, for the world seemed *darker*. Yet... no. There was nothing he could *see* that was different. But the feeling remained, as though the faintest mist of darkness floated before him. An oppressive foreboding hovered behind this perception, a feeling of infinitely distant, yet infinitely malevolent, power.

"What in the name of the *Mothers*..." buzzed Quester.

"So, you felt it too," murmured Victoria.

"What *was* that, Auntie?" Urelle was wide-eyed even as she stumbled up to them, exhausted.

The Camp-Bels were looking amongst themselves, as confused as the rest of them.

And then came the laugh.

It was a low, rattling laugh, the laugh of something dying, yet gripped by a fit of mirth that overcame even the approach of death. Looking around, Ingram saw that the eerie sound came from a Xiilistiin, one who had a nearly-human form; it smiled edged daggers at them as they all stared. "We may be dying... but your doom is now certain," it said, and snickered again.

"What do you mean, creature?" demanded one of the Clan.

"The Swarm knows, the Swarm sees many things, working with the one you call Ares. Sees, hears, knows secrets." It coughed a clot of blood or ichor, laughed again. "Cut off Aegeia is, so cut off I hear not its song. But I *remember*, know what was spoken of in secret counsels. And now I *feel* it, and laugh, for your world is doomed, and only Ares' realm will endure, when the King of All Hells walks the world."

As they stared in disbelief and dawning, hideous dismay, it gave a final buzzing cackle and collapsed.

Chapter 40
Not a Failure

Though that last terrible shock reverberated through her own mind, Urelle could see that Ingram was far worse off. *He arrived too late to save most of his Clan, and then he watched his leader, the Captain, die more horribly than just about anything, and now* this? She reached out, and touched Ingram's shoulder.

He stiffened, started to shrug her off, but then closed his eyes, and brought his hand up, touched hers. She heard a catch in his breathing, the hint of a sob, before he caught it, forced it back with that iron control his Clan had taught him. *I don't think that's really good for him... but I don't know how to change it. That's part of who he is.*

She looked instead to her aunt. "Auntie... did he mean what I think?"

Victoria looked older than she had just moments ago, the silver in her hair tarnished and dull. "I can't imagine another meaning. Even with a thousand gods, there is only one 'King of All Hells.' The Black Star walks the world?" She shook her head.

"And he would not come alone," Quester murmured. "Could the Black City itself have achieved interphase?"

Ingram's grip on her hand tightened. Then he let go and faced them. "It doesn't matter though, does it?"

Doesn't matter? For a moment Urelle was stunned by the simple assertion, but then she saw her aunt's head tilt, rather like Quester's.

A minuscule smile touched Victoria's lips. "Perhaps not. At least, not for anything we need do soon. Ultimately, of course, if he is not stopped, it will matter, indeed. But I do not feel he or his forces are in any way close to us."

"No." The new Captain straightened and surveyed their group. "No, I believe that problem, huge though it may be, is not ours, save only for what effect it has upon the world at large."

"You mean this feeling of... oppression."

Urelle concentrated, found herself frowning. "Not just a feeling, Auntie. It's... it's like a huge, sodden blanket over my spirit, weighing me down. It's going to affect any spellcaster – not much, maybe, but enough to notice. And it will *definitely* affect people's morale and attitudes – again, not to a *huge* extent, but if you turn all the great days into just good days, and the good ones into ordinary... well, there will be a lot of people whose merely bad days might destroy them."

She caught Ingram's gaze just before it dropped, held that violet regard with her own. "But that doesn't matter, either. We still have the same job to do."

His smile looked a touch forced... but it was forced for *her*, and that meant a lot. "Right. We can't stop now. *Especially* now."

"Understood," Captain Pennon said after a moment. "You and your friends need to get to Aegeia, somehow."

"Captain," Ingram said, "Do you know more? I mean, the old Captain couldn't finish..."

Urelle could see the answer in Pennon's face before she answered. "I wish I did, Ingram. Maybe the First Lieutenant did, but whatever the secrets were, they were kept *close*. I was only told that you were *important* and that on the day you returned, getting you where you needed to go was the Clan's top priority."

One of the other Camp-Bels, a whip-thin man with a narrow beard and darting, dark-brown eyes, had approached to within earshot. "Hoy, Captain, did I hear you right? *Ingram* is top priority?" His voice and bearing echoed the incredulity on his face, and Urelle saw the same expression rippling through the other survivors – and saw Ingram flinching, the confidence he exuded in their group faded to nothing as he saw the disbelieving eyes of the survivors on him.

"How *dare* you," she heard herself say.

The tall man looked at her, startled. "What?" he snapped. "This is Camp-Bel business—"

"How *dare* you doubt him?" she interrupted. "You know *nothing* of what he's done, of what he's gone through because of *your* people. By Myrionar's *Sword*, I sure hope your reasons turn out to be good, because from what I've heard you sure don't *deserve* him!"

The man opened his mouth again, but this time it was Pennon who spoke, and her soprano voice was a blade. "Silence, Guardian Paschalia."

Paschalia froze, mouth still open, and the other Camp-Bels stared.

"This was need-to-know information, Guardian, and until this disaster none of you *needed to know*." She gave a twisted, bitter smile. "I suppose we should be gratified; if so many of our people, even of the Crew-Elect, believed in Ingram the Failure, the Charity-Case? Then the imposture and the effort of conveying that impression may just have been worth it, because that means that – probably – no one *outside* of the Clan ever doubted it for a moment."

Paschalia had slowly straightened and closed his mouth. Now he saluted – the same across the chest and then upright-arm gesture Berenike had used – and spoke again. This time, however, his voice held none of the disbelief, only concern and caution. "Sir! You are saying, then, that this was all a lie? That Ingram—"

"Look on the other side of that hill," Victoria said tartly. "You'll see the corpses of eight or nine he killed in a matter of seconds, just trying to get here. I am a Guild Adventurer out of Zarathanton, young man, and I have fought alongside dozens, up to and including the Marshal of Hosts himself, and I will tell you that I have known famous Adventurers thrice his age who would despair of being as lethal, as clever, as courageous, or as tenacious as Ingram Camp-Bel."

Urelle saw there was more than a touch of red on Ingram's cheeks, but his eyes were *shining* at Victoria.

Paschalia's eyes flicked to Victoria's shoulderpatch, and he nodded, then took a deep breath and turned to Ingram. "My apologies."

With an air of vindicated embarrassment, Ingram waved it off. "It's... all right, sir. Even *I* was fooled, I guess." He looked past at the others, then winced. "But we're wasting time talking when people need help!"

Urelle winced, herself. *Maybe these things did need to be resolved... but by the Balance, these Camp-Bels are in bad shape!*

For the next hour, their every effort was focused on healing the wounded – setting broken bones, giving some of their fast-dwindling stock of healing draughts to the worst-off, countering creeping poison, lifting battle-curses, restoring lifeforce leeched by some of the things unleashed against the Camp-Bels by their pursuers.

At last, Urelle sank, exhausted, to rest on one of the scattered boulders littering the clearing. She felt an ache and sparks of luminous pain jittering through her, a pain that was neither crushing nor stabbing nor cold nor heat, but a pain clear and filled with warning that only a mage or, perhaps, a master of spirit energy such as the legendary *ki* warriors would truly understand. *Even the few spells I cast, even just unraveling these curses, it's strained me badly. Tomorrow I will be lucky if I can manage the spells to clean myself off in this jungle.* A wave of vertigo crashed into her and she wavered, even seated, on the edge of falling.

A small, strong hand caught her, steadied her. Blinking, she looked up into Ingram's eyes, two shades darker than the lavender of his hair, saw his concern. "Are you all right, Urelle?" He sat down next to her, keeping her steady; now, of course, his eyes were below hers. *So small, yet... so* reliable.

"Of course, I'm..." she began, then shook her head. *I have to be honest with him. Honest with all of us.* "...no. Not really. The Wanderer was right. I don't *think* I've done myself any real damage, but I'll be useless tomorrow, and maybe for a few days after that." She looked down, fighting the dizziness; she leaned against Ingram to steady herself.

His arm went around her shoulders with a curious hesitancy, but once there she felt his arm firm up, become something strong enough to relax against. "I... I... It's okay," he said, with an unusual stammer. "I mean, you, um, you did more than enough, that demon, what your Aunt calls a *Scutuzhak*, it was *bad* trouble if it'd stayed around. I would've done what I could, but..." he shook his head. "I don't know. Lucky we didn't have to find out." His gaze met hers again. "Lucky, we had you."

She was suddenly aware that she was leaning *very* close to him, and felt her cheeks burning. *Oh.*

A smile burst across his face, and she saw hints of pink on his lighter, tanned cheeks. "Um, I've been wanting to do this for a while." He pulled her just a tiny bit closer. "I guess... you don't mind?"

She glanced over at Victoria, who seemed to be studiously ignoring both of them, and noticed the new Captain grinning before turning away. "I... don't mind," she said, and let her head fall gently to his shoulder, hearing his surprised, happy, tremulous sigh as she did. "I don't mind at all."

Chapter 41
Conversation with a King

Raiagamor paused a moment, preparing himself. *I must always remember control. The King is not my ally yet, and he delights in provoking response, in testing control. That is my weakness. He knows it. I know it. Mother knows it. I must – must! – show that I have mastered myself.*

This was a truth he drilled into himself every day. Yet he knew, in the days when his mind was clearest, that the King *was* right to mistrust him. Raiagamor *was* mad, *was* unstable. That did not – quite – utterly disqualify him for membership in that highest of high families, the King's children, but it did, would, and must place him under vastly more scrutiny before admission.

And I had best remember that, during every second of this interview. The King had asked for a status report on his own; that implied that Raiagamor's progress either held interest for him... or that he intended to test Raiagamor's control and patience just for his own royal amusement. Either one was a possibility filled with peril. *And as Mother is not available for this conference, I am entirely on my own.* Even his closest allies did not know *this* part of his life.

Before the tension could go beyond focus and become mania or anger, he stepped before the mirror-scroll – as far as he knew, the only remaining functional link to the lands beyond Aegeia. *And even that would be impossible were the King anything other than who He is.* "Majesty, I am here."

The shining surface instantly flickered, showing a dimly-lit room with the King seated at a desk, wearing his preferred human guise: a man of perhaps thirty or so, pale of skin, golden of hair, blue of eye, with an open, friendly countenance that had convinced many a being of his essential benevolence on first sight. "Punctuality is an excellent beginning, Raiagamor," he said with a smile. "A good day to you."

"And you, Majesty."

"I am sure you have noticed a... change recently." The smile sharpened.

"I did, as did my allies. Most gratifying, Majesty. The Black City has arrived on schedule?"

"The new schedule, yes, after that little setback of Voorith's." The King gestured casually. "Other aspects of my own plan are proceeding well enough. I was interested in how your own progresses... especially since it does fill a small gap in my own plan."

Raiagamor bowed his head in what he hoped was a proper mix of personal pride and respect. It was difficult to know when Fath... the King wanted you to put yourself forward, and when he wished to ignore your contributions. *I suspect it is not quite so difficult if you are actually* accepted *as one of his people.* "I am pleased that my own work dovetails so well with your own."

"Well, now, it's not so surprising; you started it all, I suppose, I've just rather expanded and built on the whole idea. But in any event, tell me your current status."

That much was easy; he'd had plenty of time to decide on how to best summarize everything. Quickly, he sketched out the situation in Aegeia – the false Athena, the current and near-future plans for the conflict and resolution between them, the sealing away of Aegeia and how that had rendered the Camp-Bel issue moot, and the general disposition of the country's city-states and how he intended to bring them all under control.

"So," he said, winding up his description, "there appear to be only three God-Warriors active that aren't under our control – and that's fine, as we still need some honest, active opposition for a few months, at least. Berenike has made no appearances, even where we would expect her to do so – after all, a false Athena? What actual God-Warrior of the Lady of Wisdom could *possibly* let such a thing pass?"

"I find I must agree with you. If this Berenike was a true God-Warrior – and certainly your own people's testimony would seem to support that view – she could hardly allow such an imposture." The King's smile shimmered diamond blades for an instant. "Yet... you have not *killed* her, have you?"

"Not unless that force we dispatched managed it, no," Raiagamor admitted.

"Which would seem a forlorn hope, indeed. You believe it is this Berenike that was indicated by the Cards, yes?"

"I can think of no other candidate," Raiagamor said cautiously, "though of course there *could* be another. She could be a distraction. Your warnings about the Cards certainly allow for that."

"Yes, that and more, Raiaga." The blade-smile again. "But in either case, it seems you have failed to address the *actual* flaw in your plan, yes?"

A bolt of anger at the mocking tone, turned aside at the last moment by iron-willed control. "Indeed? Majesty, is it always necessary that such threats to one's plans be killed, or can they not be neutralized by other means?"

"Hm." The pause and more human smile was a signal, a concession of a small but vital point – or perhaps an acknowledgement of him not losing control. Either one was a hopeful sign. "No, I would not say that death *must* be the solution. You believe you have already solved the problem?"

"I believe I have made a good start at it," Riagamor said, after a pause to consider the best way to say what he wanted without missteps. "If Berenike is the threat, it seems nigh-certain she has been walled out of Aegeia. I believe, also, that it is a reasonable assumption that my adversary *must* actually enter Aegeia to actually topple my overall plan."

The King inclined his head. "Go on."

"If Berenike is *not* the primary threat – if she is merely an added impediment and distraction – then it was well-established by the Coins I empowered from the Cards themselves that said threat was still outside Aegeia's borders within days, at most, of the border closing. If that threat had been capable of such rapid and purposeful movement that they could have covered the hundreds of miles between their last known location and Aegeia in such a way, why did they not use it before? Thus, I conclude they are walled away, outside of the barrier, and as long as this condition holds, they are, and will remain, no threat."

The King nodded thoughtfully. "To that extent, I find myself willing to agree. But do you believe your barrier to be so absolutely impenetrable?"

"Nothing is *absolute*, of course, Majesty," he said. "For instance, there is no doubt in my mind that you yourself could pass the barrier, and likely the Elders as well; I myself can do so, through the certain talents that I share with your people. But it is established that the Seal of Athena excluded interference by gods and mortals in Aegeia's affairs, and I – with my mother's aid, I admit, though I take much credit for the research and design – have replicated that thoroughly.

"The Aegei, of course, still can be active here in Aegeia – although the agreement between the gods about direct interference prevents a number of ways they might act unless they become incarnate." He gave a bow to the King, acknowledging that it was really the King's doing that such an agreement between the gods had been arranged; a momentary smile was the response.

"So," he went on, "I am currently the only incarnate god here – having consumed Ares and become him, in essence. Athena's incarnation is almost impossible, and the others rarely have ever incarnated during the conflict portion of a Cycle. I am, of course, doing my best to prevent that possibility in any case. But even if they *were* incarnate, their powers cannot *cross* the barrier, and thus even the Aegei can't transport my theoretical nemesis here."

The King was silent, waiting, blue eyes amused behind steepled fingers. That nettled him unreasonably – which was enough warning that he was able to divert the anger back into discipline.

"That said, there *is* a very small possibility of passage through the barrier, at the point that the enchantment was secured, here in the northernmost portion of Aegeia." He caused the map to appear in the air near him, at a gesture.

"This is protected by several things. First, by obscurity; insofar as I know, such a weakness should have existed in prior Seals, but was never mentioned to have been exploited in the prior Cycles, which means that, as far as anyone else should know, the barrier *has* no weak point.

"Second, location. That pass is blocked by the Freehold, which is bound by law and tradition to let none pass when the Cycle has begun. Few are the people who would challenge the Salandaras in his Freehold, and even fewer would be able to convince him to abandon duty to let them pass."

"Third, it is *not* an opening in the barrier; it is more... a weaker point that may be slightly unraveled to make an *extremely* perilous passage, one that extends across more than one set of probabilities. Any invaders would have to succeed in passing quite a gantlet of threats before actually making it *into* Aegeia, assuming they had deduced the existence of this weak point *and* found a way to exploit it.

"Fourth and finally, I have not assumed this is impossible. I have already set guards near such possible exit points as may exist, and will be increasing their forces as time and resources allow. At the least, I will be well-warned if any such breaches occur." He raised his eyes and met the King's enigmatic gaze.

A few moments passed. Finally, the King unlaced his fingers and leaned back. "A competent and well-reasoned explanation, Raiagamor. And you maintained good control. I am, for the moment, reasonably pleased. Not *confident* in your success, mind you, but you have not yet embarrassed yourself or your mother, which *does* please me."

"Might I ask why you are not confident, Sire?"

The King laughed. "Because your preparations, dear Raiaga, are so... *rational*. I think you have worked very hard to control your irrationality, and that is, of course, all to the good. Yet the *world*, ahh, the *world* is not so tied to the rational.

"Many people – most, indeed, both in the realms of the mortals and those of the gods – who do evil *hide* it from themselves, convince themselves that they are right and the others are wrong, that they are just even while they betray all the principles of justice, and so on and so forth, a fine and amusing cycle of self-delusion that repeats both up and down the chains of power and command.

"But I – and I hope you – recognize that *we* are no such deluded souls; please recognize what an honor I extend, that I assume you share this honesty with me. We know we seek to destroy that which is reasonably called 'good,' to corrupt it, to consume it, to break its power and replace it with its opposite number. That means, my friend, that we are inevitably and inarguably *villains*. And that means, equally inevitably, that our opponents are *heroes*.

"And the single most defining traits of true Heroes, Raiagamor, is that *they do the impossible*."

"Then, does that not mean that *your* plans are also ones you have no confidence in, Majesty?"

"Ha! Symmetry would demand that, would it not? Yet I have certain... advantages even over yourself, in age, in power, in resources, in choices. I have much more reason for confidence.

"Yet... yes." The smile broadened. "Not a year ago, though far, far indeed from Zarathan, I was handed a defeat so wonderfully unexpected that even the pain I suffered was a tiny price to pay for the sake of the *surprise*. My plans, utterly destroyed by luck and mortal wit. So yes, Raiagamor, even my magnificent plans are vulnerable. Still... you have done well enough. Do you require my services?"

"Not at this time, Majesty. I wish to save your last service for as long as possible; perhaps, even to show that it was not needed."

"Now *that* would be a fine thing, Raiagamor. I will not begrudge you that third service, understand, but it will certainly reflect well on you if you succeed without requiring it." For an instant, the face shifted to its true inhuman aspect, mouth of diamond blades grinning below glowing eyes. "Of course, it would reflect *far worse* were your plan to fail because you neglected that resource out of pride. So plan well, little one."

The scroll went blank.

Raiagamor sank into a chair, trying to stem the unstable welter of emotions, then failing. Rising jerkily, he grabbed one of the chairs and broke it in half, then half again, then half again, as he let the impressions seethe through him.

He approved, overall, Raiagamor thought, and absently gouged a foot-wide chunk from the stone and crushed it in his hand. *He was warning of the vagaries of chance and the imponderables of heroes, not telling me I was stupid. Not telling me I had failed.*

He let a cackle escape, then for a few moments stopped even bothering to control himself.

"Lord Ares! Lord Ares, are you all right? What is wrong?"

The voice finally penetrated his consciousness, and Raiagamor looked around, seeing the entirety of the chamber... *destroyed*. It was scarcely possible to even recognize that there *had* been a table and chairs, workbenches, any of these things. Even the floor and ceiling were scored with slashes of claws that could carve gods; as he watched, another small chunk of stone fell from the weakened roof.

But, on the positive side, he felt... *peaceful*. It had been a while since he had truly allowed himself a rampage, and this one had been so... *limited* that he was surprised and gratified at its effect. He hadn't slain anyone. This disproved his theory that the only way to stop the madness was the consumption of a tormented soul, at least. *Though it is far more satisfying*, he thought with a flicker of a mad smile. *This peace will likely not last so long.*

"I am unharmed, Deimos," he said at last. "But bring in some artificers; my workshop and study require... repair."

Deimos entered and looked around; Raiaga could sense the consternation even from a demon at what he saw. "My... Lord?"

"A little release of nerves, Deimos. But things go well." As he contemplated how very little the King had critiqued him, his spirits rose. "They go very, very well indeed!"

Chapter 42
A New Destination

Quester watched as his strongest-flung spear rebounded from empty air a hundred feet above, the merest, momentary shimmer showing where the Seal of Athena had halted the weapon. He bounded up and caught the shaft of the weapon as it fell. "I suppose there was no reason that should have worked," he admitted.

"Not really," Ingram agreed. He glanced over to Captain Pennon, who had even tried using a weapon of their Founder, a device that fired a blast of pure, concentrated energy, against the Seal and found that it had no more effect than anything else they had attempted. "Urelle's the only one who hasn't tried."

"Not going to bother, either," Urelle said from behind them. Quester wasn't startled, as her scent had preceded her.

"Why not? I mean, in a couple days, when you're recovered."

She gestured a ways off, and Quester could see a circle scribed in the sand near the barrier. "Because with a circle, I could study it without straining myself. And that barrier?" She shivered. "Remember how I thought the spell on the *Coins* was tough? That thing... it's not just *coated* with what the Wanderer basically said was godspower, it's *filled* with godspower. Yes, there's a foundation of magic guiding it, and I can see the structure... but it's *perfect*, as far as I can see.

"It's a self-reinforcing network, any pressure on one point gets distributed across pretty much the whole thing. You can't drill through it at one point like you could a physical dome, using point force to overcome the massive strength of the whole dome."

Ingram smelled of anger and determination. "There *has* to be a way through." Then his scent wavered, and he gave a rueful smile. "Though the tales don't say there is."

"Under? Or perhaps if we go high enough, over?" Quester asked. "Surely there must be a way for air to pass; I do not see the clouds breaking up as they blow across the mountains."

"It is said that the Seal encloses Aegeia in her entirety, from beneath the floor of the world to the crown of the heavens," Pennon said absently. "How that works with the flow of waters within the land, the air and the sea, that is not told, but this is not merely magic, but the work of the gods. One presumes that their will is what defines it, and the will is to prevent interference, attack, intrusion, and presumably escape and communication from within as well. Thus, cast weapons are thrown back, people cannot pass, spells will not reach, but I would be unsurprised to find that *undirected* objects, say the remains of shipwrecks off the coast, might find their way to the shores of Aegeia."

At Ingram's thoughtful headtilt, Pennon chuckled. "But again, *will* is going to be the determinant. You will not fool it by trying to become flotsam, I think."

Ingram laughed. "I guess not." He looked pensively through the apparently-empty air towards the stretch of increasingly rocky beach beyond. "I wonder if Berenike's there or not."

Pennon blinked. "*Berenike?*"

Ingram winced, then glanced around. No one was within earshot except their own party and Pennon herself. *If anyone has need-to-know and right-to-know on this, it's the Captain,* Quester heard in his head.

This is your choice, Ingram, he thought back. *All of us know that with questions of Aegeia, it is your choice alone. That was agreed before. Save only that we will* not *allow you the choice to go alone.*

Ingram grinned back both in reality and in his mind – the latter far brighter. "Yes, Captain, Berenike."

Pennon stared at him for a long moment, then took a slow breath. "Ingram. I... we were all aware of how close you were with Berenike. And there was some... concern that you might refuse to accept her death. But..." she shook her head. "She *died* that day, Ingram. I saw her body, myself. It was injured, certainly... but I could recognize her."

"That," Ingram said, equally quietly, "was how she *wanted* it to be seen. I don't know exactly what she did to ensure the body could be mistaken for hers; she never told me, and I never really needed to know."

Pennon stared at him, mouth half-open. "Ingram... are you telling me that you have *seen* Berenike since that day?"

"Not just *me*, Pennon. Ask my friends."

Pennon looked to each of them. Victoria glanced up from where she was cleaning Twin-Edged Fate. "She has personally aided us twice thus far, Captain Pennon," Victoria said. "And the first time, she defeated a force led by Deimos himself with but two blows. Ingram says this is Berenike, she claims to be Berenike, and while I agree there is a mystery about her, I certainly have no reason to doubt that she is, in fact, Berenike."

Quester's antennae could easily scent the Captain's confusion, a mixture of disbelief and a burning desire to change that to belief, to hope. "You are *sure*?"

For answer, Urelle's hands danced through the air, catching and pulling delicately on the foundations of existence, and for an instant a vision danced before them all, of the gold-shining girl rising up, carrying Ingram up from his deadly fall, landing with a laugh and invincible confidence. "Is *that* Berenike?"

For a long, long moment the Captain stared in silence. Then... "Oh, Athena's Mercy," breathed Pennon, and tears started from her eyes. "That's... that's *her*, oh, by all the Aegei, that *is* Berenike. I don't know how it's possible. I don't understand why she never *told* us. But there cannot be two in all the worlds like her."

"She didn't tell you for the same reason you never let *me* know I was anything but a failure," Ingram said, an edge in his voice at the last phrase. "Because she was *the target*. Maybe they heard part of the same prophecy or whatever that the Clan knew about me, and thought Berenike was the one. Or did it never occur to you that if you made the real subject of a foretelling vanish, that they might decide the one they *could* see was what they were searching for?"

Pennon blinked away the tears and her mouth twisted in a bitter *moue*. "It did, indeed, occur to some of us. Berenike herself included, I will note. But in our defense, none of us imagined that the enemy would be so powerful, so widespread, and so subtle that they could land and assail Kyriarcnis with relative impunity. The few enemies who had tried such a thing in prior Cycles had been beaten so absolutely that the tales were object lessons in the humiliation of hubris."

"Right," Ingram said, and took a breath. "Anyway, that's what she told me when she visited me in the healer's hall one night; she knew she was a target; no one knew who was behind it, so she had to vanish. We had an... oath-bond, so she's been able to find and help me, even when no one else could have."

"An oath bond? Blooded?"

"She... considered that she owed me her life."

"What? How?" Then the Captain waved that away. "Sorry, not my business. The important thing is that she's alive. By the *Founder*, this could change things. If she's still inside, then there's an ally already *within Aegeia*. Maybe she'll make contact with the remaining Clan... no. She'll be doubly careful now." Her fist suddenly smacked into her hand. "Athena's Wisdom, *now* it makes some sense!"

"*What* makes sense?"

"Not long after the burial and service, orders came from the Captain – to a very, very select few – that we were to *remove* the remains and rebury them elsewhere, specifically, in the Camp-Bel graveyard, then seal the original tomb so that it looked untouched.

"At the time, I could only guess that they were worried that the remains could be desecrated somehow – gods know there are enough ways that necromancers and demon-guided can make foul use of such remnants of the pure – but it makes even more sense if I assume that they wanted to leave an opportunity for the enemy to *doubt*. Leave the wrong remains, they can always check that thoroughly and verify it was not Berenike. Leave *no* remains, you have to wonder if she is alive or dead."

"They know now, though. Deimos, unfortunately, didn't die."

"Curse the luck, then. But in any case, it is some of the finest news I could have hoped for after all our losses, that the Spear of Athena is reborn in one of those thought lost."

Quester bobbed his antennae in agreement as the others nodded their heads. Then Pennon turned to Ingram again.

"So, Ingram Camp-Bel," she said, "What will you do now?"

Ingram stared through the Seal. "Find a way in. Somehow." He rose to his feet, dusted off his knees, and looked northward. "But I won't find it here."

Pennon glanced in that direction and smiled. "A good thought, Ingram. We, too, planned to seek guidance from the Sauran King."

"And well you might," Victoria said as she, too, stood. "But know that their resources will be mightily strained. For the Sauran King we have known was assassinated but a few months agone, and unknown forces destroyed the Artan of the Great Forest." At Pennon's horrified start, she smiled humorlessly. "As we already have deduced among ourselves, young woman, we find ourselves already at the start of a Chaoswar."

Pennon swallowed. "Excuse me, then. Some of this I must convey to our people." She moved off, towards the other Camp-Bels, arranged in a small group a few hundred yards away.

"But you *do* know the new King, Auntie," Urelle said after a moment. "So maybe at least *some* help is there."

"Maybe," Ingram said. "But what are we all?"

The two Vantage women exchanged glances, and then met both his and Quester's gaze with their own. "Adventurers."

"And *there* is where we will seek our help," Quester said, continuing his Nest-Brother's thoughts. "In such times, we are the ones called upon; the Guild will expect it." He took such a deep breath that his abdomen expanded. "And we will have our own resources. I shall seek the wisdom of the Mothers Past; it lies within me, I know, and it *must* have some help to offer."

He looked at the others. "And... Lady Vantage. Urelle. If it meets with your favor... I would offer the mind and will of the Nest to you, share with you the bond that I have with Ingram."

"What?" Victoria was startled. "Are you sure, Quester?"

"I *felt* your mind, Lady Victoria," he answered. "I do not know how or why, but at the least I must take it as a sign, that you are more than worthy of such trust, if you would place such trust in me. And as for Urelle, she it was who risked herself to warn us, and for whom my Nest-Brother kept us at your home for all this time." He saw Urelle's startled glance at an embarrassed Ingram. "It would reflect poorly on his judgment were I not to see she is worthy of that trust, as well."

The Vantage women exchanged glances. "It is... a generous, and touching, offer, Quester," Victoria said, after Urelle nodded to her. "We will think very well on it, and give you a decision soon. Thank you."

"And you're right... we have our own resources." Urelle held up a lenticular jewel that grasped the sunlight and turned it into a polychromatic aura. "Maybe not *just* yet. But I have *this*, and more."

"I have experience, I suppose," Victoria conceded. "Which I believe has come in handy a time or two."

"The proper way to express it would be 'saved our lives,'" Ingram said with a grin. He sobered, looked out to sea. "And me... I have whatever this destiny, wyrd, prophecy, is. And I guess I have my Clan, now." He smiled, and his whole face seemed to light up. "I have my *Clan*."

"Though they don't deserve you," Urelle said, still obviously more than a bit angry on his behalf.

"Enough, Urelle. It's Ingram they injured; if he forgives them, that's his choice."

"Forgive them... I don't know. But *accept* them, that I can do, now that they accept me. I've always been proud of the Camp-Bels; now I just have to find out what the secrets were that the Captain knew, that only my parents still hold." He looked again to the unseeable. "Because that's what's going to tell me *why*. I'm sure of it. Why me. Why I am the target.

"And once I know that... I'll know *how*."

He reached down and picked up his pack, slung it over his shoulder; the others did the same, Quester making sure his spears were well-set in their quiver, swiftsword and longmace in their places.

"Let's go," Ingram said. "Ares is waiting."

THE END

Acknowledgements

It's easy to write A book. Writing a better book takes not just effort, but help.

First, thanks as always to Kathleen, who gives me the time to write amid an always-challenging schedule.

Second, my Beta-Readers group; they find the errors so that you will never see them, catch me if I'm getting lazy, find the contradictions and question them. Numerous parts of Godswar: The Mask of Ares would be much weaker without their constant attention and advice.

Third, Histria Books for bringing this story back to life.

HISTRIA BOOKS

HISTRIA SciFi&Fantasy

Other fine books available from Histria SciFi & Fantasy:

For these and many other great books visit

HistriaBooks.com

www.ingramcontent.com/pod-product-compliance
Lightning Source LLC
LaVergne TN
LVHW030236250426
837142LV00013B/163